MORE *than* HER

MORE THAN SERIES

- BOOK TWO -

MORE THAN HER

More Than Series #2

JAY MCLEAN

MORE THAN HER

Kindle Edition
Published by Jay McLean

Published: Jay McLean November 2013
Cover Design: Ari at Cover it! Designs

Created with Vellum

To my readers, turned friends, turned family.
Thank you for your encouragement, support and belief in me.
I would be nowhere without you.
I more than a lot love you.
So much more than a lot.
Truth.

NOTE TO READERS

Please note than More Than Her (More Than #2) is the sequel to More Than This (More Than #1) and should not be read prior to reading More Than This (More Than #1).

PROLOGUE

LOGAN

END-OF-SUMMER PARTY. PRE-COLLEGE

"What the hell just happened?" Cam said.

"Dude, I have no fucking idea."

Micky's ex just proposed, and they both left the party. Jake was on his phone calling a cab before anyone could talk any sense into him.

The rest of us sat back down, dumbstruck. I kept looking around for her. Hopefully she was okay, and she wasn't going to marry that guy. He was an asshole, and she deserved better than someone who was going to treat her like shit.

"You worried about her?"

I slowly turned to face Cam, who was sitting a few feet from me, legs straight out in front of him and crossed at his ankles. He looked at me curiously, eyebrows drawn together.

"Yeah, I am," I said, looking straight at him. I almost felt like I knew what was going to happen next. I subconsciously sat up and straightened my shoulders, waiting for the challenge, because I knew what his next question was. When he asked it, I was prepared.

"You love her, don't you?"

And even though I was expecting it, hearing him say the actual words was like a kick in the gut. I watched him, looking for any sign of what his judgment might be when I told him the truth. "Yeah, man. I think I do."

He stared at me for what felt like hours, but it was only seconds. Then he blew out a breath, pulled the cap off his head, ran his hand through his hair and replaced it.

"Yeah," he sighed out. "Me too."

"What!" I almost yelled. I looked over to where Lucy was standing, only a few feet away from us, making sure she hadn't heard what her dick of a boyfriend had just said.

"Me too," he repeated. I glared at him. "I mean, not the *love* love way. Not the way I love Lucy."

I continued to gape at him, confused as all hell. He kept going. "Micky—she's one of us now, and I get that you feel something for her. It would be hard not to, especially after what she's been through. But I don't think you love her. Not in that way. I think you love her the same way you love Lucy or Heidi. Kind of like a sister, like you want to keep them safe, protect them, you know? Or at least... I mean, if anything were to happen to me, I'd want you to be that way with Lucy." He paused. "I'm not making any sense, am I?"

I slowly shook my head.

He blew out another long breath, then sat up in his chair a little and looked up at the sky, thinking about his next words. After a little while, he faced me.

"Has Lucy ever told you how we met?" His eyes quickly went to Lucy, who was standing by a cooler, talking to a few girls.

"She just said you helped coach her little brothers and that after her mom died you started coming around to help out."

His eyes came back to me. "That's what she thinks... I actually noticed her the first time I saw her. She was in the stands with a couple of her brothers. I remember seeing her for the first time. She had a book in one hand, and the other was constantly attending to one or more of the boys." He chuckled a little. "They were always bugging her for something and getting in her face, but she never took her eyes off the book. And I remember just standing there watching her for pretty much the entire game. I mean, I'd seen her at school a few times, always thought she was kind of cute, you know? The quiet kind of cute."

I nodded my head in agreement. She was that kind of cute.

"The first week, I said nothing to her. And the weeks after that and every day at school, I tried to talk to her, but I'd be a nervous wreck, you know? And it was so weird because in every other aspect of my life I was this cocky asshole, standard semi-popular jock. Here I was getting wound up over some quiet bookworm I'd never spoken to before.

"So, a few weeks passed, and I remember looking in the mirror one day. Keep in mind I was like fifteen at the time, and I remember saying to myself, 'Today is the day. You will talk to her.' When I got to the field, I expected to see her in the stands, but she wasn't there and neither were her brothers, and that was the day I found out about her mom. The cancer and the dying, well, by then, it was her death.

I continued to listen, taking in everything he had to say.

"I went to the funeral and just watched her. She sat at the front of the plot, surrounded by all her brothers, holding this tiny little baby in her arms. Her brothers were crying, but she wasn't. She held their hands and wiped their tears, but she never, not once, shed a single one. When I went to the wake at her house, her brothers were being taken care of by other people, and that's when I saw her. She was in the laundry room, her back turned to everyone, and she was crying. Not wailing, not sobbing, just quietly crying. I remember going up to her, my palms sweating, still a nervous wreck. I could hear the blood pumping in my ears, and my whole body was shaking. I got closer to her, and she must have heard me coming because she turned around, looked up at me, her eyes filled with tears, and then just hugged me out of nowhere. And I hugged her back, but all I could get out was my goddamn name.

"Every day after that for months I went to her house after school and weekends—whenever I could—to try to help out. Because even though I wanted to protect her and help any way I could, it was more than that. I wanted to be around her, too. Like all the fucking time. And I know this is going to sound cheesy as fuck—" He stopped talking when Lucy came back over. She sat on his lap, and he adjusted them so they were more comfortable. He kissed her once on the cheek and then continued, "I really enjoyed just being with her, you know? Hanging out, talking, goofing around, whatever. And all of this was before the making out and the sex. The incredible fucking sex." Lucy just smiled.

"I guess what I'm trying to say is—is that unless you feel those things for Micky-" Lucy's head whipped to face me. Cam patted her leg a couple of times. "Unless you feel those things, the nerves, the want to be with them all the time, the missing them when they're not around...all of that shit... then it's not love you feel. Well, not *love* love. It's uh..." He thought for a moment, eyeing the sky. "It's the Logan-Lucy Love," he said.

Lucy grinned at me.

I was silent.

In shock.

Then finally I asked, "Where the fuck were you months ago when I needed that speech, asshole?"

"Fuck you." He laughed.

Pumping her fist in the air, her gaze distant, Lucy sang quietly to the tune of "Macho Man," "Lo-gan Lu-cy Loove..."

AN HOUR LATER, I was walking back to our group after talking to the DJ when I saw her. It was the first time I'd seen her since that night. I figured she might be here, but actually seeing her was harder than I thought. She was with a few other girls, standing a little away from where James and his friends were. Of course, they went to the same school.

I needed to talk to her, maybe try to explain what happened without going into too much detail. I walked toward her and wiped my sweaty palms on my jeans. I cracked my knuckles with my thumbs. It was a nervous habit I've tried to break. I basically had; I only did it when I got really nervous. And apparently with girls, or a girl, I should say.

I got closer to them, and their conversation died. Alexis, her friend, had the other two girls in her grip. "Come on," she said, pulling them away. So then it was just her and me, face-to-face, for the first time in months. And as stupid as it fucking sounded, I missed her. And I was nervous as all hell. I wiped my palms on my jeans again and adjusted my cap a little higher so I could see her properly.

"Hey." I motioned my hand in a small wave and then placed them in my front pockets.

"Matthews." She nodded her head. She had no expression. Not happy to see me, not sad, not angry, nothing.

"I, uh ... how are you?"

She inhaled a deep breath but didn't say anything. We stood, looking straight at each other. Honestly, I'd played out this moment in my head more than a few times over the last two months, and each of those moments I had something to say, some sort of plan so that she would actually talk to me again. But now, standing here, I had no words.

Just a shitload of fucking regret.

"Amanda!" Some guy behind her interrupted. We broke the stare. Her head turned to the kid, and I looked over her shoulder at him. He had a ball cap pulled low on his forehead, looking down at his phone. It was dark. I couldn't make out who he was or what he looked like. "You ready to go?" He never looked up from his phone.

She turned back to me slowly, and my eyes moved to hers. She held my gaze for a few seconds to make sure I heard her next words.

And I did. I heard them loud and fucking clear. "Yeah, babe," she said loudly, eyes on mine. "We're totally done here."

She walked backwards a few steps, then turned and went to him. He was still looking down at his phone as he spun, putting one arm around her shoulders. She wrapped both arms around his waist, looked up and spoke to him. Finally, he put the phone in his pocket, then gazed down at her. He flipped his cap backwards, leaned down and kissed her.

And I looked away.

Because I couldn't fucking stand to see it.

And this—this was the moment I knew what it felt like to lose everything I never had.

LOGAN

A Year and a Half Later

COLLEGE WAS EVERYTHING I expected it to be. I lived in the frat house, which was fine.

A few months after we got here, Jake and Micky became a thing. An official, exclusive thing. And I was happy for them. I truly was. Because Cam was right; I didn't love her. Not the way I thought I did.

I knew Amanda told Micky she was going to college here, but we never discussed it. And it sucked because I looked for her everywhere: in all my classes, walking through campus, the stores nearby and diners she might be working. Nothing. I didn't see her anywhere.

I knew I could ask Micky, and I'd thought about it on more than one occasion—but here's thc thing—if she wanted Micky to know, then she would have told her, and I'd have had my ass kicked already. She's not telling her for a reason.

So, every day I looked for her, and she's not here. And every day I got more and more pissed off and angry about what I did to her. Then I turned that anger into the one thing I knew would help: girls.

Between baseball, the parties, the girls and the sex, I had just enough time to study. If I had to give up one of those things, it would be baseball. Honestly though, I'd give it all up if it meant I could see her again.

LOGAN

The Meet

PAST - BEFORE SUMMER. PRE-COLLEGE

THE FIRST TIME I saw her was at Jake's house. It was at Mikayla's family's wake. To me—she was like a light in the darkness. I wondered now if Micky ever thought of Jake like that.

"EXCUSE ME?"

Her voice was so low I almost didn't hear it. But when I turned around, she was there. Standing in the middle of the Andrews' kitchen, plates in hand, waiting for me to say—or do—something.

Finally, a sound travelled up my throat and out my mouth. I couldn't tell you what the fuck I said, because I can't remember.

All I can remember was her.

The way she stood there, unsure of the situation. Her bottom lip was caught between her teeth, her eyebrows drawn together.

She jerked her head toward me. "I need to put these in there."

"Huh?"

"The sink, behind you? I need to put these in there," she said slowly, as if I were a child.

She lifted the plates in her hands and waited.

I took my time, taking her in. I'm pretty sure I didn't even try to hide the eye-fuck I gave her, because when my eyes finally left her body to settle on her face, she was blushing.

She tried not to smile. "Are you going to move or what?"

I smirked and lazily stepped aside.

She took two steps forward and tripped—on absolutely nothing. The plates she was holding fell to the floor and shattered. We were both quick to bend and pick them up, so quick that we knocked heads on the way down.

"Shit," she whispered, rubbing her head.

"Fuck," I said, doing the same.

I started to pick up the broken pieces and that was when I noticed the blood.

"Dude, you're bleeding," I told her.

She looked up and our eyes locked.

And that was one of the ways I remember her.

Her face so close to mine I could feel her breathing.

"Huh?" She looked down at her hand, and her eyes widened before she said, "Holy shitballs!"

And then she squealed like a little girl. Her eyes squeezed shut as she threw her hand out in front of her, waving it around, dripping blood all over the floor. "I can't see blood. I mean, technically I can see it, but I can't look at it. You have to make it stop." She hadn't taken a breath. "Seriously, it freaks me the fuck out. Make it stop! Oh my god! I'm going to throw up! Move!" She started to stand, then stopped, gripped my shirt, faced away from me, and continued, "Don't move...fix it. Please?" Then she looked at me with panic clear on her face. "I'm going to pass out. Oh God. Oh God."

"Hey." I tried to soothe her. "It's fine, I got you." I held her arm and helped her stand. I couldn't help the chuckle that escaped.

"It's not funny. I swear I'll throw up if I look at it."

She still had that panicked look, and her face had paled a few shades. That was when I realized she wasn't fucking around. It was also when I realized how cute she was. "Don't look at it then; just concentrate on my face."

So she did.

"Does it hurt?"

She nodded slowly, never taking her eyes off mine.

"Okay, I'm going to take a look. Just let me know if I'm hurting you, okay?"

Another slow nod.

I finally managed to tear my eyes off hers to check out her finger. "You're just going to need a Band-Aid."

I cleaned up the mess on the floor, led her to the bathroom where the first aid kit was and told her to sit up on the counter.

Once the Band-Aid was on, I glanced up at her. "You good?"

She bit her lip, nodding. "Thanks," she said quietly. "What are you? A doctor or something?" She smiled wide, her legs kicked back and forth in front of her.

"Something like that."

"Well, thank you. And sorry for freaking out about the blood thing. I really just...ugh...me and blood are not friends." She scrunched up her nose and made a disgusted face.

I took her in, and her big, blue eyes looked back. Her light brown hair hung loose. It was the only time I'd seen it like that.

And that was when it hit me. She wasn't just cute. She was kind of fucking hot.

She bit her lip again, and my eyes zoned in on the action. I wanted to kiss her. I wanted my mouth on hers, and I wanted it bad. For some reason, I thought it was okay to do what I did next, because I was Logan Fucking Matthews, and I was a goddamn boss. Plus—chicks loved me.

So I made a move to kiss her, but I saw her eyes widen slightly before our lips made contact, and the next thing I knew, her knee was in my junk and I was folding over myself, trying to breathe through the pain.

I leaned down, both hands on my parts, trying to soothe the ache. I couldn't breathe properly. I was doing everything I could not to fall to the ground and cry. I saw her jump off the counter and bend down to look in my eyes. "First, I don't even know you. Second, we're at a fucking wake. And third, you're an asshole," she said. One of her fingers pushed on the middle of my forehead, hard enough that it made me fall back a little.

She opened the bathroom door quickly and shut it behind her. Once I knew it was closed for sure, I dropped to the floor and rocked back and forth like a goddamn baby. The pain was that fucking intense.

I WAS OUT on the back patio with everyone else when I heard her voice. "Hi, Mikayla. I'm really sorry about your loss." She laughed once. "What a shit thing to say, like you lost something but you'll find it again."

Micky laughed. "Amanda, how are you?"

Amanda.

I tuned out the conversation and just stared at her. She wasn't hot. Not the in-your-face kind of hot. She was something else. She was still something else.

AS SOON AS SHE LEFT, I knew I had to find her.

I rushed out of the house searching for her. She was on the sidewalk, pressing her key fob to unlock a shitty red Civic.

I virtually sprinted over to her. "Amanda!" I yelled.

She turned and froze in her spot.

I stopped inches in front of her, my breathing heavy from running.

"I need your number," I told her.

"What?" she said through an incredulous laugh.

"I need your number because I need to take you out." I tried my panty-dropping smile on her.

"Um, no." She turned around to open her car door.

"What?" I asked, disbelief laced in my tone.

"No," she repeated.

"Why not?" I was pissed off. "I'm just asking for your number."

She turned to face me, huffing out a breath.

"No, asshole." She rolled her eyes. "You weren't asking for my number. You were demanding it." She eyed me up and down. "Who are you anyway?"

"Logan Matthews." I put my hand out to shake hers.

She looked down at it, shook her head, laughed once, and then looked back up at me.

"Definitely no."

"What? Why? Give me one good reason," I spat out. I didn't know why it was getting to me, her not wanting me. But I was pissed off, and I felt like I needed to win this argument or whatever the fuck it was that was going on here.

"Because."

"That's not a reason."

"Because I have a boyfriend."

"No, you don't." I shook my head and crossed my arms over my chest.

"Because you're an asshole."

"Valid, but not accepted. Next?"

"Because I like girls."

I eyed her up and down and licked my lips. "Even better."

She took a deep breath in and sighed out loud. "Fine." Her hand was out waiting, so I gave her my phone.

A huge shit-eating grin took over my face, because I just fucking won, and I couldn't wait to make her pay for it. She handed it back and rushed to get in her car. I watched her as she drove away.

Amanda.

Once she was gone, I looked down at my phone. The notes app was open:

In your dreams, asshole. Find another way to score your home run.

LOGAN

Present

WE WERE THREE weeks away from the first game of the season, and I was trying to get my classes sorted before baseball consumed all my free time. Baseball—it wasn't a big deal for me. I wasn't the best catcher on the team. I definitely wouldn't be starting. I walked onto the team by default because Jake and I were best friends and we played high school ball together for three years. They assumed we had a special connection on the field or some shit—some sort of secret communication. The thing is, Jake Andrews is that fucking good; he could pitch to a brick wall and still be a big deal. I stayed on the team because it helped clear my head and gave me a good workout schedule. It was not my passion, and it definitely was not my career.

I WAS ABOUT to walk out of the library when I saw Micky, Lucy and a third girl. I did a double take because there was no way in hell it could be her. "Luce! Micky!"

I got scolded to shut up.

I didn't care.

They both turned around immediately.

And so did she.

Amanda.

Holy shit.

My steps faltered as I got closer.

I couldn't seem to take my eyes off her. She looked the same, but different. Fuck, I don't know. Her eyes widened as she saw me walking toward them, but they quickly averted to the floor. I waited until I was right in front of them before speaking. "Hey," I said to all of them, but I couldn't tear my eyes off Amanda.

"Dude." Micky laughed, her finger clicking in front of my face. It snapped me out of my dazed state. When I finally peeled my eyes off Amanda and looked at Micky, she was smirking at me.

Lucy started giggling. "What are you doing?" she asked, trying to hide her own smirk. My eyes darted to Amanda, but she was still looking at the ground, playing with the straps of her backpack.

"Nothing, just had some shit to do. What are you lovely ladies doing?"

I don't think I realized that I hadn't taken my eyes off her until Micky was laughing and waving her hand in front of my face again. I slapped it away and glared at her. She stopped laughing, smiled, and then nudged Amanda with her elbow. "Amanda," Micky said. She finally looked up. "Have you met Logan?" she continued with a shit-eating grin on her face.

My palms began to sweat; my thumb cracked the fingers on each hand. My pulse echoed in my ears. I could see Lucy's confused expression from the corner of my eye, but I couldn't take my fucking eyes off Amanda. My hands went in my front pockets while I waited for her reaction. I needed her to say something—anything. To tell me that she remembered me. But when she finally looked up, there was nothing.

"Nope. Never." She faked looking at her watch. "I gotta go. My ride is coming, and he's in a hurry, I'll see you girls later," she said quickly and then walked away.

"We've got book club on Tuesday. Don't forget," Lucy called after her.

She raised her hand in acknowledgement.

I let go of the breath I didn't know I was holding.

Lucy put her arm through mine as we walked out and toward the parking lot. “Logan, don’t tell me you’ve slept with her, too. She’s one of the good ones,” she whined.

“What? No. I haven’t. Swear it.”

“Good.” She laughed.

I put my arms around both their shoulders. “So, what’s this about a book club? You girls sit around, reading dirty books, fanning each other’s vaginas? Because if so, count me in!”

“Ew!” Lucy yelped the same time Micky backhanded my stomach.

The girls got in Micky’s car and drove off.

I looked around for my car. I wasn’t parked on this side of the lot. I started making my way to the other side and saw Amanda sitting at a bus stop, on her phone. I was at a standstill for a moment, wondering if I should try to talk to her or if I should just leave her alone.

She glanced up when she heard footsteps, but her expression fell the instant she realized it was me. “I got to go, Lexi. I’ll call you later...yeah...uh-huh...bye.”

She regarded me, her eyebrows raised.

“Hey.” I motioned my head to the spot on the bench next to her.

She bit her lip and looked away. “It’s a free country, Matthews. You can do what you want.”

I hated that she called me Matthews. Like she didn’t even know my name. Or she just didn’t care. “So you do remember me? That’s not what you said to-”

“Are you fucking kidding me right now?” Her whole body spun to face me. “I’m not the one that—” She stopped herself abruptly and closed her eyes, forcing her breathing to steady.

I watched her, confused.

“You know what, Matthews? Just leave it alone, okay? No one needs to know that we have history—or whatever. Just leave it. Please.” Her eyes were cast downwards, picking at her jeans.

I didn’t know what to say. I opened my mouth, but nothing came out. I tried to reach for her hand, but she jerked it away.

“Amanda,” I sighed. “I’m sorry.” I meant it.

Her whole body tensed before she raised her eyes to mine.

“You’re too late, Logan.” She shook her head slowly. “You’re just too fucking late.”

A car pulled up, interrupting me from saying anything more. She rushed to stand, putting her backpack on. "I'd say it was nice seeing you, Matthews. But it really, really wasn't." I stayed silent as she got into that same piece of shit old Jeep from her graduation day.

And I was left sitting there, watching her leave.

Again.

LOGAN

The Assist

PAST - START OF SUMMER. PRE-COLLEGE

A WEEK HAD PASSED since I'd met her at Jake's house, but she still lingered on my mind. I'd forgotten that she went to Micky's school, so I didn't expect to see her at their graduation. But I was so fucking glad I did.

SHE STOOD ON the sidewalk across from me talking to another girl, both of them wearing their gowns. I crossed the road and stood behind her. Whatever her friend was saying died in the air when she saw me.

"What is it?" Amanda asked her.

I interrupted. "Well, well. I bet you never thought you'd see me again?"

She slowly turned around; a scowl had already formed on her face. "What do you want, Matthews?"

I chuckled.

Her eye twitched.

It made me laugh harder. "I don't know why you're pissed at me," I said, trying to hide my amusement. "I'm just standing here, asking you a question. It's not a big deal." I shrugged, my hands going in my pockets.

She raised her eyebrows, waiting for me to answer her.

So I did. "Your number. For real this time."

"No. Again. For real this time."

The fact that she didn't want me made me want her more. Just when I was about to tell her that I wasn't going to take no for an answer, a piece of shit old Jeep pulled up beside us. The kid driving had the top down, with two other guys in the back seat. They all wore their gowns.

"Hey," Amanda's friend cooed.

The kid driving gave her a quick head nod before he looked at me, eyes narrowed. He didn't say shit, just glared.

I glared back.

"I'll call you later," Amanda said to her friend, hugging her quickly before brushing past me and into the front seat of the car. I watched as they drove off. She never once looked back.

"So you want her number?" her friend asked.

I turned back to face her, rubbing my palm on my jaw. I eyed her up and down, confused. "Why?" I asked. "You gonna give it to me?"

"I'm Alexis, just FYI. And yes, I am." Her hand was out, waiting. I handed her my phone.

"And her boyfriend?" I jerked my head to the spot where the car had just left.

She looked up at me, mid-type. "Not her boyfriend."

She handed it back, and I made sure it was in there this time and she wasn't just fucking with me like Amanda did.

I thanked her before walking to my car. Once I was seated, I pulled out my phone and texted her.

Logan: *So, I'm thinking dinner for our first date. Any requests?*

Amanda: *Fucking Alexis.*

LOGAN

Present

"COME TO THE HOUSE," Jake said after practice. "We'll grab a few beers and order a pizza." He ran his hands through his hair. "The only thing is—we kind of have to eat out back."

"What?" I laughed.

"Yeah. The girls have book club or something. They hate when I'm around."

I raised my eyebrows in disbelief.

He rolled his eyes. "It's not that bad, asshole. I'm still allowed to be home. Just not...inside the house."

"You're so—wait. Did you say book club?"

He nodded, eyebrows bunched in confusion.

I feigned disinterest. "So, uh—who attends this so-called book club?"

"Just Kayla, Luce and their friend Amanda."

I ignored the pounding in my chest. "Hey, when she's done whipping you, do you have to carry it back to its place with your mouth?"

"Fuck off."

SHE WAS ALL I could think about the entire drive to his house.

When we got there, the girls were all sitting around the coffee table, e-readers in hand.

There were glasses of wine or champagne or whatever it is chicks drink on the coffee table, along with some boxes of tissues and a bag of chocolates.

Their heads all whipped up when they heard us walk in.

Jake went to Micky, kissed her on the cheek, and then headed to his room.

They all went back to reading, like I wasn't even here. Amanda glanced up but looked straight back down when she saw it was me.

No smile. No frown. Nothing.

I went to sit on the sofa while I waited for Jake. "So... what are you guys doing?"

"Hoovering," Micky said through a sob.

I looked around.

They were sitting on their asses, not a single cleaning product in sight.

I must have misheard them. "What?" I asked again.

"Hoovering," Lucy replied, wiping at her face.

What the hell was going on? My eyebrows bunched together in confusion. Their eyes were red and puffy from crying.

And then it hit me—what was wrong with them all.

"You guys want me to get you, like, ice cream or more chocolate...something for your cramps?" I asked cautiously.

"What?" Micky chuckled, still not looking up from her book.

"You guys have that thing—you know—when girls are together all the time and they get their periods at the same time or some shit."

"Naw, Logan. I live you." Lucy smiled at me and then went back to reading. "Now go away!"

Amanda hadn't looked up once since I sat down. Her eyes were glued to her book.

I was bored and wanted to be an asshole, so I got comfortable on the sofa. "So, did you guys hear about that lit. professor and his student?"

"Shh!" both Micky and Lucy snapped.

I couldn't help the chuckle that escaped but continued to be an asshole. "Apparently they'd been doing it for a whi—"

"SHUT UP!" Lucy yelled, as she stood up. Her face was red, jaw clenched. "Go away!" She started swatting my head and shoulders with her hands. I tried ducking and blocking her hits, but she was too quick. "You. Are. Ruining DEAN HOLDER!" Her voice got louder with every word.

She pulled me by my hands until I was on my feet, turned me to face the front door, put her hands on my back and started pushing me toward it.

I tried digging my feet into the floor, but the girl had some power.

I pulled my phone out of my pocket and started dialing Cam. By the time the phone was to my ear, she'd pushed me out the front door, slamming it shut behind me.

"Yo," Cam answered.

"Dude, your girlfriend's fucking bat-shit crazy."

"What?" He sounded pissed.

I was about to tell him what happened when he chuckled. "Dude, it is Tuesday...and they are Hoovering."

What the hell does that even mean?

CAM ENDED UP COMING OVER, putting an end to the girls' book club. Heidi and Dylan joined us, and we made a night of it.

Amanda hadn't said shit to me or even glanced in my direction. She wasn't openly avoiding me, but I could definitely tell it was an effort for her. I tried to subtly watch her, but her eyes were glued to her phone.

When the pizza arrived, we all moved to the back deck.

"We should all do something for spring break," Heidi said.

Everyone made a sound of agreement through mouthfuls of food.

"We should go to Mexico!" I said. Dylan nodded his head, fist bumping me. His mouth was too full to speak.

"NO!" Lucy gasped, her head shaking frantically. "Nu-uh! Not Mexico!"

All eyes were on her.

Cam swallowed his food and then spoke through a smile. "Lucy here..." he pointed his thumb at her, "...thinks that if she goes to Mexico, they'll kidnap her and sell her as a sex slave."

We all laughed.

She still had that panicked look on her face. "It's not funny, you guys; it happens."

"Lucy, we read that book three months ago. Get it out of your head," Micky said through a laugh. She was sitting sideways on Jake's lap while his arm rested on her legs.

"No," Lucy defended. "It's true. It happens all the time."

"Lucy," Amanda said. It was the first time she'd spoken since I got here. "I'm pretty sure you have to be a virgin to be sold as a sex slave. And you—most definitely are not a virgin!"

Everyone cracked up.

"Yeah, she's not!" Cam high-fived Amanda.

Lucy's face turned to shock, but only for a second before she looked down at the floor, smiling to herself.

"You got family there, right?" Cam asked Amanda.

How does he know that?

"Yeah. You guys would be welcome to stay there. They love having guests."

"You'd obviously be coming with us."

Obviously? What the actual fuck was going on? How long has Amanda been living here? And how the hell has she managed to get to know my friends without me knowing it?

"Maybe." She shrugged. "But if not, you guys could definitely stay there. Just let me know." She pulled her phone out of her pocket and excused herself, walking back into the house.

I watched her every move.

A few minutes later, she came back but stood at the back door. "I gotta go. E's coming to get me."

"No. Don't leave yet." Micky was on her feet. "We wouldn't have even finished book club yet. Why are you going so soon?"

"Logan can give you a ride later," Lucy chimed in. I could hear her smiling; she was so damn obvious.

"Yeah. For sure. I'll give you a ride. No problem," I rushed out.

Smooth.

Then I just stared, waiting for her to say something. She never even looked in my direction.

"It's fine. He's on his way already." She waved to everyone before quickly making her way into the house and out the front door.

I WAS IN THE KITCHEN, throwing away some beer bottles, when Cam came in. He leaned against the counter, arms crossed over his chest and a smug smile on his face. "So...Amanda..." he trailed off, expecting me to finish his sentence.

I didn't look at him. I didn't say shit.

"You know, when I first saw her with Lucy, she looked kind of familiar. But I couldn't place her. But now—I think I remember her—she's that girl from the diner, right?"

I froze mid-movement and glared at him.

"It is!" He looked like he'd just won a prize. "Did you end up taking her out? Whatever happened with her?"

I sighed, thinking about what to tell him. "Nothing, dude. Nothing happened." Lie.

LOGAN

The Reinforcements

PAST - START OF SUMMER. PRE-COLLEGE

I MET UP with Cameron at Lucy's house. He'd been watching her brothers and wanted to take them out of the house for a bit. "Let's meet up at that diner on Main, you know the one with the fifties theme or whatever."

I agreed.

Lucy had six brothers, which meant they had to take two cars almost everywhere.

"What are high school bitches like?" the kid in the front seat asked as we followed behind Cameron.

"Who cares," a kid in the back cut in. "Bitches ain't shit but hoes and tricks."

"Whoa!" I turned to the back seat. I eyed the kid; he couldn't be more than eight. "Which one are you?"

"Logan," he said.

I tried to joke with him. "What? No way, but I'm Logan!"

He rolled his eyes. "I know, asshole." Kid had a potty mouth.

"Where did you learn to speak like that?"

He shrugged, stuck his middle finger up at me, poked out his tongue, and then continued to look out the window.

Um...okay.

BY THE TIME we got into the diner, Cam had pulled three tables together and was settling the kids in their seats.

It took a good twenty minutes for everyone to order and another thirty for our food to arrive. Within two minutes, shit was all over the place. Fries, nuggets, ketchup, sodas – everything, everywhere. Cam ate with one hand, the other hand too busy cleaning a kid, or wiping the table, stopping something from spilling, or picking something up off the floor.

"Great, you're here," our waitress rushed toward the door, already taking her apron off. "You have that table of eight. Good luck with that clean-up."

"Thanks. Have a good day." I recognized that voice, and my head whipped to its owner.

Amanda.

She looked hot as hell in her uniform, which matched the theme of the diner. The skirt flowed outward, but the top half was tight, showing off her killer tits and tiny waist.

I finally managed to peel my eyes off her and faced forward.

I'd spent the last week trying to call her. She never picked up. I tried texting. She never replied.

I smiled to myself. She couldn't ignore me anymore. Not when I was right fucking here.

"What's going on?" Cam pulled me from my thoughts. His eyes must've followed mine. They were focused on the front door, where I assume Amanda was still standing. "You know her?"

"Nope," I said, popping the *P*.

"But you want to, don't you?"

"Challenge accepted, Cameron."

"Dude, I didn't—"

"Challenge accepted!" I interrupted.

He laughed.

I felt her presence before I heard her voice. "Can I get you boys anything?"

Her eyes circled the table and then landed on mine. Her face fell. My heart rate spiked. "Hey, pretty girl." I faked cockiness.

"Matthews," she greeted. "Didn't know you'd taken up stalking."

Cam stifled a laugh as he watched this play out. He leaned back in his chair, waiting for the moment of rejection. But I wouldn't accept it.

"I'm not stalking you, babe. Swear it. It's like fate brought me here."

She walked away.

One of the older boys gagged and rolled his eyes.

Valid.

"What's the plan of attack?" Cam wore a shit-eating grin.

"Who cares," little Logan huffed. "Money over bitches...am I right?" His hand was up in the air, waiting for one of us to high five him. We didn't.

I searched the table for the youngest kid.

"You." I pointed. "What's your name?"

"I'm four," he said.

"Buddy," Cam spoke, "he asked what your name is, not how old you are."

"Oh. I'm Lachlan."

I smiled at him. "Okay, Lachlan. Want to earn a quick twenty bucks?" I asked him. He nodded his head enthusiastically, eyes big, a huge baby-teeth smile on show.

He walked over to Amanda who was at the counter, returning a tray. He pulled at her skirt, making her look down at him, and then he put on the biggest pout I'd ever seen.

"I'm sad," he said.

She gazed over at me for a quick moment and then looked back down at Lachlan. She bent so she was at eye level with him. "What's wrong, sweetheart? Is everything okay?"

He shook his head. "I'm sad because you won't go out with my uncle Logan."

I didn't ask him to throw the uncle part in, but I was impressed.

She stood to full height and looked down at him. "I'm sorry, I can't go out with your uncle Logan."

"Okay then," he stated, shrugging his shoulders dramatically. He didn't move from her side though, just stood there. She went back to what she was doing, and he still didn't move.

She got called over to a table and as she left, Lachlan followed, gripping onto her skirt. She turned quickly when she felt him tugging at her. She looked down at him, confused, then continued to walk and he continued to follow, holding onto her skirt.

He followed her around like a puppy, still holding onto her, for a good five minutes. The entire time we sat and watched in silence, waiting for her to break.

When she finally did, she picked him up and carried him over to the table. She stood him up on his chair and made sure he was looking at her. "You can tell your uncle Logan that I will go on one date with him. Only one. And I can leave whenever I want. You can also tell him that I'm busy for the next week so don't bother calling or texting until a week from now, got it?"

"Twenty bucks." He held out his hand, palm up, in front of me.

I stood up, grabbed my wallet from my jeans pockets, pulled out a twenty and handed it to him.

Amanda's jaw hit the floor. She turned to walk away. I held on to her arm gently and then leaned in close. I heard her breath catch. My hand went to her waist. I think she stopped breathing. My heart stopped beating. "One week," I managed to say. "I can wait a week."

LOGAN

Present

"FUCK!" I HIT the steering wheel and rolled my head against the headrest.

I had just left Jake and Micky's and was parked in front of the frat house. I couldn't get Amanda out of my head.

I grabbed my phone out of my pocket and pulled up her number. It wasn't the first time I'd wanted to call her.

I was about to hit call, when the front door of the house burst open, then slammed shut. Four of my frat brothers rushed out. Jackson was at the front of the pack, heading straight toward me, face red, fists balled. He was pissed. The others started talking shit, trying to calm him down.

"Dude!" Jackson yelled, finger pointed at me. "You slept with my fucking sister!"

Shit.

Not again.

I'D BEEN PACKING to go home for the weekend to catch up on some studying, but mainly because Nathan, Jake's dad, had been blowing up my phone, which meant that something important was—or was about to—go down.

Dad had called and we'd spoken briefly, but he didn't know what was happening either. It was different now than it was when I was younger, mainly because now I was an adult. And even though Nathan worked mostly with kids, he made an exception for me. Nathan didn't want to discuss whatever it was over the phone, so we'd made plans for me to go to his house and talk there. Jake wouldn't be at his parents' this weekend. In fact, he was having a few people over before the season started.

At least, that was the plan, until Nathan called. He had to fly out to an emergency job, so whatever it was he had to tell me could wait. He said it wasn't urgent in a time-sensitive manner, just a need-to-know kind of thing. Whatever it was, I honestly didn't care. It could only be about them. And I stopped giving a shit about them a long time ago.

So now I was at Jake and Micky's party, buzzed, up against a wall with some girl's mouth on my neck. Go to any college party and it's the same scene. Only here, it was a little toned down, because these guys were almost pro athletes.

So. This girl on my neck was doing some crazy shit. It was definitely having the opposite effect of what she was intending, but I didn't care enough to pull her off. My attention was on my phone, trying to match up these three colored pieces of fucking candy. It felt like I was trying to work out the next move forever. I chuckled to myself, causing uh, Cindy? Britney? Tiffany? Oops. Anyway, she pulled back a little, her bright red lipstick smeared around her mouth.

"What's funny?" she asked with that high-pitched baby voice I hated.

I shook my head, switching the screen off and placing it back in my pocket.

When I brought my eyes back up, I saw her.

Amanda.

She glared at me, mouth partially open, looking hotter than I'd ever seen her.

Stomach. Floor.

8

AMANDA

LOGAN. FUCKING. MATTHEWS.

I hated him.

I hated his stupid smug ass of a face and that perfectly messy brown hair.

I hated those stupid green eyes and those perfect teeth and that hot as fuck panty-dropping smile.

I hated his stupid deep dimples that showed whenever he smirked from being an asshole—which was all the fucking time.

I hated him. I hated him. I hated him.

I hated him so fucking much, I wanted to push him up against the wall and punch him in the face.

And then I wanted to lick it.

Then rip his fucking shirt off and finger his abs while he does that annoyingly manly chuckle that I loved.

I hated him.

Stupid Fucking Logan Fucking Matthews.

Shit. I'm drunk.

And I've turned into Lucy.

LOGAN

SHE TURNED TO LEAVE, and instantly I was moving what's-her-face out of the way so I could get to her. I caught up and pulled her by her arm into the hallway and into the spare room, closing the door behind her.

She leaned against it, her eyes wide.

I moved so I was in front of her. I took her in from head to toe. "Holy shit, you look good."

She stayed silent.

I stepped closer. So close our chests were touching. I could hear her breathing heavily, her boobs rising and falling with each breath.

Our eyes locked. Our breathing got faster, heavier. I could feel my dick growing, and I hadn't even touched her. She closed her eyes and licked her lips and that was the fucking turning point. My mouth was on hers so fast, she didn't have time to react.

At first it was quick and messy, because I wanted to fucking devour her. But then I calmed myself down enough to realize that she was kissing me back.

She was fucking kissing me back.

So I deepened the kiss. My tongue came out, asking for permission. She opened her mouth for me. And instantly my mind was filled with memories of when we did this last.

She made a moaning sound as our tongues came together, and I moved closer, pushing myself into her.

We kissed for a few more minutes, not saying a word. Each second that went by—I felt myself losing control with this girl. I had no idea what she was thinking, or how she was feeling, or why she was even letting me have this. But I didn't care.

Because I wanted her.

So. Fucking. Bad.

She clutched my hair with both her hands and moved me to her neck. I resumed my kissing there. I could hear her trying to catch her breath. One of my hands moved to her thigh, creeping up and under the hem of her short dress and onto her ass. Her amazing fucking ass, barely covered with whatever panties she was wearing.

"Holy shit," she whispered, bringing my mouth back to hers. Her legs went around my waist.

I pinned her to the wall.

Fuck. Yes.

AMANDA

OH. MY. GOD.

What the fuck was happening right now?

He had me up against the wall, pushing in all the right ways. My legs were wrapped around him while my hips jerked toward his. I was two seconds away from losing it. His mouth moved from my lips, down my jaw, and onto my neck. I inhaled deeply a few times, trying to calm myself down, but his mouth kept moving lower, and his dick kept grinding harder. Then his mouth was on the swell of my breasts and I knew I should be stopping this, but it felt so fucking good. His hand reached up, pulled the top of my dress down, and before I knew it, my nipple was covered with the warmth of his mouth. I threw my head back against the door. A moan escaped from the pleasure of what he was fucking doing to me. He stopped and pulled back from my breast, causing a popping sound. I looked down at him; his eyes rose to mine. "Fuck, Amanda. I've thought about this for so long."

I froze.

And the memories came back.

My feet landed on the ground, and I adjusted my dress.

He took a step back.

"I'm sorry, Matthews. I shouldn't have let it get this far." I shook my head. "It's my fault."

I turned to open the door, but his hand in the crook of my elbow stopped me.

He spun me around to face him and bent so his eyes were level with mine. "What are you doing?"

"Nothing." I cleared my throat "I'm sorry."

We were both panting, trying to catch our breaths.

Then he had me up against the wall again, his mouth on mine, and I started kissing him back, again.

Fuck.

I pulled back.

"Stop." I pushed him off me. "Look, I said I'm sorry. I don't want to do this." I motioned my finger between us. "I don't want this."

"Well, that's not really what your body is telling me."

I blew out a breath. "I know, I'm sorry. Okay? It's just the beer and the moment. I just got caught up."

He moved in to kiss me again, but I ducked and moved out of the way.

"Quit fucking kissing me!" I was more forceful this time. My emotions were all over the place.

I didn't want him.

I couldn't want him.

Not anymore.

He chuckled.

Fucking chuckled.

"No," I almost yelled. "This shit's not funny, Matthews." My voice cracked. I didn't mean for it to, but it did. And before I knew it, I was crying.

LOGAN

SHE WAS CRYING, and I don't know what the fuck just happened. I reached out to her, but she swatted my hand away.

"I let you get to me again. You almost fucking had me," she mumbled to herself, shaking her head and wiping her tears.

"Amanda," I said, trying to soothe her. I tentatively put my hand on her waist and brought the other to her face, wiping the tears. Her big, blue eyes looked up at me. She licked her lips.

I went to kiss her again.

Because obviously I wasn't thinking with my head.

She pushed me away.

Then her hands were on my shoulders as she maneuvered me to a corner of the room. "Stay there," she said. "And quit fucking kissing me." She walked over to the opposite corner and stood with her back to the wall.

We were as far from each other as physically possible.

"What happened just now?" I asked her. I was so fucking confused.

"Something that shouldn't have."

"You keep saying that, but I don't feel like that. To me, it felt pretty fucking-"

"Stop," she pleaded. "Just please. Stop."

I watched as her body gave in and dropped to the floor.

I didn't know what the fuck to do. One second we were making out and it was hot as hell. The next second—this.

I was cautious as I took steps closer to her. I squatted in front of her so I could see her better. "Hey, what's wrong?" I hoped it came out concerned and not that I thought she was acting bat-shit fucking crazy.

When her eyes met mine, she no longer looked sad. She looked —determined, maybe? "What happened, Matthews, is that I already let you break my heart once."

Then she stood up, adjusted her dress, and walked out of the room.

I didn't call her name.

I didn't stop her.

I didn't follow her.

I just sat there, in a dark room, feeling sorry for myself.

Because as much as I tried to convince myself over the last year or so that she didn't care—or that she wouldn't care—in just a few words she proved me completely wrong.

She felt it, too.

She felt everything I did.

LOGAN

The Date

PAST - START OF SUMMER. PRE-COLLEGE

Logan: *7 days to go.*
Amanda: *Really, asshole? A countdown?*
Logan: *6 days to go. I bet you can't wait to see me.*
Amanda: *I'm already regretting this.*
Logan: *5 days to go. OMG! What am I going to wear?*
Amanda: *I thought I told you not to contact me for a week.*
Logan: *4 days to go. Seriously, though, what do you want to do?*
Amanda: *Not go on a date with you?*
Logan: *3 days to go. I'm getting pretty fucking excited to see you.*
Amanda: *Shut up.*
Logan: *2 days to go. Just thought I would remind you, in case you had forgotten.*
Amanda: *Who is this?*
Logan: *1 day to go. I'll call you tomorrow.*
Amanda: *I'll be busy.*
Logan: *I'm calling you in 5 minutes. You better answer. You promised my 'nephew' a date with me.*
Amanda: *Fine!*

EVEN THOUGH SHE asked me not to, I texted her every day, several times a day, for the week leading up to our date. She replied with smartass answers every time. If ever there was a sign that we would connect as well as we did, that should have been it.

"Hello?" she answered on the first ring. It had just hit eight in the morning, and even though it was summer, my body had gotten used to getting up at six for a morning run and training. I skipped the run. I had no training. I sat with my phone in my hand until it seemed like a decent hour to call.

"Hey, pretty girl," I replied. I tried to hide the nerves that had taken over from just hearing her voice. "What time should I pick you up?"

"Oh." She sounded surprised. "I thought you were just messing with me. I didn't know you were serious about taking me out."

I had no idea how she got to that conclusion. "Nope." I faked airiness in my tone. "Completely serious. So?"

"Um."

I waited.

And waited.

Finally she said, "I have to work. But I finish at five—if you want to pick me up from there? But honestly, you don't have to. I mean—"

"Five? I'll be there."

Silence.

"Amanda?"

"Yeah?"

"I'm really looking forward to seeing you again." Truth.

I SHOWED UP at her work fifteen minutes late, just to prove that I hadn't been sitting around waiting to leave.

She sat on a bench looking down at her phone. She probably assumed I wouldn't show.

Valid.

She stood up and walked toward my car. She'd changed out of

her work uniform and into tight-fitting jeans and an even tighter tank. Fuck. Her body was out of this fucking world.

"Quit the eye fuck, Matthews," she said, taking a seat and pulling on the belt.

She had fire. "You know what I like about you?"

"My tits?"

My eyes rose from her tits. "Huh?"

She laughed once. "Jesus, this isn't awkward at all."

I laughed with her, pulled away from the curb, and started driving to the restaurant.

I eyed her sideways. "Well, let's not do that. Make it awkward, I mean."

"Yeah? How are we not going to do that?"

I glanced at her quickly, smirking. "Well, I could pull the car over right now and we could just make out, so we don't have to worry about it later. Maybe you can let me cop a feel. Get to first base, you know?"

She laughed out loud.

I was thankful she found it funny, because that really could have gone either way.

"Okay, Romeo."

I laughed at her. Wait. "Huh? What do you mean 'okay'?"

"Pull over, let's get this awkwardness out of the way. I think you're right. I mean, what if you're a shit kisser? At least we'll know now, right? So let's go." She rubbed her hands together and rolled her shoulders.

I glanced over at her, trying to work out whether she was kidding.

She laughed. "Pull over already."

So I did.

Before the car had come to a stop, she was taking off her seatbelt and turning to face me.

I switched the car off and did the same.

And we sat there, staring at each other.

She licked her lips. My eyes focused on them. My palms began to sweat, and for some reason, I was actually nervous. I put my hand to the side of her face, my fingers laced through her hair. I brought her face closer to mine and closed my eyes. I heard her breath catch. Our lips touched slightly, right before she...laughed.

Fucking laughed.

I swear at this point I thought she might actually be crazy. Legit crazy. But then she looked at me with tears in her eyes from laughing so hard, and I couldn't help but do it, too. So there we were, laughing like idiots. Then I felt her hand on my leg and her mouth was on mine and before I knew it we were kissing.

And not the first-kiss type kissing, but kissing.

My hand went back up to the side of her face. I pushed my fingers through her hair and brought her closer to me.

She moaned.

I deepened the kiss.

Her hands reached up to hold my arms.

And we kissed.

She leaned in closer, one hand going to my hair, tugging.

I opened my mouth to lick her lips.

Then our tongues collided.

And so did the world around us.

My arm went around her to bring her closer. I didn't want to stop. Not yet.

She pulled back abruptly, her eyes wide. "Shit," she muttered.

"Wow," I breathed out. Apparently, I'd grown a vagina.

She settled back into her seat, put on her belt, and then looked over at me.

I never once took my eyes off her.

She smiled. "You can take me to dinner now," she said.

So I did.

WE ENDED UP at a steakhouse a few blocks from her work. "This place has the best banana splits known to man." She walked ahead of me toward the restaurant doors. I watched her ass.

I opened the door for her, and we walked in with my hand on the small of her back.

We were seated in a corner booth. I sat on one side. She sat on the other.

"So," I started. "You're the first girl I've ever taken out on a date."

She threw her head back in laughter.

I raised my eyebrows.

"Oh shit!" Her features straightened. "You're serious?"

I nodded.

"How awkward for you." She didn't even try to hide her smirk.

"It is." I fake pouted. "And you're being mean. You should be holding my hand and comforting me."

"Aw," she cooed, treating me like a baby.

"I mean it," I told her.

She scooted closer to me. "Better?"

"Nope." I moved so I was right next to her. "This is better." I put my arm on the seat behind her head.

She smiled up at me.

And something in me switched.

That was the moment she became more.

More than just hot, or sexy, or any of the other things I'd call her if I was surrounded by other like-minded assholes. My dad—he would call it timeless or classic. The type of beauty that no matter what time, age, or era would always still be beautiful. She was beautiful.

"How come I've never seen you before? At parties or whatever?"

She shrugged. "Not really the party type girl."

"Figures," I said. "I'd for sure remember you."

She bit her lip.

I kissed it.

She kissed back, only for a moment, before laughing into my mouth.

"You just kiss people whenever you want, huh?"

I chuckled. "No, just you, Amanda. I can't fucking help myself around you." Truth.

She started blushing, Then subtly moved closer to me. Her hand landed on my leg.

I moved my arm and placed it over her shoulders and then lifted her chin with my finger. I licked my lips. She did the same. Her eyes drifted shut. I leaned down. "Ahem." Stupid throat-clearing, douche hole waiter. "Hey, Amanda," he said flatly.

She pulled away from me and faced the waiter, her eyes wide. "Hey, Greg."

The kid didn't say shit. Just glared at me. "Problem?" I asked him.

"I'll be back," she said from next to me, Then stood up and pulled Glarey McGlare Dick away from the table.

They walked over to the bar area and spoke heatedly to each other. His arm kept pointing at me. I got up on his third point. She raised her hand to stop me. I waited. Then she spoke calmly to him, and after a few moments, she visibly relaxed and got on her toes to hug him.

She resumed her position next to me but not as close. I waited for her to speak. To tell me what the fuck just happened. But she never did. Instead, she just opened the menu in front of her, smiled at me, and said, "You wanna just get a little of everything and share it?"

"Sure." I stopped caring about what happened the second she smiled.

WE ORDERED AND ate almost silently. I made a mental note to take her somewhere else next time. Somewhere we could actually talk. Maybe I was getting too far ahead of myself. Maybe I just really wanted there to be a next time.

She was right. That place did have the best banana splits known to man and the biggest ones, too. We ended up having to share, which was a great excuse to be closer to her.

"So I need to ask you something," I told her while we waited for the check.

She moved in closer again, her hand resting on my leg. Without even thinking, I took it in mine and linked our fingers. And then froze. I wondered for a moment if it was like that with everyone, the nerves and sweaty palms of first kisses, or the seemingly natural progression of first dates.

"Logan?" She pulled me away from my thoughts.

"Huh?" I looked down at our linked hands.

She squeezed them once. "You were going to ask me something?"

My eyes lifted to meet hers. What was I going to say? Oh yeah. "That day when I tried to get your number, and you didn't give it to me. You got all weird when I told you my name. What's that about?"

She laughed. "I don't know. I've kind of heard about you." My eyebrows rose, wanting her to continue. "You know my friend, Alexis?"

"Oh yeah. I like Alexis." A smug smile took over my face. "She's good at giving out numbers."

She continued to laugh. "I know you like her, Logan. Well, you did. Once. One night—a year or so ago. You guys kind of fooled around, and then you never called her. Although, in your defense, you straight out told her you wouldn't, so she wasn't too surprised."

My mouth dropped.

She laughed at my reaction.

WE WALKED OUT of the restaurant hand in hand. Once we were in my car, I turned to her. She was already facing me. "So," I said.

"So." She smiled.

"I kind of don't want to take you home," I told her.

"Then don't." She shrugged.

"How about—I mean, do you want to maybe come back to my place for a bit? We can just hang out, promise. We don't have to do anything. I just kind of don't—"

"Okay," she cut in.

I had the car on the road and heading to my house faster than a fat kid eats cake.

I pulled into the driveway, and we met in front of the car. She smiled up at me. "Thanks for dinner, by the way." She took both my hands in hers, got on her toes, and kissed me. Then she pulled back, looking unsure about what she just did.

So I did the only thing I knew to reassure her that it was fine. It was more than fucking fine. I put one hand on her waist and the other behind her head and I kissed her.

And I don't know how long we stood there softly kissing, but I wanted more. Much more.

Somehow, she ended up on the hood of my car with me between her legs. My hand had somehow made its way under her shirt and just under her bra. "Oh my god," she moaned into my mouth.

I pulled back slightly. "I know I am, but my name's Logan."

She shook her head, chuckling. "Come here, asshole," she said, bringing me back down to her.

Then I heard the sound of a throat clearing.

We immediately stopped and both looked up.

Dad.

He stood at the front door, arms crossed, eyes narrowed.

"Shit," I muttered under my breath. I stood to full height, straightened my clothes and tried to hide my boner.

Amanda made a squealing sound and hid behind my body. "Oh my god." I heard her mumble. She fisted the back of my shirt with her hands and planted her face into my back.

I put my hands in my front pockets and looked down.

"Logan." Dad nodded once in greeting. "Don't mind me. I was just on my way out."

I nodded back, looking up, but not making eye contact.

"I take it you'll be in the pool house tonight?" he asked.

"Yep."

He got in his car and drove away. I let out the breath I didn't know I was holding and turned to face Amanda.

Her face was bright red. "That was so fucking embarrassing." Her mouth on my chest muffled her words. I chuckled and held her head close, kissing her on the forehead.

And for some reason, it felt okay to do this—to be this—with her.

"So," I said, hands in pockets. We'd just entered the pool house. She walked around, taking everything in. I walked behind her, staring at her ass.

"So," she mimicked, spinning to face me.

I quickly darted my eyes away from her ass.

"Busted."

I shrugged. "I can't help that your ass deserves to be admired."

She laughed quietly and shook her head. She took two steps forward and put her arms around my neck. Then her mouth was on mine, and we were kissing again. I didn't mind. Not one fucking bit. I loved the fact that she was the one to make the moves.

I moved us to the sofa, never once breaking the kiss. I sat down and positioned us so she was straddling me. We started grinding on each other. Her hips moved while our mouths and tongues played. Every now and then she'd moan, and I'd get so fucking turned on. She must have known it, because under my jeans I was hard as a fucking rock.

Then she pulled away. "Sorry," she said, biting her lip. "I'm not that girl, Logan."

I eyed her curiously. "What do you mean? What girl?"

"I mean, I'm not just going to sleep with you—"

I opened my mouth to interrupt, but she talked over me. "I don't mean to be a tease. I'm sorry."

"Don't say that about yourself. You're not a tease. At all. And just so you know, I don't think you could ever be that girl. Not to me." I felt it again—that nervous tension. My heart pounded against my chest. "Look, I really like you. Honestly. And I mean—I'd be stupid to not want to sleep with you. But—maybe after I take you out a few more times?"

Her eyes widened. A slow smile crept to her lips. "Okay," is all she said.

SHE SHUFFLED OFF me and lay down on the sofa so her feet were over my legs. "I'm so exhausted." She covered her eyes with her arm. "I've worked a thousand hours this week."

Before I realized what I was doing, I'd pulled her shoes off and started rubbing her feet. Her moans made me look up at her face. Our eyes locked. She licked her lips.

My dick twitched.

"Why do you work so much?" I tried to change my focus.

"Need the money for college." She shrugged, as if it wasn't a big deal. “Come here,” she whispered, scooting to the corner of the sofa so I could lie down next to her. I ended up on my back, with her half on top of me.

Her face was so close I could feel her breath on my cheek. She kissed it quickly before pulling away.

“Tell me something,” she said.

I chuckled. “What do you mean?”

“Tell me something that means something—something important to you.”

I thought about it for a long time. One hand played with her hair, the other on her waist. My thumb rubbed her stomach under her top. “If I tell you something, you have to promise not to ask about it.”

She reared back slightly and then looked me in the eyes. “Promise.”

“When I was younger, something happened to me, and for a while I didn’t talk. Like, at all. To no one. I had a hard time sleeping and couldn’t really grasp the idea of night and day, so my dad—he told me that instead of living life by time and dates, to live them by moments. And instead of trying to remember how old I was or what day it was, try to remember how I felt during those moments. So that’s what I do when I experience things.”

She was watching me, waiting for me to go on, unsure if I was done. So I continued, “Okay, say I asked you about the first time you learned how to ride a bike. The first thing you would tell me is how old you were, right?”

She nodded her head slowly, her finger moving the hair away from my forehead.

“Well, if you asked me the same question, I’d say...I felt happy or like I was flying, and I remember smiling huge and laughing. For the first time in a long time, I felt free.”

Her eyes stayed focused on mine, burning with an intensity I hadn’t seen before. Then her hand reached up to cup my jaw. “I think that maybe you—Logan Matthews—are someone I’d really, really like to get to know.”

I leaned up and kissed her again. Only this time, it was slower. This kiss—it was different. I wasn’t just kissing her because I wanted in her pants. I was kissing her because I wanted her.

And that's what we did.

For minutes that felt like seconds, we kissed. And I let myself have something I'd never wanted to feel before. I wanted her to want me—not just physically—all of me.

When we finally pulled apart, she rested her forehead on mine. "Can you take your shirt off?"

"What?" I was still in a daze, so there was no way I had heard her right.

She stood up in front of the sofa. I sat up.

"Take off your shirt," she repeated, not a trace of humor in her tone.

"What?" I said again.

She pouted. "Please?"

"No." I shook my head laughing. I tried to stand, but she pushed me down with her hands on my chest and straddled me again.

"Please?" she repeated, then enforced a megawatt pout.

I couldn't fucking say no to her. I started to lift it, but her hands covered mine. "I want to do it," she said quietly. Then her hands lifted my shirt over my stomach, my chest, and then my head. "Sweet. Baby. Fucking. Jesus," she breathed out.

I smirked.

Her finger ran down my chest, onto my stomach where they trailed along the dips of my muscles. She bit her lip again and then pulled out her phone.

"What—" I started, but the sound of the camera cut me off.

I tried to take the phone out of her hands, but she held it away. "What are you doing?" I kept reaching for it, but she was too fast.

"Alexis told me you had this killer body, I'm just sending her a text to tell her I agree."

"Are you sending a picture to her?"

"Yep," she announced, unashamedly.

Her phone pinged. She looked at the phone and laughed.

"What is funny? Give it to me." I tried to reach for it again. She slapped my hand away.

"Fine," I huffed out. "I don't wear a shirt, you take your jeans off."

She smiled. "Actually, I was going to ask if I could change into one of your sweats. You know," she paused for a beat, "I just want to get comfortable."

I didn't even think twice. I picked her up by her ass and carried her over to the bed, where I lazily threw her down. She squealed with laughter as she landed. I pulled out a pair of sweatpants from my dresser but held them behind me. "Strip," I told her.

Her eyes went huge.

I raised my eyebrows.

"No," she deadpanned.

I waited.

"Fine," she ground out.

I leaned back on my heels, anticipating a show.

She kicked off her shoes and lay flat on the bed. Then she unbuttoned her jeans. My eyes stayed focused on her hands.

She cleared her throat. I looked up at her face. Then I heard the zipper start. My eyes automatically went down to her hands. "Stop," I said.

She did.

My eyes travelled from her hands on her jeans, up her body, until our eyes locked. "I want to do it," I repeated her words.

I threw the sweats on the floor and moved so I was between her legs. I leaned over her, bracing my weight with one arm. And then I kissed her. Slowly. My mouth moved to her jaw, her neck, and her chest. I lifted her shirt and kissed her flat stomach. And then lower and lower. I felt her tense, then squirm as my mouth went lower again. I curled my fingers around the band of her jeans and slowly lowered it. She lifted her hips to assist me. I pulled them down past her hips, past her ass, and past her panties. Her fucking black lace panties. I heard her breath catch. I glanced up at her face—she was biting her lip, her eyes shut tight. I stood to full height. "Okay," I said. "You can do the rest." I quickly turned and adjusted myself, picking up the sweatpants as I did. If I was there a second longer, I would've ripped off her panties and tasted her. No. Fucking. Doubt.

"Here." I turned around and held them out to her. She was pulling her jeans off her feet. It was the first time I saw her legs. Her fucking legs. I think my eyes actually caught on fire.

"Perv," she joked.

I didn't say shit. I was too busy staring at her fucking legs.

She pulled on the sweats and walked over to the kitchen, rolling the band over her waist a few times. "I'm hungry," she announced.

I stared at her ass.

She started opening and closing the cupboards searching for something. She opened the pantry, and her eyes went wide. "Holy Moly Batman, you've got like, everything in here." She started picking up random things, looking at them quickly, then putting them back. "How do you have all this stuff?"

"My dad has a housekeeper come in twice a week to stock up," I told her, moving behind her and placing my hands on her waist. I kissed her bare shoulder; she tilted her head to the side. I started kissing her neck. "Ooh," she murmured, pulling out a packet of gummy bears.

I jumped to sit on the counter and watched as she opened the freezer, took out some ice cream, and spooned it into a bowl. Then she picked out only the red gummy bears from the packet and placed them in the ice cream.

"That's fucking disgusting."

She shrugged and picked up the bowl, then turned to face me. She froze, looking right at my chest, as if she'd forgotten that I didn't have a shirt on.

"What?" I smirked, inconspicuously popping my muscles.

Her gaze left my chest and lifted to my eyes. She bit her lip, her eyes half-hooded. "I really want to take this ice cream and smear it all over your body and then lick it off, really fucking slowly."

A strangled sound travelled out of my mouth before I could stop it.

This girl kept fucking surprising me—in a good way.

She sat down on the sofa, and I sat next to her. "So only the red ones, huh?" I asked.

"Yeah." She finished chewing before she continued. "The others taste weird." Her nose scrunched.

Fuck, she was cute.

I jerked my head toward her bowl. "Okay, let me try it." My mouth opened, waiting.

Instead of giving it to me, she got a spoonful and put it in her mouth. Then her mouth was on mine, and it was hot and cold at the same time. She pushed a gummy bear into my mouth with her tongue.

Ho. Lee. Fuck.

I swallowed, then brought her mouth back to mine and kissed her. I couldn't stop fucking kissing her.

SHE STOOD UP and started walking around the room. I watched her, waiting for my dick to calm itself down before I got up. She stood in front of the CD rack and started fingering the cases.

"Wow, you kind of listen to a bit of everything, huh?" She walked over to the iPad sitting on top of the floor speakers, turned the screen on and started tapping it. "You have all your music on iTunes, as well?"

I got up and stood behind her. "Yeah, I buy most of the stuff on iTunes, but some of my favorites I buy on CDs, too. I kind of like to have something physical to hold, you know?"

She nodded. "I'm the same way but with books. Everything's digital now, but sometimes I'll buy a paperback if I love the book. I love the smell of them, too. Like the first time you open them up and they're fresh and new. Or old books," she kept talking, animated, and I found myself smiling with her. "Old books are better—and when they're all together, oh my God, like used book stores—I love them the most. You don't find many anymore, because you know, the whole e-reader thing. But I love finding them in random places." She paused to take a breath. "Whoa, I just rambled about books. Now you know every nerdy aspect of me. I bet you can't wait to take me out again." She rolled her eyes and looked down to the floor.

I laughed. "It's cool. You're passionate. There's nothing wrong with that. Wait till you meet my friend Lucy. You guys would get along so well. She's always reading at the-"

"You want me to meet your friends?" she asked. There was confusion in her voice but hopefulness, too.

"Why wouldn't I?"

She shrugged and took a seat in front of the CD rack and started reading album names out loud, occasionally pulling one out.

I sat on the floor next to her and waited. "You really do like everything. There's hip-hop, pop, reggae, country?" Her head whipped to mine.

I shrugged. "I'm eclectic."

"You have every John Mayer album and single ever released." She pulled one out and looked on the back.

I brought her to me so she was straddling me again. She didn't refuse, but her eyes never left the CD. "So what's the deal with John Mayer?"

I started kissing her neck. I couldn't help it. Her head tilted to the side, giving me better access. "Hey, don't knock John Mayer. He's practically a god," I said, pulling back to face her. "'Your Body Is a Wonderland' is a fucking anthem. Do you know how many times I've gotten lai—" I caught myself quickly, "...ooked at...while that song's played?"

She laughed, pulling back from my mouth. "How many times have you been 'layooked' at?" She giggled some more. "I don't think 'layook' is a word."

"It is so a word. Google it."

She pushed me until I fell flat on my back. Then her hand was in my pocket. My body jerked when her hand brushed against my dick. "What are you doing?"

She smirked, holding my phone in her hand. "Googling your imaginary word." She slid her finger across the screen and started typing. "So, unless I'm spelling it wrong, layook is not a word."

She raised her eyebrows at me.

I grabbed the phone from her hand and threw it across the room. "Yeah, you spelled it wrong." I sat up and started kissing her neck again, moving lower to her chest. I heard her moan quietly. My fingers on her waist dug into her skin the closer I got to her tits. She grabbed my head in both her hands and made me face her.

"How do I always end up in this position?" she asked, her arms around my neck.

I kissed her a couple of times. "I like this position. In fact, consider this permanent."

She laughed into my mouth before pushing me back down onto my back.

"So." Her fingers started roaming my chest and lower to my

abs, her eyes following. "I'm not going to ask—about what happened when you were younger—but you said that you didn't speak for a while—what changed?" Her eyes moved up to meet mine.

I looked at her, trying to decide how much of myself I wanted to give her.

"What do you mean?" I asked, giving myself time.

"Well, what helped you to talk again? You don't have to tell me if you don't want to. I'm sorry. It's probably extremely personal. Never mind—"

"If I tell you, then you have to tell me something about you. Deal?"

She nodded.

"Okay." I sat up slightly, leaning on my elbows. "My dad made up this game to help me. It's called two truths for fifteen."

"How do you play?"

"It's so stupid, you're going to laugh."

"No, I won't. Swear it." She pouted.

"It's just—" I laughed at how stupid it was going to sound. "We asked each other a question and had to tell the truth, and we talked about it for fifteen minutes. See? Stupid."

"It's not stupid. It's really sweet. Your dad seems like a nice guy."

"He is. He's the best." Truth. "Your turn."

She eyed the ceiling a moment before answering. "You know how I hate blood?" I jerked my head in a nod. "It kind of really sucks, because I want to be a midwife." She paused and waited. "You can laugh now."

"Why? It's not funny. That sucks. Why midwife though?"

She shrugged. "I don't know. I guess I love the idea of bringing life into the world. Being one of the first to hold a miracle, you know? Babies—that's what they are. Miracles. I guess I like kids, too. Always have. So I'll just settle for childcare. Hopefully that won't involve too much blood." She chuckled to herself.

"It's called hemophobia, you know? The fear of blood."

Her eyes went wide. "I know that. But how do you?"

I shrugged. I wasn't about to tell her I googled it the night I met her at Jake's house. "They say it's normally caused by trauma in childhood or adolescence. Did something happen?"

She looked away. "Nope. Not that I know of," she said quickly. "So, that's me. I'm pretty boring."

"No, you most definitely are not boring."

She rolled her eyes, "You're just saying that because you want to get layooked."

I laughed. Hard.

She laughed with me, leaning into me hard enough that we both ended up lying down, her on top of me.

I brushed the hair away from her face "I like you, Amanda. You're something else."

She leaned down and kissed me. Slowly. Softly. Then she pulled back, covered her mouth, and let out the biggest yawn known to man.

I had to laugh. "Am I boring you?"

She shook her head, still yawning. It ended with a grunt. "No, Logan. I'm so sorry. I'm just so tired. I normally have a quick nap after work, but I didn't and I guess—"

I cut in. "It's fine."

She sat up and stretched.

I sat up, too. Then we just looked at each other. We both knew it was time, but I sure as hell didn't want it to be over.

She smiled sadly at me. "I guess you should probably take me home."

I broke our gaze and looked down. "Yeah, I guess." I ran the back of my fingers on her palm and the inside of her wrist.

"Yeah, I guess," she said quietly. I lifted my eyes to hers; she was looking down at our hands. "Or—I mean, I just need a power nap, and I'm good to go. Fifteen minutes," she said. Her eyes came back to mine; she looked unsure of herself.

I couldn't help the grin that took over. Maybe—just maybe—she felt the same for me as I felt for her.

I picked her up and walked over to the bed, lifted the covers and lowered her onto it. I kissed her on her forehead. "Good night, pretty girl."

"Where are you going?" She pulled on my hand.

I shrugged.

She scooted over.

I didn't even hesitate.

Then we just lay there, side by side, on our backs.

I felt the bed move and turned my head. She was on her side, her eyes half-closed. "Just a quick power nap," she assured. I didn't know whether she was speaking to herself or me.

"Okay," I said.

Then she scooted closer. I turned to my side and did the same. Her eyes opened fully, then locked on mine.

"Logan," she whispered.

I swallowed.

She moved closer.

I did the same.

A buzzing intensity ran through my body. We were so close.

Then I kissed her.

Our mouths moved. Our chests heaved. But nothing else.

No hands. No sounds. Nothing.

Nothing around us.

Not a single fucking thing. In that moment—it was just her.

Then she moved closer, her entire body flushed against mine.

Our breathing got heavy.

She picked up my arm and positioned it over her waist. I pulled her closer to me. And without me realizing, her hips had started moving. Thrusting. Like she needed some form of relief. I wanted to give it to her. I had to give it to her. My hand went to her stomach. Lower. And lower. Until it was just above her pants. My fingers dipped under the band. Her hand stopped me. She pulled it out but placed it between her legs, over her pants. I could feel the warmth. I started touching her. She kissed me deeper. Harder. Her breathing got heavier, more erratic. I needed to give it to her. She moaned into my mouth, then moved to lie on her back. Her knees raised. Her legs spread. Her fingers curled in my hair. I never stopped touching her. Then her hips started moving again. Pushing into my hand. All I could do was cup her and hope that it was enough. "I want to touch you," I whispered against her lips.

She never broke the kiss. "Not tonight." I kissed her deeper, my hands moving faster.

"Oh—shit—mm." She kept up with the kissing. "Shit. Stop," she said. But her hips never stopped moving.

"Why?" I asked her.

She pulled back, her head landing on the pillow. She bit her lip, her breathing sounding more and more like moans. "I'm gonna—and it's embarrassing—fuck—Logan—I'm—"

I watched as her head started thrashing from side to side.

Then her body stiffened.

I slowed my movements.

Her eyes shut tight.

I watched it all.

Then she let out a breath with a whoosh. Her eyes slowly opened, and they met mine. She kissed me once. "That was kind of embarrassing."

"No," I said seriously. "It was kind of beautiful."

Her eyes drifted shut again. "Just a power nap," she repeated.

"Okay."

She turned on her side again, with her face on my chest. Her arm went around me, and her legs tangled with mine. I did the same. "Huh." I heard her say.

And that's how we stayed. In each other's arms, holding on to this night.

I didn't want to let go.

Ever.

Maybe it was too soon.

Maybe it was too intimate.

Maybe it was too perfect.

"OH.MY.GOD!" she yelled. "Guess what fucking time it is?"

I sat up, still half-asleep. I must've dozed off, too. "I don't know."

"No, Logan, guess?!"

I rubbed my eyes. "I don't know, like, midnight?"

She showed me her phone. "It's four a.m."

"What? It can't be." I focused my eyes and took the phone from her hands.

She nodded her head dramatically, her eyes wide. "I have to be at work in five hours! You have to take me home. Like, right now!" She panicked and made a move to leave, but I held her back and pulled her into my arms. "Or..." I began. "You can just stay the night here, and I'll drive you to work when it's time."

She kissed me once and then pulled away. She eyed our surroundings and faced me again. Then she was quiet, thinking. "I don't think that's such a good idea," she stated.

I nodded, thinking about touching her again. "Yeah, you're probably right."

She got out of bed and so did I. I pulled out a new shirt from my dresser and grabbed my car keys. She walked toward the bathroom, her jeans in hand. I stopped her. "Just wear them and give them back to me next time I take you out."

She smiled. "Okay."

WE GOT TO her house faster than I would have liked. At one point, I glanced over and saw her nervously chewing on her lip. I leaned over, took her hand in mine, and gave her what I hoped was a reassuring smile. We didn't talk much; I guess we were both rehashing the events from last night. I wasn't sure what she was thinking, but I knew that I definitely wanted to see her again.

I pulled into her driveway and switched the car off, turning in my seat to look at her. She smiled softly, then turned to open her door.

"Wait," I said, "just wait there. I'll get that."

I jumped out of the car, ran to her side, and opened the door for her. She got out, and I closed it behind her. She leaned back against it and looked up at me. Her hand reached out and pulled at my shirt until my body was pressed against hers. Then her arms were around my neck, and my hands automatically went to her waist. She kissed me once. "So, I had a good night. Thank you, Logan."

"Yeah?" I asked.

She nodded.

"Not bad for a virgin dater, huh?"

She chuckled. "Nope, not bad at all."

"Okay," she sighed, removing her hands from around my neck. "I better get inside."

My hands took hers, and I locked our fingers together between us. "Okay," I said, before kissing her. A kiss I used to try to tell her how I felt. And if she decided—once she was in that house—that she never wanted to see me again, then at least she'd have that kiss to remember me by. Because I would. Remember her, I mean.

"Wow," she whispered, as we broke apart.

Good. She got it.

I kissed her a few more times, quickly, before pulling back completely.

"You'll call me, right?" Her eyes were cast downwards.

"Amanda," I said, trying to get her to see me. She looked up and into my eyes. "This." I motioned my finger between us. "It's not—I mean, it means more to me than what you're probably thinking. I'll definitely call you, okay?"

She nodded and then turned and walked away. I hated it. Seeing her walk away. I just—I don't know. I didn't want this to end. The truth was I actually gave a shit—if she didn't want to see me again—or want me at all. For the first time ever, I actually cared.

"Wait!" I ran up to her. She turned around with a confused look on her face.

"Do you have a break tomorrow? I mean—shit. Is that too soon? Is it like creepy stalker too soon? Fuck."

She laughed at me. "I have a break at two, and no, I mean maybe, but not for me. Too soon, I mean. And even if it is, who gives a shit." She shrugged. "I would love to see you, too soon."

Then she turned around and walked away, and I let her. I waited until she was in the house and I saw her bedroom light turn on. I got back into my car and pulled out my phone. I was about to text her, but she beat me to it.

> ***Amanda:*** *Is it too soon to tell you that I'm already missing the shit out of you?*

AMANDA

Amanda: *I saw him again.*
Alexis: *I assume we're talking about Logan?*
Amanda: *Yeah :(*
Alexis: *And?*
Amanda: *He kissed me.*
Alexis: *AND?*
Amanda: *I kissed him back.*
Alexis: *AANNDD?*
Amanda: *And nothing. I still hate him. And I hate myself for letting him have that part of me.*
Alexis: *I'm sorry, babe.*
Amanda: *Me too. :(*
Alexis: *Totally inappropriate, but how does he look?*
Amanda: *Totally messing with my emotions, but ah-fucking-mazing.*
Alexis: *Sigh. So dreamy.*
Amanda: *I hate him.*
Alexis: *I know, babe.*

"AMANDA?" His soft voice sounded from behind me. I turned to face him. His hands were in his pockets, his arms stiff, causing his shoulder muscles to pop. He was shivering a little from the cold.

"You're leaving?" he asked. We stood in the dark in Micky's front yard.

I nodded.

He looked around. "How are you getting home?"

"Cab."

"Alone?" He kept looking around the empty yard.

I nodded again.

He rubbed his palm against his jaw. I remembered that. It was one of the things he did that stayed in my mind long after he was gone.

"I don't really—" He sighed. "I don't want you to take this the wrong way, but I don't really think I'm comfortable with you taking a cab alone. I'd offer to drive you, but I've been drinking. So at least let me ride with you. You don't have to talk to me at all. I won't try anything. I won't kiss you. I won't talk to you. I won't even look at you. Swear it."

My eyes never left his. "It's not really your call what I do, is it?" I spat out.

"Amanda, I'm just worried—"

A bitter laugh escaped, interrupting him. "You know what? I was worried about you, too. I thought that maybe something had happened to you. That night? When you promised you'd call me, and you never did. You remember that, right?"

He nodded his head slowly, his gaze intense.

"See, I swear I thought we had something. I was so sure that you wanted me, too, the way I wanted you. God, I was so stupid. I actually thought you wanted me. Logan Fucking Matthews, with me?" I laughed to myself. "At least I can laugh about it now. But then, shit. Back then, I was genuinely worried about you. I thought for sure something bad had happened. Like, you'd been in a car accident or something—but of course I couldn't just call you. I didn't want be that pathetic girl who didn't get the hint. So you know what I did? I googled you—for days! Nothing came up.

"And you know what the worst part is? I waited—days—no weeks. Weeks. I would have still spoken to you weeks after. Every day I told myself you were going to call, or come around, or surprise me at work. How fucking pathetic is that?"

His mouth opened to say something, but I stopped him. "It was so fucking pathetic! So for days and days I waited and nothing. Not a single fucking thing from you." I was getting angry now. My words sharp, harsh. The tears started. I remembered everything. He stood there and listened silently, hands still in his pockets. He stared, right into my eyes, and he waited.

"Pathetic me, waiting for you, and I get nothing. For weeks, I sat around feeling sorry for myself. Because I fucking let you get to me. Until finally, Alexis convinces me that I need to get out. That I need to move on. So I do. I go to a stupid club, and who just happens to be there? You! You and some girl on your lap. And you couldn't keep your fucking hands off each other! And I hated it." My voice broke. "I hated that I had to see it. And I hated you!"

The anger consumed me. I started pushing him. He took every shove, not making a move to stop me. He stayed silent, while I got out over a year's worth of anger, frustration and heartbreak.

"I hated you so much that I left that stupid club and the stupid memory of you with it. I moved on and screwed some guy I didn't even care about!" Push. "And just like you, he treated me like shit!" Push. "And I didn't even fucking care anymore because it was you I hated. I still hate you." Push. "And now I'm here, and I have to deal with it. I have to deal with you and that one stupid night we had." Push. Shove. Push.

"It wasn't stupid, Amanda," he finally spoke, pinning my arms to my sides and holding me to him.

"What!"

"That night, with you. It wasn't stupid," he said flatly.

I pulled myself off him, "Fuck you, Logan."

"I'm sorry," he said, his voice quiet.

And I made the stupid mistake of looking at him.

And I saw it, the sadness consumed there.

But I didn't care.

Because I hated him.

A bunch of guys came streaming out the front door. Some of them patted Logan on the back or gave him some choice words. We never once took our eyes off each other.

I hated him.

"Amanda?" a deep voice interrupted. We both turned to see Shane, one of my brother's friends. "It is you."

He scratched his head.

"Hey, Shane. How are you?" I tried to act polite, hoping the anger inside me wasn't evident in my tone.

"Good. Are you okay?" He looked from me to Logan and back again. Logan was staring at the ground, like it was the most fascinating thing in the world.

I nodded.

"You, uh, you need a ride home?"

"Yes!" I shouted, before calming myself down. "Please. Thank you."

He waited for me to walk ahead of him, putting his hand on my back, as he led me to his car.

I didn't turn around.

I didn't look back.

Because I didn't hate him.

LOGAN

For over a year I tried to forget that night with her existed. I tried not to think about what she must have been thinking or how she must have felt. Eventually I convinced myself that she didn't care. That I was just another boy, another date, another night.

But then she stood in front of me and told me all this shit, and it took everything in me not to hold her. Not to have told her the truth, and how sorry I was, and beg her to fucking forgive me.

So I stood there and let her take out a year's worth of anger and pain on me, and I did nothing to make it better.

Because I couldn't.

How the fuck could I make things right when it was too damn late for all of it?

And then she left, with some guy she apparently knew, and I did nothing to stop her. Because she was not mine and I had no right.

I fucked up.

I fucked up bad.

And I wanted her.

I wanted her so fucking bad.

LOGAN

The Scare

PAST

I WOKE UP mid-morning the next day seedy and tired as fuck. I smiled to myself. So worth it.

Dad was in the kitchen reading the paper when I walked in. He lifted his head when he heard me. "Late night?" he asked, a knowing smirk on his face.

"Yeah, you could say that." I opened the fridge and then closed it again. Stupid habit.

"Has she left?"

"Yeah." I cleared my throat. "I took her home last night, or this morning actually."

He nodded once, not taking his eyes off me. "Do we need to talk about protection?"

"No!" I said quickly, then calmed myself down. "No. I'm good with that—trust me. But that's not—I mean, we didn't last night."

His eyes went wide; he misunderstood.

"No, that's not what I meant, I mean, we didn't...do that. We didn't have sex," I clarified.

He exhaled, relieved, and then went back to reading the paper.

I watched him. He's always been quiet, never really wanting to get too involved in my business. He got that sometimes I just needed to do things my way. I understood it was hard for him, without a woman around, to deal with certain things. He really made an effort to be both for me, but I got that it could be awkward for him.

"I really like her. Amanda, that's her name," I told him. I wanted to tell someone.

He looked up with a smile on his face. He folded the paper and put it aside, then leaned forward on his elbows, giving me his full attention.

"Yeah?" he asked.

"Yeah, she's something else. I'm actually going to meet her at work on her break today. Do you think it's too soon? I mean last night was our first date."

"Date?" he said, eyebrows raised.

I couldn't help but smile. "Yeah, date. It's strange, huh? Me going on a date."

"It's not strange, Logan. It's just about time. And no, I don't think it's too soon. If you both want to see each other then it doesn't matter, right?"

"I guess." I shrugged. "I feel like I need to do something, to tell her, or show her, that I liked being with her, you know?"

"Well, what does she like?"

I thought for a while. "Red gummy bears."

"Well, there you go." He smiled as he stood up and left the room.

I FINALLY PICKED out two bags with the most red gummy bears in them and started walking to the checkout.

That's when I saw her.

She stood in the middle of the aisle, looking down at something in her hands.

"Micky!" I yelled.

She dropped what she was holding. It fell to the floor.

I walked over to her.

She looked up, her face pale, her eyes wide, shocked. She was frozen. She hadn't moved since she saw me. She hadn't blinked. I doubt she was even breathing.

I stopped a few feet from her. I looked from her to the floor and then the shelf. She still hadn't moved. I picked up the item and looked at it. My stomach dropped to the floor. A pregnancy test. I lifted my gaze. Our eyes locked. And before I could say anything, she folded over herself as a sob overtook her.

I put the gummy bears on a shelf, brought her into my arms and led her to my car.

There was a goddamn ache in my chest, and I didn't know why.

I tried to talk through the lump in my throat, but nothing came out.

She sat there sobbing and frantically wiping her tears. She was trying to breathe through it, to calm herself down. And eventually, it started to work.

I didn't know how much more this girl could take. And I didn't know if there was anything I could have done to make it better. So I said the only thing I could think of to say. "You're pregnant?"

"I don't know." She said it so quietly I almost didn't hear it.

"So you haven't taken the test yet?"

"No." She started crying again. "Please, Logan. You can't tell anybody about this. No one. Especially Jake, please." She didn't want Jake to know. Why? Either way, I wasn't going to say shit to anyone.

"Mikayla, I wouldn't. It's not my story to tell."

Silence.

I sat there watching her for what felt like forever. "My dad's a doctor; I can take you to him, just to be sure. It's all confidential. It's the law or some shit. No one will know. I promise."

She nodded her head, looking out the window. I started the car and drove to Dad's practice.

I TOLD HER to sit in the waiting room while I found my dad.

She held on to my arm, stopping me from walking away.

I stopped and turned to face her.

She had tears in her eyes, waiting to fall. She looked up at me, and then suddenly her arms were around me, her face on my chest. She started crying again, and I don't know if she knew how loud she was, because the other people in the waiting room all looked up at her. Linda, the receptionist, saw what was going on and said, "Take her to your dad's office, Logan."

So I did.

A few minutes later, Dad came in. He closed the door behind him. He looked from me, then to Micky, and back to me again. "What's going on, Logan?" he asked suspiciously. And then it hit me, what it must look like to him. Me, bringing in some random girl, who's in tears, to see him, a doctor.

"Dad," I greeted. "This is Mikayla, uh...Jake's Mikayla."

I could see him visibly relax before a different emotion took over his features. He moved to squat in front of Micky, so they were eye to eye. "Hi, Mikayla," he started. "I'm Dr. Matthews, but you can call me Alan." He smiled at her. It was sympathetic, but it was also genuine. "What can I help you with today?"

She looked at him, then up at me. Our eyes locked for a second before tears started streaming down her face again. "I can't..." she trailed off.

I cleared my throat. Dad faced me.

"Micky needs a pregnancy test done." I told him.

He smiled at Micky. "That won't be a problem. I'll take you to see Michele, my assistant. She'll take care of everything for you, okay?"

Micky nodded again.

"Mikayla, whatever happens here, everything will be okay. I promise," he assured her.

Micky stood up and walked to the door, my dad leading her with his hand on her back. She stopped next to me, took my hand in hers and squeezed once, looking me right in the eye, and then they left the room.

And there was that fucking ache in my chest again.

Ten minutes later, she came back smiling. I couldn't help but smile, too.

"Good news I take it?"

She was crying happy tears. She wiped them away with the back of her hand. Then she laughed. It was that nervous, relieved kind of laugh. "Oh my God, Logan. I was so frickin' scared." Then her arms were around my neck as she brought me down to hug her. She was a lot shorter than me, so I had to bend down, my face landing on her shoulder. She wore perfume. It was flowery. Amanda's was fruity.

Amanda.

Shit!

As we headed back to my car, I pulled out my phone. It was 3:15. There was a text from her.

Amanda: *??*

My fingers became anxious. I had to type the text over and over.

Logan: *I'm so sorry! Something came up. I really want to see you though. I have a stupid thing I have to do tonight. Can I see you tomorrow? Please?*

I ENDED UP getting Julie from her friend's house, which happened to be the street down from mine. I dropped by the house to pick up my gear bag. I was meeting Jake at the cages after.

When we pulled up in the driveway, Jake's truck was already there. I saw him step out, and I knew instantly what he was thinking. Because I would, too.

I turned to Micky, her eyes wide, questioning. "I didn't say a word. Swear it."

We both looked back to Jake.

His fists were balled at his sides.

Jaw tense.

Eyes filled with rage.

He was pissed.

Beyond pissed.

"You girls stay here, okay?" Micky nodded before I stepped out of the car.

THE SECOND I'M out of the car he was on me, pushing and shoving and yelling, and I was two seconds from fucking punching him. But then I remembered that Julie was there.

I got why he was pissed. He loved Micky and he thought we were fucking around, but he wouldn't give me a chance to tell him what was going on. I tried to calm him down, but he wouldn't quit getting in my face. He was acting like an asshole, and I was about to shove him back when I heard Julie scream. I turned to see her in the middle of the road, standing inches away from a car that had almost hit her. I looked back to Jake, and he was yelling at both of them. What the fuck was wrong with him? I'd never seen that side of Jake before, and if I ever saw it again, we'd be done.

I SPENT THE rest of the afternoon subconsciously glancing at my phone, waiting for a text from Amanda.

Jake called and wanted to know what happened. I told him to ask Micky. It wasn't my place to say, and if she wanted him to know, she had to be the one to tell him.

There was a function that night with some pharmaceutical company Dad was involved with. I normally didn't have to go to those things, but he went on a few dates with one of the women from the company, and it didn't turn out so well. I was his buffer. If I didn't have to go with him, I'd definitely be going to see Amanda, I was sure of it.

THE DINNER SEEMED to go forever, and I was constantly checking my phone. I hadn't heard from her since her text earlier. By the time we got home, it was nearing ten.

Still nothing. I changed out of my suit and got into bed, but I was restless as fuck and I knew it was because I couldn't stop thinking about her. I picked up the phone from my nightstand and found her number, then stared at it. I didn't know how long I looked at it before I finally jumped out of bed and started pacing the room.

I took a few calming breaths and sat on the edge of the bed. Then I dialed her number.

My palms were sweaty. My heart pounded in my ears. It rang for so long I was about to give up. I pulled the phone from my ear, and that's when I heard her voice. "Hey," she said quietly.

"Hey!" I said, too loud. Too fast. "How...uh...how are you? Did you get my text?"

Silence.

Eventually I looked at my phone to see if she'd hung up, but she hadn't. "Amanda?"

"Yeah, Logan. I got it," she sighed out loud.

"Is something wrong? I mean...fuck. Are you pissed at me?" She had no right to be. I mean, I don't think she did. "Did I do something?"

"Uh, no," she said, but it came out as a question.

I took a deep breath in and let it out slowly, thinking about my next words. "Amanda, I'm new to all of this, so if I've done something, you need to tell me. Should I have called instead of texted? I mean, something really did come up. I'm not lying."

Silence. Again.

Followed by more silence.

Then finally she spoke. "Can I be honest with you, Logan?"

"No, I want you to lie to me." I tried to joke, but I don't think she got it.

The silence was unbearable.

"I feel like maybe you feel sorry for me or something," she started. "No, not sorry. I don't know what the right word is. Let me start again..." She was mumbling. "If last night was just that, just one night, then that's all good. I get it. For a second I thought that maybe it wasn't, but it's fine. Really. If you don't want to see me again, you don't have to-"

"I told you that I wanted to. I said in the text I wanted to see you tomorrow. What the hell?" I was being louder than I should be, but I couldn't help it. If this was what dealing with girls was like, I didn't know how the fuck Dylan and Cam did it.

"You're right. I'm sorry," she said quietly.

And now I felt like a dick for kind of yelling.

"I guess I'm just a little wigged out by this. I mean you. By you. You scare me."

"I scare you? How?" I spat out.

"Because..." she said, her voice softening. "I'm just scared that I might like you..." I heard her sigh loudly. "Pick me up from work at five?" she finally asked.

"Yes!" I was a little too excited. I calmed down and softened my voice. "I mean yes, if that's good for you, yes. I want to. I mean I'd like to take you out again."

She giggled a little.

"Amanda?"

"Yeah?"

"I'm trying really hard not to be the me you think I am. I'm not that person. At least not with you."

Truth.

LOGAN

The Visit

PAST

I SPENT THE next day moping around the house like a loser trying to find something that would make time go faster until I picked her up from work. I went to the store earlier and bought the gummy bears. I even opened them and sorted the red ones from the rest. The smug asshole in me was pretty impressed. The general asshole in me heard the sound of whips in my head.

I kept looking at the clock, waiting for a good time to leave. I didn't want to show up early and seem too eager. At four forty-five, I rushed out the front door and ran straight into a body.

"Holy shit," she yelped.

I held onto her and tried to regain my balance, and when I finally did, I took a step back. "Micky."

She stood with bags of groceries in both hands and an awkward smile on her face. "I thought that maybe...but I see you're on your way out. Never mind." She turned around and started to walk away, bags still in hands.

"Wait."

She spun to face me, her eyes glazed with wetness. She did that thing chicks do when their eyes go big so that the tears don't fall. "Hey, are you okay? What's going on?"

"Nothing." She sniffed once. "I just thought I'd make you and your dad dinner—kind of like a thank-you, for yesterday, I guess." She shrugged, looking right at me.

And for some reason, I couldn't fucking say no.

"Dad's not home, but I eat enough for two people." I opened the front door for her and led her to the kitchen. She placed the bags on the counter. I smiled at her. "What are you making? I'm starving."

"Pasta. It's pretty much the only thing I can cook." She started emptying the bags.

I excused myself and left the room so I could text Amanda. I wasn't sure why, but I didn't want Micky to know that I had plans. I didn't want her to think that it wasn't okay for her to be here.

Logan: *Hey. I'm really sorry to do this…something came up and I can't make it. I'll call you later though. Promise.*

When I got back into the kitchen, she had two pots on the stove and the burners on. She looked up when I walked in, giving me that same awkward smile. I sat on the island and watched her. I didn't know what to say to her, so the whole situation was a little off. But she was there for a reason, which was enough to make me sit and wait. She looked up from whatever she was cutting and faced me. "So, yesterday, with Jake—that was something, huh?"

I blew out a breath. "Yeah, it was definitely something."

"You didn't tell him what happened." It was a statement.

I shook my head. "It's not my place, Micky."

She looked at me for a long time, our eyes locked, neither looking away. Who knows how long we were there, watching each other, until finally, she looked back down. Then she spoke. "Jake, he's a great guy…" she trailed off.

"One of the best," I said.

She was still looking down, chopping whatever was in front of her. "Yeah, he really is. But what happens…I mean, what happens to me, if something happens to us?" Her voice broke. When she looked up at me, there were tears in her eyes again.

I slowly got off the stool and moved to stand in front of her. "What's going on, Micky?" I bent slightly so I could look at her face.

"I've only known him a month. I mean, I know I have feelings for him, Logan. But what happens if he decides he doesn't like me. I'll have no one. It'll be like that night all over again. You know... prom night. He can't be all I have. I can't go through that loss again." She broke down and hugged herself. "And I miss them, Logan. I miss my family so fucking much, and I can't tell him that. I can't talk to him about it because he'll think that he's not doing enough to help me, but it's not about him. It's not about..." Her body fell into mine, and she cried. Loud, uncontrollable cries.

I moved us so we were sitting on the floor and we were face to face, and I let her cry.

"I miss them so fucking much," she continued. "And I miss James, and I even miss Megan. And it's not that I want those two back in my life. I just miss the times, you know? And my sister, Emily, I miss her the most. I always thought she was this pain in my ass, but I miss her the fucking most. I miss her laugh, and I miss how we used to make fun of Dad, and I miss the way Mom smiled at us when we did it. I miss the way Dad would always make us breakfast and...I just miss them." Her tears fell endlessly as she wiped her nose with the back of her hand. "I'm so sorry, Logan. Shit, I didn't come here to put all this on you. Swear it."

She looked up at me. I hadn't said a word. I didn't think I could have said anything through the knot in my throat and that goddamn ache in my chest.

"It's just—it's been hard. Like, really fucking hard. It's not like I lost one parent, and the other was there to help me get through it. And even though I'm an adult, I'm still a child...aren't I? If I don't have parents, am I still someone's child? Oh my God. I'm not ready to do this."

She started to cry harder.

"It's not fucking fair, Logan." She was almost yelling now. "It's not fair. It's not right, and it's not fucking fair. I shouldn't have to wake up one random day and have nothing—and I feel like I can't tell the only person I have in my life any of this because he doesn't get it. He doesn't understand that I just need to miss them and that he can't fix it. He wants to make sure that I'm okay all the time, and that's great. That's perfect. But sometimes I just need to feel not okay." She couldn't control her breathing anymore.

We were both sitting against the island. I put my arm around her and held her to me. She leaned in and rested her head on my chest. "I just need to feel not okay, Logan. I just need to feel the hurt. All of it. And I don't know that I want him to see that."

I don't know what I was supposed to say. If I was supposed to say anything at all. But I got it. I knew exactly how she felt. Because I'd felt it, too. So I told her.

"Micky, I'm adopted."

She instantly stopped crying and pulled her head off my chest, her eyebrows drawn together in confusion.

"Alan, who you met yesterday—he adopted me when I was seven. He was the doctor who was working the ER the night my birth mother brought me in. My birth dad—he beat me pretty bad that night."

She gasped.

"I mean, he used to beat me all the time, so I guess it must have been pretty bad, because she took me to the hospital..."

"Oh my God." She looked at me, her eyes huge, her hand covering her mouth, tears still falling.

"Yeah, Dad...uh...Alan...he saved me that night and every night since then. My birth mom, she never came back for me. They waited a month. She never came."

"Oh my God, Logan," she whispered. "I'm so sorry."

"No one knows, Micky. Just you. And I didn't tell you because I wanted your pity. I told you because..." I took a deep breath and thought about my next words. "I told you because I get it. I get what it's like to feel like you depend too much on one person. I felt like that with Alan. I still feel like that, every day. But I couldn't have done it without him, and I think we all need someone to be our strength sometimes, and if you don't want that to be Jake, then you can let that be me...if you want to, I mean. Look, I just..." I blew out a breath. She sat and listened to everything I said. "I just wanted to tell you that I get it. I know what it's like to wake up one day and have nothing—"

"It's not the same—" she started.

I interrupted her. "I know it's not the same, Micky. I know your family died...I'm stupid, I shou—"

"No, Logan." It was her turn to interrupt me. "It's not the same because my family died. I can't see them ever again. You can see yours, but they're such bad people, you wouldn't want to. It's not the same because I'll always have good memories of my parents and you—you don't even have that." Her voice broke. I held her tighter. Her arms went around me.

I took in her words and let them sink in.

I never thought of my birth parents as a memory, as something I could bring out when I wanted to. And I never thought hard enough for a good memory of them. And even if I did, I don't know that there would be any.

"How do you do it?" she asked. "How do you wake up every day and be the person you are? That's a huge thing to happen to you, and it's not like you just go through life 'getting by.' How are you so normal?"

I thought about my answer for a while. "Because, Micky, it's my past. It's not my future, and it sure as shit isn't who I am. I'm not going to let that define me. I'm not going to let abusive or neglectful people ruin me. What they did—that's on them. That's their guilt to carry. It has nothing to do with me or who I am. And so what if it happened." I shrugged. "I lived through it. And that asshole went to jail; my dad—Alan—made sure of it. He made sure he wasn't going to be out there, possibly having more kids to beat on."

It was silent for what seemed like forever. Then, finally, she spoke. "God, Logan. You were just a kid..." Another round of sobs took over her. I placed my hand on the back of her head and held her to me as I listened to her cry. There was that same fucking ache in my chest, and I didn't exactly know what it was. But it was this moment—this exact moment—with her in my arms, that I felt something. Something I'd never felt before. Ever.

And I got it. I got why Jake wanted to be a rock for this girl. Why he wanted to make sure that she was never hurting or that she was never sad. I got why he'd do anything to make sure she was okay.

Because I felt it, too.

Her sobs grew silent, but her tears still fell. Her head lifted from my chest. I moved the hair away from her face. Then she looked up at me, her eyes huge. Expectant. Waiting. For me to say something

—anything—that would let her know that it would be okay, that we would be okay. "Micky..."

She sniffed once. I took in her face and then looked into her eyes, my gaze dropping to her mouth quickly before I spoke. And I didn't know why the next question came out, but it did. "Does Jake know you're here?"

She slowly shook her head.

Then suddenly, the smoke alarm went off.

We pulled apart and were on our feet so quickly, my head spun.

SHE DIDN'T END up cooking dinner. In fact, she left pretty much straight away. It was awkward after that, or at least I felt awkward, but it could have just been in my head.

After I cleaned up the mess in the kitchen and put away the groceries, I headed to the pool house for the night. I lay on my bed for I didn't know how fucking long, thinking about whatever the hell just happened with Micky and wishing that some of it, any of it, actually made sense.

I pulled out my phone to look at the time; it was almost nine. There was a text from Amanda at 5:05.

> ***Amanda:*** *Okay? I wish you would have told me earlier. I would have organized a ride home. Can you call me if you get done before 7? I can't get home until then. Hope you're okay.*

Shit. I felt like the biggest asshole in the world.

Fuck, I was the biggest asshole in the world.

I was about to the tap the screen to call her, but then I thought about what I was going to say, and I panicked.

The thing was I really, really liked Amanda. And yeah, we could have gone out a few times to see how things went...but I didn't want to do that to her. Not now. Not when I didn't fucking understand my feelings for Micky. Because Amanda, she was great. She was more than great. She was amazing. And she deserved to find someone who was going to treat her like that. And right now, that wasn't me. Not even close.

I sat up in bed and looked at my phone, trying to play out the words I was going to use when I told her all this. Except nothing came to me. Nothing at all. Not. One. Single. Fucking. Word.

I didn't call her that night or the night after. Or any of the nights after that.

LOGAN

PRESENT

I WENT BACK into the party and drank. Because really? What the hell else was I going to do?

I was drunk.

Girls approached me, but I made it clear I wasn't interested. I could still smell her fruity perfume on me, and I didn't want another girl's scent to cause it to fade.

If you asked me where my balls were right now, I would tell you she had them. Probably in her pockets while that asshole was making his move on her. I would say to that asshole, 'Suck it, dude. She has my balls.'

"What?" Lucy laughed from next to me. She was as wasted as I was.

"Huh?" We were lying on a trampoline in the back yard. I have no fucking idea why Jake and Micky have a trampoline.

Lucy laughed again. "You just said something about an asshole sucking a dude with my balls."

"What!" I laughed out. "You made no sense! Also, I don't think I meant to say that out loud."

Then we both laughed.

Once we settled, Lucy sighed. "Are you thinking about her, Logan?"

"Who?"

"Amanda."

"Pshh." I knew she knew something. "Amanda who?" I played dumb.

"Cam told me about the diner—how you paid Lachlan to force her to go out with you." She giggled.

"Cam has a big mouth."

She sat up abruptly, gasping, her eyes huge. She was staring at me with her mouth hanging open. She whisper yelled, "Dude! Cam says the same thing about me!"

"What?" I got out through a chuckle.

"Yeah," she said, nodding her head frantically. "He says I have a big mouth, too. You know? When he puts his-"

"Lucy!" I shouted, stopping her from saying what I think she was about to say. I pulled her back down. She laid her head on the crook my arm. "Way too much information," I told her.

"I love Cameron," she informed me dreamily, her head getting more comfortable.

"I know you do. He loves you, too."

"No, Logan. I mean I love him." She sat back up and looked down at me. "I love him so fucking much it hurts sometimes." Her voice broke. "The good hurt, you know?"

I didn't.

"Seriously, if he asked me to marry him right now and have his babies, I'd do it. Instantly. I love him that fucking much."

I smiled at her.

She went back to lying on my arm.

"Also," she continued, "this girl in one of my classes keeps wanting me to warn you that her brother is after you."

I rolled my eyes. "What girl? What do you tell her?"

"I tell her to fuck off. And that she needs to learn to control her hormones. Get it, Logan? WHORE-MOANS? Oh my God. I'm so fucking funny!"

Her laughter made me laugh. "You're my favorite people, Luce." I held on to her tighter.

"Yeah, yeah. I have a boyfriend. Don't even try it."

An hour or so later, the party began to die down. Cam came

out looking for us. We spent the rest of the time mainly in silence. We stopped drinking though, so we were a bit more clearheaded now.

"Hey, babe. We're crashing here. You ready for bed?" he asked.

She didn't move from next to me. She'd fallen asleep. I nudged her. "Lucy, your boyfriend's here."

She slowly woke up, confused, and then saw Cam. "Hey, baby," she cooed. She started to get up but swayed from the motion of the trampoline or maybe the one too many beers we had.

"How drunk are you, Luce? You drunk enough to let me do that thing you never let me do to you?" I could tell he was only half-joking.

She snorted and got off the trampoline and onto his back. He piggybacked her toward the house. "Yo!" Cam yelled out, "You crashing here, too?"

I nodded.

What else was I going to do?

I WAS OUTSIDE on the back deck having a smoke when Lucy walked out. I didn't smoke often. Actually, I barely did. Just when I drank. I didn't even know why I did it; it was a shitty habit.

Lucy walked out in her pajamas. Purple with pink hearts, like she was ten years old or something.

She waved her hand in front of her face to clear the smoke and exaggerated a cough. She pulled the cigarette out from between my fingers and put it out on the railing, then threw it in the bushes in front of us.

"Smoking kills, you know that right?" she said.

I looked away. Lucy's mom died of lung cancer a few years back. I stayed quiet.

"You know how Cam and I met?" she asked out of nowhere.

I leaned my elbows on the rail and looked out to the yard. "Kind of." I shrugged.

She stood next to me and copied my position.

"Cam used to help coach Lincoln and Liam's little league team."

"Yeah." I knew that much.

"Yeah, it was a few years back, before Mom died." Her voice ended in a whisper.

She sniffed once. I don't know if she was crying, or about to, but I didn't look at her. "After Mom died, Cam just started coming around to the house. Every day after school he was there, helping out however he could. I mean, he must've known that we'd be struggling. The first few months without Mom were devastating. Dad—he could barely get up in the mornings. I don't know how Cam knew, but he was just there. He pretty much raised the boys the first few months. I mean, I was there, too, but so was he..." She stopped to catch her breath and wipe the tears that had developed. "To this day, I don't know why he was. I've asked him a couple times. He just shrugs and says he just wanted to help. I don't even know when we became a couple. One night we were washing the dishes, and he kissed me, and that was it. For the first few months, he was there every night helping me with the boys. Eventually Dad snapped out of the funk and became a dad again...and Cameron and I... we became an us."

"Cameron's good people, huh?"

"The best," she agreed.

"So what's up? Why are you telling me this?"

"Because. I don't—I just think you should know that even though he acts like an asshole, and he's crude and obnoxious sometimes, he really is a good guy, and I love him. He's kind of like you, Logan. And one day, you'll find someone who loves you as much as I love him."

I faced her, our eyes locked for the longest time. Then I shook my head, thinking about what happened with Amanda. "I don't think that's going to happen, Luce."

She was quiet for what seemed like years, staring at me, then a smile broke through. "You don't remember me, do you?"

I looked at her and panicked. This wasn't the first time this had happened. I blew out a breath and looked away from her. I was too embarrassed to face her when we talked about this shit.

"Lucy, I'm sorry. Did I promise to call you? I didn't pop your cherry, did I?" I grimaced.

"WHAT!" she gasped. "Ew, that's gross. Yuck, Logan!" She pushed my chest with both her hands.

I fell back a step. "Shit, Lucy. Don't be that disgusted. I'm not the worst guy in the world to take your V card." I smirked.

"EW!" she screamed again.

I was all-out laughing.

She exaggerated a shudder, then calmed herself down. "When we were freshmen, I was reading a book under a tree in the quad," she said. "I was a loner back then. These juniors—they came up and started picking on me. Two girls and two guys. They grabbed the book from my hands and were being assholes, throwing it between each other. Like we were in fucking grade school and they were the bullies. I was mortified, Logan. I felt so stupid and...belittled."

"I'm sorry, Lucy." I told her. It was the truth. I fucking hated bullies and anyone who thought it was okay to treat people like shit.

"I know, Logan. I know because you walked up and stood in front of me, shielding me from them. You started yelling at them to give it back. I didn't even know you, and you were there. You were big for a freshman. I mean, you've always been big. You were bigger than both those junior boys combined. They gave it back straight away, and you handed it to me. You made them apologize to me before they left. Then you made sure I was okay before you just walked away, like what you did wasn't a big deal."

"Huh." I didn't know else to say.

"You don't remember?"

I shrugged. "Sorry, Lucy...I guess I don't."

She smiled. "That night I baked you cookies and left them on your desk in homeroom the next morning."

It began to come back to me—the memory. But I don't remember that it was Lucy.

She kept talking. "I watched you as you walked into the room and saw them sitting there, this huge smile on your face. You opened them, ate one, and gave the rest to Skinny Pete."

Now I remembered.

"Why did you do that, Logan? Give them to Skinny Pete, I mean?"

I shrugged and turned away from her.

She gripped my upper arm and forced me to face her.

"Why?" she asked again.

"Everyone knows that Skinny Pete's family was poor and he barely ate." I shrugged again.

She laughed once. "I had the biggest crush on you for like, months after that day," she said, shaking her head. "You're not such an asshole, Logan. You're one of the best guys I know. Actually, you're the best guy I know that I'm not screwing." She chuckled to herself. "One day, you're going to meet that girl who's going to make you want to be with them. And she's going to be so goddamn lucky, I swear it."

I stayed silent. Because the thing was, I think I already had.

Lucy sighed, leaned up on her toes and kissed my cheek. "Quit smoking, Logan. I don't want to lose you, too," she said before turning to go back inside. I grabbed her arm to stop her and pulled her to me. I held her. She held me back. I don't know how long we stood, holding on to each other, when she finally pulled away and looked up at me.

I kissed her on the top of her head. "It's the last one I'll ever have, swear it."

It was.

15

LOGAN

I WOKE UP the next morning before everyone else and left Jake and Micky's. I got in my car and drove the short distance to my frat house.

When I got up to my room, all my shit was everywhere.

Clothes were thrown all over the place, my mattress was up against a wall. My computer and stereo system had been smashed to pieces.

What the fuck?

Adam, the president of the house, walked into my room.

"You're out," he deadpanned.

"What the fuck?"

"I'm sorry, dude. I like you; you're a good guy. But I don't have any sisters. It's been decided. We had a meeting. You're out."

This had to be a fucking joke. "You're kidding, right?" He had to be. "Where the hell am I going to live?"

He shrugged.

Fuck.

It was early enough that the rest of the house was still sleeping. Luckily for me, it wasn't too embarrassing.

Once I was in my car, I just sat there.

Where the fuck was I going to go?

Without me realizing it, I started the two-hour drive home.

I needed the stable sanity of my own house at the moment. The events of the last few days had worn me out.

I texted Jake and told him what happened. I asked him to get feelers out, see if anyone knew of anywhere I could live. If anyone had connections, it was Jake Andrews.

By the time I got home, I was beginning to feel the lack of sleep mixed with the hangover and just wanted to crash.

I went into the kitchen, where Dad was sitting at the counter eating. It was rare for him to be home on a weekend.

"What are you doing here?" he asked, surprised.

"Thanks. Nice to see you, too," I joked. I got a soda out of the fridge and sat down on the counter with him.

"You look—uh...good?" he said, a smile pulling at his lips.

"I had a rough night."

He nodded.

It was silent for a few minutes.

Then I said, "I need to talk to you-" the same time he said, "We need to talk-"

We both laughed.

"You go first," I told him.

"Have you spoken to Nathan?"

I shrugged. "Kind of. You know what's happening?"

"Your mother's been asking around for you." He eyed me, waiting for my reaction.

"Huh. That's funny. Last I checked I had no mother." I raised my eyebrows at him, waiting for him to push the issue. He wanted me to say something more. But I didn't. I had nothing more to say.

Finally, he nodded once. "So you had something to tell me."

Shit. I played it out in my head—the words I would use to tell him. But now that I was here, I felt like an idiot. So I decide to just say, "I got kicked out of the frat house."

I wanted him to yell. To tell me he was disappointed. Something. Anything. But he didn't. Instead, he just smiled. "Do I want to know why?"

I shook my head.

"So what happens now?"

I blew out a breath. "I guess I have to find somewhere else to live. I'll get a job there. I could probab—"

"No, Logan." He cut me off. "You can't work with the course load you're taking on. That, plus baseball. No. Just find a place and use the money we have saved."

"You have saved. It's not really fair."

"Logan. Use the money in the account. I keep putting it in there, and you never use it. It's there for a reason. Use it." He paused, eyeing me. "And it is fair. You're my son. It's what I do."

I looked away. Because I'm not his son. Not really.

Just then, I got a message from Jake. Apparently one of the guys on the team knows a guy that knows a guy who has a spare room. He's desperate for someone to move in ASAP.

Hopefully my luck would change because the last few days had been a clusterfuck of Screw-You-Logan disasters.

I texted the guy whose house it was and told him I'll come by later that evening. I hoped to God it wasn't a shit hole. But right now, I'd fucking take anything.

I spent a few hours with Dad, and slept some, before taking the two-hour drive back toward campus.

I PARKED OUTSIDE the house and looked at it a moment before getting out. From the outside, it looked like a standard house. No abandoned cars, no junkies, no odors of meth labs, and no hookers in the front yard. I thought I was safe.

A kid around my age opened the door. We did our introductions, and he invited me in. Ethan, his name was.

The house itself was basic. Living room with separate kitchen/dining area but had an open breakfast bar. There was a hallway to the left where I assumed the bedrooms were. He showed me around the main areas and then walked down the hall.

"So," he started, "The rooms on the left are mine and Dimmy's. We share a bathroom."

"Dimmy?"

"My sister," he said. Then he looks me up and down. "Goes without saying, she's off limits."

I nodded, looking at him a little longer than I should. But he looked familiar, and I couldn't place him. So I asked him, "Have I seen you around before? You play anything?" He had an athletic build.

He shook his head. "Nah, man. I was good at sports in high school but not good enough for college. I was one of those 'good-at-everything-but-not-great-at-any' kind of guys, you know?"

"Yeah, I get it."

"Anyway," he perked up, "this room here." He opened the door. "This is yours. I guess you could call it the master. It's the biggest one, has its own bathroom and little outdoor area. It's more rent than what we pay, but you get that. Dimmy and I—we're kind of struggling at the moment, so as soon as you can move in—if you want to move in, that is—the better for us."

I walked into the empty room and looked around, then walked into the bathroom and did the same. It was more than decent.

I walked back to the hallway where Ethan stood. "I can move in right now." I told him. Anything that was worth packing was already in my car.

"Awesome, dude."

We shook hands and started walking to the front door.

"Uh, Logan?" Ethan said from behind me.

I turned to face him.

He rubbed the back of his neck, looking nervous. "So, when I said that Dimmy and I were struggling—I wasn't kidding. I mean, she has a job, and so do I, but we need more hours. Anyway, we're a little behind—"

"Dude," I interrupted. "Whatever you need, man. It's fine. Just let me know."

He smiled and nodded, just as I heard the front door swing open. Ethan's voice filled the room. "Oh good, Dimmy. You're home. You can meet our new housemate. This is—"

"No. Fucking. Way." I heard a familiar voice.

I whipped my head to the front door, so fast I almost pull a muscle in my neck.

"No fucking way," she repeated, her head shaking from side to side. She looked from me to Ethan. "No E, no fucking way."

"What the hell?" Ethan said behind me. He walked to stand between us.

I think I was smiling, but I couldn't be sure. My heart thumped in my chest so hard and so fast, I could feel it vibrating throughout my body.

"No, Ethan. Just no," she said.

Ethan looked from her to me and back again. "We need the money, Dimmy. It's either that or one of us goes home. You decide."

Now I knew I was grinning like an idiot because she was glaring at me, eyes narrowed.

My hands went in my front pockets as I took her in.

Amanda.

My eyes roamed her from head to toe. Her dark hair was up in one of those messy bun things, and she was wearing glasses. I didn't know she wore glasses or contacts. They're those thick black frame hipster-style ones, and they made her look fucking hot. She wore a tight, long-sleeve top that molded to her curves. She carried a yoga mat under her arm, and when my eyes moved lower down her body, I saw it.

She was wearing my sweatpants.

My cheeks began to hurt from the shit-eating grin I wore.

"Nice pants," I told her.

She looked confused for a second before she looked down. Her eyes widened as understanding dawned.

Then quickly, she threw the yoga mat onto the floor and ripped my pants off her legs. She stood in the living room in her top and panties.

I was getting turned on.

Pretty sure I would be on her if her brother wasn't standing between us.

"Fuck, Dimmy!" he yelled, eyes squeezed tight. He moved to the kitchen and ran the tap.

She threw the pants at my head, and I instinctively caught them. She brushed past me and into her room, slamming the door shut behind her.

I looked to Ethan in the kitchen. He had the water running, his head under it, letting it flow into his eyes like he was actually washing away the memory of what he'd just witnessed. "You need to fucking warn me when you do shit like that," he was yelling. I didn't think he knew she wasn't here anymore. "I shouldn't have to see that shit."

I couldn't help but laugh. "Dude, she's gone."

He opened one eye and surveyed the room. When he knew it was safe, he opened the other. "What the hell was that about?"

I shrugged. "Don't know. Your sister's obviously crazy." Lie.

"Don't let it deter you from moving in," he said, pointing at me. "You already agreed. Plus, she's not so bad. She stays in her room mostly."

He grabbed the keys off the hook near the front door and slipped on his shoes. "I'm going to the store. You need anything?"

I shook my head.

Then he was out the door. And I stood in the living room of my new house.

One that I shared with Amanda.

AMANDA

AFTER LAST NIGHT'S embarrassing outburst, I just wanted to crawl under a rock and hide out for, oh, I don't know, the rest of my existence. Give or take.

I knew that it was just one night with him, and I knew that it really shouldn't have broken my heart, but guess what? It did. And I've learned to live with that.

Not seeing him for a year helped; I was over it.

I knew that going to college meant the occasional run-in with him, especially since I was getting closer to Micky through Facebook, and once I got here and met Lucy, it was kind of inevitable. I was doing so well avoiding him, making sure that wherever I was, he wasn't. I'd even hung out with them in group situations when I knew he'd gone home for the weekend or had other things going on. I made sure of it.

Yes, I could have given up their friendships, but I didn't want to. And really, I shouldn't have to.

So every day since I got here, I was mentally high-fiving myself because I hadn't yet run in to him. It doesn't seem like a big deal, huge campus and all, but if you knew Logan Matthews, then you'd know the enormity of his presence alone.

Until that day in the library.

And when I saw him, it felt like the wind had been knocked out of me.

Not because I didn't expect to see him, because I knew I would eventually.

It was because I wasn't ready for all the emotions that would come with physically being around him.

It was like everything I had felt over the last year, but all at once. And it hurt. It was too much. I couldn't even look at him. And when Micky had asked if we'd met before, I lied.

I lied because I wanted to see if I could hurt him. If me playing dumb would have an effect on him. If he would feel anything if he knew, or at least thought, that I didn't remember him. That it was just another night, and he was just another guy.

And I really didn't want to rehash the circumstances in which we met. At least, that's what I told myself.

But the truth? The truth was that I wanted to keep the memory of that night to myself. I didn't want to share it with anybody.

Because it was mine.

And because it was the best night of my entire life.

THE LAST THING I expected to see when I came home tonight was for him to be standing in my living room.

Logan Matthews.

The guy I'd spent a year trying to forget. The guy I spent every day trying to avoid. And here he was. My new housemate.

Unfortunately for me, Ethan was right. I had no choice. We needed the money or one of us had to quit college and go home.

I WAS ALREADY LATE for work, so I was frantically going through my dresser, trying to find my uniform, when there was a knock on my door.

"Yeah?"

It was him. He walked in, closing the door behind him, hands in his front pockets making the muscles on his neck and arms pop. He had that smug smile on his face.

I continued going through my dresser until I found what I needed. I put the short shorts on, which I hated to admit covered just about the same amount as my underwear.

He stayed silent.

When I looked up at him, his eyes were trained on my legs. "Do you mind?" I said.

"Nope." He just stood there, stupid smug smile still on his stupid smug face. "I don't mind one bit."

Then he took two steps forward until we were chest to chest.

I looked at him confused, and then he brought his mouth down to mine, only I was faster this time and pushed him away before there was contact.

"What the hell is wrong with you?"

He chuckled.

I hated that fucking chuckle.

"I'm late for work. I need to get dressed. Get out!" I pointed to the door.

"I'm good here," he said.

Asshole. "Fine!"

I stripped my top off and got changed in front of him. I was wearing a sports bra, so it wasn't a big deal. I didn't bother looking for his reaction as I went to my closet to change my shoes.

"Where do you work?" He followed me into the closet.

"Elliot's."

"You mean that sports bar near campus, the one where the girls wear those-" he cut himself off, looking at my uniform. "Oh," he said, nodding his head, eyes fixed on my boobs.

I cleared my throat.

He looked up.

Then two seconds later, his mouth was on mine again.

I pushed him away. "Quit. Fucking. Kissing. Me!"

He laughed.

"I don't see how this is funny." I ran around my room, trying to get ready.

"Fine. I'll stop kissing you."

"Good! Thank you."

"On one condition."

I rolled my eyes. "And what's that?"

"You play a game with me."

I walked to him so we were face-to-face. "What game?" I was curious.

"Two truths for fifteen. I don't know if you remember-"

"I remember," I interrupted him. My voice softened. If this was what it was going to take to make sure there was no more physical contact between us in the future, I was willing to play. "Okay, but not today."

I brushed past him and out my bedroom door.

LOGAN

I WATCHED HER from just outside her room as she rushed to the front door, reaching for the keys on the hook, only they weren't there.

She had a look of confusion on her face before opening the front door. "That asshole," she muttered under her breath.

She pulled out her phone, I assume to call Ethan, who apparently didn't answer, according to the amount of curse words coming out of her mouth.

Finally, she glanced up at me, "Do you think you'd be able to give me a ride?"

She doesn't have a car? "What happened to your car?"

"Which car?"

"That red Civic you had."

Her eyes widened in shock.

"How do you—never mind. I, uh, I had to leave it with Mom. So can you? The ride, I mean?"

I opened the front door for her and led her to my car. I'd do pretty much anything this girl asked if it meant I got to spend even a second of my time with her.

I WAS FAMILIAR with the bar she worked in, so she didn't need to give directions. Which meant the entire drive we sat in silence.

It was the type of uncomfortable silence that's deafening to your ears.

I pulled into a spot and turned to her. She was biting her lip, looking out the windshield.

You know how sometimes you remembered someone, or something, and you closed your eyes but you couldn't imagine them? Like, you could kind of make them out in your mind, but you couldn't see them? It was never the case with her. If I wanted to remember her, all I had to do was close my eyes and she'd be there. I'd always picture the way she threw her head back when she laughed. The sound was so infectious, you couldn't help but laugh with her. I remembered everything about her. The way her lips felt against mine. The way my fingers felt linked with hers. The way her hair felt under my touch. Those fucking moaning sounds she made. I fucking remembered everything about her. Everything. Clear as day. Perfect. In every fucking sense.

"I didn't know you wore glasses." I blurted out.

"Shit," she mumbled, going through her bag. She pulled out her contacts case, brought down the visor mirror and replaced her glasses with her contacts, blinking a few times when she was done. "I better get inside." She jerked her head to the front door.

I followed the movement and saw a bunch of guys hanging out front. They were all drunk, cussing, and pushing each other around. She stepped out of the car, and I found myself doing the same.

I walked next to her, hands in my pockets.

"What are you doing?" she questioned, walking a bit closer to me as we passed the guys.

"I haven't eaten all day." I shrugged.

Plus, I've been here before, and I know how I treated the girls who worked here. I was sure as shit not going to let some asshole treat her like that.

ONE OF THE guys from the team happened to be here, so we sat, totally by coincidence, at a table in Amanda's section. We ordered and ate together before he had to leave to get to his girlfriend's dorm before her roommate came back.

Basically, he left to get laid.

Amanda was leaning on the bar, waiting for drinks, talking to the guy prepping them. He said something and she laughed, that same laugh I remembered so well. I eyed the guy who was laughing with her. And even though I had no right, I was jealous. Not because she was talking to him. Not even because they might be flirting with each other right now. But I was jealous because in my mind, those laughs belonged to me.

I walked up behind her and cleared my throat. The guy she was talking to stood to full height, squaring his shoulders when he saw me, like I was a fucking threat to her.

She slowly turned around and looked up at me. "You all done?" She was actually smiling.

"Uh, yeah." I was still looking at the guy who'd crossed his arms and was now staring me down. I felt a light tapping on my arm and tore my eyes away from that asshole to see Amanda's fingers on me, trying to get my attention. I brought my gaze to hers. "Yeah, I'm done. What time does your shift end?"

"Midnight."

I looked at my watch. Four hours to go. "I'll just wait here and give you a ride when you're done."

"What?" she said, laughing at me.

I didn't know why. I didn't think it was funny.

"You can't wait, Logan. It's hours from now. What are you going to do here?"

"Dude," asshole bartender interrupted us. "My shift ends at the same time. I'll give her a ride."

I narrowed my eyes at him. "Amanda," I said, looking straight at him, "I'll take us home when you're done."

Instantly, I was being dragged by my arm into a random abandoned hallway.

She pushed me up against a wall, her tiny frame blocking me in. There was fire in her eyes.

I was getting turned on.

"Did you work it out?" She cocked an eyebrow.

"What are you talking about?" My hand went out to touch her waist, because when she was this close, all I wanted to do was touch her.

She was too quick to swat it away.

"Did you work out whose dick was bigger?"

I chuckled.

Her eyebrows rose.

I moved in to kiss her.

She pushed me away. "Quit. Fucking. Kissing. Me!"

Then she turned in her spot and stormed off. Her short shorts showed off her amazingly toned legs.

Logan: *I think I may have a problem.*

Dad: *If it's red, itchy or inflamed, come straight home and notify everyone.*

Logan: *Ha ha. Seriously though, is there some sort of medical condition involved with the uncontrollable need to kiss someone?*

Dad: *Why are you asking this?*

Logan: *Because I can't quit kissing this girl.*

Dad: *No medical condition. Maybe you just like her.*

Logan: *That makes more sense. I thought for sure it was my body's way of telling me something.*

Dad: *Like what? That maybe you more than like her?*

Logan: *You may be right.*

I waited around until she was done, which surprisingly didn't drag on as much as I thought it would. She didn't argue when I told her I was staying, and no guys attempted to hit on her, so it was a win/win for me.

She was silent during the drive home, and when I pulled up to the curb, I realized it was because she'd fallen asleep.

I nudged her. "We're home."

She started to blink, those big blue eyes trying to focus. When they finally did, they landed right on me. "I was so tired," she whispered, her voice scratchy.

"You want me to carry you in?"

She laughed through a yawn. "No, I'm okay." Her eyes started to close again.

"Amanda?"

"Yeah, Logan?"

"I really am sorry." Her eyes snapped open and fixed on mine. We sat there, staring at each other for so long, neither making a move to get out. I continued, "Last night...the things you said-"

"I can't." She shook her head. "I can't talk about this with you. Not now. Not yet. Okay?"

"Okay."

She moved to open her door and was halfway out when she turned to me. "Are you not coming in?"

"I, uh, I don't have a bed. I was just gonna crash at Cam and Dylan's dorm," I finished on a yawn. I removed my cap, threw it in the back seat, and shook my hair out, trying to wake up.

"Oh yeah," she said, like she'd just remembered. "Wait. You drove me to work, stayed through my six-hour shift, drove me home, and now you're basically driving back there to crash?"

I nodded.

"That's stupid." She turned to face me. "I have one of those pullout beds under mine. You can, uh...you can sleep there. I'll swap rooms with Ethan or something..." she trailed off.

I looked into the house; it was pitch black. "He's probably sleeping. Don't wake him; it's fine. Honestly, Amanda." Another yawn broke through.

"You're too tired to drive." Her eyes met mine before looking away. "Anyway, we're both mature adults. I'm sure we can stay in the same room without killing each other, right?"

I smiled at her. "Right."

SHE MADE UP my bed and went to the bathroom. We hadn't said a word to each other since we came in. I stood in her room awkwardly and waited until she came back.

She'd changed into a high school football jersey; it was three or four sizes too big. I automatically wondered who it belonged to.

She got into her bed and pulled the covers over her. She avoided looking at me.

"Are you getting into bed?" she whispered.

I didn't answer right away, because all I could think about was getting in there with her.

"Logan?"

"Huh?" I shook my head to clear my thoughts. "Yeah. Sorry."

She giggled.

I shrugged out of my jeans and pulled my shirt off.

She stopped giggling immediately, her eyes huge, staring at my body.

"Busted!" I whispered.

She gasped. "Get in your bed so I can turn the light off, asshole."

"I totally caught you eye-licking me."

"Shut up!" she said, but she was smiling, too.

I started to get into the bed, which was practically on the floor. "You totally want me." I smiled to myself.

"Correction, Logan," she said quietly, her tone serious. "I totally did want you. A long, long time ago."

What the hell do you say to that? I stayed silent until I realized my entire body was shivering from the cold and the blanket she gave me didn't even cover half of it.

"I'm cold," I huffed out.

"Well, that explains your size misfortune." She chuckled.

I couldn't help but laugh.

"Seriously, turn the light on. I need to fix this poor excuse of a blanket you gave me." We were both whispering, giggling quietly.

She turned the light on, and I looked down at myself.

She cracked up laughing.

"You want to explain to me why I'm sleeping under a Hello Kitty blanket made for an infant?"

She laughed harder, rolling around in her bed. She managed to stop, only to look down at me, and laughed again.

"This isn't funny!" I tried to keep a straight face, but her laugh was so infectious. "Look!" I motioned my head to the blanket on my chest. I pulled it up to my neck, and it ended just below my boxers. I pulled it down past my feet, it ended just above them. I did this a few times, because each time I did it, she laughed harder.

She finally calmed herself down enough to speak, "It's all I have." She laughed into her pillow.

I stood up and looked around the room.

She was still laughing.

"There's probably something in my car I can use. Anything has to be better than a Hello Kitty rag." I picked up my jeans and went through my pockets, looking for my keys.

"Don't be stupid," she said, still giggling. She lifted one side of the covers and motioned for me to get in. "Don't get any ideas. And don't touch me. Like, at all."

I smiled huge and got into bed with her.

"I mean it. Don't touch me," she said, scooting to the other side of the bed.

"Okay," I returned, moving closer in and spooning her.

She didn't stop me.

And that was how we fell asleep, with her back against my chest, and my arms wrapped around her.

16

LOGAN

"DIMMY!"

I got pushed out of a warm bed and onto the floor, landing with a thud, which fucking hurt.

When I opened my eyes, she was leaning over the bed, looking down at me. Her eyes were wide, her hand covering her laugh.

"Dimmy!" Ethan called again.

It was morning.

"Yeah!" she replied, her index finger over her lips telling me to be quiet. Like I could freaking talk over the pain searing through my body right now.

"I'm getting ready for class. You have the day off, yeah? You don't need a ride?"

"Yeah, I'm good," she yelled back, containing her laugh.

"Have you seen Logan? He didn't come home last night. I hope you didn't freak him out and he changed his mind."

"Who cares!" she yelled, smiling right at me. "Fuck him. He's an asshole!"

I shook my head at her and then pulled her by her jersey until she landed on top of me.

"You're so mean," I whispered in her ear, then started tickling her sides.

She squealed and started squirming, trying to get out of my hold.

Then we both froze abruptly, because I was hard, and she could feel it.

"Get dressed, climb out the window, and then knock on the front door."

Then she was off me and walking out of the room.

Climb out the fucking window? What am I? Fourteen?

I did it anyway because like I said: my balls—her pockets.

Ten minutes later, we were all seated and having breakfast.

"I gotta go buy some shit today. You guys need anything?" I asked.

"What kind of shit?" Ethan said with a mouth full of cereal.

I tried to make a list in my head. "Everything. I guess I need all the furniture for my room, bathroom stuff. I need to buy a new computer and stereo system. Shit...everything."

"It is true!" Ethan barked out. "One of my boys told me your room at the house got trashed. He said a bunch of guys went there and did some damage. You screwed the wrong guy's sister one too many times or something?"

Amanda's eyes bugged out as she choked on her food. She got up and made her way to the sink.

Ethan eyed her like she was crazy. "Anyway," he continued, "you should take Dimmy with you; she loves shopping for that kind of stuff. She has an eye for it, you know?" Then he looked over at her. "Oh hey, maybe Luca will be working at the Apple store. He's been asking about you again. Just put the kid out of his misery and go out with him already." He got up and washed his bowl. "I'm out. I'll see you guys tonight."

SHE WAS WIPING down the counter when I approached her. "So can you come with me today? I mean, if you don't have plans. I could really use the help." I hoped to God she said yes. I'd do whatever she wanted if it meant that I could spend the day with her.

She turned around and faced me. "Two truths for fifteen time?"

I smiled at her. She remembered. I nodded my head and jumped up on the counter, waiting for her question.

"Is it true? They trashed your room because you couldn't keep your dick in your pants?"

I shrugged. "I guess. I didn't really hang around to find out." I hated that she knew that.

I waited for more, but she didn't say anything else. So it was my turn. "Where were you last year? I looked around for you but I—"

She interrupted before I could finish. "I had to stay home. Well, one of us had to, so I did."

She started to walk away, but I held her back with a grip on her arm. "It's called two truths for fifteen. We need to talk about it for fifteen minutes, remember?"

She nodded and inhaled deeply. "Some shit went down at home. I guess Mom found out Dad had been cheating on her since, well, forever." She shrugged like it was no big deal. "Mom—she kind of lost it. Got into drinking, heavily. She lost her job, her car, and nearly the house. Dad took everything worth anything and just bailed with his latest mistress. He hasn't looked back. So it was tough times. I stayed and worked full time, studied at the community college when I could. Helped Mom with whatever she needed."

"And Ethan?"

"Ethan got to go to college. I'm only a semester behind in classes. Hopefully, I'll be able to make it up and graduate the same time."

"Still childcare?"

"Yup."

"Still want to be a midwife though?"

She looked at me now, like she was trying to work something out. "You remember?"

"I haven't forgotten a single thing about you, Amanda."

She cleared her throat and looked away. "Yeah, still want to be a midwife. But still afraid of blood. So yeah...there's that."

It was silent for a few moments.

"And your dad?" I asked. "What's the deal with him?"

She lifted her shoulders again. "Like I said, he bailed. Don't know where he is. He hasn't bothered to call, so really—why should I give a shit?"

She tried her hardest to act like none of this bothered her, but it did. I could see the way her eyes started filling with tears. The way her voice started to crack. The way she purposely avoided my eyes.

I held her hand in mine and made sure she was looking at me. "Anyone who purposely chooses to not have contact with you is an asshole, Amanda."

She laughed a bitter laugh and jerked her hand out of mine. "I should introduce you two. You'd get along well. You being the pot, him being the kettle, guess you're both black," she said, before walking away.

A WHILE LATER we were both back in the living room, showered and dressed for the day. She was wearing denim cut-offs that showed off her legs. I don't know how the fuck she had legs like that for someone who apparently hated working out.

She silently walked around the house, gathering her shit, then turned to me as she opened the front door. "I'll see you later," she said, her hand gesturing a small wave.

I cleared my throat and pulled my eyes away from her legs. Then I remembered she has no car. "Uh, what—what are you doing? You need a ride?"

"Nope. I'll catch the bus. See ya!" she said too quickly, shutting the front door behind her.

I ran out and stopped her halfway down the driveway.

"Okay, something's definitely wrong. What's up?"

She was still avoiding my eyes.

I grabbed her chin in my hands, my fingers on one cheek, and my thumb on the other. I made her look up at me, and then I squeezed, squishing her face together, so she had fish lips.

I laughed.

She scrunched her nose. "Let go," she said, her words muffled by the shape of her mouth.

"You look so hot right now." I chuckled. "I think I might kiss you." I moved my lips down to hers, but in the corner of my eye, I saw her knee rise.

I was quicker this time, pulling back and blocking my junk at the same time.

"See that!" I pointed to her. "I learned ninja reflexes after the last time you pulled that shit on me."

She pushed at my chest. "Maybe if you'd quit fucking kissing me, I'd stop kneeing you in your junk!"

She was smiling.

And it was all I ever wanted.

AFTER I GOT the stuff I needed to replace what the assholes broke, I drove her around so she could do whatever she needed to do. We were sitting next to each other, waiting at the admin office to speak to someone about her credits being transferred.

"So you worked and studied last year?"

"Uh-huh."

She was distracted by her phone. I nudged her leg with mine until she looked up. She was smiling, trying to contain her laugh.

"What's so funny?"

"Nothing." She started giggling.

"What?!"

I tried to take the phone out of her hands, but she pulled it away too quickly.

"Seriously, what's so funny?"

"Nothing!"

I reached around her to try to grab it. I knew whatever the hell she was laughing at was about me.

She laughed harder.

"What are you saying about me?"

She kept moving the phone behind her; I kept moving to try to reach it. I realized I was practically on top of her now, with both my arms around her and our faces a few inches apart. I could feel her breasts against my chest, rising and falling with each breath.

I watched as she brought her tongue out and slowly skimmed it along her top lip. I didn't know if she did it to fuck with me because I'm pretty sure I was sporting a semi just by watching her do it. My own breathing became faster, more strained. I bit my lip to stop myself from kissing her.

Fuck it.

I moved in slowly, to warn her that I was about to kiss her, because I couldn't fucking help myself. Her eyes fell shut, and for a second, I thought she was about to let me. But then she laughed.

Fucking laughed.

I pulled back and let out a frustrated groan, shaking my head at her.

She kept giggling.

I straightened up and tried to hide my "I'm-nineteen-and-should-not-have-a-boner" boner.

Amanda: *You would not believe who my new housemate is.*

Alexis: *Who? That kid Luca with the lazy eye…but not lazy enough to stare at your tits?*

Amanda: *No! Ew! Creepy! Logan!*

Alexis: *Four random words do not a sentence make.*

Amanda: *Logan!!! Is my new housemate.*

Alexis: *Get. The. Fuck. Out.*

Amanda: *Not even joking. He's sitting right next to me.*

Alexis: *Mm…what's he wearing?*

Amanda: *You're crazy.*

Alexis: *Seriously though. What does he smell like? Sniff him.*

Amanda: *Stop it. You're going to make me laugh out loud.*

Alexis: *Fine. Don't tell me. I've seen him near naked remember? I regret not doing the nasty with him.*

Amanda: *Thanks for the reminder.*

Alexis: *No problem. Hey…honest question. Next time he's in the shower, just sneak me a pic, okay? Just his abs. I don't even need a lower half.*

Amanda: *OMG. You're too much.*

AMANDA

After I finished at the admin office, we stopped by a cafe for lunch.

We'd just finished eating when the waitress came to clear our plates and asked if we wanted anything for dessert.

"Banana split, two spoons," he told her, never taking his eyes off me.

My eyes went wide, surprised that he remembered. He must've sensed it because he smiled at me. "What? Did you think I'd forget?"

I just shook my head. I had no words.

He leaned forward, so close our knees touched. His hands under the table reached for my legs as he slowly ran his fingers up the side of my thighs. "I remember everything about that night, Amanda. Everything."

And if I lived my life like Logan Matthews, this was the moment I wished I could forget the past. Forget what he did. Forget that he hurt me. Because I wanted so badly—more than anything else—to be able to forgive him. And maybe, just maybe, we could be everything I once hoped for.

The dessert arrived, and he scooted next to me, sharing the banana split like we did on our date. Only this time, I was surrounded by the memories of him and of that night.

His arm rested on the back of the seat behind me. He moved his body closer. "Hey." His voice was low and husky when he continued, "Remember when you did that thing with the gummy bear in my mouth?"

My eyes fell shut. Of course I remembered. I could feel him move his mouth closer to my ear. His breath was against my neck.

"I remember it," he whispered, his breathing heavy. "I remember feeling your mouth on mine, feeling the heat of your breath mixed with the cold of the ice cream. I remember thinking it was the sexiest fucking thing that's ever happened to me. Ever." My hand instinctively landed on his leg. I slowly turned my head toward him, never once opening my eyes. I felt his lips brush against mine, from side to side, so fucking lightly. His fingers snaked through my hair, his palm on the back of my head, holding it in place. I caught my breath. He kissed my lips softly, just once. "I remember that about two minutes after that, you were on me, with my hands on your ass while you were grinding on my dick."

I froze.

I couldn't move. I couldn't think.

All I could do was remember. Remember the way his mouth

moved with mine, the way he touched me, the way he made me feel like he worshipped me.

"I remember thinking how badly I wanted to be inside you." His breath came faster, heavier. And somewhere in the back of my mind I remembered that we were in a public place. But I just didn't fucking care right now. He kept going. "I remember wanting to fuck you, Amanda."

I bit my lip to stop the moan from escaping.

"Breathe," he said.

And I let out all the air I didn't know I was holding. "Do you remember?" he asked, still speaking low, that huskiness in his voice driving me crazy.

I nodded my head slowly.

His lips moved against mine, so fucking softly, I could've imagined it.

Then with his hand on the back of my head, he pulled me closer to him. Our lips touched but didn't move. Against my mouth, he said, "I promised I wouldn't kiss you. So if you want this, you have to be the one to do it."

I did.

I did want it.

I turned so my entire body was facing him as I leaned into him. I started to move my mouth against his. I heard him moan, waiting for me to keep going. I opened my mouth and ran my tongue along his bottom lip—

"Logan?"

We both pulled apart and looked to the sound, to the girl standing at our table. She looked from Logan to me and then back to him again.

I heard him cuss under his breath and lean back in his chair.

"I'm sorry to interrupt." She looked at us curiously for a moment, taking us in.

"What's up, Amber?" He sounded pissed.

"I just wanted to say sorry, about my brother and his friends. And what they did to your stuff. I heard they—"

Logan sat up a little. "It's fine," he cut in. "It's only stuff. I'll see you around, okay?"

She looked taken aback for a second and then recovered. "Oh, okay. See you."

Then she walked away, having no clue what she'd just interrupted.

It was silent for a while as we both caught our breaths.

"Amanda—"

"I'm good to go. You ready?" I got up quickly, fished some money out of my bag and threw it on the table.

LOGAN

WE ENDED UP at the grocery store next. She bought groceries while I picked out a bunch of stuff I needed for my bathroom: soaps, shampoo, toothpaste, all the shit I didn't bother to take when I packed up and left the frat house.

I heard her name being called and when I looked up, I saw that same asshole from her work. He lazily walked up to her and didn't stop until he was a foot in front of her. The entire walk, he was eye-licking her, his gaze trained on her goddamn legs.

"Hey, Tony, what are you doing here?" Her back was to me so I couldn't see her reaction to his ogling, but I could hear the sweetness in her voice.

"Just buying stuff to make dinner. I'm cooking for the family tonight," he bragged. Asshat. Who the fuck does that?

"A boy who cooks? Wow."

Pshh—I could cook.

Lie.

"Yeah, I try you know." He shrugged, smiling at her. And I know what that smile was. I've used it a hundred times before. It always worked with me. But it wouldn't for him. Not this time.

I pulled a huge box of condoms and lube from the shelf and walked up to them. My arm went around her shoulders as I brought her into me.

I felt her body turn to me, but I never took my eyes off the asshole in front of me. "A little close, aren't you?" I bit out.

I could *feel* Amanda roll her eyes; she was that goddamn dramatic.

Asshole cleared his throat. "Is this kid bothering you, Amanda?" He looked me up and down, trying to size me up.

I wanted to punch him.

I turned to face her and lifted the box of condoms and lube. "This should do us for tonight, babe, but I think we have to order online if we want them by the carton."

Her eyes went wide; a shocked expression overcame her face. She started slowly shaking her head at me. "What is wrong with you?" she whispered, as she walked away.

I followed after her, forcefully bumping shoulders with Asshole as I did.

She stayed silent while I paid for our stuff, huge box of condoms and lube included. Once we were out of the store, she rushed toward my car, taking long strides. I jogged up to her and pulled on her arm to stop her. "What's wrong?"

"You can't do that, Logan. You can't just come into my life and pretend like we're something when we're not. Tony—he's a good guy. You didn't need to be like that with him."

I let go of her arm and took in her words. "What? That guy—Tony—are you into him?"

She shrugged. "Maybe. And so what if I am?" Her chin lifted as she spoke.

I walked past her and toward the car.

"He's kind of a douchebag," I said over my shoulder.

"You don't even know him."

"Whatever. I don't need to know him. Did you see the way he was looking at you?"

She moved so she was in front of me and started walking backwards, blocking my path.

"Yeah. I did. And who's to say I didn't like it?"

17

LOGAN

WE GOT HOME, and she went straight to her room. She didn't say a word the drive home and neither did I.

I was in my room, sitting on the goddamn floor, setting up my new computer when I heard yelling from the living room.

I went out to check what the fuck was happening. The last thing I expected to see was Amanda sitting on Ethan, while he was on his back on the floor. She was slapping the shit out of his head while he was yelling at her to stop.

What the fuck?

I didn't know whether to laugh, cheer, leave, or throw money at them.

"Hey!" I yelled.

They both turned to me—only for a second—before Amanda turned back around and started slapping his head again.

"Fucking quit it, Dimmy!" Ethan yelled, trying to squirm out from under her. She was sitting on his stomach, and he couldn't get out.

"I'm not fucking going back!" she yelled. "You fucking do it!"

She started slapping him harder, not just on his head, but his chest, too. His hands were covering his face to block the hits.

"Quit it!" he yelled again.

I just stood there, hands in my front pockets, confused as all fuck.

"Dude!" Ethan said, blocking her hits and moving so he could see me. "Get this crazy bitch off me!"

I lazily pulled my hands out of my pockets and walked over to them.

"Bitch? You just called me a fucking bitch?" She started hitting him harder.

He cussed some more.

I finally pulled her off him.

I held her, facing away from me, with her arms pinned to her sides, then lifted her off the ground while her legs kicked wildly.

What the fuck?

Ethan finally got up, straightening his clothes.

"Screw you, Dimmy!" he spat out. "I have to be the man of the house and support a family one day. What are you going to do? Just marry some asshole and be a mom. You don't even need college for that!"

I swear to God, what happened next, actually happened.

She roared. All out roared. Like a lion. Not even joking.

She tried to squirm out of my hold, and I let her. Ethan deserved at least one hit for that comment. She got in one slap before I pulled her by her arm and brought her back to me so she was facing me, her arms pinned to her sides again.

"That's it!" Ethan said. "I've had enough of your fucking shit, Dimmy! Ma said you weren't allowed to hit me anymore! I'm calling her, and you're going to be in so much trouble!"

He left, slamming the door behind him. Seconds later, I heard his piece of shit old Jeep peel out of the driveway.

Then I looked at Amanda, her hair wild and her face red. She was pressed against my body tightly.

"You can let me go now," she said, breathing heavy.

"Are you sure? You're not going to hit me, are you?"

She shook her head. I slowly loosened my hold on her until her arms were free.

But they went around my neck.

There was fire in her eyes. I didn't know whether it was from anger or—

"Fuck it!" she said before her mouth was on mine, her tongue was in my mouth, her hands gripped my hair and her legs were around my waist.

Fuck. Yes.

I started kissing back, my hands on her ass.

The kissing was frantic and sloppy at first until we calmed ourselves down. Then one of her hands pulled the bottom of my shirt up.

"Take me to your room, now!" she panted against my lips.

So I did.

We hit walls, corners, and furniture as we made our way there, our lips never parting. I opened the door and then I remembered—there's fucking nothing in my room.

"I don't have a bed," I said, mouth still on hers as she took my shirt off.

"Floor is fine."

Fuck. Yes.

I moved until my back hit a wall and slowly slid down it. My legs kicked out in front of me. She straddled my waist.

Her mouth moved from mine to my neck, as she started licking and kissing. Her fingers splayed against my chest. I was so fucking turned on; she had to be able to feel it.

"Oh God," she moaned out.

She started to take her shirt off, but I did it for her. My lips instantly went to the spot just above her bra.

"Off!" she moaned. "I want it all off. I want to feel you."

Within a second, I'd unhooked her bra and her tits were right in front of my eyes.

The heavens had opened.

I heard church organs.

She froze for a moment, eyes wide. "I don't even want to know how you did that so fast."

Then her hands were on the back of my head as they pulled me into her. Right onto her nipple. "Holy fucking shit," I mumbled, mouth full of boob.

Her breast was in my mouth, her hands fisted in my hair as she ground harder on me.

"Oh God," she moaned.

Fuck.

"Oh shit." She started moving faster while her hands violently moved my head. My mouth went from one boob to the other.

"Oh fuck."

She was practically raping me without penetration, and I didn't even care.

"Oh fucking shit."

Then she stopped.

She pulled back. Far enough back that her boob left my mouth with a pop.

I looked up at her, mouth hanging open. Like a baby waiting for —well—boob.

Her eyes burned with lust as her hands start undoing the draw-string of my pants.

Fuck. Yes!

"Holy Fuck. This is actually happening," I mumbled, undoing the buttons of her shorts.

"Shut up! Don't talk. Just shut up!"

"Yes, ma'am."

I watched her hands as they undid the knot, then her fingers played under the band. She paused, looked up at me for a second before her mouth crushed down on mine.

My hands went in her shorts, and for the first time, I felt her.

And she was wet, so fucking wet, two of my fingers slid right in.

She moaned into my mouth, her fingers still moving under the band of my pants.

I mentally told her to move the fuck lower.

One hand pulled on the band, making room for the other to reach down—

"DIMMY!"

Fuck!

She stopped moving. Her hand that should be on my dick was now covering my mouth.

I moved my fingers inside her.

She moaned, biting her lip to stop the sound getting louder.

"Dimmy, you better answer your phone. Ma's pissed!"

She removed her hand from my mouth, "Say something," she whispered.

I looked at her, eyebrows drawn, and then jerked my head to where my hand was in her shorts. Is she fucking crazy?

"Tell him I'm not here," she whispered.

I rolled my eyes.

She moved on me again.

"Dude, she left right after you did!"

She started moving on my fingers, her eyes drifting closed.

"Oh, God," she whispered.

"Hey, man." Ethan again. "You gotta move your car off the street. The cops are checking permits out there."

Fuck.

"Yeah, man. I'll be there in a minute," I yelled back.

"Oh, God," she started moving faster on me.

I watched as her head tilted back, her breathing became faster, and her movements became jerkier. She leaned back so my fingers had more room to move, and I started moving them.

In and out.

In and out.

"Oh shit. Oh fuck."

I took her nipple in my mouth and sucked before she started a long, drawn-out moan. I covered her mouth with mine to swallow the sound as her hips moved faster and faster. I felt her tighten around me before her movements slowed, then stopped altogether.

"Dude, he's almost at your car and it's a $360 fine," Ethan yelled, his voice sounding nearer.

"Fuck." I pulled my fingers out and moved her to the floor next to me. I stood and adjusted myself, hiding my huge fucking hard-on, and pulled my shirt over my head. "Don't you move," I told her. "We're not done. Not even close."

She nodded her head, breathing heavily, her eyes glazed over.

I moved my car and went straight back to my room.

She stood in the middle, bra back on, pulling her shirt over her head. I quickly stopped her, mid-motion. She had one arm in the air, her head half-way out the neck hole.

"What the fuck are you doing?" I whisper-yelled.

She pulled her shirt the rest of the way on. "Getting dressed." She looked at me like I was crazy.

Me!

I started to pull her shirt back up, but she swatted my hands away.

"We're not done," I told her.

"Uh, yeah. We are."

She chuckled.

Fucking chuckled.

Then she opened the door that led outside.

"What the fuck is happening right now!" I was annoyed, and pissed, and extremely fucking hard. I stomped my foot. Legit, stomped my foot. "You can't leave me hanging like this! I'm gonna have blue balls for fucking days, Amanda!"

She laughed.

Fucking laughed!

"I'm sorry." She straightened up a little. "It would have just been an angry fuck, Logan. It didn't mean anything."

"So angry-fuck me. I don't give a shit!" I motioned my hand to my dick. "My dick doesn't give a shit!"

She laughed again, moving closer to me. I thought she was about to give in, but instead, she lifted her chin and said, "You have hands, use them."

I glared at her, then thrust my hips forward slightly. "You have hands, you use them."

Then she laughed in my face and left.

And if I had anything invaluable in my room, I'd be throwing it against a wall.

Instead, I did the only thing I could do. I jumped in the shower and re-introduced my hand to my dick. They hadn't seen each other for the last four fucking years.

18

LOGAN

"I HATE IT when you do that." I could hear Amanda in the kitchen whispering. I stood frozen in the hallway, not wanting to interrupt them.

After their argument last night, the house was silent. They didn't talk. At all. Not to me or each other. I don't know if that's normal for brothers and sisters, considering I don't have any, but it was awkward as hell.

I slept in my room, in a sleeping bag, on the floor. Good times.

"Do what?" Ethan responded.

"I hate it when you put me down like that."

"How did I put you down?" He sounded pissed.

Amanda just sounded sad.

"You always make me feel like what I want to do with my life is less important than you. So what if my life goal is to be a good mom? So what if I don't want to have an epic career and make lots of money? Maybe falling in love, getting married, being happy and having a family is all I want. Maybe being a mom is enough for me."

I heard him sigh. "You're right, Dim, I'm sorry. I'm an asshole."

I was still in the hallway, listening in on their conversation. I felt like I should turn around and go back in my room. But I needed to leave for class, so I was stuck.

"It's okay," she said quietly.

"No. It's not okay. You already stayed all last year. I'll just find another job."

"No," Amanda said quickly. "You get another job, you may as well quit. I'll go back home. It's fine. I'll just go back to school there."

Then it was silent.

I made sure to make a lot of noise as I entered, so they knew I was coming.

They were both in the kitchen, coffee in hands, looking at the floor.

Ethan looked up when he heard me, then to Amanda he said, "We'll work something out, Dim, promise." He squeezed her arm before brushing past me and into his room.

I poured myself a coffee and stood next to her, leaning against the bench.

She hadn't raised her eyes since I'd come in; she was still staring at the floor.

I gently nudged her with my elbow. "You okay?"

Her head lifted and her eyes met mine. They were red from crying. She had tears falling but didn't bother to hide it.

I put our coffees on the counter and pulled her into me. She didn't resist. Her face was on my chest as her arms went around me.

"What happened?" I slowly ran my fingers through her hair. I hated seeing her like this. I hated that she was sad. I hated that she felt anything bad enough to make her cry.

She inhaled deeply, then pulled back slightly to look up at me, those big blue eyes full of sadness.

And it was this moment that I knew—I knew I'd do anything at all in this entire world to make sure she'd never feel sadness again.

"I have to go home, Logan." She sniffed and wiped her nose on her arm. "I have to leave and go home."

I tensed at her words.

She couldn't leave.

I couldn't let her go.

Not again.

"You can't leave, Amanda."

She stared at me. Unblinking.

A million emotions ran through me.

"I won't let you go." I said. "Not again." It was barely a whisper.

"Logan?" She was looking at me confused, not understanding my words.

Valid.

I didn't truly understand them either.

Finally, she pulled away and started to gather her stuff.

My mind was still reeling with her news, so I wasn't focused when she said she was leaving and walked out the door.

I WAS DRIVING to campus when I saw her waiting at the bus stop. I pulled over so fast, the car behind me nearly hit me.

"What are you doing?" I yelled out to her.

She looked up from the ground. "Huh?"

"Where are you going?"

"Class," she shrugged.

Ten minutes later, we pulled into a parking spot on campus. I turned the car off and faced her. She looked out the windshield, blank expression on her face.

"What happened? I mean, why do you have to go home?"

She faced me and shrugged. "It's nothing, Logan. Nothing we can actually do anything about."

Turned out she had book club with Micky and Lucy that evening, so we planned for me to pick her up from there after practice. She said she wasn't in the mood for socializing with anyone, so it worked out well.

SHE WENT TO her room when we got home from Micky's, shutting the door behind her.

She didn't say anything on the drive home, and neither did I.

I did, however, offer her my hand.

She took it.

I sat on the sofa, getting some homework done when I felt Ethan sit down next to me.

"I feel like an asshole," he said, running his hand through his hair. He looked like he'd been working out.

"Why?" I shut my laptop and faced him.

"For the shit I said to her yesterday. I mean, I didn't mean to say it. Not the way it came out. But it is kind of true, you know? If anyone needs to be here, it's me." He lowered his voice and looked to the hallway. I guess to make sure Amanda couldn't hear us. "I get it—that she doesn't want to go back. And I don't even think that it's the missing out on college thing. I just—I think she doesn't want to be home—with Ma. And I think she just doesn't like to be there, with the people and the memories. I mean it happened a year and half ago, I don't—" He cut himself off before I got the chance to ask him what the hell he was talking about. "Shit," he spat. "Don't tell Dimmy I said anything. I forget sometimes that not everyone knows."

"Knows what?" I asked, confused.

"Nothing, man. Just—never mind." He put his leg up on the coffee table and started kneading his hip with his hand. "I can't fucking believe Ma got fired again."

And there it was.

"So she lost her job and that meant Amanda had to go home, and what? Work? Look after your mom?"

"Unless a miracle happens, yeah. I guess so."

AMANDA

I'D BEEN LAYING in my bed, in a dark room, for who knows how long, feeling sorry for myself, when really, things could be a lot worse.

The thing was, I just didn't want to go home. I already gave up a year of my life to stay there and make sure everything was okay. I get that Ma was upset and that she lost it a little, and honestly, she had every right to.

But it was hell.

It wasn't just the schoolwork added with the full-time work at a crappy diner and then the coming home to a borderline alcoholic mom. It was also because somewhere between the day Dad walked out on us and the night it happened, I lost myself. I lost who I was as a person and became someone else. Someone weak and stupid and pathetic. Someone completely not me at all, and I didn't want to be reminded of that.

There was a light tap on my door before Logan popped his head in. "You decent?"

It was too dark to see anything. "Uh-huh."

"Dammit!" I could hear the smile in his voice, and for some reason it made me happy, and so did the fact that he was in here right now.

"What are you doing?" He moved closer to the bed.

I sat up a little. "Sitting here feeling sorry for myself. What about you?"

"Can you please turn a light on? Contrary to your obvious perception of my body, I'm not superhuman. I don't have night vision."

I laughed and did what he asked.

He stood there, bowl of ice cream in one hand, gummy bears in the other.

My eyes went big as a gasp escaped my mouth, "Did you go out and get me these?"

He nodded.

"You didn't!"

"I did." He smiled that beautiful smug smile of his.

He sat on my bed and watched me scarf down the ice cream, which surprisingly made me feel better. "So I have an idea," he said.

I put the bowl on the nightstand and gave him my full attention. "And what's that?"

"Let's go a little crazy and beat the shit out of Ethan."

I laughed so hard I snorted. It was my most attractive quality.

He watched me—that panty-dropping smile of his on full display.

The thing with Logan was that he had that power over me. His presence could make me forget all the emotions I felt before he entered a room. Because the second he was here, it was all him.

I hated it.

And I loved it.

"What was that about anyway?" He mocked as he scooted closer so our legs touched. "I felt bad for the kid. I felt like yelling at him to tap out. How the fuck did you even get him to the ground?"

I threw my head back with laughter.

"So I have my two truths for fifteen question. Are you ready for it?" he asked.

I nodded, still smiling.

"I don't know why I didn't ask you this earlier—but why the hell does Ethan call you Dimmy?"

Shit. I didn't want to answer. "Pass."

"You can't pass." He had that shit-eating grin on his face. "This story must be good." He moved closer again, until his hands were on my knees. We were face-to-face, sitting cross-legged on my bed.

"I pass. There has to be a 'pass' rule. You can't answer every question truthfully."

"Yes, there is a pass rule, and it's that you're not allowed to pass."

"What? You have to answer every question? So if I asked you: 'How many girls have you had sex with?' you'd have to answer?"

He nodded, but he was unsure, "Is that your question?"

Did I want to know? I think I made a gagging face because he chuckled.

"No. That's not my question."

"So why does he call you Dimmy?"

I pursed my lips tight and shook my head.

"I'll find out," he said, eyebrows raised in a challenge.

I continued shaking my head.

He sighed out loud, slumping his shoulders, like he'd given up. He dropped his head forward, causing his hair to fall into his face.

My hand shifted to move it out of the way. I didn't know I was doing it until it was done. But when I went to pull back, his hand held it in place, linking our fingers together.

Then he looked up at me, and slowly, a smirk pulled at his lips. He took in a deep breath, and then it hit me, what he was about to do. "Yo, Ethan!" he yelled, before I got a chance to cover his mouth.

Ethan walked into my room and took in our position, before leaning on the dresser. "What's up?" He looked at us suspiciously.

I didn't care.

"Why do you call her Dimmy?"

"Don't you dare tell him!" I narrowed my eyes at him.

He crossed his arms over his chest with a smug grin on his face. The exact same one Logan wore. I looked between the two of them.

"Amanda the Demander," Ethan sang.

"Shut up!" I said.

"She was a little brat when we were kids. You know that girl from Willy Wonka?"

Logan thought for a beat. "The 'I want it now' girl?" he said through a laugh.

Ethan joined him. "That's the one. She was exactly like that. Mom, Dad and I used to call her Amanda the Demander; eventually it just got shortened to Dimmy. It stuck." I threw a pillow at his head. He blocked it, chuckling to himself.

"Is that all?" he asked. Smug asshole.

"That's all," I said through gritted teeth.

He walked out laughing to himself.

"Amanda the Demander," Logan repeated in Ethan's annoying tone. "I like it."

"Shut up."

He laughed.

"You're lucky you don't have any brothers or sisters so I can dig up dirt on you."

The moment the words were out of my mouth, his features straightened and he tensed slightly, looking away from me. "Yeah, lucky me," he deadpanned.

I don't know why, or what'd changed, but he stood up and started to walk out of the room.

I stood and pulled him back down to the bed.

"Did I say something?"

He avoided making eye contact.

"Logan?"

He looked at me.

I pouted.

He smiled.

And it was all I ever wanted.

"You got your question?" he asked.

I thought for a second, while he got more comfortable sitting in front of me. He took my hands in his and kissed the inside of each wrist, the whole time smiling up at me.

I bit my lip to stop myself from leaning in and kissing him. Because I wanted to. So damn bad. "When was the last time you had a moment? Like the ones you told me about. Remember?"

He nodded.

I continued, "What was the last thing worth remembering like that?"

He looked at me for so long, I didn't know if he was going to answer. Then he took a breath. "That day I saw you at the library, after we talked at the bus stop. That was the moment, that for the first time in my life, I wanted to believe in second chances."

LOGAN

WHEN I WOKE up the next morning, she wasn't in her bed.

She was sitting in the living room, coffee in hand. I sat next to her, but her eyes didn't move from staring down at the floor.

I put my arm around her and brought her into me. She didn't resist. "When do you have to leave?"

She removed my arm and stood up. "Tomorrow."

"What?" I followed her as she walked to the kitchen. She put her mug in the sink, then turned to face me.

My forearm landed on her shoulders. "I don't want you to go."

"I don't want to go, Logan." Her voice broke.

"So what do we do?" I put both my arms around her neck and pulled her into me.

Her arms went around my waist. We held each other tight.

"We do nothing. You stay here and go to college, and I go home and work."

"But I don't want you to go," I repeated. Maybe if I said it enough, she wouldn't. I pulled back and rested my forehead on hers.

"So you've said," she whispered.

I licked my lips.

I saw her lick hers.

"So I've said," I breathed out.

I felt her fingers tighten, gripping the back of my shirt. Her eyes fell shut, and she moved her head to the side so her nose rubbed against mine.

"Amanda?"

"Mm?"

"I really, really want you to stay."

I brought her in closer again so her body was flush with mine.

She moaned.

"In fact," I started. "I really, really need you to stay."

And then I kissed her, softly. Just enough that our lips touched.

And that's how we stayed, for seconds, minutes, hours, who knows.

Our arms around each other, holding on. Mouths touching, but not moving. Eyes closed. Breaths heavy.

And then I moved.

I pushed her slowly until her back was to the counter, and my mouth moved on hers, slowly kissing her.

But she didn't kiss back. And it fucking hurt. Because as much as I wanted her, I think I needed her more. I've never needed anything more than her.

When I pulled away, I could see the tears forming in her eyes. "We can't, Logan." Her voice broke again. She straightened up.

"Why not?" I whispered, still holding onto her tightly.

"Because." She pulled back and moved her head to my shoulder. "Because you'll be here and I'll be there."

"So what?"

She was quiet for a while, before she removed herself from my hold completely and leaned back on the counter, crossing her arms in front of her. "So college relationships are hard. You may be with someone, or even love them. But when you don't get that something physically, it's hard not to be tempted. And there are way too many temptations in college."

I shook my head at her, "Any asshole that has you, and is stupid enough to lose you, is a fucking idiot, Amanda. Trust me. I would know."

Logan: *I need your help.*

Dad: *Anything.*

I WAS WALKING to the field entrance for practice a few hours later, when I saw her. There were always a bunch of people waiting around outside the gates, but I didn't expect to see Amanda. She was sitting cross-legged on a bench, loose shirt hanging off her shoulder and those cut-off shorts. Her eyes cast downwards, focused on the textbook in her lap.

A couple girls called out my name, getting her attention. I ignored them and walked straight to her.

"What's up?" I dropped my gear bag on the ground in front of the bench and sat next to her. "How did you know I was here?"

"Micky." She shrugged, closing her book and putting it in her bag. She turned to face me, legs still crossed.

The sun hit her eyes, making them extra blue. She squinted. Her nose scrunched. She was pretty fucking adorable.

Her hand moved to her head to block out the sun, but it didn't work.

I laughed.

She giggled.

I took my cap off and put it on her head. It was way too big and fell over her eyes. Her body slumped, and she pouted. I laughed again, adjusting it so I could see her face, and moved to the side to block out the sun. "Better?" I asked.

"Much."

"So?"

"So."

"What?"

"What?"

"Huh?"

"Huh?"

I laughed and gently shook her with my hands on her upper arms. "Quit being cute. What are you doing here?"

I shook her so much my cap fell over her eyes again.

She pouted, again.

It was fucking adorable, again.

The sound of whips formed in my mind.

"So my mom rang earlier."

I tried to contain my smile. "Yeah?"

"Yeah. She got a job. Can you believe it?"

"Huh. Luck must be on her side."

"Yeah, it could be luck. Or it could be something else. I mean, she got a job as a receptionist at a doctor's practice."

"Yeah?"

"Yeah. A Doctor Matthews..."

I bit my lip to try to stop the huge grin that'd taken over my face.

She continued, "Yeah. He called her...said a friend of his recommended her services. Apparently they were desperate. She starts tomorrow."

"Well, that's good, right?"

"Yeah. It just seems like a coincidence, you know?"

"What is?"

"That she gets a job with a Doctor Matthews..." She paused for dramatic effect. "Hey!" She shoved me lightly, exaggerating a gasp. "Your dad's a doctor, right? A Doctor Matthews?"

I shook my head. "What are you saying? Are you accusing me of something?" I took her hands in mine.

"Yeah, I am. I'm accusing you of being awesome!"

I laughed.

"Thank you, Logan." She scooted closer to me. She had our linked hands between us.

I moved them to the side so I could get closer to her. "You're welcome."

And then she kissed me. On my lips. Just once. But it was enough. I'd done at least one thing right by her.

"What are you doing now?" I asked, our fingers still locked.

"Probably catch the bus home."

I really didn't like her catching the bus. It's not far, but it's far enough. Plus, I think I remember Micky telling me about a guy licking her elbow once.

"I've only got a short session. I'll be done in an hour. Can you hang around here?"

She bit her lip, looking down. "Okay."

"Okay." I nodded my head.

She took my cap off and placed it back on my head, then scrunched her nose and flipped it backwards.

"Better," she said, before moving in and kissing me.

AMANDA

I KNEW THE girls outside the stadium were laughing at me, and I get it. Logan Matthews talking to me. It was funny, but whatever. Fuck them. It'd only been about half an hour since he left, but the temperature had dropped a shitload and I didn't bring a sweater. I was freezing my ass off waiting for him. I was about to text him and tell him that I'd just meet him at home when I heard those girls giggling again. I looked up to see him walking toward me. My eyes went wide when I took him in. It's the first time I'd seen him in his baseball gear and holy shit, he looked good, better than good.

"Busted!" He smirked.

Shit. I can't even deny it.

When he got closer, I could see him holding his team jacket in his hand. "You cold?" He started to open the jacket.

"Yeah," I yelled. I don't know if he could hear me over the sound of the wind.

He stood in front of me and put his jacket over my shoulders. I put my arms in the holes.

"Turn around," he said.

I was confused, but I did it anyway.

He pulled out my hair from under the jacket, and I zipped it up. When I looked up, I could see the girls glaring at me, their hands covering their mouths as they talked shit.

He turned me to face him, but his eyes were narrowed at the girls.

"You came out just to give me this?" I asked, trying to get his attention.

His eyes moved from them to me. "Well, yeah. I can't have you sitting out in the cold."

And just then, a crack of thunder sounded, and the rain poured down, instantly soaking us.

"Holy shit!" He picked up my bag, grabbed my hand and led me inside the stadium.

The few seconds it took for us to get in was all the rain needed to get us drenched.

Once we were safely inside, he took his cap off and shook out his hair. I watched him, this boy—no, this man, looking hot as hell in his uniform. And I wanted him. Bad.

He put his cap back on and turned to face me. Then a smile pulled on his lips, and I knew he'd caught me, again.

He moved closer to me and started walking me backwards until I hit a wall. His hands gripped my waist, and his body covered mine.

"Busted," he whispered in my ear. "If I catch you looking at me like that again, we're going to have a huge fucking problem." One hand moved under the jacket, so it touched my bare back. His skin on mine was scorching. "Because from now on, when I close my eyes, I'm going to see you, in my uniform and nothing else." He made a moaning sound from deep in his throat. "Fuck, baby, I'm getting hard just thinking about it." He gripped my thigh and lifted it so my leg wrapped around him and he was between me. I could feel him, hard, against my center.

I couldn't help the moan that escaped. I tried to swallow, but my throat was too dry. Then his mouth was on my neck, sucking, slowly moving higher. I tilted my head, wanting more of him. His lips brushed against mine. His tongue darted out and licked my bottom lip. And then he backed away. But I gripped his shirt in my hands and pulled him back, bringing his mouth to mine.

And I kissed him.

Because if he needed to know that it was okay for him to kiss me, then I'd show him.

The second our tongues met, he let out a low groan. His hand on my back moved lower, and lower, until it was under my shorts and under my panties, cupping my bare ass. "Mm," he moaned, never taking his mouth off mine.

I started to untuck his shirt. I wanted to touch him, too. I wanted to touch him everywhere. I wanted to feel him everywhere.

His mouth never stopped moving, and our tongues never stopped playing. It was slow and soft, but he was in full control.

I lost mine the minute he looked at me with lust clear in his eyes.

He pressed further into my center and I felt him again, rock hard against my core.

He started a rhythm, grinding into me. One of my legs was on the floor, the other wrapped around him. I started moving, too. And slowly, we started moving together. "Oh God, Logan." I kissed him harder, softly biting his bottom lip.

His mouth moved from mine, down to my jaw, to my neck, to my collarbone. He slowly ran his tongue along there, lower, and lower, until he reached my chest.

"Oh, shit," I whispered. I was panting, moaning, moving, gripping, all of it, all at once. My nails dug into his back. "Oh, shit," I said again. I had no control over what came out of my mouth when he did these things to me.

He gripped my ass tighter. I let out a sound I had no idea I was capable of. I was so fucking turned on. His movements on me were making me so fucking wet, I could feel it soaking my panties. His mouth moved from my neck to my ear. "You gotta quit making those sounds, baby." He kissed the spot behind it. "I'm starting to lose it."

Then he took my mouth in his, moving into me harder, pinning me to the wall. My leg on the floor moved to wrap around him. I needed him closer to me; I needed more of him.

He started to build a rhythm again. I felt that slow burn building low in my stomach. I didn't know how the fuck he was doing it. Or what the fuck he was even doing. But I didn't want it to stop. Ever. "Oh my God, Logan." I was panting, my head threw back against the wall. He was on my neck. Sucking. Hard. He was going to leave a mark. I wanted him to.

"Matthews! What the fuck are you doing?" a deep voice yelled.

I screamed, dropped my legs, ducked, and hid behind him.

Oh. My. God.

Reality set in.

What the fuck were we doing?

"Fuck," he spat. His hand went down his pants to adjust himself, before turning around.

"What the fuck do you think this is, Matthews?"

"Sorry, Coach."

Oh. My. God.

Kill me now.

"Go home!" I was too embarrassed to look past Logan to see his coach's reaction.

"Yes, sir." Logan sounded like he was about to laugh.

What the hell?

"I'll cover for you." His coach sounded different now, like he was trying to contain his own laughter. "Fuck, I wish I was in college again," he said, before I heard his footsteps walking away.

I didn't know what emotion was on my face when Logan turned to me, but he laughed.

Fucking laughed.

"This shit's not funny!" I whispered loudly. "I almost let you have me." I motioned with my finger at our surroundings. "Right here!"

He didn't respond. Just looked me up and down and licked his lips. His eyes settled on my face, as he brought his hand up to cup my cheek.

And then his face was so close to mine, I could feel his breath on my lips. He rubbed his nose against mine. "Wait here," he said, his voice low, laced with desire. "We're not even close to being done. I'm going to take you home, and I'm going to fucking finish what I started. And when I'm done with you, you won't even remember what happened just now. All you'll remember is how I make you feel when you're screaming my name."

LOGAN

She hadn't said a word since we started driving home. I couldn't even glance at her long enough to figure out what she was feeling because the rain was so heavy, I could barely see a foot in front of the car.

"I can't see shit," I told her, wiping the windshield with my sleeve.

She stayed silent.

I slowed down enough so that I could look at her quickly. Her eyes were squeezed shut, and she was gripping the sides of the seat so tight, her knuckles turned white. Her face was pale. I could see her chest heaving from her erratic breathing.

What the hell?

I was about to ask if she was okay when her phone sounded.

My concentration went back to the road, but I heard her answer. "Hey," she greeted.

"Yeah, I was on my way home...."

"Logan's driving..."

"Okay, hang on..."

To me, she said, "E wants to talk to you; I'll put it on speaker."

The next sound was Ethan's voice. "Dude, can you pull over somewhere safe?"

I did as he asked, took the phone off speaker and put it to my ear. I never took my eyes off Amanda.

"What's up?" I said into the phone.

"How is she?"

Her feet were on the seat, her knees drawn up, her head between them. "What's going on?"

"She just...has a thing...with this weather." He spoke cautiously. "Could you just stay put until it clears?"

"Sure." I hung up, put her phone in the console and stroked her hair gently. "Amanda?"

She made a sound but didn't look up.

I don't know what the hell was going on, but it was more than just being afraid of rain.

A crack of thunder sounded. She flinched and started rocking back and forth.

I leaned over and tried to get her to calm down. I tried to hold her, but she wouldn't stop rocking.

"Baby," I said.

That single word made her look up at me. She was crying. "I'm such a fucking baby." She sniffed.

"No, you're not," I soothed. "Come here."

I helped her so she was lying on top of me. I loved feeling her this close. It wasn't a sex thing, not all the time. Sometimes I just wanted her. I moved the hair that'd fallen in front of her face to behind her ear. "Are you going to tell me what's going on?"

She shook her head. "I want to, Logan. Just not now."

I nodded and kissed her cheek before lowering my seat to a lying position. I got us comfortable while we waited out the storm. Honestly though, I could lie like this, with her in my arms forever, and it still wouldn't be long enough.

"I hate this," I told her.

"What?" She sniffed again.

"I hate seeing you like this, crying. I hate that you have to feel like this, and I hate that I can't do shit about it."

Her head lifted from my neck. "You are doing something. You're here. That's something."

My hand started running through her hair. "It's not enough."

"It's more than I expected," she said, lowering her head to my chest.

AMANDA

He put his free hand on the small of my back, and that's how we stayed, with his arms wrapped around me, his fingers in my hair, my head on his chest, and my heart in his hands.

Minutes went by before I felt his hand that was stroking my hair begin to slow, and his breathing evened out.

He'd fallen asleep.

I lifted my head slowly, hoping not to wake him.

And I looked at him.

And I forget where I was and how I got here. I forgot the storm outside and all the memories associated with it. Because all I felt was him. I watched as his chest slowly rose and fell, his hair—that perfect mess, his lips slightly parted as his breath blew in and out.

My gaze lingered on his lips longer than it should, but I didn't kiss him. Instead, I laid my head back down and let his rhythmic breathing lull me into my own slumber.

I got jolted awake by the ringing of my phone. It surprised me so much that I jumped and hit my head on the roof of Logan's car.

He was already chuckling as his hand soothed where I hit my head. "It's Ethan," he said, handing me my phone.

By the time we got home, the rain had stopped and the sun was out. We didn't talk about what happened in the stadium, and we didn't discuss my crying in the car.

A bunch of Ethan's friends were in the living room watching the game, including James. James walked past us to go to the kitchen. "Amanda." He nodded in greeting, then looked at Logan, his eyebrows bunched in confusion. I didn't know if he knew Logan lived here or if he suspected something else. "Matthews." He did the same head nod toward Logan.

"Asshole," Logan replied.

We waited for James to be done in the kitchen before going in; I sat up on the counter while he got out two bottles of water. He handed me one at the same time Ethan walked in.

"You okay?" he asked, clearly concerned.

I smiled at him. "Uh-huh."

Logan leaned back on the opposite counter, crossing his arms over his chest.

"You sure?" Ethan asked again. He's always been a good brother, and even though we're twins, he's always acted like an older one, a protector of sorts. He understood who I was, and he put up with my shit, even when I didn't deserve it. But the summer after senior year, things changed. He became more than just my brother; he became my best friend.

"I'm sure, E, it's fine. Logan took care of me."

Logan choked on his water, then tried to contain his laugh. He wiped his mouth with his sleeve, while Ethan looked from me to him, a look of disgust clear on his face.

"I don't even want to know," E said, shaking his head. He continued, "So, you don't..." a slow smirk developed as he took a step closer. I was confused for a second before his arms came up. "You don't need a hug, do you?"

My legs automatically kicked out in front of me. "No. Ew. Gross."

He started laughing, backing away.

"What's that about?" Logan said through his own laughter.

Great. My brother and my whatever-the-hell Logan was, both laughing at me.

"Dimmy hates being hugged. Ask Tyson. It was the one thing he didn't love about her."

My face fell at the mention of his name. I could see Logan watching me from the corner of my eye. I knew what his next question was going to be. I mentally prepared myself for it.

Ethan left the room.

And then it was deadly silent.

I kept my eyes trained to the floor. I saw him take the few steps until he was right in front of me. He separated my legs so he could stand between them. Then he placed both hands on the counter on either side of me.

I never looked up.

I waited.

And I waited.

"So," he said, his voice low. "You hate being hugged?"

Not the question I was expecting. I couldn't help but smile as my eyes moved up to meet his. I nodded once.

His arms went around my waist. Mine moved on their own until they rest on his shoulders. His smile matched mine. He pulled me closer.

"I would have never guessed," he whispered in my ear. Then he rubbed his nose along my jaw until his mouth was aligned with mine. "I must be special," he said into my mouth, right before he kissed me.

And I lost myself.

In his hold.

In his kiss.

I completely lost myself in Logan Matthews.

He started to pull away but came back in for a few more chaste kisses. I giggled into his mouth.

He rubbed his palms up and down my bare legs. "What are we doing tonight?" he asked.

"We are doing nothing. I am going to work."

He threw his head back, frustrated.

"But," I continued. "I have tomorrow day and the next day completely free, but I have to work tomorrow night."

"I have practice in the morning, and then I'm free the rest of the day." He paused, thinking. "And the next day, too."

He backed away and left the kitchen.

I knew he was lying, but I didn't care. Right now, I couldn't think of anything I wanted more than him.

LOGAN

CLEARLY WHOEVER THE fuck that Tyson asshole was—he wasn't holding her right.

20

LOGAN

Amanda got a ride to work from a friend. A non-Tony friend.

The guys ended up leaving as soon as the game was done, and some girl came over. I didn't see her; I just heard her heels as she walked into the house. They went straight to Ethan's room without saying a word. I stayed on the sofa and studied.

I didn't know how much time passed before Ethan came out, with a brunette in tow. If you had asked me a few months ago, I would've told you she was hot. She just wasn't Amanda.

It was close to eleven, and I was still on the sofa surrounded by books. It was a sight not many people saw. The brunette with him stopped suddenly when she saw me. I hope I hadn't screwed her because this could get real awkward.

"Kellie, this is Logan." Ethan had his hand on the small of her back as he introduced us. I motioned a small wave.

She smiled, throwing her hand out for me to take. "Kellie, with an *I E*, just so you know," she cooed, stepping closer to me. I looked from her hand to her face. She was checking me out. I looked behind her to Ethan, who was yawning.

I shook her hand once, firmly, and said to Ethan, "What are you guys doing?"

He finished his yawn with a grunt. "Kellie's going home. I was about to pick up Amanda."

"I don't know why you need to pick her up all the time. Surely

Tony could bring her home." She turned to face him. "I wanted to sleep over tonight," she whined.

His shoulders lifted with a carefree attitude. "I don't want her riding with guys I don't know. Just leave it alone, okay?" I picked up on his angry tone straight away. I'd have to ask him what he meant later.

"Whatevs," she sang, making her way to the front door. "I guess I'll see you tomorrow." She kissed him on the cheek before he lazily shut the door behind her.

He made his way back to the living room and sat on the recliner opposite me.

He looked at the books surrounding me. "I thought you were a dumbass."

My gaze shifted from my book to him. I lifted an eyebrow in question.

"You study. A lot. More than anyone I know. When you're not in class or practice, your head's in a book. What's the deal? What's your major?"

"Pre-med."

"No shit?" His shock didn't surprise me. I'd gotten used to it.

"Shit," I replied, sighing and closing the book. I threw it to the side. "So. Kellie?" I contained my smirk.

"No, dude. Kellie with an *I E*." His voice rose to a mockingly girly tone.

Then we both laughed.

"Fuck," he moaned, rubbing his eyes. "I need to save up and buy Dimmy a car. I'm sick of driving her around all the fucking time. I'm tired as hell right now, and I can't be fucked." He threw his head back against his chair.

"I'll pick her up tonight; we could share the workload."

He didn't answer, just looked at me curiously. "So, I think we need to talk about this."

I lifted my chin. "About what?"

"You know what."

"I really don't." I tried to act bored.

"You've lived here a few days. There still isn't shit in your room. Where do you sleep?"

I kept my mouth shut.

"Dude," he continued. "I'm not an idiot, and I'm not an asshole. I'm not going to sit here and give you some speech about how you can't be with her or whatever, not that you'd listen. I see you guys together, you know? I hear you guys laughing at night. I know you sleep in her room. And I hope that's all you do—sleep. Because she's not ready for much else."

I opened my mouth to interrupt him. He raised his hand to stop me. "Look, if you guys are going to do whatever you're doing, just be careful with her, okay? I'm not going to give you a reason or tell you why...but it's more than just a brother looking out for his sister, you know?"

I was confused. I had no idea what the fuck he was saying.

"She's changed with you."

That got my attention. "What do you mean?"

"You guys knew each other before you moved in." It was a statement, not a question. "I mean, I assume because of the way she acted when she saw you. I don't need to know how or why, but she's happier when you're around. I don't get it, but whatever you're doing, thank you."

He stood up and put his fist out for me to bump.

I did.

I still had no fucking clue what he was talking about.

"If you could pick her up tonight, that would be awesome." He started walking to his room. "She finishes at midnight." He stopped just before walking in and placed both hands on either side of the door. Then, with a smirk on his face, he said, "Holy shit, Kellie I E wore me out." He chuckled to himself before entering his room and closing the door behind him.

AMANDA

I COULDN'T KEEP the smile off my face when he arrived at work to pick me up, but by the time we got into his car, something had switched. I could see him looking at me from the corner of his eye, but he wouldn't face me. I saw him open his mouth to say something, but he didn't speak. It felt like the longest car ride in history.

When we finally pulled up to the house and got in, he went straight to his room.

I dressed for bed and knocked on his door.

"Come in," he said.

He was in his sleeping bag on the floor.

"What are you doing?" I asked.

He sighed. "Nothing, just studying." His books were spread out in front of him.

I sat on the floor next to him. "Two truths?"

He slowly closed all the books and stacked them in a pile. "Sure." He tried to smile, but it didn't reach his eyes. "I go first, though."

I nodded.

"Tony?"

I rolled my eyes.

He continued. "I ran into him outside the bathroom, right before we left your work. He said you guys are a thing? Or will be? I don't know...but he told me to back off, that you were his. What the hell?"

I shook my head. "I don't know why he told you that, but it's not true. I mean, we've fooled around a couple of times..." I trailed off, not wanting to go into too much detail.

He raised his eyebrows. "That's all?" He was pissed.

I reared back, "What do you want me to say? Why are you pissed?"

He shrugged, avoiding my eyes.

I stood up and walked to his door. "You're being an asshole."

I WAS IN my room for all of two seconds before he came in, a different emotion set on his features. "I'm sorry," he said.

I shook my head, not looking at him. "You're being a dick. You've been in my life for what? A week? And you want to act like this when you find out that I've fooled around with someone. You have no right!" He stayed silent. I got out my anger. "And what about you? I know the number of people I've slept with. Do you? Can you give me a number?" I finally turned to face him. His hands were in his pockets. His gaze fixed on the floor. I went on. "Two, Logan. I've slept with two people." He lifted his head now, eyes penetrating mine. "And neither of those people were you. So you have no right to be like this. Quit acting like an asshole and get over it."

He just stared at me. I could feel the air rushing in and out of my lungs as I tried to level my breathing. Then a smug smirk developed on his face, and he finally spoke. "I fucking love this feisty side. It's such a turn on."

"Get out!" I pointed to the door, then turned to get into bed.

I sensed him move, before I felt his hands on my waist, his breath on my ear. "I'm sorry," he said again. "I'm sorry I'm being an asshole. But the thought of you, and some other guy with his hands all over you—I hate it, Amanda." He gently turned me to face him and then rested his forehead against mine. He kissed me once, softly. "I want to feel everywhere he's felt. I want to replace the memory of his touch with mine. I don't want a single part of your body to not know my hands, do you understand?" His voice was low, husky, filled with desire.

My eyes drifted shut at his words. A sound of agreement left my mouth. He started kissing my jaw. "Has he kissed you here?" he whispered, his words muffled.

I nodded.

His lips moved from my jaw and worked their way down to my neck, kissing, licking, and slightly sucking. I could feel his hard-on against my stomach. One of his hands moved to cup the back of my head, his fingers curled into my hair, softly pulling and tilting my head back to give him better access.

I moaned.

His other hand moved under my shirt, the back of his fingers skimming my stomach before I felt him grip my side, just under my breast. I wasn't wearing a bra.

He released his grip on my hair just enough that my head fell forward; he kissed me again, just once. Then I felt his thumb rub against my already straining nipple. He made a moaning sound from deep in his throat, pushing into me. "Has he touched here?"

I nodded again.

He replaced his thumb with his hand, covering my entire breast, gently squeezing.

"Oh my God," I whispered. My chest heaved with every breath. My legs squeezed together trying to find some form of relief.

His other hand moved from my head to under my shirt and onto my bare back. Then he started to slide it lower, and lower, slowly making its way under my panties and onto my ass.

"Fucking shit," he spat out, grabbing a handful. "Please don't tell me he's touched you here?"

I kept quiet.

"Fuck." He knew the meaning of my silence.

It was quiet for a few moments, his head resting on my shoulder, one hand gripping my ass and the other holding my breast. The only sound in the room was our heavy breathing. Then his hand on my ass slowly moved, from the back to the front, his fingers playing under the band of panties. His head lifted from my shoulder, and his eyes darkened as he took in my flushed face.

"And here?" Anger was laced in his tone.

My lips thinned to a line.

He moved his hand lower, and lower, until the tip of his finger met my wetness.

And he had to know.

He had to know what he did to me.

I bit my lip to try and contain whatever sound was about to escape. But then I felt his finger inside me, and any and all control I had was gone. I threw my head back; my legs gave out underneath me. His arm curved around my back, holding me to him. And then I was airborne. With his finger still inside me, I was moving. I heard something fall to the floor, before my ass landed on my desk. Then his single finger was replaced by two, and he moved them, in and out. He drove me crazy. My head started thrashing from side to side, my hands on his shoulders, trying to hold on. His mouth caught mine, and finally, he kissed me, his tongue coming out and invading my mouth.

And I wanted him.

I fucking wanted him.

More than ever.

I didn't know how much time had passed, before he pulled back, just enough to speak. "Did he make you feel like this?" he said, moving his fingers inside me.

"Oh, God," I moaned out.

"Did he?" he asked again, a little louder.

"Not even close, Logan." I curled my arm around his neck and brought him back down to my mouth.

I was on the freaking edge, and he must've known because he started pumping his fingers faster into me, his palm rubbing on my clit at the same time. It seemed like a well-practiced move, but before I could think about how or why, he pulled back from the kiss and replaced his mouth and tongue with his thumb. He watched me intently as I slowly licked it and sucked it into my mouth. His eyes rolled back along with his head while he groaned out the sexiest fucking sound I'd ever heard.

Then he pulled his hand away from my mouth and moved it under my shirt, where his now wet thumb rubbed against my nipple again.

And then he stopped.

Time stood still.

My breathing got even heavier.

Then he looked intently into my eyes, his face carrying an emotion I couldn't decipher.

"Amanda," he whispered, shaking his head.

And then it was silent.

For so long I didn't know if this was as far as we were going to go.

And I watched him. I watched his eyes roam my face. Those green eyes I remembered so well. For months after that night, I could close my eyes and see them. The way they lit up when he made me laugh or the intensity in them when he listened to me speak.

I swallowed down my emotions.

When I opened my eyes, his face was so close to mine. And I was no longer confused by what he was thinking or what he was feeling, because I felt it, too.

Only he felt the guilt, the regret. And I could see it in his eyes, how sorry he was for all of it.

And this—this was the moment I forgave him.

"Logan." I held his face in my hands. "No one makes me feel the way you do." It was the truth.

Instantly his mouth was on mine, his fingers moved, his thumb rubbed.

It started at my toes—that tingle feeling—then moved its way up to the pit of my stomach, and I think I must have blacked out from the pleasure of it, because all I could remember was his name leaving my lips over and over and over.

Once the buzz faded, I finally managed to open my eyes, and he was there, inches from my face, a smile on his lips. Only he was blurry. I blinked a few times to correct my vision.

"Hey, pretty girl," he said quietly, the same time he removed his fingers. "Welcome back."

21

LOGAN

I QUIETLY OPENED her bedroom door to let her know I'd be back. I didn't want her to think I'd forgotten our plans to spend the day together.

I shook her gently, but she didn't wake. I shook her a little harder. "What the hell?" she said, her words muffled by the pillow.

"I just wanted to let you know that I'll be back later."

"Logan?"

"No, the other guy you let finger-fuck you."

She gasped and sat up straight, a look of shock on her face.

I chuckled.

She opened her mouth to say something but then closed it. Her shoulders slumped as she said, "What time is it?" She reached to her nightstand for her phone. "Five-thirty? Five fucking thirty! Who the hell gets up at this time?"

"College athletes," I said, sitting on her bed and rubbing my palm across my jaw.

"Fuck practice; come back to bed." She rested her chin on my shoulder, while her arms went around me from behind.

"I can't." I started to pull her arms off me, because if she asked again, I didn't think I could say no.

Instead of letting go, she tightened her hold and wrapped both legs around my waist. I laughed. "What are you doing?"

She made a grunting sound as she pulled us both back until we were lying on the bed. She got out from underneath me and shifted so we were side by side. She panted, exhausted from the energy it just took to do what she did. Her face was flush and hair was a mess on her head. I laughed at how cute she looked. She smiled, too, looking right in my eyes. And then something took over her face, a completely different emotion. Her smile slowly faded. One of her fingers brushed my cheek. "I love it when you smile," she said quietly. "I love when your dimples show." She kissed one and then adjusted my head to kiss the other. And then she pulled back, her eyes never leaving mine.

And this—this was the moment when I forgot my past. I forgot that not everyone who loved you was out to hurt you. It was this moment—when I let it be okay for someone to love me. Because Amanda and I—we could. I didn't think we did yet. But we could. One day—soon I thought—we could really fall in love, with each other.

I got my phone out of my pocket and brought up Jake's number. "What are you doing?" she asked, watching me.

"Sending Jake a text."

"Why?"

"To tell him to make up a reason why I'm sleeping in your bed instead of going to practice."

She made a squealing sound as she got back under the covers, making room for me. She wore a huge smile. I took my pants and shirt off and got into bed with her.

"Are you going to be able to get back to sleep?" she asked from beside me.

I put my arm behind her head and pulled her into me. Her head was on my chest, my fingers in her hair, and her body half on top of mine. "Now I will," I told her, kissing her on the head.

A FEW HOURS later we were in the living room, sprawled out on the sofa. We wanted to have a day to just be together, without really doing anything. I planned on taking her out to dinner tonight and maybe a movie or something afterwards. As much as I wanted to, I was going to try to hold off on sex for a few more dates.

The keyword was try.

I was sitting down, with the laptop on the arm of the sofa, doing some homework.

She was laying down with her head on my lap, while she read on her e-reader. My fingers played with her hair.

We both looked up when Ethan walked in. He watched us for a moment, before sitting on the arm of the recliner opposite us. "Hey, Dimmy, what's that girl's name, you know the one who's friends with Kara? The one with the big..." he trailed off but motioned his hands to indicate boobs.

Amanda snorted. "Kara," she answered, going back to her book.

"No. Not Kara," he said annoyed, "her friend! Are you even listening to me?"

"Yes, asshole, Kara's friend with the big boobs is Kara. There are two Karas."

"Oohhhh," he smiled, then got up and began to leave.

"Wait. Why?" She sat up now and turned to him.

"I'm picking her up later."

"What?" It was my turn to speak. "What happened to Kellie I E?"

"Don't even," he said, shaking his head.

"What happened?" I couldn't help but chuckle.

He sat back down in the recliner. "Dude. She was so annoying. She speaks Internet talk. Like it's an actual thing. I'm not joking. She never laughed. Ever. You know what she'd do instead?"

I could hear Amanda giggling next to me. "What?" she managed to get out.

"She'd say 'LOL' or 'ROFL.'"

Amanda laughed harder.

"She said 'OMG' all the time. Every sentence, 'OMG'." He mocked her voice when explaining. "Instead of acting or saying she was confused, she'd actually spell out 'W T F'."

Amanda was all-out laughing now, and so was I. She scooted closer to me and hugged my arm, plastering her face onto it to muffle the sound. My hand landed on her bare leg.

I saw Ethan's eyes catch the movement, but he didn't say anything, just smiled and continued to speak. "I twisted my ankle playing basketball, and when I told her, she didn't ask if I was okay. Guess what she said?"

Amanda shook her head, still laughing.

"Guess!" Ethan said again.

"What? I don't know." Amanda's giggle took over the room. All I could do was watch her.

Ethan answered, "She pouted and said 'sad face emoticon!'"

She threw her head back in laughter, her eyes starting to water.

"She did not." She shook her head in disbelief.

"Swear it." He got off the sofa and started walking out of the room. He turned just before the door and took in our positions again. "You need to call Ma and let her know everything's okay."

Her face sobered, but she nodded.

Then her head was back resting on my lap, and my fingers were in her hair.

And it was pretty damn close to perfect.

"I've got a good truth question today." She smiled big, excited. She sat up and got comfortable, turning her body toward me.

"Go for it," I told her, as I positioned us so we were face-to-face, our knees touching.

"Okay. You get the chance to travel the world. All expenses paid. You get flights, accommodation, and food, everything taken care of. But you have to somehow make money to go sightseeing and buy souvenirs and stuff. You can bring three things with you to help you make money. So, you can be like, a street performer or something. Whatever. What do you bring?"

I watched her as she said all this, legs crossed, her hands clasped in front of her, eyes wide, waiting for my response.

And seeing her like this—I knew what I wanted.

I wanted more.

I wanted her.

"I'd only need one thing."

"But you can bring three," she said, still excited.

I shook my head, looking her straight in the eyes. "I don't need three; I just need one."

"Okaaay...are you going to tell me what it is?"

"Honestly, I don't think you could handle it."

She rolled her eyes. "Come on! Tell me," she pleaded, her hand on my leg trying to shake the answer out of me.

"Fine!" I told her. She stopped shaking me, but her hand stayed on me. "I'd bring you, Amanda. Just you."

Her eyes widened, before looking down between us. My hands moved to hers and linked our fingers together.

"But...I can't make you any money," she said quietly.

"Amanda." Her eyes lifted to mine. "It doesn't matter where I am in this world, there's nothing else I'd rather see. Just you."

She closed her eyes slowly. I didn't know how long I sat there staring at her, her eyes staying closed, before she finally whispered, "Kiss me now, Logan."

So I did.

I slowly moved forward, licking my lips. I rubbed my nose against hers.

She sighed.

My lips brushed hers so lightly I didn't know if she felt it.

Then her phone sounded.

We both jerked back from the sudden interruption.

She let her ringtone play. It was "Hey There Delilah" by the Plain White T's. She smiled dreamily.

"Excuse me," she said, standing up and leaving the room. She put the phone to her ear and spoke. "Well, well," she started, "you finally found time in your busy schedule to call me." I heard her laugh before the bedroom door closed.

Fifteen minutes later she was back. She stood in front of me, biting her lip, playing with the hem of her shirt.

I waited.

She opened her mouth to speak and then snapped it shut. She did that a couple more times before finally sighing and sitting down next to me.

I raised my eyebrows, waiting for her to speak.

"So." She looked down at her phone. "That was my friend Ty."

"Friend? You need to leave the room to talk to a friend?"

She shook her head. "He's, uh, he's my ex-boyfriend."

I nodded. "And?"

She blew out a small breath and then took my hand in both of hers. This must be bad. "Please don't get mad—"

I interrupted her. "You should never start an explanation with that."

"I know. But you will, and I don't want you to."

Now I was really worried. "What is it?"

"Promise me you won't get mad?"

"I can't promise that."

"Fine." She stood up to leave.

I pulled on her arm. "I promise."

Whipped.

She sat back down, closer this time. "We need to go out and buy your own bed. Like, now."

"What the fuck?" I almost yelled.

"You promised," she warned.

I tried to settle down. "Explain."

"Ty's coming to visit for a few days and I need you to not-"

I opened my mouth to interrupt her, but she covered it with her hand.

She closed her eyes and took a few calming breaths, her hand still covering my mouth. Then she opened them and continued, like she was talking to a child. "I need you to sleep in your own bed tonight."

She slowly removed her hand.

"That doesn't explain a fucking thing, Amanda. What the fuck?"

"He can't know that you and I are—whatever you and I are."

I waited for her to continue, but she didn't.

"I don't understand." I stood up and started pacing. I was so fucking confused. "Are you still holding out hope that you guys will get back together or something?"

"What?" she guffawed. "No. Not at all."

"Then what, Amanda? I don't get it." I was yelling.

She stood up, too, then forcefully sat me back down on the sofa. Then she sat so she was straddling my hips with a hand on each side of my face. "Quit it. Stop being pathetic."

I rolled my eyes; my hands went to her ass, bringing her closer to me. She leaned her forehead against mine and kissed me quickly a few times.

"Stop using your body to distract me," I told her.

She kissed me again, deeper this time.

I gripped her ass, tighter this time.

"Wait." I pulled away. "Why don't you want him to know about us?"

She pulled back, her eyes roaming my face. "It's complicated. I can't tell you. Not now. But soon, okay?"

"I don't like all these secrets you're keeping from me."

She smiled sadly. "Neither do I, Logan. Trust me."

My phone had been blowing up from the coaching staff, I guess because I missed practice this morning. I was still deciding whether or not it was worth whatever punishment I was about to receive.

She came to the field with me but waited in the car while I went in and took whatever punishment they had for me for bailing on practice.

Turned out they were calling me for a whole other reason.

She must've sensed it, because the second I was back in the car, she turned to me. "What's wrong? What happened?"

"They need me to start."

She looked at me and waited. I guessed she didn't get it.

"The first game of the season is two weeks from now. They want me to start. Jackson, the starting catcher, he's injured. They want him to sit it out. So I'm playing."

Her eyebrows drew in. She started to pout.

"I don't normally play. Not catcher. I don't normally have much game time. This will be the first time Jake pitches to me at college level."

It was quiet for a moment, as she took this in. "Well, that's good, right?"

I shrugged, before pulling out of the spot and driving to Ikea. "I guess," I mumbled. "I don't really know."

We met Dylan at the parking lot and swapped cars. I never had to ask him twice; he loved driving my car. I told him he could have it for a week. He tore out of the lot, wheels spinning as he did.

He was on his own when he arrived. In fact, come to think of it, I hadn't seen much of Heidi around at all lately.

Amanda walked around with her tablet and knew where everything was. I let her buy whatever she wanted. Honestly, I didn't give a shit what was in my room.

I did, however, step in when she asked the guy at the electrical store which TV had the 'prettiest picture.'

22

LOGAN

WE'D ONLY BEEN HOME for a few minutes before there was a knock on the door.

She froze mid-movement. I watched her closely. "Ty," she breathed out, before practically running out of my room.

This guy must be a god of some sort, judging by her reaction. Or ridiculously good in bed. I swallowed down the vomit that'd formed in my throat. The mental image of her being boned by some other guy was literally making me sick. Slowly, and attempted casually, I walked to the door so I could meet this asshole. She had her arms around his neck, his arms around her waist, lifting her off the floor. She was crying, but it wasn't the sad, fucked-up tears which I cause. These were happy tears.

He looked up when I walked into his vision. He placed her back on the floor, before taking the few steps to reach me.

"Oh," Amanda spoke. "Sorry, this is, uh..." she trailed off.

"I'm Tyson." He spoke for her, hand out waiting. "Her ex. She's so damn awkward about it."

I shook his hand. "Logan."

His eyes widened and his body tensed. It was a small movement, and if I wasn't glaring at him, I wouldn't have noticed at all.

He looked back at Amanda, then me again. "Huh," he said, as if something had just dawned on him. He faced her. "Dinner? We got a lot to catch up on."

She nodded.

I CALLED DYLAN to help assemble all the shit Amanda bought. He was with Cam at the time, so they both came over. Lucy called Cam to hang out at Jake and Micky's, but he told her he was busy so everyone ended up coming here.

Amanda was having dinner with Ty, so I left all the smaller shit for her to do.

I was pissed she was with him instead of me, but I couldn't do shit about it. I told her I'd leave it alone, so I was trying. She only just left, and already I was looking forward to seeing her again—to having her all to myself.

WITH FOUR GUYS ASSEMBLING, it only took an hour until everything was built.

"Shit," Cam said. "It looks just like your-"

"Pool house," I finished for him, taking a look around the room.

She remembered.

"DUDE," DYLAN SAID to Cam, who'd just taken his cap off and was now shaking his head wildly. "You need to get a haircut."

"Yeah," Jake agreed, "you look like that kid from One Direction."

We all looked at Jake before bursting out laughing.

We were all in the backyard, having a quiet night in.

"Which one?" Heidi asked, giggling.

Jake shrugged and sat up. "I don't know their names," he spat, defensively.

We laughed harder.

"What?" he huffed. "Julie's going through a phase. Shut up!"

We kept laughing.

"I can't get a haircut," Cam said, interrupting the laughter. "Lucy won't let me."

"What!" Dylan practically yelled, the same time I spat out my beer. Cam was seriously the most whipped of all of them.

I wiped my mouth with the sleeve of my shirt. "Sorry, Cameron, you're going to have to repeat that. I couldn't hear you over the sound of your throbbing vagina."

Jake threw his head back, his body shaking with his laugh. Dylan and I bumped fists while Heidi snorted, which made her giggle harder.

"You assholes laugh it up," Cam said, pointing a finger at me. "Luce likes something to hold on to when I go down—"

"OH MY GOD!" Lucy yelled, the same time Heidi squealed.

We were all in fits of laughter when the back door opened and Amanda walked out, sans Ty. Thank fuck.

"You've been at work?" Micky asked her.

Amanda brought a chair from inside and placed it next to me before taking a seat. She faced Micky. "No. Just out for dinner. Um, Ty's in town," she said. There was no hint of any emotion in her tone. Not happy, not excited. She was just stating facts.

"Ty's here?" Micky perked up. Jake sat up a little straighter.

Amanda grinned. "Yeah, just visiting for a couple of days."

"Oh really?" Micky crooned. "I want to say hi to him."

Amanda gripped the side of her chair, leaning forward and rubbing her cheek on her shoulder. "He just went to catch up with some friends quickly, but he should be back soon. Hopefully you'll catch him."

"Oh my God," Micky gasped, facing Lucy. "Remember when I told you about that guy from my school who sang 'Hey There Delilah' by the Plain White T's at his graduation?"

I glanced at Amanda. It was her ringtone.

Lucy's brows furrowed, thinking. "Yeah, what about it?"

Micky's eyebrows rose, and her head jerked toward Amanda.

"No way!" Lucy's eyes went wide.

Amanda chuckled a little and then nodded her head slowly.

"Wait." Lucy sat up, looking from Amanda to Micky and then back again. "That musician with the Juilliard scholarship? That's Ty? That's your ex?"

Juilliard? Really? How much do I not know about her?

Amanda laughed a little. "Yeah, that's him," she stated proudly.

Great.

Heidi piped up. "What am I missing? Who did what now?"

Cam held his hand to his heart, batted his eyelashes dramatically, and said in a high-pitched voice, "Oh my gaaahhd. He's so dreamy. Motherfucking swooooooo—" He got cut off when Lucy back-handed him in the stomach.

We laughed.

"So," Micky started, while Jake rolled his eyes. "Ty's two years older than us, right?" She looked at Amanda for confirmation. She nodded. Micky continued, "At his graduation ceremony, he convinced the committee to let him perform, in front of everybody. He sang 'Hey There Delilah,' just him and his guitar, on stage, but changed it to 'Hey There Amanda.'" Her smile widened. "I swear to God, every girl there cried. And it was all-out ugly cries. Everyone was so jealous of her."

"No way." Heidi shook her head slowly, looking at Amanda.

"True story." Amanda nodded, smiling back.

"Oh!" Micky yelled at Heidi. "It's on YouTube. Look it up. Look up Tyson Landry graduation." Then she sat back in her chair with a wistful look on her face.

Jake eyed her. "Are you done?" he said.

She pulled his cap down over his eyes and kissed his cheek before mumbling, "Shut up, idiot."

So Ty was a big deal at their school.

So what?

So he was fucking amazing.

So fucking what?

I decided that tonight was the perfect night to get a little wasted. It had nothing to do with the fact that her ex was in town. And that apparently he could make a bunch of grown-ass women turn into gushing pre-teen fan girls.

Seriously.

Not related.

At all.

The next ten minutes consisted of everyone loving the shit out of some guy no one had ever met.

Whatever, not a big deal.

Until said guy actually showed up.

Then I decided that tonight was a perfect night to get completely wasted.

He walked out from the back door and paused for a beat when he saw everyone, then casually introduced himself. Micky got up and gave him a quick kiss on the cheek before sitting back next to Jake, who instantly put his arms around her shoulders. He was crazy if he thought Micky even looked at other guys. Ever.

Ty did a little spin, I guess looking for somewhere to sit. Cameron got off the bench he was on and walked to Lucy, who stood up and gave him her seat, before sitting back down on his lap.

Ty sat down the same time as Amanda stood. I watched as she walked away from me and sat on the bench next to him. He stretched his arms out, resting his hands on the bench behind him, enough so that one arm was behind Amanda. He leaned in close and whispered something in her ear. A slow smile overtook her face.

Jake broke the silence. "So, how do you know Kayla? I mean," he looked to Micky, "you and Amanda weren't really friends back then, were you?"

Micky's expression changed, just slightly, before she recovered. "Uh, James and Ty played ball together. I think Ty's last year, James made varsity, right?"

Ty nodded. He could probably sense that Jake didn't need to know any more.

"Anyway," Cam tried to ease the awkwardness. "The girls were just gushing about your performance at your graduation."

Ty's face lit up, and then he looked at Amanda and nudged her side. "Oh yeah, remember that? It was good times, huh?"

She nodded. "Yeah. You made me cry like a frickin' baby."

"So worth it though." And then they stared at each other for what felt like a lifetime. I swear I thought he was going to kiss her. My fists clenched at the thought, but eventually she looked away.

She was the first to look away.

That had to mean something.

I didn't know how much time passed, with me in my buzzed state, before I saw him whisper something to her. She nodded before they both walked past me and into the house.

Lucy got off Cam's lap and sat on the abandoned chair next to me. "You okay, babe?"

"Nope."

EVERYONE LEFT SOON AFTER, and Amanda came to my room to finish whatever final touches she wanted to do. Ty was settled for the night in her room. I'm assuming the floor, because I didn't think I could handle anything else.

"Do you like it?" she asked, sitting on the bed next to me.

I looked around the room and adjusted us so my arm was around her waist.

It was perfect.

Perfectly me.

"Holy shit, Amanda. This is awesome." I faced her.

"Yeah?"

"Uh-huh. I love it."

"I tried to make it like your pool house, you know?"

I nodded.

"So you really like it?" She waited expectantly for my answer.

I faced her. "I love it, Amanda. Really."

"Good." She smiled.

I finally tore my eyes off hers and looked around the room. "So you're really good at this—the design stuff. You don't want to study that? Make that your career?"

She looked down. "No. I mean, I love doing it. And I think I'm good at it. But it's just having a good eye. It doesn't take a miracle to do it. But—"

"But babies," I interrupted her, "babies are miracles."

Her jaw dropped, as her eyes widened.

"You remember?" she breathed out.

I took her hands in mine.

"I remember everything about that night, Amanda. I told you. Everything."

TWO HOURS LATER and the house was finally quiet. I'd been lying in bed, wide awake, waiting for the talking and giggling from her room to stop. Now, it was dead silent, and I didn't know which one I'd prefer. My fucking imagination was driving me crazy. All I could think about was if people could fuck in silence.

I was about to get out of bed, just to focus on something else, when the bedroom door opened. She stood in the doorway, in her oversized jersey, looking unsure of herself. I couldn't help the grin that took over my face.

She chose me.

AMANDA

HE SMILED WHEN he saw me. Without saying a word, he lifted the covers and waited for me to get in. Once I was, his arms were instantly around me, holding me closer to him. His warmth surrounded me, my back to his front. His hand on my waist gripped me tighter. He moved my hair away from his face and kissed my neck a few times. Then he pulled back. "Huh." I heard him say.

"What?"

"Nothing."

"Bullshit, what?"

His hand moved from my waist and flicked the name on the back of my jersey. "Who's this Marquez kid? It's not Ty's."

I tried to contain my laugh. "Why?"

"Because I kind of want to punch him."

I let out a snort and looked over my shoulder at him. He was leaning on his elbow, his head resting on his hand. I turned to face him. I couldn't hide the smirk that'd developed.

"What's so funny?" he asked.

I rubbed my face on his chest. He placed his hand on the small of my back and brought me to him. I could feel him through his boxers. "So?" he asked.

"So what? Are you jealous?"

"Quit being cute; you know I'm jealous. I'm in bed with you while you're wearing some other asshole's jersey."

I laughed.

"What?" he repeated.

"What are you going to do to this Marquez kid when you see him?"

"Punch him."

I laughed again.

"What's so funny?"

"You'll be punching my brother. That would be awkward."

"What?"

"This is Ethan's. I just wear them because they're comfortable to sleep in."

"What?" His brows bunch together. "How did I not know what your last name was?"

"I guess it was more important for you to get in my pants." I block my chuckle with his chest.

"Me?" he almost shouts. "What about you?" he continues. "You basically ripped my shirt off me that night."

I laughed, harder this time, and so did he.

"Are you complaining?"

"Not at all, babe. Not one bit."

Then I moved up so my entire body covered his, our parts against each other. My hands came up to his face, my fingers tracing his dimples. "I love these," I whisper.

He leaned up and kissed me quickly.

"Fuck, I'm so glad—" he said, the same time I say, "Shit, I missed you like crazy today."

My eyes widened the second the words were out of my mouth. I moaned into his chest, annoyed that I let the words slip.

His hand went into my hair, gently pulling until I was face-to-face with him.

"What did you say?" He was trying to contain a smirk.

"Nothing. I shouldn't have said it."

His smirk turned into confusion. "What? Why?"

"I don't know." My eyes cast downwards. "I mean, you don't think it's too soon to be saying stuff like that?"

He kissed me again, longer this time.

"Maybe," he said, smiling. "But not for me, too soon, I mean. And even if it is, who gives a shit."

LOGAN

SHE WASN'T IN my bed when I woke up the next morning. It was the ass crack of dawn, which meant she must've snuck out at some point in the middle of the night. I texted her and let her know that I was out for the day. Even though I told her I was free, I did actually have classes. I'd rather have spent the day with her. Too bad ex-assholes get in the way.

I'd organized with Jake yesterday for early practice this morning to get me ready for game day. It was still two weeks away, but I should be prepared.

IT WAS LATE afternoon by the time I got home, and I was dead tired. No one was there when I got in, so I napped for a few hours.

I was woken up by a rustling sound coming from somewhere in my room. I slowly opened my eyes and saw her sitting at my new desk, her hands working away at something. I sat up, rubbing my eyes.

"Don't look," she said, never looking up from her task. "It's nearly done. Just wait."

I didn't bother replying.

"Okay," she said, standing and walking over to me. She had her hands behind her back, hiding whatever she was holding.

I moved to sit on the edge of the bed, my feet hitting the floor with a thud. Her eyes widened when she saw I just wearing boxers. I'll never, ever get sick of her reaction to my body. Ever.

"I got you something really lame. Are you ready?" She laughed.

I chuckled, placing my palms flat on the back of her thighs and bringing her between my legs.

"But first..." she raised an eyebrow, "...you need to put a shirt on."

I shook my head.

"Fine," she exaggerated, then brought her hand forward and gave me something wrapped in newspaper.

I ripped it open. It was John Mayer's *Room for Squares* album on vinyl. "Holy shit!" My eyes rose to meet hers.

"You like it?" she asked excitedly.

"I love it. But when? I mean how? What?" I couldn't seem to form a clear sentence.

She laughed. I just watched her, shaking my head. And I did the only thing I could think of to thank her. I kissed her.

Her body melted into mine. She moaned as the kisses got deeper. We took each other in, drowning in each other.

"Oh God," she said into my mouth, pushing me down until we were lying down, her body on top of mine. She was straddling me, her hips jerking forward, her heat rubbing on my already-hard dick. She was grinding harder and harder into me, and if she kept going, I wouldn't be able to stop. My right hand went under her shorts, grabbing her ass and encouraging her to keep going, to keep moving. The other hand was in her hair, bringing her closer to me.

God, I wanted her.

She pulled her mouth away and moved to my neck. She started to kiss me, but soon the kisses turned to licks, and then sucks. Hard sucks. My legs jerked at the attention she was giving me. Both my hands held her ass, pulling her shorts lower and lower off her hips. She kept moving on me, her body taking up a rhythm.

She sucked harder again.

"Are you trying to mark me?" I asked, only half-joking.

"Yes," she said, the word muffled by my neck.

"Seriously?"

She laughed. "Yep."

"What?" I chuckled. "Why?"

"Because bitches need to know you're mine," she deadpanned.

My dick twitched in response.

I think she knew it, too, because she started kissing lower, down to my chest. I honestly had no fucking idea why it was such a turn-on—for her to claim me—but it was.

She sat up and took her shirt off, her black lace bra barely containing her stiff nipples.

"Fuck," I breathed out, before flipping us over until I was on top. I started to kiss the spot just above her bra; my hand went into her shorts.

"Shit," she gasped, grabbing it before I reached where I so badly needed to touch. I looked up at her. Her eyes were half-hooded, her chest rose and fell, mouth slightly open, ragged breaths causing her lips to tremble. I tried to release my hand from her grip so I could continue. "No, Logan, I have to go to work soon."

I grunted.

Grunted.

My head fell to her stomach. "I'll be quick." I was desperate.

She giggled. "Wow," she said sarcastically, "how can I resist when you say it like that, asshat."

I laughed and moved off her, coming to a stand. I wasn't going any further if we couldn't go all the way.

I grabbed my phone off the nightstand and pressed a few buttons while I watched her expression turn to confusion.

Then the familiar sound of a guitar filled the room, before John Mayer's voice joined in.

She threw her head back with laughter. I climbed onto the bed and crawled up next to her. She grabbed my face in her hands and raised her eyebrows. "'Your Body is a Wonderland?' Really?"

"Uh-huh." I nod, turning my head to kiss her wrist. "You're totally about to get layooked," I joked.

AMANDA

STUPID WORK. STUPID money. Stupid customers. Stupid food. Stupid drinks. Stupid bar.

I could be at home right now getting layooked by Logan Matthews.

23

LOGAN

ETHAN DROVE HER TO WORK. I offered, but he said he was on his way there anyway. I left my room to get a drink when I saw Ty sitting on the sofa; I'd kind of forgotten he was here.

"Hey." I tried to make small talk. "When are you heading home?"

"Tonight, actually. My buddy is picking me up in an hour or so."

I nodded and then just stood there awkwardly.

"Actually," he pointed the controller to the TV and switched it off. "I'm glad you're here. I kind of wanted to talk to you, without Amanda, you know?"

Fucking awesome. I looked forward to this conversation. "I don't think we need to talk about shit." I started walking away.

"You need to quit being an asshole. It's about Amanda," he said. And it was enough to stop me in my tracks and turn to face him.

"What about her?" My eyes narrowed at him.

He motioned for me to sit opposite him. I tried to resist, just to be an asshole, and to show him that he had no control over what I did. But he just waited.

And waited.

So I finally gave in and made a show of how inconvenient it was for me to sit my ass down on a chair. Because I'm eight years old, and this was clearly a form of punishment.

He rolled his eyes at me.

Valid.

"So, she didn't tell you about me, huh?" He got comfortable.

I shook my head. I didn't know what the protocol should be for current whatever-the-hell-I-am to ex-boyfriend conversation. It was awkward as fuck, and the fact that we were alone didn't help.

"Did she tell you about what happened two summers ago?"

Instantly my eyes snapped to his. I was paying full attention. I wasn't sure if this was about me or if he even knew about that. But he had this look on his face, like he was ready for a fight. And I didn't want to have it. Not with him.

"You know Dimmy and I, we dated for years." He said this looking straight at me.

"Yeah?"

"Yeah. We started dating six months before I went off to college. She was a sophomore. I mean, when I went after her, I really didn't know anything would come of it, you know? I didn't expect that I'd be going through college still with her. The six months before I left were intense. We fell in love so quickly. And it wasn't just that first-love bullshit people speak of. It was that real love. The 'one day I'll marry you' kind of love."

"Yeah?" I called bullshit on this asshole. Whatever he was trying to do here—this intimidation shit he was trying to pull—it wasn't going to work. At all. "If that's true, then what the fuck happened?" I knew I sounded pissed, but I thought I had every right to be.

"She broke up with me."

"Huh." I tried not to sound like a smart ass. Really, I did.

"Yeah." He nodded. His eyes narrowed at me. "See, the thing is—we talked about my move to college before I left. And we had this stupid agreement that we could kind of see other people while I was away. I think she was scared that college would be too tempting for me. And the truth is—it was. At the beginning, anyway. I made out with a few girls, but it was all physical. None of it meant anything. And the minute it was over, I called her. I fucked up. Made a mistake. And Dimmy—being Dimmy—she just shrugged it off. Said she understood, that it made her sad, but she agreed to it, so what could she do? That's the thing about Dimmy; she's just that fucking perfect."

I shook my head and laughed once. "What are you trying to say?

That you want her back? You want to have it out to see who she wants? Is that it?"

"No, asshole. Not even close."

"Then what? What's your problem?"

"My problem is that she called me that summer." He was the one pissed now, speaking through clenched teeth. "Five o'clock in the fucking morning, to break up with me. Said she'd just gotten home from an actual date with some jerk. She said she could see herself being happy with him. That this guy made her feel things she never felt before—not even with me. It broke my fucking heart. But what could I do? We were states away. And she sounded happy. If she wanted to be happy with some other asshole then who the fuck was I to stand in her way?"

I stayed silent, looking at the floor, shocked by what he was telling me. That she broke up with her boyfriend of what? Two, three, years? To be with me. And I fucked it up.

"So I let her go," he continued. I didn't want to stop him. Whatever he had coming, I deserved it. "I let her fucking go, this girl I wanted to be with forever. And you know what the worst thing is, Logan?" He spat out my name. "The worst thing is that she called me back a few weeks later, crying her eyes out, begging me to take her back. And I wanted to. I so badly wanted to. But I couldn't. And you know why?"

I swallowed. "Why?" My voice cracked. I cleared my throat. "Why?" I said again.

"Because I made a mistake, I fooled around with girls. I gave them my body. A physical act. But that's all it was. Just physical. Dimmy though, she wanted more. She gave a part of herself to someone else. She was willing to give her mind and her heart to this jerk. She wanted to actually live a life without me and be with someone else. And as much as I wish I could've forgiven her—or at least tried to understand it—I just couldn't."

It was silent for a long moment while I took in every single fucking thing he said.

"Apparently the kid never called her back after that night. It's strange though..." He's using that same knowing, mocking tone as before. "She swears she never slept with him. So I don't get it. I don't get what the deal was. He didn't use her for sex, so what the hell happened?"

I kept my mouth shut.

He sighed.

I looked up at him. "That's it?" I wanted to get the fuck out of this room.

He stared back, holding my gaze for what felt like a lifetime.

"That's not even close to being it."

"What the fuck does that mean?"

He stood and started pacing the floor.

Now I was edgy, and I wanted this conversation done. "What else?"

An hour passed while he told me, in detail, everything that happened that summer.

All of it.

"So what happened?" I finally got out. I couldn't look at him. Because if he saw me, he'd know. He'd know it was all my fucking fault.

"To what?"

"To that asshole?" I could feel the vomit creep up my throat. I swallowed it down.

"Ethan and his friend took care of him."

"How?"

"Not important," he deadpanned.

"Fuck," I breathed out.

"Yeah. Fuck." He eyed me for a long time, deciding what to say next. "Ethan doesn't know, Logan."

"What?"

"He doesn't know it was you. That you're the guy she broke up with me for. He doesn't know. And if he did, I don't know that you'd be standing here right now."

TY LEFT, AND so did I. I called my buddy from the frat house. We used to party hard when we were freshman.

"I was wondering if you'd ever come back around," he said when he pulled into the driveway. I got in and didn't say a word.

I just wanted to forget. I wanted to forget everything Ty just told me, and I wanted to pretend like it never happened. I needed to pretend like Amanda didn't exist. I couldn't be with her, and she sure as shit couldn't fall for me. Not now. Not ever. I wouldn't fucking let her.

"You wanna drink or smoke?" he asked.

"All of it," I told him.

AMANDA

I GOT HOME from work just after midnight, but he wasn't home. I thought he would've texted to let me know he wouldn't be here, but I guess we're not really at that stage where we need to tell each other where we are at all times. I called him twice, but he didn't answer. I didn't know whether to wait for him in my bed or his, so I just stayed in my room, missing the shit out of him.

At three a.m. I started to get worried. I called a couple more times, but still no answer.

At four a.m. I heard the front door open. I couldn't help but smile.

He truly had me.

I jumped out of bed and opened my door. He was stumbling down the hallway, clearly drunk.

"Hey, babe," I whispered, not wanting to wake Ethan. I chuckled to myself as he tried to take his sweater off, but his cap was in the way. I held onto his arm, trying to steady him. He continued to struggle with the sweater that was covering his head.

He pushed my hand away. "Get off!" he sneered, "I don't need your fucking help."

"Whoa." I took a step back, surprised. "Mean drunk much?"

"I'm not drunk, Amanda. I just don't need you in my space all the fucking time." He finally managed to take his sweater off, throwing his cap behind him and adjusting his shirt.

I just stood there, not knowing what to say.

He brushed past me and into his room. My legs followed of their own accord. "What's going on?" I asked cautiously from the doorway. "I tried calling you."

"Jesus Christ!" He threw his hands in the air. "Clingy much?

You're not my fucking girlfriend," he spat out, slumping onto the bed. "You shouldn't be blowing up my phone when I'm out. It's fucking embarrassing."

I swallowed down the knot in my throat, and my eyes stung from holding back tears. I squared my shoulders and tried to act stronger than I felt. "Did something happen?" I said quietly. Something must have happened for this switch in him.

"Yeah, Amanda." He said my name like it was a curse. "You happened. I don't need your shit. Not now. Not ever."

He looked at the floor, avoiding eye contact. He started to unlace his shoes. "Look at me," I said.

He laughed. His shoulders bounced with the movement. Then he lifted his head; there was fire in his eyes, but not the good kind. "You don't tell me what to do," he stated, standing and taking a step closer to me. "You don't control me. And I shouldn't fucking control you. What you do is on you. I don't control a fucking thing you do."

I frantically wiped the tears that were falling. "What the hell's gotten into you? Why are you being an asshole?!"

"I'm not being anything!" His tone got harsher with every word. "I'm not being an asshole," he repeated, a little softer this time. "I just am one. You should have known that when I didn't call you after that night."

My stomach dropped to the floor, and for a few moments, I forgot to breathe.

I stared at him wide-eyed. My head shook back and forth. I bit my lip to stop myself from breaking down. He couldn't see me like this. He couldn't win. Not again. Then shock and disappointment quickly turned to anger. "Why the fuck didn't you call me, huh?"

I stepped forward.

He stepped back.

"I'm not fucking doing this, Amanda." He was yelling. I knew for sure it was going to wake Ethan.

I continued shaking my head, angry with myself for letting him get to me again. I knew why he didn't call, but I wanted him to admit it. I wanted the words to come out of his mouth. "Was it a pity thing?"

I saw him flinch.

Asshole.

"I'm right, huh?" I tried to talk through my tears, and my voice broke. "You thought it would be fun to fuck around with some loser girl, so you could tell all your friends that you went slumming?"

"What?" He took a step back, confusion on his face. But I didn't care. He needed to own up to it.

"It's true, isn't it?"

He didn't say a word. Just stood there. Hands in his pockets.

"Fuck you, Logan," I seethed.

I turned to walk away, but his words stopped me. "Too late," he announced. "Some other girl beat you to it."

24

LOGAN

MY EYELIDS WERE HEAVY. My body ached. My head was pounding. The room was spinning. My mouth was dry. My fingers itched. Somewhere in the distance, I could hear her voice.

Amanda.

Fuck.

I'd love to say that I didn't remember what went down last night, but I did. I remembered being an asshole to her. I remembered doing it all on purpose, so she would leave me alone and not want to be with me, because there was no fucking way I deserved her. Not even a little.

I remember hearing her cry in her room. She must have cried for so long, because by the time I'd passed out, she was still going.

She thought I pitied her. The second the words were out of her mouth, I flinched. Not because she was right, but because I couldn't believe that she'd ever think that about herself. How the fuck could she think that I was better than her? I let it go. Maybe she needed to believe that. Maybe it would make it easier for her to accept that I didn't want her. But I did; I wanted her so fucking bad. But that was my problem to overcome. Not hers.

I'd love nothing more than to lay in bed all day, but I promised Jake I'd meet him at the field. Fucking baseball.

I slowly got up and walked to the kitchen, needing something in my stomach to make this whatever-the-fuck feeling go away. I stopped in my tracks when I heard their voices.

"Were you arguing with Logan last night?" Ethan said.

"Nope," she said quickly.

"Huh. I swear I thought I heard you and—"

"Nope," she repeated, interrupting him. "Not me. He had some other girl in there."

Why would she tell him that?

"Oh." Ethan sounded surprised. Then it was quiet for a moment, before he spoke again. "Are you all right, Dim?"

"Yeah, why wouldn't I be?" I could hear the airiness in her voice, and for some fucked up reason, it pissed me off.

"I just thought that you and he—"

"Are nothing. We're nothing."

I cleared my throat to announce my presence before taking the few steps into the kitchen.

"Hey, roomy!" she boomed.

I flinched from the magnified loudness in my ears.

She downed the rest of her coffee and washed it out in the sink.

"Dude." Ethan sniffed the air, then glared at me with a disgusted look on his face. "You smell like ass. I don't care if you smoke weed or whatever—that's your thing—but don't bring that shit into the house, okay?"

I jerked my head in a nod; it was all I could do.

Amanda laughed; it was that perfect, bitter laugh she used. Then she turned away from the sink, crossed her arms and faced Ethan. "Didn't you know?" she started, her voice laced with sweetness. "You can't tell Logan what to do. You can't control him. No one can." Then she kicked off the counter and walked toward me, turning on her side so she could pass me in the doorway, only she stopped half-way, her breasts rubbing on my arm. "I hope she was fucking worth it," she whispered in my ear.

THE DAY SUCKED ASS.

I was hung-over as fuck, and the day sucked ass.

Also, I was an asshole.

Oh yeah, the day sucked ass.

I was sprawled on the sofa while Ethan was on the recliner. ESPN was on, but neither of us were watching.

He was on his phone.

I was wishing I was dead.

Then I heard the clicking of heels get louder and louder. "I need the keys," I heard her before I saw her. She walked in front of the sofa to get to him. Her bare leg brushed my hand. My eyes finally focused enough to see that she was wearing the shortest of short dresses. It barely covered her ass. Her perfect ass. Her fucking legs. Where the hell was she going?

Ethan adjusted so he could pull the key out of his pocket. He held them out but didn't give them to her. "Where are you going dressed like that?"

"Study date," she answered.

"Dressed like that?" he quirked an eyebrow at her.

Exactly, Ethan. Good man.

"Tyson said I should start dating again." She shrugged. "Tony's going to be there."

I made a groaning sound, unaware that I was doing it until it was done. If she was trying to piss me off and make me jealous, it was working.

They both turned to face me. I focused my attention on the TV.

She grabbed the keys off him and walked past me again. This time, I pulled my hand away. If I touched her, I wouldn't be able to stop myself from doing something more. Which would be awkward for two reasons, one—she wasn't mine, and two—her brother was in the room.

So I stayed silent.

AMANDA

I DIDN'T DRESS this way to make Logan jealous, but the fact that it did was a bonus.

I was about to put Ethan's car in gear when my phone chimed with a text.

Logan: *Why are you dressed like that for a study date? He's going to get the wrong idea.*

Assface has a lot of nerve.

Me: *Why? Because fuck you, that's why. Also, whatever idea he gets – he's probably right.*

I peeled out of the driveway and made it a block before my phone chimed again. I pulled over and parked, already furious at whatever his reply might be. Only this time, it wasn't from Logan.

Ty: *I'm sorry.*

What was he talking about?

He answered before it even had a chance to ring. "Look," he said, before I could get a word in. "I'm sorry. I thought at the time I was doing the right thing. But you have every right to be pissed; I shouldn't have told him. It wasn't my story to tell. It was yours, and you kept it a secret for a reason. I feel so bad. Please don't be mad."

"Told who what, Ty?"

LOGAN

THE FRONT DOOR slammed shut, and a second later she was in the room. Ethan and I looked up as she entered. Our positions hadn't changed since she left. But she had—her eyes were bloodshot and the little amount of make-up she wore was smeared.

"What happened?" Ethan sat up.

She ignored him and glared at me. "He told you?" she seethed, her eyes narrowed.

My head was still pounding, so it took me a while to catch up to what she was asking.

"He fucking told you?" she repeated, louder this time.

I sat up and rubbed my face with my hands.

"Dim," Ethan soothed. He stood up and walked over to her. "What's going on?"

She kept ignoring him. "Answer me!" she yelled.

I stood up and faced her and nodded—just once.

"He had no fucking right!"

"Dimmy." Ethan put his hand on her arm, trying again to calm her down.

"No!" She jerked away and then faced him. "No," she said again, her body overtaken by a sob. "He had no right, E. He shouldn't have fucking said a word—not to anyone!" Then she turned to me, "So that's why? You didn't want to be with me because you didn't want anyone to find out? Are you embarrassed?"

"What?" I shook my head. Where the fuck did she get that idea? "That's not-"

She cut in, "You fucked some other girl because you were ashamed of me?"

"What the fuck?" Ethan said, glaring at me.

I didn't know what the fuck to say. So I did the worst thing I could possible do right then—I stayed silent.

"You're a fucking asshole!" she shouted, her voice cracking. Then she turned in her spot and walked away.

Her door slammed shut a moment later.

Then it was just Ethan and me. I saw his fists clench at his sides. The muscles in his jaw tightened.

I still didn't know what the fuck to say.

He cleared his throat.

I looked up at him.

"I told you when you moved in she was off limits. I told you she wasn't ready. I told you to be careful. And you didn't listen to me then. So I'm telling you now: leave her the fuck alone."

AMANDA

IT'S NOT LIKE I was harvesting some major secret. It was my choice not to tell Logan, because honestly, I was at the point where I was over it. It happened—I moved on.

When he drove me home after our date, I didn't speak, because my mind was consumed with what I was going to do about Ty.

Ty—my boyfriend—who was miles away. Five hundred and six miles, to be exact.

When he left for college the beginning of my junior year, I was torn. He wanted to stay together and do the long-distance thing. I felt like I'd be holding him back if he did. So I made that stupid rule. At the time, I thought it was best for both of us. If he was there and found someone else, then he could leave, and I would be fine with it. The first time he called and told me he'd kissed a girl, he was so upset. He'd felt so guilty for what he did, and later on he said that he did it just to see if I'd care. Of course I cared, but what could I do? It was my stupid rule.

The second and third time he did it, he was drunk, which in normal circumstances was no excuse, but I was not naive. I know what it would have been like for him in college, surrounded by beautiful girls, all interested in the same thing. Add to that the pressure from his friends, who didn't understand why he'd tie himself up with some high school girl back in his hometown—and I got it. I really did. He felt horrible about it and called me as soon as he could to confess.

So it happened the first few months he was gone and never again. But, with the distance and his busy schedule, we barely got time to speak, let alone see each other. Whenever he was back home, we were inseparable. It was perfect. Ty was perfect.

I never even thought about other guys while Ty was gone. Not really. Everyone in school knew I was his girl and he was kind of a legend, so no one tried anything. Which was a good thing, I guess.

I worked and studied my ass off and got accepted to NYU. Making that phone call to Ty was one of the happiest moments of my life. He didn't even know I was trying to get in. I didn't want to get his hopes up if I didn't get accepted, so you can imagine his reaction. He wanted to go out and look for an apartment right away. I told him to hold off until I flew there to visit after graduation. I thought it would be a good idea to look together, so we could find something that suited both of us. He agreed. I didn't think he really cared. He was just happy we were going to be together again. And so was I.

Then shit hit the fan. Mom caught Dad with another woman in her own bed. In their own house. He was screwing someone half his age, with pictures of his kids hanging on the walls in their room. And the worst part? He wasn't sorry. Not even a little. Because while Mom was standing there yelling at him—shattered and heart-broken—he went to the closet, pulled out his suitcase and started packing while his mistress stood in their bedroom and quietly watched it all go down, half-naked, with Mom's husband's shirt on. And you know how I knew all this? Because she told me. She'd repeat the story over and over on the nights she'd get drunk and ramble incoherently—which was every single night for months after he walked out.

It gets worse.

The day after he was caught, he cleared out all the bank accounts, including Ethan's and my college funds.

He never said goodbye to us.

Devastated doesn't even come close to how we felt.

Mom had to call my grandma for a loan, but there was only enough money for one of us to go to college. Grandma, being old school, was adamant that Ethan be the one to go, considering he would one day have a wife and kids to take care of. So really, I was out of options. Which didn't make things any easier when I had to make that phone call to Ty.

At first he was pissed off for me. And then he was just pissed.

We'd both been so excited to start our lives together, and just like that, it was all over.

I DON'T KNOW exactly what happened, but after that news, it felt like something in him switched. Almost like he'd given up on us. He became so tied up with school and work and had even taken up an internship over the summer. He barely had time to answer my calls. Occasionally, when he did call, it was in the middle of the night and he'd just be getting home. The night before graduation, when he hadn't called all day, I decided to try at two in the morning. Only it wasn't him that answered. I didn't know who it was, honestly. Just some girl, in a loud room full of people, who was more than happy to let me know that she had no idea Ty had a girlfriend.

He didn't call me for three days after that.

When he did call, he was completely closed off. He complained that he was exhausted and rushed to get off the phone.

And to me, it felt like the beginning of the end.

That was the last I'd heard from him by the time Logan Matthews walked into the diner. I'd been ignoring his calls and his texts hoping that he would just go away, because for the first time since I'd started dating Ty, I was physically attracted to someone else. But that's all it was. Just physical.

Even if you asked me now, I couldn't tell you why I agreed to the date. I even gave us a one-week cooling-off period. It didn't help. He called or texted every day. And when my own boyfriend didn't call me once during that week, the attention from Logan made me feel something. It made me feel wanted. And after the shit my dad pulled, it was exactly what I needed to feel.

NOT FOR A SECOND did I expect to have the kind of time I had with Logan. He brought out parts of me in that one night I hadn't felt for a long time. Not since the beginning of my relationship with Ty. With Ty—it was different. It was a gradual build-up, a slow burn before acceptance. With Logan—there was nothing to accept. It just was.

So the entire ride home at four in the morning, after an amazing first date, I began to panic. It wasn't like I was instantly head over heels in love with him. But I thought, that given time, maybe I could be. I had no idea if he felt the same thing I did. In fact, I had no idea how he felt at all. And then he reached over, took my hand in his, gave me a small smile, and that was it.

That was all I needed.

Stupid.

Ty answered on the second ring.

"Hey," he said quietly, followed by a sigh.

It sounded like I was the last person he wanted to speak to.

"Were you sleeping?"

Another sigh. "No, Amanda. I just got home."

He never called me Amanda. Since the day I brought him home to meet my parents, and he found out they all called me Dimmy—and why—he started calling me that, too.

"What's up?" he said. "Why are you calling me so late? Or early?

Or whatever."

I swallowed down the knot in my throat. My eyes stung with tears.

"We need to talk," I managed to get out.

Nothing.

"Ty?"

"You're breaking up with me, right?" He said it so quietly, I thought for a second I imagined it. But then it all made sense. He was expecting it. Waiting for it. Wanting it.

"I met someone else," I told him.

I could hear him blow out a breath, then movement, like he was standing up and walking somewhere else.

"You did?" he asked.

That's when the tears fell. Like a dam that had been broken. And I didn't know if it was just Ty, or the lack of college plans, or any future plans at all, or if it was the fact that I still hadn't heard from my dad. Most likely, it was all of it.

"Who is he?" he said, when I hadn't spoken.

"Just a guy. You don't know him."

"And?"

"What?"

"You want to be with him now?" His voice broke. "You don't want to be with me anymore?"

I thought about my next words carefully. "Are we, though? I mean, are we together? I haven't spoken to you in weeks."

"The phone works both ways, Amanda."

He was right. It did. But the first few times I called him, he didn't answer. He was always so busy that I didn't want to disturb him. "You're always busy."

He laughed once, but it was a bitter laugh. "Yeah, fuck, Dim. I'm sorry I'm in college and working and doing this stupid half-assed paid internship just to be treated like scum every day. I'm sorry I don't have time to talk to my girlfriend five hundred miles away. I'm sorry that I'm here and you're stuck all the way over there, and there's not a goddamn thing we can do about it. I'm sorry my life is so busy and complicated, while you're what? Meeting random guys and going out with them? I'm really fucking sorry." His voice got louder with every word, his tone icy.

I bit my lip, trying so hard not to break down.

"So that's it, huh?" he continued. "We're done? You want to be with him?"

I nodded, and even though he couldn't see it, he must've sensed it.

"What the hell happened to us?" he said, but it was more to himself.

I wiped away the tears and gripped the phone tighter. "I don't know, Ty; you tell me. Where have you been? We barely even talk anymore. Ever since I told you I couldn't go to New York, it's like you've shut me out completely. And I don't know why-"

"It's not important...not anymore," he cut me off.

"Ty..." I tried to reason with him.

"Look, Dim. I just need some time." He paused. "Just please don't call me, okay? I'll call you when I'm ready."

And then he hung up.

He didn't call me.

But neither did Logan.

TWO WEEKS PASSED, and I was a mess.

I had come to terms with the fact that I was also a fucking idiot.

Because I let some guy I didn't even know uniwittingly work his way into my heart. So I did what I thought was right at the time. I called Ty and begged him to forgive me. I begged him to take me back. I needed him to take me back.

The first thing he asked was whether I slept with Logan, and when I told him I hadn't, he said it was worse. He said that maybe he could have forgiven me if it was just sex—if it was something physical. But the fact that I actually wanted to be with someone else, spend time with someone else, give my heart to someone else – that he couldn't forgive me for. He couldn't understand how after years of making things work long distance and how strongly we felt for each other—I could just throw it all away.

I sat there, on the edge of my bed, and listened to everything he had to say. And he was right, about all of it.

But then I brought up the fact that I thought he wanted me to break up with him. I mentioned that he stopped calling and that he was always busy and it seemed like he stopped caring about me—and that's when he told me. He told me he was trying to keep up with classes while working two jobs, as well as a shitty internship, because he was saving money to get an apartment for us, so that even if I wasn't going to school there, we could at least be together.

And I ruined it. I ruined us. I broke his heart. I broke mine. I broke us.

I fucked up.

And I couldn't even blame Logan.

As much as I tried, I couldn't.

It wasn't his fault I was stupid enough to believe him.

THE NIGHT I saw him at the club, making out with another girl, just happened to be the same night Greg was there. Greg—Ty's best friend. He caught me on my way out, with tears streaming down my face—tears I was shedding for a boy I barely knew.

He was with a bunch of his friends, most of whom I knew—only in passing—because they were Ty's friends, too. "Hey," he soothed, lifting my chin so he could see my face. I'm sure I looked as messy on the outside as I felt on the inside. "Are you okay?" His brows creased with what I believed was genuine concern.

I bit my lip to stop the sob escaping, but it didn't work. The next thing I knew I was in his arms as he led me to his car. He didn't say anything, and he didn't ask me to, either. When the crying finally stopped, all he said was, "You want to tell me how sucky your life is?"

It made me laugh, and I did. I wanted to tell somebody. So I told him. I told him about my dad, and about Ty, and how I felt shut out after I told him I couldn't be in New York with him. I told him about how I thought it was over between us, and I even told him about the stupid date with Logan and the phone call I made after. I told him about how I fucked up with Ty, and even though I begged for him to take me back, he wouldn't, and I had to accept that.

Greg—he remained silent, listening to every word I said. And when I'd finished pouring my heart out to him, he just looked at me, a sad smile on his face. "You know what you need?" he said.

I shook my head.

He smiled. "A banana split."

So that's what we did.

I texted Lexie and told her I was safe and I'd call her later.

Greg took me to the grocery store and bought all the ingredients to make the perfect banana split, the same type they make at the steakhouse where he worked. We then went back to his apartment, which he shared with two other guys, and he proceeded to cheer me up.

By the time the sun came up, we hadn't even realized how much time had passed. He drove me home and asked if he could see me again. It didn't even have to be a date, he said. He just enjoyed my company.

The rest of the summer, he made every effort to woo me. He'd surprise me at my work with flowers and called or texted regularly. He told me often that he missed me, and at one point he even said he was falling for me. And soon after that, I found I was beginning to hate myself less and less. The guilt of what I did to Ty was slowly fading, and even though I thought of Logan often, I began to not hate him as much, too.

I didn't even think about how a maybe-relationship with Ty's best friend would affect Ty. Like I said—stupid.

By the end of summer bonfire party, Greg and I had unofficially become exclusive. We spent as much time together as possible, and he even made an effort to hang out with Ethan and my friends, which was why he was there at that party. He was almost 21 – and could really do without the high school parties, but still—he was there.

And so was Logan.

As much as I could try to deny that seeing him that night didn't affect me, it really did. It brought back memories of that one night we had together and all the feelings I had when I decided to break up with someone who could have so easily been my future.

Greg knew something was up the rest of the night. I don't know if he knew that it was Logan I was speaking to when he interrupted us, but he didn't ask any questions. He just allowed me to drink away my emotions. Looking back on it now, it was almost as if he encouraged it.

I decided to stay the night at his house, too ashamed to go home in my drunken state, even though Mom was probably passed out on the sofa, worse off than I was.

That night, he climbed into his bed with me and he held me, and then he told me he loved me. And I needed it. I needed it more than anything in the fucking world. I needed someone to love me, and he said he did.

So I slept with him.

And then I must have passed out.

Because I didn't remember him pulling the covers off me.

I didn't remember the flashes as he took the pictures.

And I sure as hell didn't remember him fucking me without me knowing.

Or taking more pictures of my most private parts as he was doing it.

What I did remember—was loud banging and then Ethan, his best friend Tristan, and Lexie kicking down his bedroom door.

I remembered Lexie wrapping a sheet around me and then helping me walk out to the car.

I remembered throwing up on the way there.

And I remembered Ethan coming back with a cut lip, broken nose and blood all over his knuckles.

I couldn't look at him—too much blood.

"What happened?" I said to no one in particular. My head was throbbing. I finally managed to face Ethan. "What happened?" I repeated.

He didn't say anything, just wrapped me in his arms. I could feel his body trembling, and he started to cry.

Ethan never cried. Ever.

Not when Dad left.

Not even when we were twelve and he pushed me out of the way of an oncoming car and got hit.

Not even when he broke so many bones in his lower body that they broke skin and blood was everywhere. It was the reason I couldn't stand the sight of it.

He didn't even cry when he had to have surgery to put pins in his hip and all throughout his legs.

But now—he was crying.

"What happened?" I asked again, my voice strained from holding back my sob.

He held me tighter. "I'm so sorry, Dimmy. I'm so fucking sorry." He repeated the words over and over.

Then he showed me the pictures on his phone.

I spent the next two days and nights throwing up.

And the next two weeks in a zombie state. I didn't eat. I didn't sleep. I didn't talk to anyone.

Ethan begged me to press charges, but I just wanted to forget it. He said I was stupid, and we fought about it. I didn't say goodbye to him when he packed up and left for college.

I didn't take care of my mom, who hadn't even realized that something had happened to me.

Ethan drove two hours home, almost every day to take care of me.

And then one day, out of nowhere, I picked myself up, sold all my shit, left Mom behind and flew to New York.

I knocked four times before Ty answered. And when he did, he was shirtless, his jeans roughly pulled up, his fly undone. But that's not what I noticed. All I could see was the girl in his bed, with the sheets pulled up to her neck, hiding what I'm sure was her naked body.

"Dimmy?" I heard. I knew it was Ty, but he sounded far away. The girl in his bed's jaw dropped, her mouth forming a perfect O.

"Dimmy?" she repeated.

"Huh?" I said, then managed to pull my eyes away from her to look up at Ty. I don't know which one of the two hurt more to see.

"Tyson?" the girl asked. Her voice was laced with confusion, but behind that, there was a plea.

He stood there, between his past and his future, looking from one to the other.

Finally, I spoke. "I'm sorry, Ty," I said, looking him clear in the eyes. And then I turned and walked away. He called out, but I didn't stop. I just wanted to be somewhere else. I didn't know where I would go. I didn't want to go home. I couldn't face it another day. I couldn't stay in New York. And I was broke. I left his dorm and sat on a bench just outside, waiting for something to change. Hoping that something would happen soon. Because I wasn't sure how much more I could take.

It was only a few minutes before he came out, bed girl in tow. I watched as he kissed her goodbye. I could see the panic on her face, but his body language was reassuring. He kept shaking his head, holding her hands in his. He walked her to her car and waited until she drove away before looking around. I saw his body visibly relax when he saw me, his hand going up in a small wave. I tried to smile, but I just couldn't.

He took a seat next to me and nudged my leg with his. I didn't speak, and neither did he. Not for the first hour.

"Where are you staying?" he asked quietly.

"Hotel," I lied. I had no idea what I was doing.

"Have dinner with me first?"

I couldn't. "I don't think that's such a good idea, Ty, with your girlfriend and all."

"Yeah," he agreed. "Ali—that's her name."

I nodded and tried to compose myself. Seeing a girl in his bed hurt, but not as much as him admitting that he belonged to her. Ali and Tyson. I rolled their names around in my head.

I couldn't even be mad about it. I had no right. It was my fault.

"So you and Greg, huh?"

My eyes snapped to his. "You know?"

He looked confused for a moment. "That you started dating my best friend? Yeah, I know. I'm not gonna lie, Dim. I'm pretty pissed off about it."

I breathed out, relieved.

But then something else took over, and I broke down.

For the next four hours, I sat on that bench and told him everything. About Logan, about breaking up with him, about what happened the weeks after, all the way up to the night of the bonfire.

He sat quietly and listened to it all. When I got to the part about the pictures, his head fell between his shoulders. His grip on the bench caused his knuckles to turn white. I could see the muscles in his jaw flexing.

"You should have told me earlier," he stated, when I was done speaking.

"I couldn't," I cried.

"Dimmy." He sniffed back his own tears. "I'm so fucking sorry that shit happened to you. I should have been there. You should have told me. I could have come for you. I could have done something—anything. You'll always be important to me. I'll always love you," he said.

But just not in that way.

Not anymore.

After a few more minutes of silence, I stood up, wiped my face with the back of my hand and said, "I better go check into the hotel."

He nodded, standing too. "When do you leave?"

"Tomorrow morning."

"You came for one night?" he asked. I could tell he knew I was lying, but neither of us was going to call each other out.

"Uh-huh," I lied. I planned on staying forever. "I guess I'll see you around, Ty."

He jerked his head in agreement but said nothing.

I held back my sob.

Then he pulled me into him and wrapped his arms around me. I closed my eyes from the sensation. I hated being hugged, and he knew it, but right then, it was perfect. He was perfect.

And then he kissed me.

It was the saddest fucking goodbye in the history of the entire fucking world.

I didn't want him to pull away. I wanted to stay in his arms, with his mouth on mine, forever.

But he did. He pulled back and said, "Take care, Amanda."

I cried the entire walk to the twenty-four hour diner three blocks away. I didn't even care about the concerned looks people were giving me. At the time, it felt like I had lost everything that meant anything to me.

I got to the diner, ordered a coffee and pulled out my phone.

"Ethan?"

"Where are you?"

"New York."

"I'll be there soon."

Nine hours later, he was there.

TY CALLED EVERY day after my visit. At first it was quick check-ups, and then slowly, it built to longer, deeper conversations. Initially, I answered because I knew he wouldn't stop calling if I didn't. And then one day I found myself looking forward to his calls. Eventually, without me knowing, he had somehow helped me heal. And by the time I moved to start college, I was almost back to normal.

Until the day I saw Logan at the library, and it felt like my past, my life, my world—all of it—came crashing down around me.

Like I said—almost.

25

LOGAN

I BARELY SAW her for two days. If we were home at the same time, she ignored me. The truth was I wanted to see her, more than anything. But I knew I shouldn't. So I didn't. Instead, I let her believe that I was an asshole. I was. But not for the reasons she thought.

"Amandaaaa! Your boy's home!" an unfamiliar voice boomed from the front door. I could hear Ethan laughing, then Amanda squealing. I opened my door the same time she did, but she didn't notice me.

She practically ran down the hallway. I followed because I'm a nosy, jealous asshole.

Some guy had his arms around her, spinning her around. Her legs were wrapped around his waist. It was like Tyson all over again.

"Dude," she said, as he placed her back on the floor. "E didn't tell me you were coming!"

"I wanted to surprise you."

She had a huge grin on her face. "How long are you here for?"

They talked for a few more minutes. Nobody bothered to introduce me. I just stood there with my hands in my pockets feeling like a loser.

"I gotta go to work," she said, "but afterwards, you're all mine, okay?"

He nodded as she turned and went back to her room, brushing past me. She didn't even acknowledge me.

I watched the dick stare at her ass as she walked away. "Holy shit, Amanda!" he shouted. "Yoga must be working. Your ass is fucking incredible."

She laughed.

Fucking laughed.

Who the fuck was this dick?

Ethan went to the kitchen; Dick followed behind him.

I was still fucking invisible.

"Ethan, man," I heard Dick say, trying to keep his voice low. "Amanda's gotten hot. Like really fucking hot."

I cleared my throat as I entered the room, glaring at Dick as I did.

"Oh hey, man." He had his hand out. "Tristan."

I looked at his hand, ignored it, and then opened the fridge for a bottle of water. I glared at him. "You think it's okay to talk about your friend's sister like that?"

His eyes widened slightly, then slowly, a smirk appeared. This dick was actually smirking at me.

"Aah," he said, nodding his head.

What the fuck did that mean? I crossed my arms over my chest. "Maybe you should have a little more respect, don't you think?"

I don't care who this guy was; he couldn't talk about Amanda like that.

I heard him chuckle. Then Ethan walked up to him, patted his shoulder a few times, and left the room.

Dick straightened up and squared his shoulders.

I sized him up. I could take him.

I took a step forward.

He did the same.

"I've known her since we were five," he started, "then through her teenage years, you know, when her body started to develop." He motioned tits with his hands, because clearly he was twelve fucking years old.

My eyes narrowed.

He continued. "She was cute in high school, but she was Ty's. Now though..." he trailed off and licked his lips.

"Watch your next words, asshole." I cracked my knuckles with my thumbs. I wanted him to continue. I wanted a reason to hit him.

His smirk got wider.

I wanted to remove it with my fist.

"Now though, I bet she'd be fucking dynamite in the sack."

I shoved him. Hard.

He fell back and hit the wall.

Ethan walked in.

Dick started laughing.

Ethan shook his head.

"Tris, don't fuck with him like that."

Dick, aka Tristan, continued to laugh. I shoved him again.

"Logan," Ethan warned. "He's being an asshole. He's just fucking with you. He's gay."

"What?" I looked him up and down. He didn't look gay.

"Don't look at me like that," Tristan said. "I might get the wrong idea."

Ethan chuckled.

"You don't look gay," I stupidly said.

"We're not all fairies and feathers, you know."

Ethan chimed in, "I'm taking Amanda to work. I'll be back soon."

"Looks like it's just you and me," Tristan said, blowing me a kiss.

I couldn't help but laugh.

I grabbed a couple of beers from the fridge and handed one to him. We spent the time Ethan was gone getting to know each other. I remembered his name from Ty's story. And even though he fucked with my head, I couldn't not have respect for him.

"I DIDN'T COME out to my parents until the day I left for college."

"Yeah? That must've sucked."

"Yeah," he said, shrugging. "I spent most of my high school years so far in the closet I was having adventures in Narnia."

I choked on my beer, swallowed, and then laughed.

So did he.

"Amanda's actually the first person I told."

"Really?"

"Yeah. I mean, I didn't know how Ethan would react, you know?"

"He's your best friend, right?"

"Yeah, he is. It's not that I thought it would ruin our friendship or anything. It was just the initial reaction that scared me. I knew he'd be okay with it eventually."

"How did he react?"

He chuckled. "He asked if I thought gay dudes would think he was hot. I told him yes and he high-fived me. That was that."

THEY ALL PLANNED a party that night. I didn't even know if I was invited. It was in my own damn house.

"You should invite your friends," Tristan told me. At least he cared about me. "Invite Jake Andrews, he's hot. You're friends with him, right?"

"You're using me for my hot friends?"

"Are you gay?"

"Nope."

"Then you're useless to me."

I INVITED MY FRIENDS, and they all showed up. Turned out Amanda had already invited them. Sometimes I forgot she was friends with them, too.

I did my best to avoid her, but when I got into the kitchen and saw her sitting on the counter, with that asshole from her work standing in front of her, something in me snapped.

AMANDA

HE WALKED INTO the kitchen and froze mid-stride. I was sitting on the counter, with Tony standing in front of me. Tony and I had fooled around a little before Logan showed up. I called it off the second I felt the slightest thing for Logan. I'm not one of those wishy-washy girls who stayed with someone or led them on if there was a chance that my mind might—even for a second—wander to someone else.

Obviously.

Exhibit A – Tyson Landry.

Logan casually opened the fridge and pulled out a beer. My eyes stayed focused on him, waiting for him to leave. But he didn't. Instead, he leaned on the counter opposite us, crossed his legs at his ankles, and folded his arms over his chest. He took a long sip of his beer. His eyes never left mine. Then with beer in hand, he saluted me. "Carry on," he said, like it was the most natural thing in the world.

Tony shook his head before leaning in to say something, his hand rubbing my arm, but I didn't know what he said, because all I could see was Logan. His eyes were bloodshot as they narrowed to slits. He pushed off the counter and walked up to us. "A word?" he said lazily.

Tony turned to him. "Rude much? We're in the middle of something here."

Logan glared at him, then lifted his index finger in the air, twirling it around. "You see this?" he asked, his chin lifting.

Tony looked around the kitchen, confusion all over his face. "See what, asshole? There's nothing."

"Exactly." Logan smirked, moving so he was in front of me. "That's all the fucks I give."

Then he lifted me over his shoulder, walked us out of the kitchen, and into his room.

LOGAN

"WHAT DO YOU want, Matthews?"

I narrowed my eyes at her. "Why the fuck are you letting him touch you like that?"

I knew I'd lost it—the control I should have had in this situation. But I couldn't fucking help it.

"Like what? His hand on my fucking arm!" She was pissed. "Why the fuck do you even care? You've made it clear that you don't want me. So what is this? You don't want me but no one else can have me?"

"Yes!" I yelled, before settling down. "I mean no. Fuck, Amanda. I don't know!" My hands went into my hair, clasping my fingers behind my head. I started pacing the floor, wondering how the fuck I was going to make sense of this shit.

"You don't know?!" she repeated, anger laced in her voice. "You don't fucking know!" she screamed louder. "Maybe that's the problem, Logan. Maybe that's always been the problem. You just Don't. Fucking. Know!"

She took a deep breath in, calming herself down. "I can't believe I fucking let this happen again. What the hell is wrong with me?" She shook her head, talking to herself. "And the thing is—I forgave you. After the shit you pulled that summer, I just forgave you. Like it didn't even happen. Like it didn't matter. When it fucking did. You know how much it mattered."

I just stood there, hands in pockets, because I had no words.

Nothing.

"You know when you moved in, I had no choice. I thought, fuck it. Just treat him like you would any other asshole. I would have been happy to forget about it, Logan. I would have been happy to just be friends with you and move on. But you—you were the one that kept pushing this. Not me. And now? Now you don't know what you want."

Silence.

Followed by more silence.

Because as much as I wanted to tell her something—anything. I couldn't.

So I didn't.

I just stood there and let myself be the pathetic fuck-up I was.

"You know what the worst part is, Logan?" She moved so she was right in front of me.

I kept looking at the floor.

"Look at me!" she yelled.

So I did.

And the second I did, I regretted it. There was rage and anger and sadness in her eyes. But what hurt the most were her tears. Those same fucked-up tears I always caused.

She took in a deep breath, making sure I saw her. "The worst part is that you and me—we could have been amazing. We could have had it all, Logan. Everything. And you fucked it up."

Then she laughed once. That bitter fucking laugh. "I'm done, Logan." She motioned her finger between us. "You and me—we're done." She wasn't angry anymore. She wasn't bitter or even upset. She was exactly what she said she was—done.

She brushed past me and walked toward the door, stopping just before her hand reached the handle.

"Logan," she said over her shoulder, "you need to find somewhere else to live."

She wiped her face, before opening the door and leaving.

She bumped into Jake on her way out, who looked confused to see her. Then he glimpsed into my room, saw me, and then looked back at her and then me again.

He cautiously walked into my room and sat on my desk chair.

"What's up?" he said casually.

"Nothing." I threw my body backwards onto the bed and covered my eyes with my forearm.

"That didn't look like nothing to me." He cleared his throat. "What's the deal? You into her?"

"Have you been living under a fucking rock? You know I'm into her. Don't be an asshole."

He laughed. "Dude, I just didn't want to make any assumptions. You know what happened the last time I assumed you were into someone."

I did. It was that day with Micky.

"So what's the problem?" he continued. "She doesn't want you?"

I sighed out loud and sat up so I could face him.

"She does want me, which is the problem."

His eyebrows bunched together. "I'm sorry, man. I'm a little buzzed, so you're going to have to help me out here." He shook his head slowly. "What's the problem?"

"She's too good for me, Jake. I don't fucking deserve her. Not now, and not the first time."

"The first time?"

Fuck. I forgot he didn't know. "Nothing."

Then he looked at me, and I glared back. Like we were eight and this was a stare off. He took his cap off, ran his hand through his hair, and then replaced it. "Shit. You're more than into her, huh? You're like, into her."

I nodded slowly. He was right.

"Fuck, man. I never thought I'd see the day," he said, disbelief laced in his voice.

"Like you're one to talk."

"Valid."

Then it was quiet for a while as I thought about the colossal tower of fucked-uppery I'd gotten myself into.

"Don't you think it's her decision?" Jake broke the silence.

I looked over at him. "Huh?"

"Don't you think she should be the one making that choice? Whether to be with you or not? I mean, if she wants you, then there's something there, right?"

I kept staring at him, waiting for him to go on.

"Look, I know you enjoy being this asshole or whatever, but you're a decent guy. I mean, you were there for Micky when she had that pregnancy scare, and the next day when she went to see you, you were-"

"You know about that?" I cut in.

He eyed me. "Of course I do. She didn't tell me right away but a few months later. We don't keep secrets, Logan. Ever."

I nodded.

"All I'm saying is that you're a good guy. And maybe you can't see that. But maybe she does. And maybe that's enough, you know?"

I was about to say something, but shouting coming from the living room interrupted us.

We both got up quickly and made our way out. When we got out of the hallway, it was mayhem. Someone had turned the music off, and everyone was looking at the corner of the room.

We broke through the crowd to see Ethan with his forearm against some kid's neck, pinning him to the wall. The kid looked familiar, but I couldn't place him.

"We fucking told you not to come around here," Tristan spat, pacing behind Ethan.

The kid's eyes narrowed. "Fuck you, Tris. You fucking faggot!"

I swear to God time stood still as people gasped. Ethan's

forearm went further into his neck. Tristan just shook his head and laughed it off.

"Everybody out." Ethan's voice was flat but dead serious.

Nobody moved.

Dylan got up from his seated position on the sofa. "You heard him, out."

This time, half the room left.

The other half just stood there, waiting for a show.

And I had no idea what the fuck was happening.

"Out!" Ethan was a little louder this time.

Nobody moved.

Then from the back of the crowd, "You heard E, everybody get the fuck out!" It was James. And this time, people listened. One by one they filed out the front door. James was the last to leave.

"You good?" he asked Ethan and Tristan.

They bumped fists and he left. James must have had power at their school; it was like the seas parted when he spoke.

"What the fuck are you doing here, Greg?" Ethan snapped.

Greg.

Mother. Fucker.

I was about to step in, but Jake pulled on my arm to stop me.

Greg pushed Ethan off him. "I just wanted to tell your slut of a sister here that I don't appreciate her sending around her ex-boyfriend over to the house, causing shit for me and calling me a fucking rapist!"

Instantly my ears fill with the familiar sound of bone crushing bone.

I have no fucking clue how long we stood there, watching Ethan beat this kid's face with his fist, but eventually Cam and Dylan pulled him off.

Ethan fell to the floor, his breathing heavy, jaw clenched, head bowed between his raised knees.

Cam and Dylan held Greg back, as he spat blood. Then he raised his head, eyes narrowed at Ethan. "She wanted it, you know? I told her I loved her, and she fucking wanted it. It was that fucking easy. She was that fucking easy."

And this—this was the moment I lost control of the one thing I've tried my entire life to avoid. I may have talked shit and wanted to punch people, but I never had. I never thought I would. Because in the back of my mind, I was always too afraid I'd turn into him.

The second Greg's words left his mouth, I was on him. And I didn't know how exactly I got to the point of my fist repeatedly slamming into his jaw, his nose, his mouth, his entire fucking face—but it did.

Suddenly, there were arms around mine and I was being pulled back, Jake's voice in my ear. "That's enough, dude. It's done."

"You need to get him out of here," I told someone. Anyone. "And make sure he doesn't fucking come back. Ever."

"Done," Dylan deadpanned. He dragged that asshole out of the house, Cam following behind him.

And then I heard her.

Her sobs took over the room, and when I looked at her, my stomach dropped to the floor. She was huddled in a corner, her knees up to her chest, and her head between them. Her arms were crossed over her head, shielding herself, as she rocked back and forth, crying.

I moved closer to her. "Amanda," I tried to get out through the lump in my throat.

Slowly, her head rose to look up at me, eyes red. She was about to say something, but then her eyes snapped to Ethan, who was still sitting on the floor. She let out a sob and slowly, she crawled over to him, crying harder as she got closer. She wiped her face with her forearm and moved to sit in front of him. Then she saw the blood on his hand and made a noise as she looked away. He removed his shirt, covered his hand with it, and then whispered something to her. She looked back at him and broke down, falling into him, while he wrapped his arms around her, saying something in her ear. She slowly nodded her head. He picked her up off the floor, cradling her like a child, as they walked into her room and closed the door quietly behind them.

I didn't follow. I didn't say a fucking word. Because in my mind, all I could think—was that it was my fault.

It was all my fucking fault.

"Fuck," I muttered under my breath, as something cold was placed on my hand. I looked down to see Lucy covering it with a bag of frozen peas. And then I remembered everyone else was here.

"You all good, man?" Jake patted my shoulder.

I nodded, held the bag to my hand and sat on the sofa. "What the fuck just happened?"

I DIDN'T KNOW how much time passed before Dylan and Cam came back in the house. "One of his boys just picked him up," Dylan stated.

"Yeah, you don't need to worry about him coming back either. D took care of it," Cam confirmed, taking a seat next to Lucy and putting his arm around her. She sank into him.

My mind was still buzzing from the adrenaline, and the pain in my hand had started to throb. My head rolled to the back of the sofa as my good hand rubbed my eyes.

I heard a door open and shut and whipped my head to the sound. Ethan came out of the hallway, shrugging on a new shirt. He stopped abruptly when he saw us all sitting around, waiting...I didn't really know what for.

"How's your hand?" he asked, as he got closer.

I glanced at his. "Not as bad as yours."

He shrugged. "She, uh, she wants to see you." He jerked his head to her bedroom.

I took a deep breath in to calm myself. I didn't know if I could see her. I didn't think I'd have the right words to tell her how fucking sorry I was. For all of it. For being an asshole. For not calling her. For not being there. But mainly, for not being what she thought we could be. What she wanted us to be.

"We're gonna head out," one of the guys said. I didn't know who because I was already walking toward her room.

I knocked lightly on her door and opened it. She lay in the middle of her bed but slowly came to sit on the edge. I sat next to her, looking down at the floor.

Then I felt her soft hands on mine, removing the frozen bag. I jerked it away.

"Logan." It was barely a whisper.

I cleared the lump in my throat. "There's still blood; you can't see it."

"Whose?"

"Huh?"

"Whose blood is it?"

"I don't know." I still couldn't face her.

Silence.

"Logan, what's wrong?"

I shook my head.

"Look at me, please?" she pled.

So I did.

And then we were just staring at each other, trying to understand what this was. Where this left us. She looked at me so intently, her eyes boring into mine, that I think I forgot to breathe. I dropped my head again, too uncomfortable to hold her gaze.

"I'm sorry," she said.

I let out the breath. "What?"

"Your hand..."

My mind was too filled with guilt for thoughts to make sense.

I felt her move closer to me. My head lifted to face her. She was biting her lip, watching me.

"It's my fault," I told her. Truth.

She shook her head. "I don't want to talk about this anymore. Please? I want it to be done."

I raised my good hand and held the side of her face as she leaned into it. I wiped her tears with my thumb. "Did he hurt you?"

She closed her eyes softly. "Honestly?" When she opened them, they were focused on me.

I nodded.

She covered my hand with hers and held it closer to her face. "Not as much as you did. But it's done. It's over."

She laid back down, her head on my lap. I started running my fingers through her hair.

We were silent for so long that eventually her breathing evened out. She'd fallen asleep. I tried not to disturb her as I moved from under her, but she woke. Her arms went around me, holding me to her.

"I just need some water." I lifted my hand. "And aspirin. You want anything?"

She shook her head as she got more comfortable under the covers. "Come back, okay?"

WHEN I GOT BACK to her room, she was sitting up, the covers bunched at her waist. "You took your time."

"Sorry." I stood at the foot of her bed, not sure what to do.

She lifted the covers on one side. "Are you coming in?"

I unbuckled my belt and started to take my jeans off. I noticed her watching me. I kicked them off and removed my shirt. Not wanting to see her reaction, I quickly got into her bed and turned off the lamp.

We were lying side by side, not talking, not touching.

Then I felt her move to her side. "Why didn't you call?" she whispered, sadness consumed her tone.

I turned to face her. A single tear fell from her eyes. I wanted to reach out and take away her pain. But I didn't. I just lay there and tried to ignore the ache in my chest. "I promise, I'll tell you. But not tonight, okay?"

She nodded as she moved closer. I wrapped my arms around her, holding her head to my chest. Her arm went around my waist while her legs tangled with mine. We were as close as we could possibly be.

And for the first time in days—being with her—like this—holding her—I finally felt like I could breathe again.

26

AMANDA

I WOKE UP the next morning to Logan's phone alarm going off, then his deep rumble from underneath me. My head was on his chest, our legs tangled and his arms around me.

His hand was gentle in my hair as he pulled back from me. Then we were face-to-face.

He smiled. "God, Amanda. I'd be the luckiest asshole in the world if I got to wake up like this, with you in my arms, every goddamn day." He kissed my forehead, and my eyes fell shut.

When he pulled back, he just looked at me. "I need you to forgive me," he breathed out, both hands on my face. I didn't know if he was asking or telling or if he was even talking to me. It was like a thought in his head that had to be voiced.

I opened my mouth to speak, but he interrupted. "Don't say anything. I need to show you something," he said, his eyes moving all over my face. "Can I show you something, please? Ethan and I are going to see the team doc, but after that, will you...let me take you somewhere?"

I nodded slowly.

"Okay," he said, taking my hand and kissing my wrist.

LOGAN

I TOLD ETHAN it was me that summer—the one who she broke up with Tyson for. I told him in the car on the way to the field, and he didn't say shit. But now we were here, outside of the car, standing face-to-face. I could see he wanted to hit me. I'd take it. I'd take whatever beating he gave me.

He glared, squaring his shoulders.

I did the same.

"I kind of want to punch you," he said.

I nodded.

"Why did you even tell me?"

"Because I wanted to. And because you needed to know. So that when I asked you—no—told you—that I couldn't not be with her—then at least you'd know the truth."

"Fine," he muttered.

And that was that.

AMANDA

HE DROVE TO a strip of stores near campus and parked on the side of the road. I got out and made it two steps before I felt his hand on mine, linking our fingers.

"So, have you checked out this area much? The stores and stuff?" he asked, his hand squeezing a little tighter.

I shook my head. "Not really. It's kind of hard with the one car."

"Good." He stopped in the middle of the footpath and then moved us to the side so we were out of people's way. "I want to show you something. If that's okay?"

I nodded.

His grip on my hand got tighter as he led me down a few streets and into a sketchy alleyway. It was a dead end with no signs and barely any stores.

"Are you going to murder me?" I asked, only half-joking.

He chuckled, pulling me to the end of the alley and into a doorway.

When we walked inside, I froze.

I looked up at Logan, who was smiling at me.

"Smell it," he deadpanned.

So I did.

I closed my eyes and took a deep breath in.

It's that familiar smell of books I loved so much.

"How did you find this place?"

I wanted to ask him how he remembered, but he's made it clear he remembered a lot from that night.

"I'll tell you later," he said. But I'd already tuned him out as I looked around. It was shelves upon shelves of books, magazines, comics, everything. He squeezed my hand to get my attention. "There's a coffee spot hidden in the corner there." He pointed, but all I could see were shelves of books. "Go play." He smiled at me. "I'll be waiting."

So I did.

Like a frickin' kid in a candy store, I walked down the aisles as slow as I could, taking everything in.

I had a handful of books before I got to where he was sitting, drinking a coffee, head in a biology textbook.

I dropped the books on the table, causing him to look up. He saw my pile and smiled up at me. "That was quick."

"That was two aisles, Logan. I'll be back."

No shit—two hours later—I ordered a drink and sat at the table with him, with a basket full of books I couldn't afford and a huge, goofy grin on my face.

He stared at me, smiling.

"What?" I asked, staring back.

"Nothing." He shook his head, licking his lips. We couldn't take our eyes off each other.

The barista brought over my drink, smiling like the Cheshire Cat. I didn't know why. Then she looked over at Logan. "So this is her?" she said.

Logan smiled and nodded once.

"Hi, Amanda," she said to me, her hand out, waiting.

I shook it, confused. I looked from her to Logan and back again.

"I've waited a long time to meet you." She giggled to herself before walking away.

"What was that about?" I looked at Logan, bug-eyed. "How does she know me? What does she mean about waiting?"

He opened his mouth to say something but closed it almost instantly.

"What?" I asked again.

"You're going to think I'm the world's biggest creeper." He laughed to himself, shaking his head.

I laughed, too. "I won't. Promise. Tell me."

"Okay," he said, leaning forward in his chair a little. He blew out a breath. "I hadn't forgotten you, Amanda. Some stuff happened after our date, but I never forgot you. I wanted to see you. I wanted to speak to you. To apologize or whatever. But then I saw you at that bonfire party, and you were with that guy and I just couldn't. I figured you'd moved on or didn't care—"

I wanted to interrupt him, but he put his hand up to stop me. "Just let me finish, please. I need to get this out."

"Okay."

"I knew you were coming here; well, I thought you were. So I looked up all the places where I thought I might run into you. I went to all the cafes and diners where you might be working. Basically, anywhere I thought you might be." He paused. "See? I told you you'd think I was a creeper."

I stayed silent, afraid of what he might be saying. For the year and a half I tried to forget him, he did everything he could to try to remember me.

"Finally," he continued, "I started scoping out bookstores, because I knew how much you loved them. It wasn't so bad, there are only four around this area, but when I came into this one...I just —I don't know. I just felt like it was you. I just felt this connection with you the minute I walked in. And I know it sounds stupid, like one night together could give me that feeling—that pull feeling— but it did. And so every chance I got, I came here. Eventually, Chantal—the owner," he said and nodded his head to the woman behind the coffee machine, who was still smiling at me, "she asked me to leave. She said that if I wasn't buying anything and was just coming in for the coffee, then I should go sit at a coffee shop. Honestly though, I think I just creeped her out—the way my head would whip up every time I heard someone walk in. Or the way I'd just sit here for hours. Hours, Amanda. I'd sit here for fucking hours and just think about you."

I tried to swallow down the lump in my throat. I knew I was two seconds away from crying, and when I did, it would be worth every single fucking tear.

"So I told her," he said. "I told her everything. I told her all about you. About our date. And about how I fucked it up. I told her that I came here all the time because I was just hoping that one day the girl of my dreams was going to walk through those doors and forgive me for being an asshole. That you were going to come in and tell me that it was okay. That you'd give me another chance to make it right. Because I needed that. I needed you. And I sat here in this exact chair, for hours, and poured my heart out to her. Because no one else would get it, Amanda. No one else would understand how one fucking night with a virtual stranger changed me. How I never wanted to be close to anybody my entire life. Not until I met you."

I knew the tears were flowing, I could feel the wetness on my face, but I couldn't move a muscle. I couldn't breathe through the ache in my heart. And I still couldn't tear my eyes away from his.

"How long?" I asked him.

"What?"

"How long were you coming in here, waiting for me to show up?"

"Every day until the day I saw you at the library."

27

LOGAN

SHE DIDN'T SPEAK to me the rest of the day, or night. She hadn't spoken to me at all since we left the bookstore. Chantal—the owner of the store—gave me this sad, pathetic smile when we left. That was yesterday.

The team doc said I had to rest my hand for a few days, so when Nathan called to tell me he was back from whatever business he had to attend out of town—I figured it was the perfect opportunity for me to go and see him.

I opened the bedroom door and practically walked into her. She was lugging a huge gear bag behind her. It looked heavy as hell. I stepped forward and took it from her hands. She resisted, but only for a second. "Where do you want it?"

She laughed. "The bus stop." It came out as a question.

"What?" I chuckled. "Where the hell are you going with this thing?"

"Uh." She hesitated for a second. "Home."

She was leaving? "What? Why?" I rushed out. I didn't want her to leave. If anyone was moving out, it was me.

My emotion must've been evident because her eyes widened slightly, "No, Logan. Just, uh, just for the night."

"Oh." My shoulders relaxed, then a grin took over my face.

An hour later she was in the passenger seat, and we were driving home. It was awkward. She was on her phone, a concentrated look on her face. She wore those short denim cut-offs she always wore. My eyes kept drifting to her legs. I couldn't help it. They're that fucking amazing.

Without warning, a crack of thunder sounded and rain started bucketing down. She sat up, putting the phone away.

"You want me to pull over?"

"Um, no. You don't have to. I'm sure you have things you need to do at home."

I pulled the car over on the side of the road. You could barely see anything through the rain. Her knee started bouncing, most likely from nerves. She bit her thumb, looking around.

I leaned over to adjust her seat to laying position; we may as well get comfortable. She tensed when my body covered hers. When she was settled, I did the same with mine.

Then we lay there on our sides, in silence, facing each other.

"It's funny," she whispered, loud enough to hear over the sound of the rain pounding against the metal. "It's like we're in our own little bubble."

She closed her eyes, her lips trembling.

She was afraid.

My hand reached out and touched the side of her face. She leaned into it, her eyes still closed.

"Logan," she whispered, quieter this time.

She opened her eyes.

Then I felt it—that ache in my chest—but it was different this time.

And this—this was the moment.

The moment I let myself fall completely in love with her.

I let out all the air in my lungs. "I didn't call you because I thought I was in love with Mikayla."

"What?" she squeaked out, sitting up a little.

I swallowed. My heart thudded against my chest. This could make or break us.

I knew I could lose her forever.

I shifted and lay on my back. My arm covered my eyes. I couldn't watch her face when I told her the reason why she had to experience all that pain. All the pain I caused.

So I told her.

I told her about running into Micky at the store on the way to see her. I told her about the pregnancy scare and taking her to see Dad. I told her about the next day, when I was so fucking excited to see her, but when I opened the door to leave, Micky was there. I told her how she cried about missing her family. About how I held her as she did. I even told her the exact moment I thought I felt something.

She stayed quiet, even when I was done speaking. I was shit scared to face her, so for minutes, we just sat there, silence filling our own little bubble.

Then she cleared her throat.

I finally moved my arm and opened one eye to look at her.

She was watching me.

I turned to my side and faced her again. "I'm sorry, Amanda."

She faced the roof. "Ethan was hit by a car." She spoke so quietly, I almost didn't hear her. "Actually, he pushed me out of the way and got hit by a car. We were twelve. I was stupid. I didn't even look. It was raining. Just like this." Her voice was strained. She sniffed once. "That's why I'm scared of the rain. Everyone has their reasons. It may seem stupid, Logan, but to me, it's enough." Her eyes lifted to meet mine. "Do you still have feelings for her?"

I stupidly nodded.

Her face changed.

"Not like that," I said quickly. "Not in that way. I never did, Amanda. I was just stupid and confused. But no—I never had those types of feelings for her."

A huge gust of wind caused the car to shake. She reached her hand out to grip my arm. Her eyes snapped shut. "Come here," I said, helping her move until her body was on top of mine, my arms around her, exactly where she belonged.

Another gust of wind.

She tensed.

I held her tighter.

A pained sound escaped her.

"Am I hurting you?" I stroked her hair.

"No," she said into my chest. "You're healing me."

I COULD FEEL my heart thumping against my chest. She must've felt it, too, because she raised her head to meet my eyes. "Your heart is going a million miles."

"Mm," I hummed in agreement. My eyes were closed. My breath was shaky. I placed a hand on the back of her head, trying to get her to resume her position.

She resisted. "Logan?" She tried to get my attention.

I glanced down at her.

"What's going on?"

I watched her—her eyes carried an intensity I'd never seen before. Truth time. "I'm nervous," I said flatly.

"Why?" She had a puzzled scowl.

"You make me nervous."

She laughed once. "How do I make you nervous?"

"I don't know." I shrugged. "I'm afraid that it's not enough. That what I've said and what I've done and what I'm doing right now aren't enough. That you won't forgive me and you won't want to be with me. And you do this thing—where you shut yourself off and you don't talk to me—or anyone—for hours, or days, and I have no idea how you're feeling or what you're thinking. So yeah—I'm nervous as all hell that this is the last time I'll get to hold you. I'm afraid that we'll never be as close as we were. I'm scared you'll want nothing at all to do with me."

She let out a long, drawn-out breath, her eyes glued to mine.

I waited.

Then she sighed, her forehead falling onto my chest.

"I'm sorry," she said. "You're right. It's not enough. Not anymore."

I HELD HER as the rain beat down on the car.

I held her tighter as it got worse.

I let go of her when it cleared.

And then I drove her home.

All while not saying a goddamn word—because really—what was there left to say?

She said she couldn't be with me.

I'D BEEN DRIVING AROUND for four hours. That's how long ago I left Jake's house. Nathan was right; what he had to tell me wasn't time sensitive. Not at all. In fact I could have waited another twenty years to hear it.

Without realizing, I found myself sitting in her driveway.

I knew I shouldn't be here. I knew that she was done with me. With us.

A woman I assumed was her mom eventually answered the door. She wore a dressing gown over her pajamas, running a hand through her disheveled hair. She squinted up at me.

Then a slow smirk pulled on the corner of her lips. "Dimmy!" she shouted, directing her voice up the staircase. "Lucas is here."

"Uh, it's Logan actually," I tried to tell her, but she'd already moved to the bottom of the stairs. "Dimmy!" she yelled again.

I heard a door open and then heavy footsteps. I stood outside and waited.

Her mom glanced at me quickly, then back up the staircase. "Does he know what time it is?" she whispered loudly.

I didn't. I had no fucking clue what time it was. Shit.

I saw her legs first, completely bare, before I saw the rest of her. She was wearing a basketball jersey and her glasses. Her steps faltered when she saw me, but she recovered quickly.

"Hey," she said, confused. Her hand came up in a small wave. She pulled the hem of her jersey down a little. "What's going on?"

I was about to speak, but her mom beat me to it. "Lucas," she said, "would you like something to drink?"

I rubbed my hand against my jaw. "Uh, it's Logan, actually."

"I'm fucking with you, kid." She and Amanda laughed. "I know who you are."

I'd be laughing, too, if I my head wasn't consumed with other thoughts. "Um, I'm okay, ma'am. Thank you." I hurriedly took off my cap before continuing. "If it's okay with you, I just need to speak to Amanda real quick. I promise I won't stay late."

She smiled at me. It was different from the smirk she gave me when I showed up. "Huh." She looked me up and down. "You're just like your father," she said.

Only I'm not. Not at all.

She left us alone and walked into what I assumed was the living room.

Amanda took a few steps forward, eyeing me as she did. "You okay?"

I swallowed. "No. Not really."

She nodded once, taking my hand and leading me up the stairs.

She let go of my hand and closed the door quietly, then paused, looking around her room awkwardly.

"Um, have a seat, I guess." She jerked her head toward the bed.

I didn't move.

She stood, leaning her back against the door, her hands behind her.

I tried to smile, but I knew it didn't follow through.

"So...what's going on, Logan?"

AMANDA

"WHAT ARE YOU doing here?" I had my back against the door, facing him.

He stood up and looked around my room, his hands in his pocket, his hair all over the place from combing his fingers through it. His eyes lingered on my bed longer than they should.

"Logan?" I tried to get his attention, but his mind was somewhere else.

He threw his cap on the bed, then faced me. "I'm sorry," he said.

"What?" I asked, confused. "What for?"

He shrugged, his hands going back in his pockets.

"Please don't take this the wrong way," I said, "but why are you here? I mean, I don't mind. I just—I mean why?"

Truth is, I did mind. I came home because I needed to get away from him, even just for a night. I needed to clear my head and work out what I wanted. But then he gave me that speech in the car, and I felt forced to make a decision before I was ready. And when he asked if it was enough, I knew in my heart it wasn't. Maybe if he hadn't slept with someone else. Maybe.

He took a seat on my bed and gripped the edge. His head fell forward. He took in a huge breath, his shoulders heaving with the weight of it. And then he looked up at me. There was a pained expression on his face that even he couldn't hide.

"I'm sorry," he said again. "I just—I don't know. I needed to see you."

Whatever was going on with him, it was bigger than us. Bigger than whatever issues we had to work out.

I kicked the door and opened it. "Mom!" I yelled, "Logan's staying the night."

Without waiting for a response, I climbed into bed and waited for him to join me. "Are you sure?" he said through an almost shy smile. But he wasn't asking. Not really. His shirt and jeans were off, and he was lying in my bed before I had a chance to reply.

Then we just lay there, side by side, on our backs, not touching, not speaking.

"I lied," he said, just as I was about to surrender to sleep.

"What?"

"I lied," he repeated. "I was being a dick. I didn't sleep with anyone. I said it because I wanted you to hate me. So that you wouldn't want to be with me. Because it's my fault you went through all of that shit after our date. It's my fucking fault, and I don't deserve to have you."

My eyes snapped open. I was fully awake. "What?" I said again.

His arm moved up to cover his eyes, even though it was already dark in the room. "I tried," he started, "I really did. I tried to leave you alone, but I don't think I can do it."

I blew out a quick breath. "What are you saying?"

"You own me, Amanda. All of me."

I STAYED UP for a long time after his confession. He fell asleep almost instantly. I could tell the moment his breathing had evened out. "Logan?" I whispered. He didn't respond. Then I reached over, took his hand in mine. And let myself have him. All of him.

I FELT HIS hand separate from mine before I could wake myself up. The heat from his body escaped from under the covers as the bed raised.

He was leaving.

I slowly opened my eyes and watched as he put his shirt back on. I sat up. "What are you doing?" I said quietly, switching on my night light. I checked my phone; it was two in the morning.

He sat on the edge of the bed and turned his body to face me. "I'm sorry." He kept saying he was sorry and I had no clue why. "I shouldn't have come here. Go back to sleep; I'll find my way out."

I sat up on my knees and moved closer to him. "What's going on, Logan?"

"Nothing." His eyes darted around the room, everywhere but on me. There was a sadness consumed in his features. I knew he was lying.

I sighed. "Obviously it's something. You're here, aren't you?"

He didn't respond.

I moved closer and then linked our fingers together.

His eyes snapped to mine. They drifted down to our joined hands and back up again. He swallowed. "Is this—I mean are you—"

I cut him off with my mouth on his. I kissed him slowly, letting my lips linger on his. "Stay?" I asked.

"Yes," he replied but didn't move from his position.

I waited.

He looked right at me, his gaze so intense. I refused to look away.

Finally, he broke the stare. "I just found out I have a sister," he said out of nowhere.

"What? How?" Clearly, I was confused. And shocked. But mostly confused.

His thumb came up to straighten the lines between my brows.

"I'm adopted," he informed me.

"WHAT?! And you just found out?" I almost yelled.

His hand covered my mouth, and then he chuckled. "No, Amanda. I knew. It happened when I was seven. So...it's not a big deal. But she's been looking for me. I guess she found me."

I settled my frantic heart. "I'm confused," I told him, pouting a little.

"Yeah," he agreed, looking away. "Honestly, so am I."

He kissed me once, then took his shirt off and made a move to lie back in bed. I followed him. Then he positioned us so his arm was under my head and I was lying sideways with my head resting on his chest.

He looked up at the ceiling. I looked up at him.

Then he spoke. "My birth parents were assholes, Amanda. And I'm not talking just neglectful assholes. I'm talking abusive, drugged-up, fucked-up assholes."

I gasped.

He continued. "When I was seven, my dad beat me so bad, that even in her messed up state, my mom knew enough to take me to the hospital."

"Oh my God," I breathed out.

His hand went under my top, rubbing slow circles into my back. Like he needed to comfort me.

"You remember my dad, the one you kind of met that night?"

I nodded. "The one Mom works for?"

"Yeah." I could sense his smile. "He was my doctor when she brought me in. My birth parents never came back for me, so he adopted me."

I tried to keep my breathing even. I tried to hold back the tears. I tried so damn hard to hide the fact that my heart was breaking.

"Anyway." He spoke so casually, seemingly unaffected. "Supposedly the asshole wasn't just a dick to me, but to his wife, too, because he had a kid with another woman. Apparently she's my age. He knew about her. Used to visit her all the time. I guess he loved her—used me as a punching bag."

I wiped my tears on his chest. I sniffed once. "Logan," I managed to get out through the giant lump in my throat. "I'm so sorry."

He adjusted us so I was completely on top of him. His hand on my back kept circling. His other hand played with my hair.

"How did you find out?"

"Jake's dad. He's, um, my lawyer—kind of. She—my sister—she's been looking for me. It's a long story."

Silence filled the room while I tried to imagine his life. "Do you remember it?" I asked.

"Remember what?" he answered, his voice low and scratchy.

"That day. When he—" I looked up and into his eyes. "When he hurt you. Do you remember why? Or how?"

He swallowed hard, his eyes drifting shut. He nodded his head once. "I remember the phone ringing and my mom answering. Straight away she was glaring at me. I tried to remember what I could have done that made someone call her. I couldn't think of anything. I mean, even as a kid I understood that whomever she was speaking to, it was about me. I remember her hanging up and then yelling at me, saying that Dad was going to be pissed. She only hit me once across the face before going for her smokes. I knew straight away what was going to happen. I remember trying so hard not to cry. Crying only made them madder. The second she lit her cigarette, I tried to run, but she cornered me. I remember pissing my pants." His voice broke. He paused to clear his throat and then inhaled a huge breath before letting it out in a rush.

I had my mouth on his collarbone, letting the tears fall silently. I could feel my body shaking. He must've been able to feel my tears soaking his skin. But he never stopped the movements of his hands. Not once. The circular motions on my back, the stroking of my hair. All of it. It never stopped. He was comforting me. And I couldn't do a damn thing to comfort him.

"She always put it out where no one could see. Her favorite spot was under my arms. She always covered my mouth with her hand so I couldn't scream. So no one could hear my cries."

I couldn't help it. I let it out—the sob that overtook me.

"Shh," he soothed.

How? How could he be so calm?

"Then she locked me in this tiny cupboard for hours. No food. No drink. Sitting there crying quietly in my own piss and shit. Those were the worst times, because I never knew how long it would be until someone came for me. I swear sometimes it was days. It felt like fucking days." His words ended on a whisper.

"You can stop. You don't have to keep going. I'm sorry." I frantically shook my head. I didn't know if I could take anymore. But he didn't stop. He just kept going. I didn't know if it was for me or for him. "I remember hearing his voice. It always scared me, you know? Even when he wasn't angry. It was this deep fucking rumble. I remember thinking that maybe he was a monster. And not really my dad. Some nights I'd fall asleep and dream that it was true. That my real dad was out there and that this fake dad was a monster. And one day someone would kill him. Could you imagine?" He laughed once. "A little kid hoping to hell that someone would kill his dad. What the hell was wrong with me?"

Nothing. Nothing was wrong with him. I wanted nothing more right now than to kill him myself.

"He opened the cupboard. The first thing I saw was his fist. It was already clenched. His face was red. For months afterwards, whenever I closed my eyes, I saw his face. It was the cause of all my nightmares. This fucking monster. The first punch was to my face. The next few to my ribs. I knew it was going to be bad, because normally he spoke to me while he did it. The son of a bitch would ask if he was hurting me, while he was hurting me. He'd laugh while I screamed. But this time—he didn't say shit. Just kept with the punches, the kicks, until I was a ball on the floor. I remember being on my hands and knees. He grabbed my hair in his hands. I was spitting blood, barely conscious. Then he lifted my head and squatted to meet my eyes. He said, 'Your bruises aren't for show and tell, you little cunt.'"

I flinched as he repeated the words.

He continued, "And then he stood up and kicked my head with his steel-cap boots. That's when it went dark. That's all I remember."

Oh my God. "Logan," I said again. I didn't know what else to say. "Stop. Please. I can't. I'm so sorry. I just can't." I was all-out crying. I tried to muffle the sound with his neck. But it didn't work.

"Shh," he said. But he was distracted. "It's okay."

"How is it okay?" I lifted my head, looking into his eyes. His green eyes so clear of any emotion.

"Because," he said, kissing me softly. "It's over. We move on, right?"

I nodded. I didn't know why I did. Because it wasn't. It wasn't okay at all.

Then I felt his hands on my back stop moving. His fingers in my hair froze. I looked up at him.

"I've never told anyone that," he said, his brows drawn in.

"What?"

"Remember how I told you that I didn't speak for a while when I was kid?"

"Yeah."

"They were trying to get me to tell them what happened, but I never did. I never told anyone. Not until you."

I took in a long, slow breath. My eyes dropped from his gaze. "Why me?"

"Because Amanda." He lifted my chin with his finger. "Because you and me—we're going to be amazing."

THERE WAS A banging on my door.

"Dimmy! You better not be making babies in there!"

Oh my God. "Mom! We're sleeping."

Logan's eyes snapped open. He looked from me, then to the opposite side, where Mom continued to knock. "Should I leave?" he whispered.

I shook my head.

Then the door swung open. Mom stood in the doorway, her arms crossed. "It's midday, Dimmy. Get out of bed. Were you guys having sex?"

"Oh my God." I heard him mutter. He began to blush.

"Mom!" I warned. "We're not having sex. We were sleeping."

She rolled her eyes.

"We're clothed. See?" I lifted the covers so she could see for herself.

"Shit," Logan huffed, quickly covering his hard-on with his hands. He rushed to grab the blanket from my grip and covered himself. "What the hell?" he whispered to me, shaking his head, his eyes huge.

I laughed.

"It's not funny," he said.

Mom slowly closed the door. "Your dad sure as hell never looked that good."

The second she was out, Logan was on me. "What the hell?" he said again.

I laughed. Again.

I got out of bed and stood at the edge. "Come on, Lucas. Let me make you some breakfast."

LOGAN WANTED TO go to his house and speak to his dad about the whole long-lost sister issue. I told him I'd wait for him in his pool house.

So that's where I was, going through his clothes and pulling out all his old sports jerseys.

He walked in a half-hour later. His eyes instantly went to the pile of clothes on his bed. "You ready?" he asked, his eyes remaining on the pile.

"Nearly," I told him, packing the clothes into an old gear bag I found.

He strolled over to help me, picking up an basketball jersey and putting it in his bag. "What are you doing?"

I shrugged. "I can't be in bed with you while wearing some other asshole's jersey." I reached up and kissed him quickly.

"Okay, pretty girl."

I LEANED OVER the center console and took his hand in mine. He was driving us home. "What are you going to do, Logan?"

He eyed me sideways and then pursed his lips. "I really don't know." He shrugged. "It's not going to change with time, right? So I guess I'll just think about it, you know?"

I nodded. "Thank you for sharing that with me. I know it must have been hard for you."

He brought our hands to his mouth, kissed the inside of my wrist, and then rested them on his lap. His shoulders lifted. "You're my person, Amanda. It's what we do, right?"

28

LOGAN

It's official.

She has my balls and she was not giving them back. Ever.

It'd been a week since Amanda and I became a thing, but we've both been so busy with practice and classes and work and study that we barely had time to see each other. I was so busy doing double practice sessions because of the upcoming game that I didn't even have time to drive her to work. I picked her up every night, but by the time we got home, we were both too tired to talk about our days, let alone fool around. I copped a tit touch every now and then, but that was as far as it went.

She asked the night we got back if I wanted to talk more about what happened when I was a kid. I said no. I also told her that no one else knew about it. Not even the adoption side. No one but Jake and Micky. It wasn't that I didn't trust anyone; I just didn't want people's pity. I especially didn't want hers. So she left it alone and hasn't asked since.

I was sitting in my bed, books all over the place, when I heard the front door slam shut. "Babe?" she yelled.

"Bed."

She came into the room, dropped her backpack to the floor and fell forward onto the bed with her head on my lap. "I'm so deliriously tired," she muffled into my leg.

I tried to contain my laugh. "Take a nap."

Her head lifted to face me so she could show me the most exaggerated eye-roll ever. "If I had time to nap, I wouldn't have this issue, asshat."

"Sorry," I grimaced. "You're in a good mood."

She grunted. "I have to be at work in an hour." Her head fell back on my lap.

"Can someone cover your shift?"

"No!" she snapped.

Clearly I was an idiot for even asking.

She lifted her head again, staring at my lap for a few seconds. Then she raised her hands lazily and started to undo the drawstring of my pants. "Let's have sex," she announced through a yawn.

What? "What?" I tried to jerk my hips back, but there was nowhere to go.

"I don't know," she rushed out, starting to put her hand down my pants.

I grabbed it. "What the hell are you doing?" I laughed out.

She let out a frustrated moan. "I don't know. I don't know what's happening right now. I'm so tired. Is this real life?" She pouted. She looked so damn cute. "Logan?" she sighed, flipping over and looking up at me.

I stroked her hair, trying to relax her. "Yeah?"

"Please don't be mad, but I have to work during your game tomorrow. Everyone else already had tickets, and I couldn't get out of it. I'm sorry. Don't hate me." Her eyes began to drift shut.

"That sucks."

"Logan?"

"Yeah?"

"Why haven't we had sex yet?"

"Because it's not just sex with you. It never will be."

29

AMANDA

GAME DAYS WERE ALWAYS SO busy at the bar. But today was hectic because it was the first game of the season. I tried to watch as much as I could on the big screen, but I was completely distracted and useless at my job.

Everyone's eyes were glued to the screen; Jake was pitching and Logan was catching. It was the top of the ninth; the opposition had two outs, two strikes. This pitch could make or break their perfect game. The buzz so far was that it was the Andrews/Matthews dynamic. Personally, I just thought my boy was that fucking amazing.

I didn't see it, but I heard it. Loud cheers on the screen, as well as in the bar, broke the intensity. Everyone was on their feet, celebrating. I walked through the patrons so I could see the TV. The camera was on Jake and Logan, talking shit as they walked to the dugout. Both wore huge grins. Logan had his mask off, his dimples on full show. My heart swelled—if anyone deserved to have a moment like this—it was him.

I got lifted off the floor by someone's arms around me. At first I panicked, but when I realized it was just Shane, Ethan's friend, I celebrated with him. "I'll see you at your house!" he yelled.

"What?"

He threw his head back in laughter. "Ethan called!" He had to scream over the celebrations around us. "Party at your house!"

Normally, I'd be pissed. But right now, I just didn't care.

The game got closed out, and the bar emptied out pretty soon after. Because we were so close to campus, most of the patrons were students, which meant I'd probably see them at my house.

TWO HOURS LATER, I finally pulled into the driveway. Ethan let me borrow his car because he knew he'd be drinking. There were people all over the house, and the music was blaring.

I saw a bunch of girls and guys on the front lawn. I recognized the guys from the team. Was everyone here? All of a sudden I was nervous. It was different when it was just me and Logan and our close friends, but I didn't know what it'd be like in front of everyone. I knew I shouldn't be, and a part of me hated that I was, but I couldn't help being insecure when it came to him. I was confident with how he felt about me. It was just how other people felt about us. I shouldn't give a shit. But I did.

I made my way into the house and walked to the kitchen. And he was there, leaning against the counter, beer in his hand, his arms crossed over his chest. He had two girls in front of him. They held hands, clearly trying to flirt. Probably trying for a threesome. He shook his head, clearly uninterested in whatever they were offering.

He must've sensed me in the room, because his eyes moved around until finally they locked on mine.

I stood there and waited. Anticipating his next move.

Slowly, he began to smile, and it got wider and wider until his dimples got as deep as possible. He wordlessly kicked off the counter, walking between the two girls, until he stood in front me, so close our chests touched. Then we just stared at each other, wearing the same stupid, goofy grins. Without a word, he took my hand and led me to his room, closing the door behind him.

"I wish I was there," I said, the same time he said, "I wish you were there."

Then we laughed at each other.

I sat on the bed.

He paced the floor. It was obvious the adrenaline from the game was still flowing through him.

"Oh God," he started, his fingers linked behind his head. "I couldn't even explain what it was like."

"Try!" I told him. I needed to know. I wanted to share the excitement with him.

He faced me, his smile huge. He shook his head, like he couldn't believe it. "It was just—I don't know. Being out there—and the crowd cheering—it was so loud!" He started to get animated. His words were coming out in a rush. "It was unbelievable. I mean—I've played before, but it was never about me. And this time, it kind of was, you know? And the crowd was wild. Like, crazy wild. And I got to share that with my best friend. How fucking good is that?! You know, not many people could say they experienced something like that. I mean Jake—he's probably used to it. But for me, it was kind of a big deal—being out there. I just—" he stopped abruptly, then stepped up to me. He looked in my eyes. "Why are you crying?"

I wiped my face, surprised. I didn't even know I was. "I'm sorry," I sniffed, wiping them with the back of my hand. "It's just—" I leveled my breathing. "After everything that's happened to you, and you just—it's like you don't even let it get to you. And you—you deserve to have this moment, Logan. You deserve all the amazing moments in the world. I just—I'm so happy for you and I'm being a sucky person because this should be about you and I can't stop crying." I was doing that half-laugh, half-cry thing. "I just—I want you to be happy."

He laughed a little, taking a seat next to me. "I am happy," he said, pulling my head to his chest. He took my hand and kissed the inside of my wrist. "And you're not a sucky person. And even if you are—you're my sucky person."

LOGAN

We ran out of alcohol an hour ago. It was around the same time most people bailed. Funny how that happened. Now it was just us and our friends in the backyard. We were all a little buzzed. It was good times.

Amanda changed out of her uniform and into a dress. I didn't know shit about girls' clothes, but I knew they made her tits look huge. I'd been staring at them all night. She had nice tits. I should probably tell her that more often. She knew how I felt about her ass. I wonder if her body parts got envious of each other. Maybe I should tell her I loved her entire body. Maybe I should tell her I love—wait. No.

"Oh, okay," Micky said, pulling me from thoughts. "Maybe I should remind you that I answered a call on your phone from Marissa just last week."

Lucy gasped.

The guys stayed silent. We knew when to keep our mouths shut.

Amanda obviously didn't. "Who's Marissa?" she said from next to me. I shook my head at her. She shrugged.

"Jake's supermodel ex-girlfriend," Micky answered.

"She's not my ex-girlfriend."

"Whatever," Micky huffed.

"Dude," Jake said to me. "Tell her."

I took in a deep breath. "She's not," I said to Micky. "They never dated. She wanted to. She invited herself as his date for prom. I think they fooled around a couple of times." Micky's face contorted to a look of disgust. "Not sex," I clarified.

"Oh, well that helps." She rolled her eyes.

Then Dylan spoke up. "Who gives a shit? You guys are all good now. That's all that matters, right?" There was a hint of anger in his tone, but no one dug further.

It was quiet for a moment. No one wanted to speak. Dylan had that kind of presence. Amanda nudged my side, a questioning look on her face. I guess she hadn't seen this side of Dylan before.

I just smiled at her, my arm going around her shoulder. I leaned in to tell her something but my cap hit her head, and she laughed. She faced me, turned it backwards, and then resumed her position. "Are you buzzed?" she asked.

Yes. "I think maybe a little. But fuck, I missed you," I whispered into her ear.

The others had started talking again, ignoring us.

She bit her lip, turning her head and facing me. I saw her slowly leaning in. My heart started to pound faster. I licked my lips and waited.

But then the back door opened, and I heard Heidi. "Hey, guys," she greeted, causing Amanda to pull away. I threw my head back, frustrated, and then caught Lucy smirking. She tipped her beer toward me. I did the same.

"Nice of you to fucking join us," Dylan spat.

Heidi took a step forward, getting closer to him. "I told you I had sorority stuff to take care of." She sounded pissed. Amanda leaned closer into me. I rubbed her arm up and down.

Everyone watched Dylan and Heidi.

"Sure. Sorority stuff." He rolled his eyes, mocking her tone. "You mean stuff with that asshole, Jonah."

"Not now, D." She was getting more and more annoyed.

"Not now, she says." He faced everyone, then looked up at her. "Then when? When do you think you might be able to schedule your fucking boyfriend into your life, huh?"

He was on his feet, in her face. We never saw Dylan and Heidi argue, so the fact that this was happening right now had us all a little on edge.

"Oh wait..." Dylan continued. And I didn't know much about girls, but I was pretty sure this would be about the time he should shut the fuck up. Whatever it was that was going on between them must have been boiling for a while. Dylan never talked shit to Heidi. Ever. "Maybe I should ask Jonah when he's free, maybe clear it with him."

"You're an asshole!" she yelled, wiping tears.

"Dude." Jake tried to calm the situation.

"Shut up, Jake," Dylan warned. He must be wasted.

Then the pre-Heidi Dylan came out. "I'm getting sick of your shit, Heidi. You wanna be with him. Do it. Leave. But you have to do it. You have to be the one to break up with me."

What the fuck was happening?

He went on. "You don't think girls are up in my shit every day. You don't see it, do you? You know why? Because I make it fucking clear that I'm not interested in anyone but you. So how do I get treated? Like shit. You ignore me for days and spend all your time with that asshole!"

"Fuck you, Dylan!" She turned and walked away.

"Fuck," Dylan breathed out. Then he chased after her before any of us could get a word in.

It was dead silent.

No one wanted to speak.

Then a slapping sound was heard.

I heard Cam yelp and his chair being pushed back. He was on his feet rubbing his head, facing Lucy. "What the fuck, Luce?"

"Why the fuck don't you ever go all jealous-and-hot-alpha on me?"

"Are you fucking kidding me right now?"

"Fuck you, Cameron. I want that same fucking treatment. I'm gonna start chatting up assholes on a daily basis." I looked at the ground next to her chair; there were five empty beers.

Then Jake laughed.

Everyone faced him.

"Shit, dude, does she know about Mike?"

I laughed, too, remembering Mike.

"What?" She turned to Jake and then to me. "What were you talking about?"

"Shut up," Cam instructed, mostly directed at me.

I laughed harder. And just to be an asshole, I didn't listen to Cam. Instead, I told Lucy the story. About how I overheard this kid, Mike, who went to our high school, talking about Lucy in the locker rooms. He was her partner in some class, and he bragged about how he could see her tits whenever she bent over. She gasped at this point, but I kept going. I told her how I mentioned it to Cam, and the next day Mike came to school with a black eye. He wouldn't tell anybody how he got it. Cam looked at me with a 'shut the fuck up' look on his face, but I didn't care.

Lucy was staring at Cam in shock, her face flushed from the alcohol.

Then Amanda gasped from next to me. "Oh my God," she started. "Remember that guy—your partner from journalism class? The one who asked you out last semester? Cam was behind you... and he didn't know..." she trailed off.

"Oh God," Lucy whispered.

Amanda giggled. "That was the last time you saw him in class, remember? He dropped the class."

Cam looked at the ground, shaking his head.

She continued, leaning closer to me again, "And every time you see him, he beelines it in the opposite direction!" She was all-out laughing. So was Micky.

"Is it true?" Lucy asked Cam softly, standing up from her chair.

"Whatever," Cam snapped. "I'm pissed at you, Luce. Don't treat me like that."

"Holy shit, Cameron," she said seductively. We all watched, trying to hold in our laughter.

"Dammit, Lucy. I mean it," he said, squaring his shoulders and facing her.

She bit her lip and looked him up and down. Amanda held onto my arm, her face pressed against it to block her giggles.

Lucy's eyes zoned in on Cam's junk.

He covered his dick with both hands. "I mean it, Lucy."

He took a step back.

She took a step forward.

"Quit objectifying me!" he yelled. "I have feelings, you know!"

She took a few more steps forward until she was in front of him. She placed her hand over his, still covering his parts, and raised her eyebrows.

"No," he warned.

She pouted.

"No," he said again.

She licked her lips.

"Oh, fuck it!" he grunted, before lifting her over his shoulders. He bumped fists with me on the way out.

"I want you to fuck me rough tonight," we heard her say.

The second we heard the door shut, we all let go of our laughs.

A minute later, Ethan came home with James in tow. Jake stood up. "We're out." Micky just shook her head, following behind him.

"Have a good night." She smiled at us.

WE WERE BOTH a little wasted by the time we got into bed. She stripped off her dress and was sleeping in her bra and panties and that's all. I was doing everything I could not to touch her inappropriately.

"So are you likely to get more game time now?" she asked, settling under the covers.

"No. I'm done. I'm telling them tomorrow. I quit."

She gasped. "Really?"

"Uh-huh. What a way to leave the game, huh?"

She just smiled. "It sucks that I wasn't at the game today, but I'm glad I still got to share some of this moment with you."

I brought her into my arms. "I'm glad I'll get to share all my moments with you."

30

AMANDA

HE WASN'T IN bed when I woke up the next morning, but there was a text from him. He was in a team meeting and would be home soon. I jumped in his shower but forgot my clothes, so I put on his jersey that was lying in his hamper. When I opened the bathroom door, he was there, sitting on the edge of his bed with his back to me.

His jersey barely covered my ass, and even though he'd seen me like this before, the fact that I was completely naked underneath had my skin feeling hot. I knew I was blushing. I cleared my throat. He looked up surprised.

"Hey," he said. "You just getting up?"

I nodded, nervously pulling the hem down further.

His eyes narrowed in confusion, then went from me to the bathroom door and back to me again.

I stood in front of him.

He was looking down, I assumed at my legs. I've seen him do that a lot. He wet his lips and sat up a little straighter. His hands twitched at his sides. He didn't said a word. "Logan?" I tried to get his attention.

Slowly, his gaze travelled from my legs, up my body, and rested on my face. His eyes were hooded, burning with lust. He bit his lip as he moved forward; his hands reached and cupped the back of my thighs, bringing me closer to him. His touch was soft and demanding all at the same time.

He blew out a heavy breath before dropping his head forward and letting it rest on my stomach.

And I let him.

For a few moments, I let him stay there. Not moving. Not saying a thing.

Then slowly, and so fucking lightly, his hands moved.

Higher.

And higher.

And I knew that I wanted him there.

I wanted him to touch me.

My legs rubbed together. A moan escaped before I could control myself. Because I couldn't. I couldn't fucking control myself around him.

He cleared his throat.

My eyes darted to see him looking up, watching my face.

My hands clenched at my sides, and my eyes fluttered shut. I needed him to touch me.

One hand cupped my bare ass. He didn't grab, he didn't squeeze; he just held it there. He finally lifted his head to meet my eyes. There was a question on his face, but he didn't need to ask. Not anymore. I was his. My fingers started undoing his jersey. I started from the top, slowly parting the material. His eyes followed my fingers, waiting. When I undid the last button, his free hand splayed flat on my stomach. He started moving the material aside. His mouth came to my belly button, as his tongue tasted my skin. My muscles tensed at the sensation. When he pulled away, he looked up at me. His eyes were dark and penetrating. "Fuck," he breathed out, before pushing his jersey off my shoulders. It easily fell off my arms and onto the floor. Then I stood there naked, in front of him, for the first time. He stayed silent. His eyes raked all over my body for so long, I started to feel self-conscious. My arm shifted to cover myself but before I could, both of his hands were on my ass, pulling me closer to him. I stepped forward the same time his mouth covered my nipple. At first he was slow and gentle, but it didn't last long before the gentle kisses turned to sucks and my knees began to weaken. His mouth was warm on my skin. He kept moving from one to the other, making sure they got the same treatment. My hands moved to his hair, gripping tight, trying to hold on. Then he slowed down, his mouth pulling back slightly so that his tongue could make slow circles around my nipples. It drove me crazy. I needed more. But he wouldn't give it to me. He just kept going from one to the other. I was panting. "Logan," I pleaded.

"Shh," is all he said.

He pulled away, all the way away, and then blew a heated breath on each wet nipple. My knees buckled, but he held me up with his arm around my waist.

Then his mouth was on me again.

Kissing. Licking. Sucking.

I needed more.

My legs squeezed together, trying to ease the tension that was building. Then I felt his hand between them, trying to part them. And then his finger—oh my God—his finger gently separated my folds. He started at the top of my slit and moved down, then back up again. He repeated the motion over and over, but never enough to push me over the edge. I started squirming, but he just held me tighter.

"Logan, please," I begged. My eyes were shut tight. I'd lose my fucking mind if I saw him. I tried to move my pelvis down so I could take more of him, but he wouldn't fucking let me. Just when I was about to yell at him to do something, anything, his finger was inside me.

I let out a gasp. "Oh fuuuuck."

He pulled out his finger and replaced it with two.

And then he started the in and out motion, so slow, so gentle. My juices poured onto his fingers.

He used his thumb to rub slow circles on my clit, and I lost all control. His tongue on my nipple copied the same lazy circles. I started thrusting my hips, fucking his fingers. "Fuck, Logan," I managed to get out.

"I got you, baby."

I could feel it building, my toes curled, my fingers tightened around his hair, but he never stopped fucking moving. His fingers, his tongue, he was everywhere, all at once. "Holy...fucking...uh."

"Mmmm," his deep, throaty rumble made me open my eyes. I

looked down to his face, his mouth still attached to my nipple. His eyes were filled with lust. His gaze was trained on my face, watching me enjoy the way he made me feel. My breathing was short, heavy. My hips kept thrusting onto his fingers. Our eyes locked, watching each other.

And then he smirked.

With a mouth full of boob, he fucking smirked, his dimples deepening.

Then winked at me.

Fucking winked.

And then his fingers curled inside me, his thumb rubbed harder and his mouth covered my entire nipple and sucked. Hard.

And I lost it. My walls tightened around his fingers. My legs gave out. My head threw back; I bit my lip to stop from screaming. He held me up, the entire time never stopping, never changing his rhythm.

When my breathing settled and I could stand on my own, I peeled my eyes open, and he was watching me, biting his lip. He slowly removed his fingers from inside me, kissing my stomach a few times before pulling away completely.

"Hey," he greeted, "welcome back."

LOGAN

SHE DIDN'T RESPOND. Just straddled my lap. There was fire in her eyes. They roamed all over my face. "I need you inside me now," she informed.

I grunted.

She ripped my shirt off.

I grabbed her ass, bringing her closer. And then I took her mouth with mine.

Her nails dragged along my chest, lower and lower. They paused on my abs, fingering the dips. She did that a lot.

Then her fingers curled in the band of my sweats, pulling them away from my body. She kissed me harder, and her tongue invaded my mouth. I almost came when my fingers were inside her—this—this was almost too much. Then I felt the heat of her fingers closing in on my dick, as she wrapped her hand around it. But she was there less than a second, before she moved completely off me and away. All the way away. Her naked body was pressed against the wall opposite me. She had a shocked look on her face. Her eyes bugged out. Her mouth hung open. She was slowly shaking her head.

I looked down at my dick—just to make sure it hadn't turned into a dragon or some shit.

It looked fine.

I sniffed once.

It smelled fine.

My eyes lifted to hers again. "Logan," she whispered, looking around the room.

I unintentionally did the same. Just in case we weren't alone.

What the hell was happening?

I looked back at her. She hadn't changed positions.

Her head began to shake more frantically, but her eyes were glued to my dick.

"Logan," she said again, whispering a little louder. "That's not gonna fit."

I tried hard to contain my smirk, but I don't know if it worked. "It will fit," I tried to assure her. She continued to shake her head. I stood up and pushed my pants down to my ankles. A gasp got caught in her throat. I was all-out grinning now.

I sat on the bed with my back against the headboard. "Come on." I motioned for her to join me. She slowly moved off the wall, still hesitant. "You can be in full control. We'll take it slow. I promise."

She nodded, biting her lip. She crawled onto the bed and over to me, throwing one leg over mine and straddling me again.

She ran her tongue along her top lip. I stopped it with my mouth, and that's what we did, for minutes, just kissed. And without knowing, both our hips had started a rhythm, thrusting, rubbing on each other. I pulled back. "I need inside, baby."

She sat up on her knees and took me in her hand, then slowly guided me into her. "Holy...oh my...shit," she moaned, lowering herself onto me.

And then she moved.

Up and down.

Grinding and making little circles once I was all the way in.

And even though I've had sex way too many times to count, this time, it was different. It was more.

Her eyes were shut, her head thrown back, her mouth slightly open, panting. Fuck. "Oh God," she whispered. "You feel so fucking good."

Then she started moving faster and faster, and I was so fucking close. My legs tensed, and I did everything I could to hold off so I could watch her come again.

"Fuck, Logan."

My hands gripped her ass while she rode me. She looked so fucking amazing, and I was so fucking close— "Fuck. Stop."

She did. But only for a second before she started to move again.

I held her still. "Stop. Just—shit." If she kept going it'd be over, and I didn't want it to be over. Not yet. But I'd never had a problem holding off before. Ever. "I just—" I let out all the air in my lungs with a whoosh. "I've never had this problem." I grabbed her face in my hands and made sure she was looking at me. "I've never felt like this." My eyes roamed her face, looking between her eyes. I didn't know what to say. I didn't know how to make her understand that this was different. "It's all you, Amanda. Just you."

Then I flipped us over until I was on top of her. I started kissing her neck, down her body, her breasts, her stomach, lower and lower. She needed to blow once more, because I sure as shit couldn't go on much longer. I got to her pelvis and kissed either side. I could smell her. It made me dizzy. I needed to taste her.

I started to dip my head, but her fingers gripped my hair and pulled, stopping me.

AMANDA

I LOOKED DOWN at him. His eyebrows were bunched.

"What the hell are you doing?" I whispered.

He rolled his eyes. "What does it look like I'm doing?"

My mind was swimming with lust, so I didn't even register what was happening until it was too late. Now he was down there and I didn't know what to do. I shook my head, "You can't. I mean—"

He cut me off with a smirk on his face. "Has this happened to you before?"

I shook my head slowly.

His smirk got bigger.

"Good," he said, moving off the bed and kneeling on the floor. "Enjoy, babe."

Then his hands were on my ankles dragging me further down the bed. He spread my legs with his palms flat on the inside of my thighs and then lifted them over his shoulders.

I threw my head back against the pillow and shut my eyes tight. Then I felt his warm breath on me, and I waited.

"Ready?" he asked. I imagined his half-smile, single-dimple face and could probably come just from that image alone; I was so fucking turned on.

Then his tongue was on me.

My hips raised off the bed because it was so much more than I thought it would fucking be. He held my hips down to stop me from moving. "Relax, babe," is all he said before I felt it again. He moved slowly, up and down. I tried to squirm and pull back and away because it was just too fucking much. But he held me there and made sure I took every single second of this intense pleasure he gave me. Unknowingly, my hips started thrusting into his face. I was making him fuck me with his tongue. Oh my God. What the fuck was happening?

"Fuck, I love your pussy," he said, his mouth never leaving me.

"Oh my God," I moaned out, thrusting faster. I couldn't fucking help it.

"Ready?"

"Huh?"

Then he covered my clit with his mouth and sucked. And it's all I needed to push me over the edge. I bit my lip to stop from screaming. Not squealing. Not moaning. But screaming.

When I finally came back to earth and opened my eyes, he was above me. Watching me. "Hey, pretty girl." He wiped my wetness off his face. He leaned down to kiss me but paused half-way, hesitating. After the way he made me feel, I couldn't give a fuck if I could taste myself on him. I put my arm around his neck and brought him down to me. He moaned into my mouth. Tasting myself on him turned me on more.

"Fuck," he groaned out, before effortlessly entering me. His head fell to my shoulder, his weight held up by his forearms. He started moving in and out, harder and faster. "I'm not going to last long, Amanda. You're ruining me right now."

"Uh." I couldn't say anything else because I felt it building again. I'd never felt like this before. Ever. And I knew why. It was him. And I didn't know if it was his skill or the feelings I had for him, but I felt myself climbing again. He kept moving over and over, and I was there the exact same time I felt him get even bigger. Then he let out the sexiest, manliest fucking sound I'd ever heard.

31

LOGAN

"So I think I want to meet her," I said, looking up from my textbook. We were in my bed; I sat against the headboard, shirtless. She didn't let me wear shirts. Ever.

She was on the opposite end of the bed. She did this so she could look at me shirtless without making an effort. I did whatever she said.

Balls. Pockets.

"Who?" she asked.

"My sister—or whatever. I think I want to know more about her."

She sat up and scooted closer to me. "Are you sure?"

"Yeah." I shrugged. "What have I got to lose, right?"

Everything. I had everything to lose.

I called Dad to let him know we were coming. He practically choked on his words when I told him I was bringing Amanda home. He jokingly asked if she was pregnant. I laughed it off, remembering how she wigged out after our first time. That was three weeks ago. I was clean, and I knew she was on the pill because I saw her taking them. Still—it was stupid that we got so lost in the moment that we didn't discuss it until after the fact.

Two hours later, we were at the grocery store near home. I pushed a cart while she pulled items off the shelf and placed them in there. I told her we'd probably just order a pizza for dinner. She said she wanted to cook for us.

She walked in front of me, her short shorts barely covering her ass. I watched it sway from side to side—hypnotized by the movement. It was probably why I wasn't paying attention when my cart ran into the side of someone.

My eyes lifted. "Sorry," I tried to say, but my words died. And so did my heart. At least for a second.

"Logan?" the woman in front of me said. She took two steps until she was standing only feet away. She looked me up and down. I didn't blink. I didn't move. I didn't breathe. "It is you," she whispered.

She was older. But then again, so was I. If you took away the effects of time, she looked the same. The same drugged-up, fucked-up person who carried half my genes. The only difference was her eyes. They looked tired. Or maybe that's just how the seven-year-old me remembered her. Maybe I remembered the fire in them. The crinkle in her eyes was always due to the anger inside her. She never smiled. I remembered that then—that she never smiled. Not when I was a kid. But right now—she was smiling. It didn't make sense.

"Logan?" she said again.

What was I supposed to say to her? *What's the protocol for mom meets beaten kid fifteen years later?* I wanted to ask her why she did it. I wanted to know how she let it happen for so long. I wanted to ask her how—how she could do that to a kid. But really, I just wanted to tell her to get the fuck out of my face.

I could feel the muscles throughout my body start to get tense. My jaw locked from flexing so hard. My fists balled so tightly I could feel my nails breaking skin.

She took a step forward, eyeing me closer. I squared my shoulders. "Jesus, son, you've grown."

"I'm not your fucking son; don't call me that." My teeth clenched. My heart pounded in my ears.

Then I felt Amanda's hand curl around my arm, and instantly, I relaxed, as if she had some sort of power that made everything better. Maybe she did. Maybe that's why I needed her.

"Excuse me," I heard Amanda say from next to me, but she wasn't talking to me. "I'm sorry, I don't mean to be rude, but fuck you." She released my hand and took a step closer to my mother. She was between us, blocking me like a shield. "Of course he's grown," she said quietly, so only we could hear. "What? Is he too big now? You only enjoy beating on little helpless, defenseless kids?" She took another step forward. "You sick fuck. You need to crawl back in the demented hole you came from, and I hope you die there. Because I swear it, lady, if I ever see you again, I'll kill you myself."

AMANDA

He didn't want to talk about what happened. So I left it alone. When we pulled into his house, he told his dad he wasn't feeling well and he was just going to crash in the pool house for the night.

He sat down on the sofa, pulled me toward him, placed me on his lap, wrapped my legs around him, and held me. And that's how we stayed. For fifteen minutes. Our arms around each other, chest to chest with our hearts beating as one. Then he sighed and pulled back. "We've had some shitty things happen to us, huh?" he said, his face so close to mine his breath brushed my lips. I closed my eyes and nodded. "It's not going to happen anymore, Amanda," he stated, almost like a declaration. "You and me—together—it's not going to happen anymore." He was talking to himself, but I nodded anyway.

It was clear from just looking at him that it was Jake's dad who answered the door the next day. He smiled when he saw Logan, but the smile turned megawatt when he saw me—and our linked hands. "Asshole," he greeted Logan.

I laughed.

Logan chuckled, that deep, manly chuckle I love so much. "You trying to make me look bad in front of my girl?" he questioned, stepping into the house.

We walked hand in hand to an office where Jake's dad motioned for us to sit. We did. Then he took a seat in the chair opposite and linked his fingers under his chin. And waited. For what—I didn't know.

Eventually he broke the silence. Leaning forward with his hand outstretched to me, he said, "I'm Nathan, you must be—"

"Shit," Logan broke in. "Sorry, this is Amanda." He shook his head, clearing his thoughts.

We shook hands.

Then a loud screaming came from somewhere in the house. "Is that his car?" an excited voice rang out.

The office doors burst open, and a girl strolled in, followed by a woman. Jake's sister and mom, I assumed. The girl halted immediately when she saw me. "Who are you?" she said, her eyebrows creasing. She looked me up and down.

I felt self-conscious. "Um..."

"Don't be rude, Julie," her mom reprimanded.

She rolled her eyes dramatically, but their direction never left mine. "Logan?" she said, still eyeing me. "Who is she?"

Logan stood up slowly and stretched out his arms. "Julie, how are you?"

She smiled as she wrapped her arms around his waist—still glaring at me. I swear to God—she mouthed 'back off, bitch' just before he let go of her. I didn't know whether to laugh or piss my pants.

She finally tore her eyes away from me, and I let go of the breath I didn't know I was holding. Pre-teen jealousy is a bitch—a bitch named Julie, apparently. "What are you doing here?" she cooed, looking up at him.

"It's adult business, Julie," Nathan interrupted. "Go to your room and play with your Barbies." He had a shit-eating smirk on his face.

"I do not play with Barbies, Daddy! Guh! You're so embarrassing!" she cried, before leaving the room.

"That's mean, honey," his wife scolded.

Logan sat back down.

Then the woman smiled warmly at me.

Nathan cleared his throat.

Logan's gaze snapped to him.

They glared at each other. Then Nathan shook his head, "You are an asshole," he stated to Logan. Then to his wife, he said, "Mandy." He motioned his hand to me. "This is Amanda, aka the Logan Tamer."

Her head threw back in laughter.

"Well, it's about time." She nudged Logan's side, then shook my hand. "I'm an Amanda, too. But it's been a long time since anyone has called me that."

She faced Logan. "I made those cookies you like. You want me to bag 'em?"

Logan's grin took over his face. "You know, Mandy, if you weren't married and I didn't have a girl, we'd kind of be perfect for each other."

"That's enough," Nathan playfully warned. "Get out of here, wifey, before he works his magic."

She laughed, closing the door behind her.

Then it was silent as the mood turned serious. Nathan looked from Logan to me and back again. "You're happy to have someone else—"

"She knows it all, Nathan; it's fine." He took my hand and squeezed once.

"Okay then." Nathan pulled out a folder from his drawer and set it on the table. "What do you want to know?"

Logan shrugged, his eyes staring off into the distance. He gripped my hand tighter. I didn't know if he knew he was doing it. I cleared my throat. They both turned to me. I said to Logan, "How about her name? Do you want to know that?"

He nodded, turning back to Nathan, who inhaled deeply, and opened the folder.

And then he told us her name.

32

LOGAN

SHE'S BEEN QUIET since we left Jake's house. In fact, she's been quiet since Nathan told us her name. I'm not really sure why.

"You don't know, do you?" she asked, turning down the stereo on the drive home.

"Know what?"

"Who she is?"

I shook my head.

"It's Megan Strauss..." she trailed off.

Her saying the name a second time didn't change the fact that I had no idea who she was talking about.

I raised an eyebrow, begging her to elaborate. "As in Mick and Meg? Mikayla and Megan and... James?"

"No shit!" I exclaimed, clearly shocked.

"Shit," she deadpanned.

"Shit..." I responded.

"SHIT," JAKE BREATHED out. I told him to meet me at the little league field between both our houses. He paced up and down in front me. His fingers linked behind his head. He took off his cap and threw it to the ground, running his hand through his hair. "Shit," he repeated.

"So," I started. "I mean—it's not going to change anything—between us—right? If I want to get to know her, I mean?"

He paused mid-step and eyed me, as if deciding what to say next. He sat down on the bench beside me and leaned back. I was leaning forward resting my elbows on my knees.

"It's not that. It's just—it's more complicated. I think maybe—I mean—you might need to speak to Kayla."

"What do you mean more complicated?"

"Exactly what I said. You need to speak to Kayla. Come by my place."

I looked at my watch. "I gotta pick up Amanda soon."

I felt him lean forward, mirroring my position. "So you and her..." he trailed off.

"Me and her," I confirmed.

"We got lucky, huh?"

"Dude, you have no idea."

AMANDA FELL ASLEEP on the way to Jake's house. She works way too frickin' much. I told her I'd pay more rent so she could at least take a night off, but she won't let me. Apparently Ethan couldn't work too long on his feet because of the pins in his leg, so his job prospects were limited. He delivered pizza a few days a week and also had a side business with a few of his boys where they filled kegs with half-water half-shit beer and sold and delivered to underaged kids around the area. He said he was doing the world a favor by not letting fourteen-year-olds drink. Valid. But still—Assholes.

I gently nudged her until she woke. "You wanna stay in the car?"

She shook her head and sat up straight, pulling down the visor to check her face.

"You look beautiful," I told her. "You always look beautiful." I outwardly cringed.

Lame.

She just smiled, faced me and spoke. "So I know this is going to sound stupid, or whatever, but you and me—us," she paused; a blush crept to her cheeks. She sucked in a breath and let it out slowly. "We're a thing, right? Like—exclusive or whatever. I just don't want to think one thing and you think something else." She was rushing her words now. "Because if it's not, that's fine. But I don't not want to be not that—if that makes sense. I mean—I hope that I'm the only gi—"

"Amanda," I interrupted her. "Honestly, I'm kind of pissed that you're second-guessing what this is. Do you need a written contract? You know how I feel about you, and if you don't, then I obviously need to do more..."

She shook her head slowly. "No." She sighed. "You don't need to do more—but I know you—and your past—"

"Is my past," I cut in, "and you—you're my future."

JAKE PULLED THREE beers out of the fridge and handed one to Micky and one to me. Amanda took my keys from my hand and jerked her head in approval. We took a seat at the dining table. "So," I said, running my palm across my jaw. Amanda placed her hand on my leg under the table. "Uh...you know how I told you about my parents—my birth parents, I mean?"

Micky nodded with a confused look on her face.

"Well—it turns out my birth dad had another kid—a girl—uh..."

"Just tell her," Jake encouraged. "Like a Band-Aid."

I closed my eyes. "It's Megan. Your friend." It came out as a question.

Her eyes went huge, and instantly, tears were streaming down her face.

I looked at Jake. He shook his head and held up a finger to stop me from saying anything. Micky frantically wiped at her face. We all stayed silent.

"Her dad?" she finally croaked out. "Her dad is the same as your d-d..."

"Birth dad—yes."

She let out a breath with a whoosh. "How did you—I mean, how long have you—does she—have you spoken—is she okay?"

Jake's eyes narrowed as his head whipped to face her. "It doesn't matter if she's okay, Kayla."

Micky held his hand that rested on the table, and I saw her squeeze it. "Jake..." she cautioned him.

What the hell?

"Have you?" she continued, facing me. "Seen her, I mean."

I shook my head, but my gaze was fixed on Jake. He had his fist balled and eyes shut tight. His jaw clenched shut from the effort of holding his breath.

Amanda broke the tension. "Have you seen her since...what? Prom, right?" she asked Micky.

Micky's eyes drifted shut; a silent sob took over her body. She sniffed once, nodding, but not speaking.

"Baby," Jake soothed, "you need to tell him."

So she did.

She told us all about seeing her at the cemetery on the anniversary of her family's death. She told us about the baby she was carrying and the way she looked. And then she told us about what went down the night her family was killed. She cried the entire time. Her body molded to Jake's side as he stared into the distance, not moving, not speaking. It seemed as though she let out years' worth of pent-up anger, hurt, and sadness. But most of all, it felt like she was relieved. Relieved to get it out and share it with someone.

And then I understood it. I understood why Jake had reacted like he did when Micky asked if she was okay. Because he was right. It didn't matter. It didn't matter to him. But for Micky—it did. And for me, too. I didn't know why, but it did.

"I get that what she did was wrong," Micky stated.

I hadn't said a word. Amanda held on to my arm tightly, her own tears soaking through my shirt.

"But I've had almost a year to deal with it and to think about it —and I don't know." She shrugged. "I can't see her as a murderer. At the end of the day—even if you take away the James factor—there was a reason we were best friends for so long." Her voice was strained from the knot in her throat.

"Fuck that," Jake sneered. "How can you be so goddamn forgiving, Kayla? She helped murder your family."

"Jake!" It was my turn to warn him.

"I'm sorry," he said. "Look, I know you guys were friends." He looked at me. "And I know that she's your sister or whatever the fuck—but no. Just no." His eyes darted from me to Micky. "She has to be out of your life. She has to be done. The fact that she didn't mean for what happened to happen doesn't change the fact that she knew. She fucking knew who it was, and she didn't say shit. She didn't turn him in. She didn't do anything."

Micky's voice rose. "She left the state and ended up pregnant by some guy who isn't around—"

"And that's not your fucking problem, Kayla. And you sure as shit aren't going to make it one!" His accent got thicker. He was pissed.

Amanda and I sat in silence as we watched them argue. It seemed like this was the first time either of them had discussed it.

"Jake. She didn't mean to." She was all-out crying now.

"I don't fucking care, Kayla." He stood from his chair, causing her to leave his arms. "She knew he was out there. What happened if he did it again? What if he'd done it to one of our houses? What if it was Lucy's and all her brothers were home? What if he'd done it to mine?" Then he walked away and into their room, slamming the door behind him.

"I'm sorry," Micky managed to get out. She stood up and started for their room.

"So," Amanda said as we got into the car. She didn't make a move to turn it over. "That just happened."

"Yeah," is all I could get out.

I understood where they were both coming from; I really did, which made the whole situation even more confusing.

"It's your decision," she said quietly, pulling me from my thoughts.

"What?" I faced her.

"It's your decision. It's your sister. It's your relationship. I get that what happened was fucked up, and I know that confused look on your face—I've seen it plenty of times. But whatever you decide—if you want to meet her—or if you don't—I'll support you no matter what."

Perfect.

She was fucking perfect.

I leaned across and kissed her slowly, softly, almost sickeningly sweet. "Thank you, pretty girl."

She smiled against my lips. "You're my person, Logan. It's what we do, right?"

33

LOGAN

"THE DOOR," SHE said, her words muffled by my chest. She kicked my legs. We were in bed. The sun hadn't even come up yet.

I kicked her back.

"The door," she repeated, kicking me harder.

"Uhh," I moaned.

Then Ethan bellowed, "One of you assholes get the fucking door."

"Uhh," I moaned.

"The door," she said again, kicking me harder again.

"Uhh." I kicked her back.

"Assholes, get the fucking door," Ethan yelled.

"Uhh."

And then my phone rang.

"Uhh," I answered.

"Dude." It was Jake. "Answer your fucking door."

"Uhh."

I opened the door to him standing there, shirt off, tucked into his sweatpants, sweating and smelling like ass. He'd been running.

"Shower," he panted. It was way too early for me to give a fuck, so I opened the door, got some sweats for him to change into and showed him the bathroom.

I threw myself on the bed and tried to wake Amanda. "Babe," I whispered, flicking her ear.

She flinched.

"Babe." I did it again.

"Get off me, asshole." She buried her head deeper into the pillow.

I sighed, lying on my back and putting my arms behind my head. "Jake's here," I informed.

"So?"

And just to be an asshole, I thought I'd test her. "Yeah, he was out for a run. He's in the shower right now."

"And?" She still hadn't lifted her head.

"He was all shirtless and sweaty," I mocked in a girly tone.

She sat up then.

"What's your point?" she asked through a yawn, her eyes only half-open, her hair squished on one side. She reached blindly around the nightstand for her glasses.

"So." I grabbed her waist and positioned her to sit on my stomach with her legs on either side. My hand went under her top—my high school baseball jersey—and splayed open on her flat stomach. "Girls go crazy for a shirtless Jake Andrews."

Her nose scrunched, causing her glasses to lift slightly. "Really?" She sounded genuinely confused. "Huh—I just don't see it."

I rolled my eyes.

"Besides," she said, shifting her body to lay flush with mine. I moved my hand to her back. "I kind of have a thing for green-eyed assholes and dimples." She kissed my neck.

I dragged my hands lower down her back until I could squeeze her bare ass.

"Mm," she hummed, her mouth opening wider on my neck.

I thrust up between her legs, and she pushed down.

"Oh God," she moaned, her mouth moving lower, her tongue exploring further.

I squirmed underneath her. "You know," she said, removing her glasses and throwing them on the bed. She was at my abs now, her finger dragging lightly across the dips. "There's something I've never done before..."

A sound escaped from deep in my throat. I threw my head back against the pillow. "Never?" I croaked out, my eyes shut tight.

"Never," she assured.

Then I felt her hand rub against me through my shorts. I did everything I could to stop from jerking my hips further into it. Then her warm breath was there, as her teeth nibbled gently along the length of me.

My dick throbbed.

"Mm," she moaned again, palming the head.

It wasn't even skin on skin and it was driving me fucking crazy.

I need to hold off.

Think, Logan. Think.

Grandmas.

Grandmas smell like Band-Aids, mothballs and oranges.

Good.

Then her hand reached through the leg of my boxers and cupped my balls.

"Fucking shit," I grunted, jerking my hips back in surprise.

I glanced down at her—she was watching my face. My eyes rolled to the back of my head. I bit my lip as I felt her hand wrap around me.

The throbbing got worse.

Then her other hand reached in through the band of my shorts, her palm rubbing against my head, so fucking lightly.

Grandmas.

Mothballs.

Band-Aids.

Oranges.

"Fuck," I grunted when I felt her fingers curl around my shorts, pulling them down. My dick twitched. She must have seen it. Her eyes got huge before a smile pulled on her lips. Then she dipped her head—

"Dude, I need—Whoa! Fuck! Shit!" Jake stammered from the doorway.

Amanda squealed and rolled off the bed, falling to the floor with a thud. She hid her body from Jake's view.

"Shit!" Jake repeated, his eyes huge, but his head faced the ceiling. "Dude, I—I mean—I didn't know—uhh—the room, shit..."

Fuck.

I lazily put my dick back in my shorts.

"Uh." Jake again. "I'll be in the kitchen...you guys...finish? Shit." Then he closed the door behind him.

Amanda came to a stand. "What the hell?" she whispered, her eyes bugging out. She slapped me on the chest.

I laughed.

"I'M SORRY." JAKE ran his hands through his hair. He'd been waiting for me in the kitchen.

I shook my head. "It's fine. What's up?"

Amanda walked in, her face red. "Hi, Jake," she greeted, her eyes trained on the floor.

"Hey," he responded, refusing to look at her.

Awkward.

He added, "Kayla made me come. Not come—like you guys just —not—I mean, here. She made me come here."

"Oh God," Amanda groaned. Her hands covered her face.

I laughed and jumped to sit on the counter. I pulled her between my legs; she plastered her face to my chest.

"Is she okay?" I asked Jake.

He nodded, leaning back against the counter opposite me. "Yeah. I um...she made me come here to apologize."

My eyebrows drew in. "What do you mean?"

"I was an asshole last night—about the whole Megan thing. We've never spoken about it, not like that. And I guess we just had different takes on it. Kayla said I was being insensitive to you—and your situation—so she made me come here and apologize. But I'm not gonna lie. You're my best friend, she's my girl...Megan—she's nobody to me. And I want it to stay that way."

I sighed. "I get that, dude. I honestly don't know what I want yet."

"She wants to be there," he rushed out.

"What?"

"If you decide to meet her or whatever. Kayla—she wants to be there."

We tried to get back to sleep after Jake left, but we couldn't. We both skipped classes and opted to lie in bed and waste the morning away. I tried to get her to finish what she started, but she denied me, saying it was her form of punishment for not knowing that she gets horny when she's delusional and tired. I tried to convince her that I told her Jake was here, but she didn't believe me. She let me watch her while she showered—I guess that was something.

"Did you know her? Megan?" I asked, running my hands along her legs.

We lay opposite each other in bed. I convinced her on a no shirt—no pants rule.

She looked up from her e-reader and shrugged. "Kind of," she said but avoided my eyes.

I sat up and pulled on her arms until she was upright. I raised an eyebrow in question. She sighed, switching off the e-reader and throwing it next to her. "I don't want to say anything that's going to sway your decision. It's your decision, and like I said, I'll support you no matter what."

"Yeah, but your opinion counts," I told her.

"It shouldn't."

"How can it not? You're the most important person in my life. Of course it counts."

She smiled, looking down at the sheets. Her cheeks turned a shade of pink. I rubbed them with the back of my fingers, and she kissed my wrist and shifted until she was sitting cross-legged in front of me. She opened her mouth to speak but snapped it shut. She did that a few times before she finally spoke. "We didn't run in the same circles in high school. Apart from when she was trying to steal Tyson or made an effort to let me know I wasn't good enough for him, she just flat-out ignored me."

"What?"

She bit her thumb, her eyes cast downwards. Shrugging, she said, "Yeah, it happened a lot. I don't think I ever really got over it—hence why I was so insecure when he went to college." She tried to smile, but it didn't reach her eyes.

"I wonder why Micky was friends with her."

"Yeah, I never got it. Micky was always so nice to everyone; she wasn't catty or bitchy, even when Megan was around. But one day my car broke down and Micky pulled over with Megan and she offered me a ride. She had to drop by her house to pick up her sister for some dance thing. We had half an hour to spare, so we went in the house and hung out for a bit. Her whole family was there—and Megan—she was different with them. I don't know. It's hard to explain, like she could be herself around them or something. She joked and laughed with them. She even gave Micky's sister a Justin Beiber poster for her room. I don't know." She shrugged again. "I think maybe that was who she was, you know? But she just struggled with it, and I remember thinking even then that maybe she didn't have that at home. That family togetherness..."

"Huh," is all I could say.

"But that's not—there's more."

"Okay," I said cautiously.

"So, Ethan dated this girl, who was kind of friends with her—or whatever—I'm not sure. Anyway—she told him she was in LA the year after we graduated, and she bumped into Megan there. Only it wasn't really Megan. Not the one everyone knew. She said she tried to get her to have a meal with her because it looked like she hadn't eaten for days. She was so thin, and her eyes were hollow looking. She told Ethan she looked and smelled homeless. So this girl takes Megan to a diner, and she's completely out of it. Like, can't-even-finish-sentences out of it. Then she took off her jacket and there were bruises all over her arms and chest and neck, and she had track marks."

"Bruises?" My voice cracked.

"Yeah," she said, holding my hands in hers. "Rumor has it that after Micky found out about her and James, she tried to make it work with him, but he didn't love her the way he loved Micky, and it was obvious, so she met some guy and moved to LA with him. The guy ended up being an asshole drug dealer. Apparently when he was here, he wooed her off her feet, promised her the world. When they got there, it all went to hell. They lived in this awful house with a bunch of junkies, and she got involved in it, too, I guess. And then it got worse."

I shut my eyes, not wanting to hear what I thought she was about to say.

"Logan?" she said quietly. She released my hands and sat on my lap, her legs around me, where she knew I wanted her. "You want me to stop?"

I opened my eyes, and she was there, a concerned look on her face. I shook my head slowly. I needed to know.

"Apparently the guy started beating her."

I swallowed the bile that rose in my throat. My heart pounded against my chest. Blood rushed in my ears.

"According to the way she looked that day, he beat her pretty bad. She told Ethan that you could see an entire hand print, fingers and all, bruised on her neck."

I inhaled a huge breath.

She wrapped her arms around my neck and held me to her. "A few other people tried to visit her there, and she always made excuses. Then one of the girls from her cheer squad went there and tried to force her to leave and come home. Apparently, Megan broke down and told her about all of it, the drugs, the beatings..." She paused and swallowed, her voice strained. "And the sex. Apparently her boyfriend used to trade her for sex when he couldn't make payments to his dealers."

"What?" I pulled back to look at her face.

She was crying. "Yeah." She nodded, staring off into the distance.

Then it was quiet for a long moment as we both tried to comprehend what happened to her.

"I get it now," she said. "I thought that maybe she took it hard, losing her best friend or whatever. But I don't think that was it. I mean—after what Micky told us, I think it was her way of dealing with the guilt, you know? Like she let all that shit happen because she needed bad things to happen to her. Karma—kind of. I don't know."

34

LOGAN

I THOUGHT MAKING the actual decision was the hardest part. Amanda stayed neutral while I reeled off the pros and cons of the situation. She tried her hardest not to let her opinions or emotions sway my decision. I wasn't lying when I told her that her opinion counted. Because at some point in the last few weeks, she became more than just some girl I slept with or some girl I shared a bed with every night. She became more than just my girl. She became my everything.

When she wasn't around, I missed the shit out of her. When she was around, I didn't want to leave her side. If you called me a pussy right now, I'd tell you it was valid.

"So, you're sure Micky doesn't know any of this?" I asked her again. The problem I was faced with was that whatever choice I made, it wasn't just about me. I could make it that and be a selfish asshole, but I cared about Micky. Obviously. And Jake, too—he was just as invested in this as I was.

"I'm sure. No one's spoken to her about it. Ethan said that James hadn't brought up her name at all with Micky. You know, sore subject and all."

"Does James know?"

"Yeah, but what can he do?"

I sighed. "Nothing, I guess."

She reached over and held my hand. We were on our way to

Jake's house to speak to Nathan and then spend the night at my house. I wanted to talk to Dad about the whole situation, and he still wanted to meet Amanda.

"I'm kind of glad you quit baseball," she said out of nowhere.

I chuckled. "Yeah? Why's that?" I picked up her hand and kissed her wrist.

"You just have more free time. I like having more of you. I don't think I'd ever get sick of having you around," she snorted, rolling her eyes. "Lame," she announced.

"It's not lame." I kissed her wrist again.

"You do that a lot."

"Huh?"

"Kiss my wrist—you do that a lot—why?"

I shrugged. "I don't know. It's like my lips—on your pulse. I can feel your heart beating and know you're here. I guess sometimes I find it hard to believe that you're real—and that you're mine."

NATHAN HAD ALL the information ready when we got there. He held off on a lot of it when we came the first time because he didn't want to overwhelm me—whatever that meant.

"You sure you want to do this?" he asked.

"No," I answered. It was the truth. "But I think I'd always wonder if I didn't, you know?"

Amanda and I decided not to tell Nathan everything we thought we knew about her, just in case it would sway my decision. That was Amanda's biggest concern. That I made the choice I wanted.

"She's, um..." He cleared his throat. "She's not at a good place at the moment."

Amanda and I looked at each other. We figured she wouldn't be, but we didn't know to what extent.

He continued, "She's in a home."

"A home?" I asked.

"Yes, a mental facility."

I exhaled loudly. Amanda held my hand tighter. I didn't know what to say, so I just stared at the desk in front of me.

"Logan?" Nathan got my attention. "She's on suicide watch."

Megan Strauss. Patient #163 at Dalton Psychiatric House. At least that's what the file says about her. The picture they have of her is nothing at all like Amanda remembered her to be. If I had to describe her in one word, it would be lifeless.

"Do you think she looked like me?" I glanced over at Amanda, who was eyeing the file on her lap as we drove to Dad's house. "I mean, before all that shit happened. Are there any similarities?"

She looked up at me then, her eyes squinting in concentration as she took in my features. "Apart from being ridiculously good-looking?"

I had to laugh.

"No, Logan. I don't think so."

I didn't think so either.

It was no real secret about what happened when I was younger, but I guess people had enough decency not to talk or gossip about it too much. By the time I reached middle school, I'd worked out that not so many people knew about my past. I remember talking to Dad about it once. He never tried to hide my past from me; he was always honest and straightforward. Apparently the fact that my birth parents never came back for me made the entire adoption process simple. I remembered thinking how amazing it was that I'd somehow been chosen to have a second chance at life. Even at a young age, I knew better than to waste it. I guess that was what happened when you cheat death. I remembered thinking maybe Dad would keep me around and not hurt me if I kept my room clean. It was such a stupid thing to think—now that I looked back on it—but when you're a kid and you're scared of monsters' voices—then you did anything you could to not have to go back to that place in your life.

I still kept my room clean.

When I was fourteen, word got around town that my birth mom was looking for me. Apparently she went to Dad's work and created a scene. That was when he went looking for the best lawyer in town just in case anything went down. And that was when we met Nathan. You can imagine my surprise when I made friends with some asshole with a weird accent, who was apparently some kind of baseball God, and went to his house to shoot the shit one day after school. Nathan—he didn't even flinch when he saw me. I stuttered my way through introductions and hoped to God it didn't show. It's not that I was ashamed of my past, but I had just met Jake, so coming out and saying, 'Hey, I'm adopted, my parents were abusive junkies and your dad's my lawyer' wasn't really in the cards. Not then. It took me a good year to tell Jake I was adopted—and even then—I still didn't tell him why.

Sometimes I forgot I was adopted. Like this kid, Phuong, in one of my classes—he told me once that sometimes he forgot he was Asian. I found it so funny when he said it, but now—I kind of understood it.

I wondered if Megan ever forgot who she was before she became who she was. I wonder if she knew what was happening to her, as it was happening, or if one day she just woke up and she didn't know who she was anymore. There was a part of me that feels for her. She was this sad and pathetic little girl who didn't get what she wanted, so she stole it. Maybe she needed that attention, craved it in a way. Maybe it was because she didn't have that family togetherness at home, like Amanda said. Maybe she did something that was just supposed to be some innocent prank because she was a bitter bitch, and it ended in the worst form of tragedy. Maybe I just felt bad for her because of what happened to her afterwards. Because even though we didn't know each other at all, and even though the worst type of circumstance led us to kind of knowing each other—maybe I didn't want another human being to die in the hands of fucking drugged-up assholes. Maybe this was my way of paying back what my dad did for me. Maybe I wanted to help her. Maybe I needed to help her.

I told all of this to Dad while Amanda was at the store buying stuff to make dinner. He just shook his head and said, "Maybe she needs you to help her."

So that was that.

Amanda arrived not long after the conversation, grocery bags in tow. I'm pretty sure the last time the kitchen was used by anyone other than the housekeeper was when Micky was here.

I washed my hands and pushed up my sleeves. "What can I do to help?"

She laughed the same time Dad did.

We'd moved to the kitchen, and she was unpacking while Dad sat at the counter.

"What's funny?" I asked them.

Dad answered, "I don't think I've ever seen you do anything cooking related."

Amanda laughed again. "Ever?" she asked him.

"Ever," he confirmed.

Assholes. Both of them.

She opened the fridge and pulled out two beers. She handed one to Dad and started to give me the other, before she hesitated and pulled it away. Her eyes went huge, realizing what she'd just done.

My dad chuckled. "Sweetheart, he's been drinking openly since he was sixteen. It's fine." He gave her a reassuring smile.

I saw her body relax as she handed it to me.

When I was sixteen, Dad noticed the amount of parties I started going to. It was before I got my license, so we walked almost everywhere. When I got my permit, he sat me down and told me he was fine with me drinking, that he knew I was going to do it, so he wanted me to be prepared about the consequences of alcohol. He went through the entire medical side of things and how often he saw kids having to get their stomach pumped and shit like that. Then he told me about Tina. Tina was his high school sweetheart. They'd dated since freshman year and all through college. He told her he'd propose to her the day he graduated. And he planned to. The night of graduation, she was hit by a drunk driver while crossing the road to get to the hotel room he had booked. The room he had littered with candles and roses and where he waited on bended knee for her to open the door. He said he could still hear the sound a car made when it impacted with a human body. He even showed me the ring he still held on to. He said he believed in one true love and that she was it for him.

She was his person.

"HOLY SHIT, WHAT IS THIS?" Dad and I both said during our first mouthful of whatever Amanda made. I swear I saw Dad's eyes roll back in satisfaction.

Amanda laughed. "Good, huh?"

"Sweetheart," Dad cooed. "This is better than good."

"It's taco casserole."

"It's amazing is what it is," I told her.

We moved to the living room after dinner to watch TV. She lay down with her head on my lap and was out within five minutes. I could see Dad watching us while I stroked her hair. "She asleep?" he asked.

I nodded, looking down at her. "Yeah. She's always so overtired. She works way too much."

"Does she need to work that much?"

"I offered to pay more rent; she won't let me."

Then it was quiet for a moment, while I continued to watch her sleep.

"She makes you happy, son?" he asked quietly.

"No," I said, shaking my head. "She makes me whole."

I had to wake her to move us to the pool house for the night. By the time we said goodnight and left the main house, she was wide awake.

"It's such a nice night out," she said, her head tilted, looking up at the sky.

I agreed.

"Let's just stay out here for a bit."

So we did.

I walked us over to the daybed near the pool and laid us down. She put her head on the crook of my arm and her leg over me.

"So I've made a decision," I told her.

She looked up at me. "Yeah?"

"I think I want to go see her."

"With Micky?"

"I guess."

"Good for you, babe."

There was also something else I wanted to tell her, or ask her actually, but I didn't know how. So I just came out and said it. "What are your plans after college? I mean, are you planning on hanging around here?"

She sat up a little and eyed me curiously. "Not sure." She shrugged. "Why?"

I cleared my throat and faked confidence, locking my fingers behind my head. My heart pounded against my chest. I didn't know how she'd react to me asking, but I kind of needed to know. "Just—I mean—when I choose med schools to apply for, I kind of need to know where you'll be or what your plans are, you know?" I rushed out my words in one long breath.

She closed her eyes slowly and visibly swallowed.

Shit. "Shit," I said aloud. "Forget I said anything. I'm sorry. It's way too soon for this conversation."

She smiled. "Maybe it is—too soon, I mean—but who gives a shit, right?"

I laughed once. "Right."

Then she lay back down and rested her head on my chest again. Her hand went under my shirt, fingering my abs. "I'll follow you wherever, Logan. For as long as you'll have me."

Forever, I thought. But I kept that to myself.

35

LOGAN

I COULD TELL it was hard for Jake to stay quiet while I told Micky that I wanted to visit Megan.

"Suicide watch?" Micky asked, her voice breaking. She'd been crying since Amanda told her the rumors of Megan's life in LA.

I nodded. "I'm going a week from now; it's a five-hour drive."

"I'm going, too," she insisted.

"So am I," Jake said.

Amanda held my hand tighter. She didn't have to say the words. I knew she would be coming to support me.

WE TOOK DYLAN'S truck for the trip. Mine was too small, Jake had no back seat and Micky's car was too unreliable.

Five hours later, we stood in the foyer of the Dalton Psychiatric House. Amanda and Jake stayed outside. I had researched visiting protocols and times, so I was prepared when they asked us to hand in anything loose that was on us. A metal detector and a security search later, we were inside what looked like a visiting room. Like in jail. Not that I'd know what that looked like in real life. Just TV.

"It looks like a jail," Micky said, reading my thoughts.

"Uh-huh."

"Are you nervous?" she asked.

"Are you?" I retorted.

"Shit yes," she choked out.

I turned to face her. She was already crying. I covered her hand that rested on the table with both of mine. "We'll be okay, Mick —promise."

Then the doors opened and she walked in. A nurse followed but stayed in a seat next to the door. Micky gasped the same time Megan's steps faltered.

She was worse than in her picture.

"Is that her?" Micky whispered, turning her head to me.

"Yes."

"Shit."

"Mikayla," Megan greeted. Her voice came out hoarse, like she smoked two packs a day. Then she looked at me. "Bro." She tried to smile, but she couldn't.

She looked old. Her skin sagged on her face and was covered in blood. Her hair looked dead on top of her head, she had bags under her eyes and her cheeks were hollowed out from how skinny she was. She sat down in the chair opposite us and rested her arms on the metal table. I could see the bruising on her arms from where the needles would have constantly punctured skin. She sniffed once, getting my attention. She raised her eyebrows in question. I must have been staring.

"Meth?" I asked her.

"Winner winner," she croaked out. She had a twitch, the type junkies got when they needed a hit.

For a second, I wanted to get Micky on her feet and get her the fuck out of there. I'd seen that face on other people before. Hell, I lived with those kinds of faces—but Micky—I didn't know if she'd be able to deal.

"Megan," Micky whispered.

Megan's eyes went from me to Micky, and it was instant. Whatever emotion she was trying to hide disappeared the moment her eyes locked on her best friend. Her body slumped and a sob took over. "You're not supposed to see me like this," she said through a cry.

"Megan." Micky sighed. She reached her hand over and tried to hold Megan's, but she pulled it away and stood up. The nurse stood, too.

"No!" Megan yelled. "You're not supposed to be here. You're not supposed to see me like this, and you're definitely not allowed to fucking pity me!" She started pacing. I saw the nurse pull out her walkie-talkie.

"No!" Megan yelled again. "Micky, what the fuck? Why are you here?"

"Because I need to forgive you," Micky said quietly.

"Forgive me?" Megan spat out. "No, Mick, you don't need to do that. You can't do that. You—and your family—you were all I had—and look what I fucking did!"

"Megan," she repeated again, tears streaming down her face. "You may have been a shit friend, but you don't deserve what's happened to you. Nobody deserves that."

"So that's it?" Megan stopped pacing and faced us. "You came because you felt sorry for me? You can't do that Micky. You can't pity me. You just can't. I won't let you." She shook her head back and forth, her eyes wild. "I won't fucking let you, Micky." She started walking backwards until she hit the corner of the room. "I won't fucking let you." Then her body slid down the wall until she was sitting in a fetal position, rocking back and forth. "I won't fucking let you." She kept repeating the words over and over. "I won't fucking let you."

Micky stood, but I pulled on her arm. "It's okay," she said.

I looked at the nurse, who nodded once in confirmation.

Then she walked over to Megan and kneeled in front of her. She placed her hand on Megan's shoulder and whispered loudly in her ear, "Megkayla brings all the boys to the yard, and they're like..."

Megan looked up then. "It's better than yours."

Then they both said, "Damn right, it's better than yours."

They both laughed. Through tears of anger, sadness, despair, pity, and sorrow, they laughed.

"Oh, Micky," Megan said, leaning closer to her.

"Shh." Micky comforted her and then turned to me. "Give us a minute?"

I looked at the nurse again. "I'm here the entire time," she assured me.

AMANDA

"DID YOU HAVE a pet kangaroo?" I asked Jake. We were sitting on a bench just outside the building. We didn't know how long they'd be, so we walked to get a coffee and some food.

He turned to face me with a slight scowl on his face. "You're shitting me, right?"

I shrugged. I was. But Micky told me once that he hated getting stupid questions about Australia and his accent. "I'll take that as a no."

A few moments later, I asked, "How big is Australia? Is it the same size as Texas?"

Jake shook his head slowly, eyeing me like I was stupid.

I tried to contain my laugh.

"It's like the same size as America," he said slowly.

"Oh," I pretended to sound surprised. Then, "Did you guys have bowling?"

"Bowling?" he repeated.

"Yeah, like ten-pin bowling."

"Oh my God." He laughed. "It's not all red-dirt country. Of course there's fucking ten-pin bowling."

"Oh," I said again. "Do they let you bring your pet kangaroos bowling?"

He looked at me like I was crazy.

Then I threw my head back in laughter.

"Oh, you're fucking with me!" He finally got it and laughed with me.

Then Logan's voice boomed from the doorway. "Hey, asshole, you better not be hitting on my girl."

"Where's Kayla?" Jake asked, all humor gone from his voice.

"She's in there—it's fine." Logan raised his hand. "She's safe."

"What are you doing out here?" I came to a stand and moved in front of him, wrapping my arms around his waist.

He did the same. "They just need a minute." His face came close to mine, rubbing his nose along my jaw. He laid his forehead on my shoulder. I saw Jake watch us, and then he walked away, giving us some privacy.

"How is she?" I asked him.

He blew out a long, slow breath. "Bad. But I don't want to talk about it right now."

"Okay."

"You know what I want to do, though?"

"What's that?"

He rubbed his nose against mine, and then he kissed me long and slow. I hadn't even realized that he was holding me up by the time he pulled away. "I just want to appreciate you. Everything about you. All of it."

LOGAN

"SHE'S READY FOR you." Micky came out a while later, wiping tears from her face. She walked straight into Jake's waiting arms. He hadn't said a word since we got here. Not about Megan anyway.

I kissed Amanda and walked into the building, palms sweaty, heart racing, blood pumping. I didn't know what to expect when I went in, but she just sat at the table, looking calm and ready.

"Hey." Her smile was genuine this time. She looked at the nurse and then to me. "I'm sorry about my outburst earlier. It's a lot for me to take on. I mean, you being here is enough—but Mikayla—it just—it was too much."

I nodded and took a seat opposite her. "She wanted to be here," I said.

"Yeah." She blinked tightly a few times. "She told me."

Then it was silent for a few moments until she finally sighed. "So..."

"So..." I repeated.

"Lucky we never slept together."

I choked on air.

She laughed.

Then it was silent again.

"He talked about you."

My eyes darted to hers, surprised. "Who?"

"Our dad," she answered.

"Not my dad."

She rolled her eyes. "I get it." She nodded and then continued, "When I was younger, like really young, maybe up until I was six or something...he used to talk about you."

I laughed once. I didn't even know what to say. "He wasn't specific or anything; he just said that you existed. I knew your name. That was it. And then he stopped coming around. I wasn't sure why, but he was gone a few years. Anyway, my counselor at my old rehab said I should try to find you—maybe it might help motivate me to get better." She paused to take a breath.

I leaned my elbows on the cold metal table and waited. Whatever the fuck she was saying, there had to be a point to it all.

"Anyway, I think it must have been around the same time you got adopted out or something—when he stopped coming around."

"Maybe." I shrugged.

"Did he hurt you, Logan?" Her voice was still harsh, but underneath it was a layer of sympathy.

"Why?" I asked her. "Did he hurt you?"

"No." She shook her head. "My mom, though. I saw it a few times. But not me—not when I was a kid at least."

"What does that mean?"

"What?"

"Not when you were a kid. Has he hurt you recently?" My eyebrows drew in.

Her eyes welled with tears, but she looked down to the floor. "He's just not good people, Logan. You need to stay away."

"No shit. What the fuck did he do to you?" My jaw clenched and my fists tightened. She reached over to cover them, but I pulled away. It was too soon for her to be touching or comforting me. I didn't need that shit. And even though I had to feel something for her—I wasn't ready to feel that.

She sighed and leaned forward. "Micky told me that you know... about my life in LA...she said that word got around and Amanda told you?"

I nodded.

"Also, Amanda Marquez?" She said her name like a question.

"Don't say her name again," I warned.

"Okay. Touchy asshole. No problem." Her hands went up in surrender. "So our Dad—"

"Your dad," I cut in.

"Fine, my dad—he went to LA, apparently to check up on me. But he was more excited to find out that my boyfriend was dealing drugs and that he could score off him. One thing led to another—it started with weed, then ecstasy, meth and then cocaine. It was like the most fucked-up form of family reunion possible. For five months straight it was just..." Her words trailed off. Then a single tear fell. "And then we had to pay for it all, and I mean—how could we? So my boyfriend decided to pay with me."

"And your dad let it happen?" I yelled. I couldn't help it. The nurse sat up straighter. "I'm sorry," I told her and then repeated the question, quieter this time.

"Like I said, he's not good people."

My head fell back. I eyed the ceiling, wondering how the fuck people got so unbelievably bad.

"Now they run some sort of drug ring," she continued. "Pauly from LA, Dad from here."

I shook my head.

"And me?" she said, her eyes falling to the bruises on her arm. "I have the same nightmare every night. Except it's not a nightmare. It's almost like a dream. It's too good that it hurts when I wake up. I dream every night of them. Of Mikayla's family. I can still hear Emily's laugh. And I shouldn't be allowed to. I shouldn't be able to feel the joy that one sound can bring. I shouldn't be able to close my eyes and see them. I don't deserve to."

"WATCH IT, ASSHOLE," some dick in front of me said. Valid. I'd just walked out the visiting room doors and wasn't looking where I was going, I would have run into him if he didn't say anything.

"Sorry, man."

"Yeah." He tried to square his shoulders. "You better be."

I took him in. He had the same lifelessness that Megan had. His hair was thin, almost like it was going to fall out at any time. He had those same fucked-up blood spots on his face. You could tell he made an effort to dress up; his suit hung off his body and was sizes too big. He had flowers in his hand that were clearly picked from the bushes just outside. I don't know how old he was. He could've been forty—or he could've been twenty.

"Chill out," I said calmly, opening the door for him. I watched as he walked in and started for Megan's table. She looked up at him. She didn't flinch. She didn't gasp. Her breath didn't even hitch. But I saw it in her eyes. She was scared. Scared of monsters.

Logan: *I need your help*
Dad: *Anything.*

"I WONDER WHAT fucked-up things Dylan and Cam are going to do to your car," Jake said through a laugh. He turned his head to glance at me from the driver's seat.

"I know. Those assholes. We should do something to D's."

We were driving back home. Amanda had fallen asleep in the back seat with me, but she was starting to stir.

"Like what?" Micky asked.

Amanda sat up. "What are we talking about?" Her voice was scratchy from sleep.

"Fucking with Dylan's car," I replied.

She turned her head to face me, her eyes squinting, trying to focus. She bit her lip, looking me up and down.

"What's with you?" I laughed out.

She leaned into me and rested her hand on my dick, rubbing it softly. "I'm so fucking horny right now," she whispered.

My dick twitched.

She kissed my neck and then bit my earlobe. "I can't wait to get you home and fuck you."

I groaned. My dick got harder.

I pulled her into me and kissed her. Hard.

She palmed my dick through my jeans.

"You got any ideas?" Jake asked.

Fucking cock-blocking Jake Andrews.

Amanda laughed and pulled away. "We can get soda and pour it on the car, get it really sticky, and then cover it with bird feed. A few hours from now, it'll be covered in bird shit."

Jake threw his head back in laughter. "You guys are fucking perfect for each other."

I watched her face as a grin overtook her features. "Yeah," she said, her legs coming up on my lap. "We kind of are."

36

LOGAN

THE DAY AFTER we visited Megan at Dalton, my dad called. He said he made a few phone calls and was able to get her transferred to a facility in Washington, far away from any monsters that might chase her. He didn't tell me how he did it or where the money came from to do it, and I didn't ask. I knew that if I did, he'd lie.

Apparently Micky called her the next morning to check on her. She said she was fine but didn't want either of us calling her until she was clean or on her way to recovery. She said she was happy to email and write, but everything got checked and filtered, so it might be a while until we heard from her. That was almost a month ago.

I was still processing everything.

You'd think that finding out you had a sister, and your sister turning out to be who she was, would turn your world upside down. But it didn't. Not for me. Maybe because a part of me had so much to look forward to in the future that I really didn't give two shits about my past.

Maybe it was because I had Amanda.

"Amanda," I said. "I'm thinking about maybe buying you a car."

I was sitting on the floor leaning on the bed, playing on the Xbox. She was lying on the bed, reading a book, her hand playing with my hair. "I'm thinking of punching you in the junk," she said flatly.

I laughed. "So that's a no then?"

"That's a fuck no, and don't bring it up again."

"Fine." I sighed. "What if it doesn't cost me anything?"

"You into grand theft auto?"

"No, what if I trade my car in and get two?" I threw the controller on the floor and faced her. I'd been thinking about it for a while. At first I wanted to just buy her a car, but I knew she wouldn't take it. So I asked Ethan to help me out and lie, say that he bought it for her. He said he couldn't lie to her, that she had some crazy twin sixth sense and knew whenever he was bullshitting. He couldn't even sneak food into the house without her knowing. I continued trying to convince her. "I mean, what kind of twenty-year-old college student needs a Mercedes? I could get a truck, it'll be bigger, and we can fool around in there more." I sat up straighter and held her face in my hands. She bit her lip, refusing to look at me. "You can get whatever you like, something small. Whatever you want. I already asked my dad, and he said it would be fine."

She looked at me then, her eyes shining with tears, and she swallowed loudly. I didn't know what to say, so I just kept talking. "Um, Cameron, his mom's boyfriend owns a dealership. I called him the other day; he said he'd work out a great deal for us."

Tears fell then.

"Baby, don't cry."

She didn't respond, just leaned in and kissed me.

And that's what we did, for I don't know how long, just kissed. With our hands on each other's faces and the taste of her tears on our lips, we kissed. "I need you to make love to me now," she whispered.

So I did.

AMANDA

BOYS IN BOOKS are so not better. Not compared to Logan Matthews.

I love him.

"So that's a yes to the car?" he asked, kissing me on the forehead. We lay naked in bed, face-to-face.

"That's still a no to the car. But the fact that you thought of it..." I trailed off. I didn't have words.

"Fine." He sighed like a disgruntled kid.

Then a crack of thunder whipped and rain hit hard against the roof.

He smiled. Huge. "Get dressed!" he ordered, getting out of bed and pulling on his sweats.

"What!" I sat up.

He leaned on the bed, his weight being held up by his arms. He kissed me once. "You trust me, right?" There was excitement in his eyes, and for a second, I let myself think of him as child. But then I remembered—he didn't have that.

"Baby?" He had a huge grin on his face, his dimples the deepest I'd ever seen them. "Please?"

I nodded and got out of bed. He pulled something out of his desk drawer and waited for me to finish getting dressed. Then he took my hand and led me to the front door, opening it wide for me to step through.

"What are you doing?" I yelled over the sound of the rain. It was thick and heavy. I could barely make out the road in front of the house. He just smiled bigger and lifted me by my waist until my legs were wrapped around him.

"Ready?" he yelled.

"For what?"

And then he stepped into the rain. It only took a few seconds for us to be soaked. I held on to him tight. He kept walking until we were in the middle of the yard where his car was parked.

"It won't hurt you!" he yelled.

I wiped my eyes with one hand; the other was still wrapped tightly around his neck. "What?"

"The rain. It won't hurt you. I won't let it."

He placed me back on the ground and held my face in his hands.

And then he kissed me.

In the middle of our yard in the pouring rain, he kissed me.

And it was like no other kiss in the history of kisses.

You know in movies, where the kiss happened, and the cameras panned around in a circle, and you almost got dizzy from watching it? This was that kiss. This was the make-you-dizzy type, the I'm-giving-you-all-of-me type kiss. And I did, somewhere along the way—I'd given him all of me. And nothing in the past mattered, because Logan—he was my future. My world. My everything.

And then he pulled back. "I'm not going to let anything hurt you. Ever." His hand went in his pocket, and he pulled out a gold chain with a glass vial pendant. He opened it and held it in between us, letting the rain fall into it, and then he screwed it shut and put the chain around my neck. "And now you have this." He lifted it for me to see. "And this." He pushed me backwards until my legs hit the hood of his car, and he slowly laid me down, and then he kissed me. And everything around me disappeared. The rain, the sounds, the cold of the metal underneath me. All of it disappeared. And all I could feel was Logan. His warm body pressed against me, his hands in my hair, and his mouth on mine. And then he grabbed my hand and placed it over his heart. "You and me," he shouted. "We're going to make new memories. Ones that you aren't afraid of. And it's going to be amazing."

I swallowed down my nerves.

I loved him.

I loved him so fucking much it hurts.

I opened my mouth to tell him.

LOGAN

"DON'T SAY IT."

Her eyes widened. "What?"

"Don't say what you're about to say—what I know we both feel. Just don't."

"Oh," she said quietly. She slowly moved to get up from under me, but I held on to her tighter.

I shook my head slowly. "It doesn't mean that I'm pulling away from you. Or that I don't feel the same way. Or that I don't want you." I took her face in my hands and made sure she was taking in every word I was saying. Because I needed her to hear them. "You have no idea how much I need you—I need you more than the air." I paused, thinking about how I could make her understand how I felt without saying the actual words. "You know what my favorite part of the day is?" I shouted, hoping she could hear me.

She slowly shook her head.

"It's those few seconds in the morning, when my mind wakes up but my body hasn't, and I feel you in my arms. And I know that when I open my eyes, it's you I get to see."

She stared at me, her eyes wide. She looked like she wanted to say something, but she didn't know what. So I continued, "I know you've said those words before. I get that you've been in love with someone else, and that's fine. But I haven't. Not before you."

She gasped.

"I can't give you much, or anything at all. But when I say those words to you, it won't just be words—it will be me giving you something that means something. And you deserve to know that, to feel that. So please, let me be the first to say it—because I need to be able to at least give you that...and when I do—those three words will be yours, forever. And so will I."

And then I kissed her.

"What are you guys doing?" Ethan shouted.

I pulled back the same time Amanda turned her head to see him running up the driveway. "Making memories!" She laughed.

Then she faced me.

And smiled.

And it was all I ever wanted.

"It's fucking cold," Ethan informed us, rubbing his hips. He was laying on the recliner, watching TV.

We'd come in soon after he did and showered, dried and dressed. We also managed to have sex twice during that time, but I couldn't tell you what order we did it in.

We were lying on the sofa, Amanda on top of me.

Amanda kissed me a few times and got up. "I'll be back," she said, kissing me once more. I watched her leave.

"Dude, don't look at my sister's ass when I'm in the room."

I laughed.

"I'm not even joking."

I laughed harder.

She walked back in with a mug and handed it to Ethan, who

smiled up at her. "Marshmallows?" he asked her, with eyes big like a little kid.

"Of course," she answered. "Only the best for you, big bro."

Then she walked out of the room again, only to return a few seconds later with his comforter. She placed it over him and tucked it around him like he was a goddamn baby.

"Thanks, Demander."

"You're welcome, asshole."

"Seriously, though." His face turned thoughtful. "You're going to make a good wife to some asshole someday."

She lay back down on top me. "Aw, thanks, Ethan."

Then he smirked and jerked his head in my direction. "Hopefully not that one."

Amanda chuckled.

"Aw." I mock-pouted at him. "Sad face emoticon."

37

LOGAN

"I HAVE SOMETHING to tell you, and I don't want you to be mad."

Her eyes narrowed at me. "Logan, that's like saying here's a fucking cookie, don't eat it."

"Okay," I agreed. "Probably not the best way to start a conversation."

"Nope," she said, not looking up from her toes. She was painting her toenails in bed, one headphone in her ear. I'd just come home from a run and was sweating my ass off. "Also," her nose went up and sniffed, "you smell like sweat-stained balls."

I laughed. "I know. I'm getting in the shower now." I leaned forward on the bed to kiss her.

She squealed. "No! Shower first." Then she looked up at me. "Whoa. You run shirtless?"

I nodded.

"All the time?"

"Not when I start off, but after a while, yes. Why?"

"Don't do that anymore," she deadpanned.

I laughed once. "What? Why?"

"I mean it, Logan." She capped her nail polish and put it on the nightstand. "That shit you're selling," she pointed up and down my body, "it's not for sale anymore. I own it. And I say it's for my eyes only."

I had to laugh. "Are you kidding me right now? You own me?"

"Problem?" She raised her eyebrows.

I dropped my shorts and walked into the bathroom. I heard her moan. "No problem at all, babe, but it goes both ways. Remember that."

I WALKED OUT of the shower and put on a pair of sweatpants. She had both earphones in now, reading a book on her e-reader. I didn't think she heard me come out because she laughed quietly, her eyes never leaving the book. She shook her head. "Reid Knox," she whispered. "You hot piece of alpha male asshole."

"What?" I said, loud enough for her to hear.

She looked up and gasped, then slowly pulled her earphones out.

"Uh..." she stammered.

I raised an eyebrow.

"Just..."

I waited.

"Lucy told me to read this book, and it's..."

I waited.

Then she laughed. "Baby," she cooed, "you're better than all the book boyfriends in all the world. Promise." She was all-out laughing now.

"What's funny?" I sat on the edge of the bed. She came up behind me.

"Just that you're insecure or jealous over a fictional character."

I rolled my eyes. "Cameron says Lucy reads dirty shit. Do you?"

"Yup," she said, almost proudly.

I turned around to face her, surprised. "Really?"

"Yup," she repeated.

"Huh. You ever want to re-enact some of those scenes, you let me know." I was only half-joking.

"Actually," she whispered, moving so she was lying with her head on the pillow, her knees bent. She motioned with her finger for me to join her, spreading her legs as she did. I swallowed and moved up in between them. I was already sporting a semi caused by my imagination. Her arms went around my neck, bringing me into her. Then she kissed me. Her tongue didn't bother asking for permission. Her hips pumped up to me; I was hard as all hell. Her hands moved from my hair, down my bare back and into my pants. "Mm," she moaned. Her mouth left mine and made their way down my jaw, my neck and only my shoulder, back up and into my ear. "I read this book once," she whispered, her hips raised and rubbing my hard-on. I started pushing into her, harder.

"Yeah?" I managed to get out.

"Mm-hmm—mm, baby." She started moving faster, her body squirming on the bed. Her hands on my ass squeezed. "This guy... uh..his...girlfriend..." she panted.

"Mm?" I asked, thrusting into her now. Her hands moved further down my ass.

"...fingered his asshole."

I don't even know what happened next, but I was up and against the wall adjusting my dick in less than a second.

"That's fucked," I spat out.

She threw her head back in laughter.

"I'm not fucking kidding, Amanda."

She laughed harder, coming up to a sitting position. She held the sides of her stomach from the pain of laughing so hard.

"It's not fucking funny." There was panic clear in my voice. "Hard. Limit."

She was wiping tears now.

I shook my head at her. "Are you done?"

She tried to contain it, holding one finger up at me to wait. Her breathing started to slow, and her laughs became sporadic. After five minutes, she finally spoke. "So what did you have to tell me?"

I sat back down on the edge of the bed. She sat with me. "It's my birthday today."

She gasped loudly, almost too loudly. I turned to face her. She was fucking with me. "You knew, didn't you?"

She nodded. "Yep. I was wondering when you'd tell me." She came to stand between my legs. Her arms went around my shoulders. "How come you didn't say anything?"

I shrugged. "Not really a day to celebrate, you know, with my parents and all."

She leaned down and kissed me slowly. I held her closer to me.

She pulled away and moved the hair away from my face, and then she smiled. "We're making new memories, remember?"

"Right," I agreed. "And you're my favorite one."

She sighed. "I wish I could tell you how I feel about you."

"You don't need to tell me. I know."

"You do?"

"Of course." I picked up her hand to kiss her wrist, but she quickly pulled it away.

"I got you something!" she said, excited. She leaned over me and felt under the bed on the opposite side. "Here it is!" Then she came back to stand. "Okay," she breathed out. "It's small, and stupid, and I think about it now and I don't even want to give it to you. Maybe I'll just—" She started to pull it away.

"No." I grabbed it from her hands. "You got me something?"

"Yeah—but it's stupid." A blush crept to her cheeks.

I smiled. "Babe, I'm sure I'll love it."

"Fine," she sighed out. She sat on one of my legs so I could unwrap it. "It's dumb," she said, as if she was warning me.

A plain, white box was underneath the wrapping. I glanced at her quickly before lifting the lid.

A stethoscope.

My eyes snapped to hers.

"See? Stupid," she said.

"No, baby, not stupid at all. I just – I mean this is amazing."

"You like it?" she asked, unsure of herself. She bit her lip anxiously.

I picked it up and placed the empty box next to me. "Of course I like it."

She took it from my hands. "I got your name engraved on it, see?"

I looked down. Dr. L. Matthews was engraved in the middle. "This is amazing. Thank you."

I tried to act cool, as if all she was doing was giving me a gift. But that's not all it was. Not to me. Not at all.

I loved her.

I opened my mouth to tell her.

"I figured you'd need one soon." She spoke, interrupting me. "This can be your first one. It's not the best. I couldn't afford anything amazing, but the research I did said that this is the one most doctors start off with. I hope it is. I hope I did okay."

"You did better than okay."

She smiled huge. "Good!" She kissed me once. "Now we gotta get ready!"

"WHUU." A SOUND got stuck in my throat. I think I stopped breathing. My jaw dropped to the floor; my eyes moved down to her legs. My dick went up at the sight of her. "Holy shit," I breathed out. I don't think I'd ever seen her look so fucking hot before. She was wearing the shortest dress I'd ever seen; it clung to her ass and left nothing to the imagination. The sleeves were long, loose, but buttoned up at the ends. It had no back. At all. And the front dipped between her tits down to her navel. I didn't even know how it was holding up. "You can't leave the house looking like that."

She just laughed at me.

I didn't know why. I sure as shit didn't find it funny.

"Hurry up, asshole!" Cam shouted.

"You guys got me a fucking limo?" I waited for Amanda to get in before getting in myself. It's what gentleman do, right? It was also a great opportunity to look at her ass, again.

"You only turn twenty-one once, right?" Dylan handed me a beer.

I put my arm around Amanda's shoulder; her hand went to my leg. "I guess so."

Jake cleared his throat and raised his beer. "To my best friend," he said seriously.

Micky eyed him, then me. "To douchebags who spill beer on random girls." She raised her glass and laughed.

We all did.

Lucy hiccupped next to them; she was sitting on Cameron's lap, clearly drunk. "To the best guy I know that I'm not screwing." She hiccupped again.

"Gee, thanks, Luce," Jake mocked.

Then Cam chimed in, "To the asshole that my girl would be screwing if I weren't around."

We all laughed.

Then Heidi giggled. "To the guy who took my V-card."

"What!" I'm pretty sure that was everyone.

Nobody knew about Heidi and me. Not until now.

I shook my head and looked down. "Nooo!" Amanda gasped. This could get real bad, real quick. She kept looking from me to Heidi to Dylan. "Doesn't that get awkward?" she chuckled.

Thank fuck.

Dylan shook his head frantically, his eyes shut tight. "Nope. I try not to think about it, and I sure as shit don't want to picture it." Then he opened his eyes, his gaze on me. "To good friends and good people," he said. There was an underlying tone in the way he said it. Everyone felt it, because we all went silent. Dylan and Heidi hadn't been around much lately; in fact, we barely saw Heidi at all. And Dylan, he was always broody, but I didn't know, lately it seemed like something was going on with him.

"What about you, Amanda?" Micky broke the silence.

She turned her head to face me. I was already looking at her. "To a boy who makes every moment a new memory."

WE GOT TO the club after an hour of driving around. I only had one beer. I didn't want to drink tonight. I just wanted to remember it. And I wanted to remember exactly how Amanda looked. Also, I needed to be sober to punch any asshole who looked at her wrong. Because there were going to be a lot of them.

Like now.

"Ho. Lee. Shit," Alex—a kid on the team—said, bro-hugging me. I hugged him back with one arm, the other holding onto Amanda's as we entered the VIP section on the top level. Jake said he knew people who knew people and got us a private area. Everyone was here, the boys on the team and some of my frat brothers. Alex continued, "Where the hell have you been hiding her?" His eyes roamed Amanda's body up and down. She shyly hid behind me.

"In my fucking bed, asshole. Watch your words. And your eyes."

His hands went up in surrender. "Dude." He chuckled. "I got it. She's your girl. No problem."

We all sat in a corner booth; it only took an hour or so before the room filled. "How the fuck did you guys organize all this?"

Jake pointed to Amanda. "She did it."

I faced her, but she was mid-conversation with Lucy. Probably about that Reid Knox asshole from that book.

She threw her head back, laughing at something Lucy was saying. I loved watching her laugh. I turned my entire body to face her and placed my arm on the seat behind her head.

AMANDA

I could feel his breath on my neck. His hand lightly rubbed my leg under the table. My skirt was short, shorter than I was comfortable with. But I wanted to wear something he'd enjoy. His hand moved higher. And higher. I turned to face him. "Stop," I warned.

He smirked. "I can't," was all he said.

I crossed my legs.

His hand wedged between them. "You're just going to make it harder." He licked his lips. His eyes were hooded, burning with lust. Then he kissed my neck. My eyes fell shut. "I want to touch you so fucking bad." His voice was hoarse. I opened my legs. I didn't mean to, but I lost control. I always lost control with him.

His hand moved higher again, separating my legs further.

Higher.

And higher.

I moaned from anticipation. Then I felt his finger run along me through my panties. I moaned louder.

He grunted. "So fucking wet," he said. I was. He did that to me. Then I felt his fingers shift to move the material aside. And then it hit me. Where we were. What we were doing. My eyes snapped open. No one was in the booth. "They're dancing," he said. I threw my head back against the seat, unknowingly spreading my legs further for him. No one could see what we were doing, unless you were watching us. But I didn't care.

Then I felt his fingerx slowly move up and down my wetness. "I wish I could taste you," he moaned.

"Oh God," was all I managed to say.

Then his finger was inside me.

"Holy fuck."

He chuckled. "You have such a potty mouth when I'm about to make you come. I love it."

My hand went to his dick, over his pants. I started rubbing.

"Fuck." He pulled his finger away.

My eyes went wide. I looked around. No one was watching. "Huh?"

"We have to stop." He put his hands down his pants and adjusted himself. "If we don't, I'm going to fuck you right here and I don't care who sees."

"Okay." I nodded. But it wasn't. Not really. I had whatever the equivalent of blue balls was for girls. Blue bean?

I look around for the others; they'd made their own dance floor in the middle of the VIP room. "You want to dance?"

He scrunched his nose.

"You don't dance?"

He shook his head.

I laughed.

He reached for my hand and linked our fingers under the table, his other hand coming up to my face. "You did all this."

I nodded.

"Why?" His brows drew in. His eyes were intense as he roamed my face. He had to know why. He had to know how I felt about him. He had to know I loved him.

"Because..." I trailed off. Then I sighed. "You won't let me say the words."

His shoulders stiffened, his eyes cast downwards, looking at our linked fingers. I lifted his chin with my finger, the way he'd done to me so many times. I looked into his eyes. He licked his lips and then kissed me slowly. "Me too," he said.

Ethan, Tristan and Alexis showed up a couple hours after we got here. Ethan brought Kellie I E with him. Alexis was pissed. She always joked to me about being with Ethan, but I think deep down she actually had feelings for him. We were on the dance floor. I was buzzed; she was trashed, barely able to stand up.

"He brought Kellie I E. What a joke!" she slurred out.

"I know, babe." Her arms around my neck tightened. I tried my best to hold her up. She still managed to dance, moving her hips from side to side. "Maybe you should just tell him how you feel."

"Fuck off," she scoffed. "I don't feel anything. Just drunk."

"Okay, Lexi."

"Hey, James is here, maybe he'll do me."

"Oh my God."

"James!" she yelled, stumbling over to him.

I looked around for Logan, but I couldn't see him anywhere. I started to walk to the balcony to see if he was downstairs when someone grabbed my hand and pulled me into a room. My eyes shut tight instinctively but opened when I heard a latch lock. I was in a bathroom. It was high-class, not dirty, scummy run-of-the-mill club bathroom. "I can't wait," a voice whispered in my ear.

Logan.

I turned around. "I was looking for you."

"I was watching you." He licked his lips and stepped forward, placing one hand on the small of my back and the other on my leg, moving higher and lifting my skirt with it. He kissed me slowly. Painfully slowly.

"Logan," I whispered, out of breath. "We can't. Not here."

"Why?" he asked against my lips.

I bit his bottom one. "I have a surprise for you at home."

He pulled back, his eyebrows raised. "A surprise?"

I bit my lip and nodded. "I got a naughty little nurse's outfit to go with your birthday present."

He visibly swallowed. "You're not fucking with me, right?"

I laughed. "No, baby." I stepped forward, the alcohol making me braver. "When we get home, I'm going to change, and you, Dr. Matthews, are going to bend me over and spank me."

Instantly, I was being pushed back until my back hit the counter. There was fire in his eyes—the good kind. His mouth mashed with mine, his tongue darting out, invading my senses. I lost control. Then his hands were everywhere. On my breasts, on my legs, in my hair, and somehow, in my panties. "You're so bad," he murmured. His fingers made their way inside me, spreading my wetness. And within a second, he'd spun me around, bent me over, and had my panties around my ankles and his dick inside me.

"Oh God!"

Then he started to move, in and out. Slow at first, and then he built his rhythm. He kissed my bare back while one hand cupped a breast. He slowed down, pulling away. Then he grabbed on to my hips and started moving again. "Fuck, baby. I could watch this all fucking day."

A moaning sound escaped.

He started again. Faster. Harder. Then his hand moved from my hip and his fingers rubbed my clit, and I was done.

Done.

LOGAN

I OPENED THE bathroom door and Cam was there waiting. He was looking at the ground, but his eyes trailed up when he saw the door open. Then a huge shit-eating grin took over his face when he saw us and whatever state we were in. He kicked off the opposite wall and faced the wall next to the door. Then he started pumping his hips into it, singing, "Birthday sex, birthday sex...it's the best day of the yearrrr, girl..."

You couldn't not laugh at that.

"DID SHE CALL YOU?" Micky asked.

"Who?" I bent down so I could hear her over the music.

"Megan. She called me today looking for you."

"No." I shook my head.

"I offered to take a message, but she said she needed to speak to you directly. Maybe it was just to say happy birthday."

"Maybe." I shrugged.

"FUCK YOU, TRICIA!" Lucy yelled, her hands coming up, most likely to pull hair. Cam easily held her back. "You need to quit spreading rumors about me and go back to spreading your legs!"

I laughed, but Amanda shook her head in warning.

Tricia—whoever the fuck she was—was being held back by a few other girls. She kept trying to reach for Lucy, but no one would let her get close enough. Amanda leaned into me. "This Tricia bitch thinks that Lucy tried to steal her boyfriend. Apparently the boyfriend told her he had feelings for Lucy. Lucy had no fucking clue."

"Are you calling me a slut?" Tricia spat out.

"Fuck you!" Lucy yelled. "I'm not fucking calling you a slut!" She took a step forward. "But if cocks had wings, you'd be a fucking airport."

Tricia reached forward, trying to grab Lucy. Cameron moved her behind him. Then to Tricia, he said, "You tell your boyfriend or whatever the fuck he is—that if he keeps calling Luce, I'll find him and I'll fucking beat his ass."

Tricia calmed down, then eyed Cam up and down. She lifted her chin. "You call me when you're sick of playing house with Plain Jane and want a taste of something better."

Lucy scrambled from behind him and raised her fisted hand. Cam was quick enough to hold it back. But somehow, a slapping sound was heard.

Amanda.

She towered over Tricia. "Get. Your. Shit. And. Leave. Now. Bitch." Her jaw was clenched. "Now," she repeated calmly.

"Holy hell," Amanda said through a yawn. "Tonight was good times."

Her head was on my lap; we were the last ones out of the limo on the way home. "Yeah," I agreed.

"My favorite part was when you took my innocence in the bathroom."

I laughed once, rolling my head on the back of the seat. "Yeah, that or when you bitch-slapped that girl."

A laugh rolled out of her, getting louder by the second. "I feel bad for Lucy. I mean—if anyone knows the effects of rumors, it's me."

I stroked her hair. "How bad was it? I mean...that summer?"

She shrugged. "I'm not going to lie. It was bad. But we move on. We get over it. Make new memories, you know?"

I smiled down at her. "Yeah, we do."

Then she sat up and kissed me. And I got lost—in this moment and in her—until she giggled into my mouth. "What's funny?" I asked against her lips.

She pulled back, trying to contain her laughter. "If cocks had wings, you'd be an airport."

I laughed with her.

"I so don't want to work tomorrow," she whined.

"Sucks."

Then it was quiet for a minute.

"So," I started. I didn't know if what I said next was—I don't know—normal—but I'd been thinking about it for a while. "I think you should just move your stuff into my room. We could rent out yours and save you some money. Then maybe you can cut back—"

"What?" she cut in. "Like, move in with you?"

"Well, you already live with me—"

"Yeah, I know, but I mean, if we fight or break up—"

"I don't see that happening. Ever."

She smiled.

Shit. She was so fucking beautiful.

"We're here," the driver stated, pulling up to the front of the house.

I got out first and helped her out. We didn't release each other's hands.

"Okay," she said.

"Okay?" I stopped walking up the driveway and faced her. The only light was from the moon. There were no streetlights on our road.

"I'll move in."

"Yeah?" I couldn't help the smug grin that took over. Honestly, I was happy she had nowhere to go if I ever pissed her off. She'd have to stay with me.

She nodded. "You're so getting layooked tonight."

I chuckled and continued walking up the driveway. "It's so fucking dark."

"I know," she agreed. "Ethan always forgets to put the security light on."

We walked to the door and I got my keys out and then faced her. "Hey."

"What's up?" She was shivering from the cold.

I put my arms around her and held her close. "Thank you for tonight. For all of the nights you give me. Just...thank you."

She pulled away and looked up at me. "You're my person, Logan."

I just shook my head. I had no words. I opened the door and stepped in behind her.

"Hello, son."

Monsters.

Voices.

38

LOGAN

A LIGHT TURNED ON. There were three of them.

"Your mamma told me you'd gotten big, boy." His deep rumble voice echoed in my ears.

This was what nightmares are made of.

"You not going to introduce me to your girl?"

I stood there, frozen.

Then her hand curled around my arm. "Logan?"

I turned to her. Her face was pale. Her bottom lip quivered.

I picked her up and rushed to the front door, opening it and placing her outside. Her panic-stricken face turned to shock. "What are you doing?" she cried.

I pulled out my phone and gave it to her. 'Call the police,' I mouthed, then slammed the door shut, making sure to lock it.

"Logan," she shouted, her hand pounding on the door. I ignored it. I had to.

I turned around. The monster stood in front of me.

"You took my girl," the one next to him said. My eyes went to him. I knew him. It was Megan's monster, the one that was there when I visited her. "You took my girl," he repeated. "And now you have to pay."

I didn't know which came first: the fist to my jaw or the bat to my stomach.

AMANDA

"LOGAN!!" I BANGED on the door harder. I turned the knob. It kept slipping from my hands. "Logan!!"

There was shouting.

Glass breaking.

He told me to do something.

"Logan!" I was crying. My heart pounded against my chest. It hurt so fucking much.

He told me to do something.

I moved to the window and tried to pry it open.

"Logan!!" I looked around. "Help me!! Somebody! Help me!" I yelled into the pitch-black night.

Then I felt his phone in my hand.

Call the cops, he'd said.

"You have to hurry!" I yelled into the phone. I gave them the address. I gave them what they asked for. "Logan! Please!" I banged on the window. There was so much shouting. It felt like hours. I cried harder. My body shook. I needed to break the window. "Oh my God, oh my God." I couldn't see. It was too fucking dark. "Logan!!"

The spare key. In a magnetic holder in the wheel well of Ethan's car. Fuck. Fuck. Fuck. I walked with my hands out in front of me, feeling for his car. Fuck. "Help!" I shouted again. I hit something solid and dropped to the ground. I felt for his wheel and where the key was supposed to be. Even if there were light, my tears would stop me from seeing clearly. "Come on, come on!" I felt around. It wasn't there. "Fuck!" I yelled. Then I felt it. I pulled it off and pried it open. The keys fell with a clanking sound onto the concrete. "Fuck!" I felt around blindly until my fingers hit the cold metal. I didn't even know how I got to the door.

And then I opened it.

And he was there.

"Logan!" I shouted. But he didn't respond.

He was being held up by two of them, while the other held a bat in his hands. His head drooped in front of him. There was blood everywhere.

"Logan!" I shouted again, running toward him.

This time he heard me.

"Amanda," he croaked out. His entire face was swollen and bloody. "Go!"

I grabbed onto the arm of one the guys holding him. "Let him go!" I shouted, trying to pry his hold of Logan. "Let him go!"

LOGAN

"GET OFF ME, you little bitch," I heard.

Then a loud thump. I tried to raise my head. But I couldn't. It all hurt too much. It took all my effort to open my eyes. And she was there.

And something in me snapped. "Amanda," I screamed.

Her body was on the floor; she was trying to get up. Then I saw footsteps in my blurred vision, getting closer and closer to her. "Don't you fucking touch her!" I tried to break free, but I couldn't. I couldn't fucking get to her. "Amanda!" In my head I was yelling. But outside, I didn't hear a sound. It was static. White noise. Monsters' voices.

"Fuck you!" she spat out, her eyes trying to focus on him. He bent down and then raised his hand.

"Don't you lay a fucking hand on her!" The words were only in my head. My eyes were heavy. I felt nothing everywhere else.

And then he slapped her.

That's the sound that broke the static.

Something came over me. Adrenaline strength I'd only ever read about. I pulled from their holds, but I fell to the floor. They'd been holding me up. I was too weak to stand. I started to crawl.

"You take away my girl," the asshole on Amanda said to me. "Now I take yours."

Then he kneeled between her legs and undid his belt.

I crawled as fast as I could. It all happened so slowly.

She tried to fight him off. She raised her arm to hit him. But he blocked it and roughly pinned it onto the floor. She cried out in pain, tears falling faster. I crawled as fast as I could to save her.

He pushed his pants down to his knees.

"Logan," she cried out, tears falling down the side of her face.

She was helpless. Her body broken. Her eyes focused on me as I crawled pathetically to her.

But I couldn't. I couldn't get to her fast enough. "Logan," she sobbed. She'd given up.

Amanda.

This time, I saw it before I felt it. A boot headed toward my head.

And then darkness.

But only for a second.

They say your life flashes before your eyes.

It didn't. Not for me.

All I saw was her.

Her smiling.

Because it was all I ever wanted.

39

LOGAN

Beep. Beep. Beep.

It sounded so familiar.

Beep. Beep. Beep.

I tried to open my eyes.

Beep. Beep. Beep.

I coughed.

Then I heard footsteps.

"Hey, man. You awake?"

I didn't recognize the voice. I tried to open my eyes again. This time it worked. Barely.

Tristan. He was sporting what would soon be a black eye.

"Shit, okay." He started to panic. "I'll get your dad, just wait, okay?" He started to leave.

"Wait." My voice cracked. I tried to sit up. "Is she—did he?"

He slowly came back. "He didn't," he said. "We got there in time, just before the cops. He didn't—do that—to her."

I nodded and lay back down.

What the fuck was happening?

Dad walked in a minute later. I struggled to sit up.

"Broken arm and bruises, she'll be fine."

I breathed out, relieved.

"You on the other hand—"

"I don't care."

"Son, she's okay," he tried to soothe. But he shouldn't have. I'm not the one who deserved to be comforted. They were in that house because of me. They hurt her because of me.

My breathing got heavy. My body shook. My muscles tensed. The beeps got faster. My heart was breaking.

And then for the first time since I was in this same position, fourteen years ago, I cried. In the arms of a man who loved me more than blood. "Dad." I held on to him tighter. It was the first time I'd ever called him that to his face. He didn't say anything. He didn't need to.

AMANDA

I WAS IN the hospital for two days. For two days, Ethan never left my side. He never went home. He never showered. Mom brought us food. Logan never showed.

He was at home, I told myself. He was preparing our room. He was moving my stuff into his. Like he said I should do. And when I got home, it would be perfect. The girls came by. They didn't mention him. I didn't ask. He was at home, waiting for me.

Only he wasn't.

I got home to his empty room. "Baby?" I looked around the house. He wasn't there. Ethan was carrying all the flowers and balloons from the hospital into the house. Mom had come and cleaned up the living room, so there was no more blood. No more broken furniture. No more bad memories. "Babe?" I yelled again. I went to my room first and then his. I looked in his bathroom. He wasn't there. Was his car here? I didn't even bother to check. "Logan!" I started to panic. I walked to his desk, where he normally kept his keys. They weren't there. But there was a wad of cash and a note.

The money should cover rent for six months.

What?

I dropped to sit on the bed. I re-read the note over and over. It never made sense. Not once.

Ethan came in.

"Where is he?" he asked.

"Gone." I sobbed into my hands and dropped the note.

I felt him pick it up.
Then the bed dipped as he sat next to me.
He wrapped his arms around me. “I’m sorry, Dimmy.”
I cried harder. “What did I do wrong?”
“Nothing, Dim. You just loved him.”

AMANDA

One Week Later

I DIDN'T KNOW how or why I ended up here, but I needed to be here. I couldn't go another day not knowing what happened.

His dad answered when I knocked on the door, a look of surprise clear on his face. "Amanda?"

I didn't even care to know what I looked like right now. I'd walked a mile in the pouring rain from the bus stop to his front door, my arm wrapped in a plastic bag to keep the plaster from getting wet.

"You're shivering; come inside."

So I did.

I couldn't stop my teeth from chattering.

"Goodness, Amanda, you must be freezing. Just...wait, okay? I'll get Logan."

I nodded.

It was the only thing I could do.

I stood in the entryway for only a minute before I heard his voice. He walked from the back of the house, his eyes widening when he saw me.

"Get her dry and a change of clothes, son. She's going to catch pneumonia." I watched his dad make his way up the stairs, giving us some privacy.

When he was out of earshot, I faced Logan. "I had to see you," I tried to get out, but my body wouldn't stop shaking.

He blew out a deep breath. "Come on. Let's get you dry." He jerked his head for me to follow, but he didn't wait for me to walk ahead of him. Instead I followed behind him. Neglected. Because maybe that's what I was now.

We walked into the pool house and he led me to the bathroom, holding the door open for me. "You should have a shower, warm your body. I'll bring you a change of clothes." He looked down at my plastered arm and then lifted it to inspect it. "Try to keep it out of the water."

I wasn't going to call him out on the fact that I'd had it on for a week already. A week when he'd been MIA. When I've had to take care of this myself because he decided to just up and leave me. Leave us.

Ten minutes later, I was out of the shower, and true to his word, fresh clothes were waiting for me. When I was dressed, I walked out of the room and he was there. Hands in his pockets, leaning against the kitchen island, his head was bowed, his shoulders slouched.

When he heard me, he slowly raised his head, but he didn't look at me. "What are you doing here, Amanda?"

"You just disappeared." I took steps forward until I was right in front of him.

His eyes finally moved to mine. His jaw clenched, hands still in his pockets. "Is that your answer or a question?"

"I don't know." I moved to hold his hand, but he jerked it away and moved so he was behind me.

And now I was pissed. Because I didn't know what the fuck I did wrong. I turned to face him. "Did I do something? What the fuck happened, Logan? One second, I'm in a hospital bed, and then the next second, you're gone. Your shit's all packed up and you're gone. What did I do?"

He shrugged, eyes staring off into nothing. "You didn't do anything, Amanda."

"Really, asshole? The 'it's not you, it's me' speech. Really?"

He shrugged again.

I took a minute to calm down, because as much as I hated that I was here right now, I was here for a reason. And I wasn't leaving until I knew what the fuck happened.

"Can you at least look at me, Logan, please?"

And he did.

He looked at me, and it was that exact same feeling I had the first time I saw him again. Standing in that library. With all those misplaced emotions. All at once.

"Do you think I want to be here?" I started. My voice broke and I knew I was about to cry, but I didn't give a shit, because he needed to see it. He needed to understand how badly he was hurting me. "I don't want to be this girl. I don't want to be standing in front of you, pouring my heart out, because I don't know what happened. I don't know why you haven't come home. I don't know why you won't answer my calls." The tears were flowing, and I didn't bother to wipe them. "I don't know what the fuck I did, Logan. I'm sorry. Whatever it is, I'm sorry. You just have to forgive me, and you need to come home. And I need you to tell me what I did. Please. You have to tell me." I hated me. I hated me so fucking much. I hated this pathetic, weak excuse of a person that I'd become, but I couldn't fucking help it. Because I needed him. Like air. I just needed him.

He sniffed once, looking right into my eyes. "I don't know what you want from me, Amanda." His voice was strained.

I knew he was holding back his tears and his own emotions. He had to be. Because this couldn't be it. This couldn't be all there was for us. To our story. This couldn't be how it ended.

"I want you to want me," I tell him. "I want you to need me. I want you to fucking choose me. I want you to fight for me. You have to fight for me, Logan! You can't walk away. Not again." I moved so I was standing in front of him, my hurt and anger taking over. I grabbed his shirt in my hands as best as I could. And sometime between walking into his house and now, I'd become desperate. "You have to choose me." My fingers gripped the material tighter. And this—this was the moment I lost all control. "You have to fucking choose me. Please, Logan. You just have to."

I was crying so hard, I didn't know if my words were clear.

Outside of my head, it was silent.

But in my mind, every single conversation we'd ever had played out. All the times he told me how he felt about me. The ways he showed me how he cared. The late-night conversations with those stupid truths. The times we talked about our lives, our future. And now? This. Me—begging him to stay. And I have no idea what the fuck happened to us.

I tried to calm my breathing, but the sobs wouldn't quit, not even for a second.

"Amanda," he said it so softly I almost didn't hear him.

I lifted my eyes to his and held my breath, waiting for him to say something. To tell me I was right. That he wanted me, as much as he needed me. Like air. Those were his words.

He pried my fingers from their hold on his shirt and pushed my hands away. "I can't."

The second the words were out of his mouth, something in me changed. I slowly closed my eyes and took a deep breath in. When I opened them, I refused to see him. Instead, I walked straight to the door and opened it.

"Wait," he said.

So I did.

I stopped halfway out but didn't turn around. Because I couldn't stand him anymore.

"It's still pouring out; I'll give you a ride to your mom's."

Whatever.

I didn't move, but I didn't decline.

I heard him grab his keys before he brushed past me and led me to his car.

The drive home was silent apart from my soft cries.

When he pulled into the driveway, he didn't turn the car off, and he didn't look at me. Not until I opened the door to get out.

"Wait," he said again.

So I did.

Finally, he turned to face me.

And we stared at each other. Like we did the first time I sat in this car. Not knowing that one night would lead us here—to this moment.

He swallowed and cleared his throat, his eyes starting to glaze with his own tears. He sniffed once, trying to hold it together. And I didn't know why he chose this moment. Why he said what he said next. Or why he even said it all.

"I love you, Amanda."

And then he quickly turned and faced forward again, refusing to look at me. Refusing to acknowledge what he'd just said. What he just did.

And I know why.

It was because he didn't.

He didn't love me.

Not at all.

Those words he promised would belong to me forever—they didn't.

And I didn't have him.

Not forever.

Not even for now.

Not anymore.

So I told him the one truth that wasn't a truth, but one I had to believe to get through the rest of my life without him.

"I hate you, Logan."

And then I was out of his car, slamming the door shut, and walking away. Because it was my turn. It was my fucking turn to leave him behind.

LOGAN

DAD LOOKED UP when I entered his office.

"Everything okay?"

I nodded.

"You ready?"

I nodded again.

41

AMANDA

Five weeks.

It's been five weeks since I'd seen him. I hadn't heard from him once. Not a thing. And I think it was for the best. I think that maybe I needed a clean break. A way to completely erase him from my life. I'd told Micky and Lucy, and they understood. They knew that being around them might mean being around him or even hearing about him. And I couldn't do that to myself. Not now. Not yet. I was back to where I was when I first got here. Trying to do everything I could to avoid him.

"I have something to tell you." Ethan turned the TV off and I faced him. He was home more often now, and I knew why. He was worried about me. He thought I'd turned into the girl from that summer. But I wasn't. Not really. I was nowhere near as broken as I was then. Maybe it was because I was immune to the fucked-up ways of Logan Matthews. Maybe it was because I'd come to accept the fact that maybe—just maybe—it was my fault. That I never should have taken him back the first time. Or the second time. Or the third. Whatever it was. I didn't care. I was over it.

"Dimmy." He tried to get my attention again.

"What? What do you have to tell me? If it's about his room—not yet, okay? Just wait. Another week. I've got to go in there and clear out my stuff."

Okay, so maybe I wasn't over it yet. But I was close.

"No." He shook his head. "That's not it. But uh, it's about him."

I looked away. "Then I don't want to know."

"Dimmy, I think you need to know."

"I don't think I need to know shit about him anymore, E. I'm done with him."

"He's gone."

My head whipped to his. "What do you mean he's gone?"

"Like, gone. Away. Out of the country. He's traveling the world or some shit. I don't know." He shrugged.

"What? How? What about college? What about med school? Traveling where?"

"Dim, I don't know. I bumped into James today, and he asked how you felt about Logan experiencing the world indefinitely or something."

"Indefinitely?"

"Seriously, I don't know. I know as much as I just told you. Look, I'm just telling you so that you know it's okay. You don't have to worry about bumping into him on campus or anything. You can hang out with your friends again. He won't be there. I just wanted you to know. And honestly, Dim, you fucking deserve to know. He should have at least told you that much."

EPILOGUE

Logan

I WAS THE match that started the inferno.

EXCERPT

MORE THAN HIM

A KNOCK ON the window caused me to jump out of my skin. I held my hand to my heart and turned to see a familiar face.

He knocked again.

I should've expected to see him; we were parked at the front of his work. I wound down the window.

"Hey, Amanda," he greeted, then rubbed the scruff of his beard with the back of his fingers. "You got a minute? I'd like to have a quick word if that's okay?"

It could only be about one thing, and for a second, I hesitated. But I wouldn't let this ruin what I'd spent months trying to build. "Sure." I smiled at him and got out of the car.

He motioned for me to sit on a bench a few feet away. I did. "How have you been, Dr. Matthews?"

"You know to call me Alan, Amanda."

I laughed. "How have you been, Alan?"

He blew out a breath, his smile completely gone. "I've been better." He cleared his throat. "That's actually why I wanted to speak to you."

My eyebrows drew in. "What do you mean?"

He took my hand in both of his. I let him. I swallowed down my emotions and blinked back the tears. I don't know how he'd suddenly made me feel like this.

"I owe you an apology—"

I opened my mouth to interrupt, but he lifted his hand to stop me.

"Please, sweetheart," he said. "I need to apologize to you. Logan—"

My breath caught. No one's mentioned him by name since he left.

"He was in a bad way after what happened to you. And even though it happened to him, too, he never saw it like that. All he ever saw was you. He blamed himself. He thought it was his fault that it happened. And he thought that if you hadn't met him—well —" He let out all the air in his lungs. Then he looked at me. Right into my eyes.

I let a tear fall.

"I thought I was helping him. It was my idea for him to leave and travel. I thought that maybe it would help him if he saw things differently...but hell, I never even thought about you."

I let the dam break.

"And I'm sorry," he continued. "I'm sorry that he's gone."

"Please." I managed to say, trying to stop him from continuing. I wiped my face. "I appreciate what you're saying. I really do. But you're not the one that should be apologizing."

He nodded. "Do you want to know about him?"

"No," I said quickly. "I can't."

"Okay," is all he said.

Then he removed his hands from mine and leaned back on the bench.

I mimicked his position.

We stared straight ahead.

"You know," he said, his tone a little lighter. "When he left for college, it started to get real lonely in that big, old house, but he would come by and visit on weekends. Now though—I miss him."

I swallowed the knot in my throat. "Yeah." I did, too. But I wasn't going to admit that to anyone.

He laughed once. "I looked up taco casserole recipes on the internet."

I smiled. "Yeah?"

"Yeah," he replied. "Mine came out black, though."

I laughed, that awkward crying-type laugh. I wiped my face and sniffed.

"Just saying—if you ever feel the need to make it and want to visit a lonely, old man in a big, empty house, the invitation is there."

I turned my head to face him. "Maybe."

"There you are!" his voice came from behind me, interrupting us.

I stood up.

So did Alan.

I waited until he was next to me before I made the introductions. "Um, this is Tyson." I pointed my thumb at him. "Tyson, this is Dr. Matthews." I felt Tyson tense from next to me.

They shook hands.

Alan smiled and then faced me. "The invitation will always stand, pretty girl."

Read More Than Him now.

ABOUT THE AUTHOR

Jay McLean is an international best-selling author and full-time reader, writer of New Adult and Young Adult romance, and skilled procrastinator. When she's not doing any of those things, she can be found running after her three little boys, investing way too much time on True Crime Documentaries and binge-watching reality TV.

She writes what she loves to read, which are books that can make her laugh, make her hurt and make her feel.

Jay lives in the suburbs of Melbourne, Australia, in her dream home where music is loud and laughter is louder.

For publishing rights (Foreign & Domestic) Film or television, please contact her agent Erica Spellman-Silverman, at Trident Media Group.

Made in the USA
San Bernardino, CA
09 September 2019